## YOU BELONG TO ME

Malcolm saw the flicker of doubt in Nicole's eyes before she lowered her gaze.

"After you walked out on me, I never thought you would willingly come anywhere near me again," she said. "But Denise told me Celestial Productions approached her."

Malcolm pushed away the guilt her words evoked, reminding himself he wasn't the only one to blame for their relationship failing.

"Nicky, you pushed me away. After—"

"Don't." She held up a slim hand, pain clouding her ebony eyes. "I don't want to talk about it, Malcolm."

He dropped his gaze to hide his own pain. "Fair enough." *Business. Stick to business.* "Ty and I are very excited about the idea of owning the movie rights to *InterDimensions*. We enjoy science fiction, and we'd do a good job with your book."

Nicole turned toward the window. "And you'd give me everything I asked for. Allow me final approval on the screenplay and input on the shooting locations, the cast, and the final cut."

"Yes." Malcolm frowned at the tightness of her tone.

"Tempting." Nicole turned back to him. "But deals with the devil usually are."

# YOU BELONG TO ME

## PATRICIA SARGEANT

Kensington Publishing Corp.
http://www.kensingtonbooks.com

*To my dream team: my sister, Bernadette, for sharing the dream; my husband, Michael, for supporting the dream; my brother, Richard, for believing in the dream; my brother, Gideon, for encouraging the dream; my friend and critique partner, Marcia James, for sharing the dream; and to Mom and Dad always, with love.*

*Thanks to Diane Castell for cheering me on, Roberta Brown for agreeing to represent me, Karen Thomas for giving me this opportunity, and Nichole Bruce for returning my call.*

DAFINA BOOKS are published by

Kensington Publishing Corp.
850 Third Avenue
New York, NY 10022

All Kensington Titles, Imprints, and Distributed Lines are available at special quantity discounts for bulk purchases for sales promotions, premiums, fund-raising, educational or institutional use. Special book excerpts or customized printings can also be created to fit specific needs. For details, write or phone the office of the Kensington special sales manager: Kensington Publishing Corp., 850 Third Avenue, New York, NY 10022. attn: Special Sales Department, Phone: 1-800-221-2647.

Dafina and the Dafina logo Reg. U.S. Pat. & TM Off.

First Dafina mass market printing: November 2006

10 9 8 7 6 5 4 3 2 1

Printed in the United States of America

# CHAPTER ONE

"What are you doing here?"

Nicole Collins pitched her voice low in the elegant hotel restaurant. Still, she managed to interrupt the introductions between her literary agent, Denise Maitland, and the two men who stood in front of their table.

Malcolm Bryant turned toward her, a wariness in his cocoa eyes. His chiseled brown face hadn't changed much in the past four years. Perhaps it was even more appealing now, as was his six-foot-plus frame. No, *appealing* was the wrong word. The writer in her searched her mental thesaurus for something more appropriate. *Compelling*, she decided. He was more compelling and more confident. A self-assured stranger in a tailored, dark blue suit.

"I co-own the company that optioned for the movie rights to your book." His deep-sea voice washed over her. It still had the power to sweep her away.

"You own the production company?" She spoke through numb lips.

"Co-own." He inclined his head toward the tall, well-dressed man beside him. "This is my partner, Tyrone Austin."

Nicole glanced at the smiling stranger before returning her attention to the man in front of her, and the memories of broken vows and tragic loss. She folded her hands in her lap, hoping that would stop their shaking.

"Nicky, what's wrong?" Denise asked.

She turned toward her agent. "Did you know he owned the company?"

"Of course." Denise regarded her with a confused expression on her dark, round face. "Does it matter?"

"It matters." If she had known Malcolm was Celestial Productions, she wouldn't be here.

Nicole scanned the room. Couples and groups of friends enjoyed lunch and quiet conversation. Now and then, bubbles of laughter floated across the silence, then faded away. He had brought her here. Paid for her to fly first class across the country to Los Angeles, back to his territory. Reserved a suite for her in a luxury hotel. Invited her to a business lunch in the hotel's four-star restaurant. And then, once she was lulled into a false sense of security, he'd changed her dream to a nightmare by reappearing—and bringing the painful past with him.

Nicole returned her attention to him as she stood. His gaze tracked her, and his firm lips stopped moving. She hadn't heard a word he'd said.

"I can't do this," she stated.

"What?" Denise half-rose from her chair.

Nicole picked up her purse and walked out of the dining room. She squared her shoulders, tilted her chin, and kept her vision straight ahead. She couldn't do anything about her shaking knees, though. She'd lost her temper—and probably her agent. She hated herself for running away from Malcolm. But she'd hate herself more if she stayed and did something stupid, like burst into tears.

A crowd waited in front of the elevators. The doors opened as Nicole approached. She stepped on and noticed someone had selected her floor. The crowd thinned as the elevator rose, seeming to stop at every floor. Nicole stood, outwardly calm in the center of the packed car, but inside turbulent emotions filled her. Anger. Sorrow. Regret.

Finally reaching her floor, Nicole and several other passengers disembarked and separated in the hallway. She located her room and pulled her key card from her purse.

YOU BELONG TO ME                    7

She started to slip it into the security lock when a dark hand grasped her wrist, the long fingers warm against her pulse.

"We have to talk," he murmured.

Malcolm Bryant felt the pulse jump in Nicole's delicate wrist as he leaned over her, his chest against her slender back. He could feel her warmth as he breathed her soft fragrance—a mixture of the soap she used and her natural scent that still stirred him, even in his dreams.

"We have to talk," he repeated.

An older couple stepped from the room across the hall. Malcolm caught their curious stare before they moved along.

"We can stay out here if you want," he murmured into the shell of Nicole's ear. "But we'll probably attract a lot of attention. Personally, I'd prefer to talk in your room. Either way, we will talk."

"Fine." She pulled free of him and pushed open the door. "We'll talk in the room."

Nicole crossed the thick, turquoise carpet, walking past the dining section and small living area to the sliding glass doors on the opposite side of the suite. She tossed her purse on the mahogany conversation table between two matching overstuffed chairs, folded her arms across her chest, and turned to face him.

She was backlit by the window, which offered a glimpse of the sun straining to penetrate the Los Angeles skyline. The cream-colored pantsuit flowed over her, masking her figure. But he could tell from her face that she was a lot more slender, almost fragile. Her thick, nearly black hair was longer and was gathered in a clip at the nape of her neck. Small stud earrings were her only accessory. The conservative, polished businesswoman before him was very different from the free spirit he had known four years ago.

*The scene is set,* Malcolm thought, strolling into the living area. He shoved his hands into his trouser pockets, biting back the urge to ask how she'd been the past four years. *Business,* he told himself. *Stick to business.* Emotions always got him into trouble.

"Celestial Productions offered a fair market price for the movie rights to *InterDimensions.* And we've agreed to your other terms," he began.

"You misrepresented your company, Malcolm. You knew I wouldn't have anything to do with Celestial Productions if I knew you owned it. Can you deny that?" she prompted when he didn't speak.

"No." He watched resentment darken her catlike eyes. She lowered her arms and balled her hands into fists. Even from across the room, he could feel her vibrating with anger.

"You were probably disappointed when I insisted on meeting Celestial Productions's principals." Her smooth inflection barely masked the throb of fury in her voice.

"No, I wasn't." Malcolm kept his tone reasonable. "If I'd wanted to keep my identity a secret from you, I could have. I didn't have to come to lunch today."

"Then how would your partner have explained your absence?"

"We would have thought of something. The point is, I never hid from you. When your agent asked for information about our company, we gave her everything. You must not have asked to see it. My name was all over those papers."

Malcolm saw the flicker of doubt in Nicole's eyes before she lowered her gaze.

"After you walked out on me, I never thought you would willingly come anywhere near me again," she said. "But Denise told me Celestial Productions approached her."

Malcolm pushed away the guilt her words evoked, reminding himself he wasn't the only one to blame for their relationship failing.

"Nicky, you pushed me away. After—"

"Don't." She held up a slim hand, pain clouding her ebony eyes. "I don't want to talk about it, Malcolm."

He dropped his gaze to hide his own pain. "Fair

enough." *Business. Stick to business.* "Ty and I are very excited about the idea of owning the movie rights to *InterDimensions*. We enjoy science fiction, and we'd do a good job with your book."

Nicole turned toward the window. "And you'd give me everything I asked for. Allow me final approval on the screenplay and input on the shooting locations, the cast, and the final cut."

"Yes." Malcolm frowned at the tightness of her tone.

"Tempting." Nicole turned back to him. "But deals with the devil usually are."

Malcolm felt his nostrils flare. Heat rushed into his cheeks. "You've gone too far. I understand this is a shock to you. I had time to get used to the idea of seeing you again. You didn't have time to get used to seeing me. But there's no reason for personal attacks."

"There's every reason." Nicole seemed to gather herself. Her deep breaths lifted her chest beneath the loose-fitting jacket. "Does Denise know about us?"

"Of course not. That's personal. This is business."

She looked troubled. "Malcolm, I can't do business with you. There are too many . . . difficult memories behind us."

"Nicky—"

"Please leave." Her tone emerged between a plea and a command.

Malcolm started to speak, then reconsidered. She was too agitated to continue this discussion. A discussion that hadn't started well and had deteriorated badly. His gaze lowered to watch her hand press against her abdomen. He flinched, and her hand dropped away.

"You're right." His voice sounded rough to his ears. "We both need some space. We'll talk more tomorrow."

"No, we won't. I'm getting a flight back to New York tonight."

He frowned. "Nicky—"

She shook her head, her voice resigned. "Good-bye, Malcolm."

He looked into her shuttered eyes. She'd closed him out

as firmly as if she'd locked a door against him. Pleading with her wouldn't remove the barrier; beating against it wouldn't make it go away. He'd tried those tactics unsuccessfully more than four years ago.

He studied her, this remote, composed woman, and wondered with regret how deep she'd buried the Nicole Collins he'd known. And how much of her demise was his fault. A part of her must still be alive, though, Malcolm thought. The part that had created the fantasy world of the *InterDimensions* series with its warm, close-knit family. That was the Nicole he needed to reach. But, he realized, looking into her eyes again, not today. She wouldn't listen to him today. Without a word, Malcolm turned and walked out, shutting the door behind him.


Nicole was shaking so much, she couldn't convince her legs to carry her to the overstuffed chairs. Instead she sank onto the carpet.

Her mind stayed blank for several minutes before clicking back on. But the memories weren't happy ones. She pressed a damp palm to her stomach. Years ago, their lives had been perfect. But then the foundation had crumbled, and she and Malcolm hadn't been able to regain their footing. At least not together.

An impatient fist pounded on her door. Nicole closed her eyes. *Please let it not be Malcolm.* They had nothing more to say to each other.

"Nicky, open up," Denise commanded. "I know you're in there."

*Denise.* Nicole groaned. *Could we try curtain number three?* Still, Denise was her agent and her friend. She knew the other woman deserved an explanation for her seemingly bizarre behavior. After all, Denise had worked hard to put this deal together for her—at her request. Nicole scrubbed her palms over her face, then pushed herself to her feet and walked across the room on still-wobbly legs. She checked the peephole to make sure her agent was alone, then let her in.

Denise marched across the plush carpet in three-inch, fire-engine-red stilettos. A form-fitting, scarlet dress wrapped her curvaceous figure. She stopped in front of the glass doors and spun back toward Nicole.

"What's the problem? Why did you call off the deal? Do you know how long and hard I worked to pull this off?"

"So this is about you?" Nicole knew from past experience that putting Denise on the defensive was the fastest way to calm her so they could discuss things reasonably.

"You know this isn't about me." Denise frowned, pointing one cherry-red fingernail in Nicole's direction. "But after all the time and energy I put into this deal, I deserve to know why you pulled out of it."

"Because I knew I wouldn't be able to work with the producers."

"How did you know that?" Denise's voice hovered less than one pitch below exasperation. "You hadn't even met them."

Nicole wandered into the living area and sat on the armchair facing the window. Denise was right, Nicole thought. Her agent deserved to know why she had walked away from Celestial Productions's offer. Nicole wondered how much she could tell Denise without revealing the painful details. What would her friend accept?

"You knew Malcolm," Denise accused. "You've met him before. When?"

Nicole sighed. "I met him in college."

"And?"

"And, Denise, the rest is private."

Denise studied her with a shrewd, dark gaze. Nicole hated that look. It made her feel as though her friend could reach into every dark corner of her mind and find out what she'd had for breakfast, how many hours of sleep she'd had, and the date of her last confession.

"So, this is personal?" Denise's understanding tone put Nicole on instant alert.

"Very personal."

"And you're going to let it affect your professional life? Our professional lives?" Denise baited.

Nicole drew a sharp breath and inclined her head. "Direct hit."

It was frightening how well they knew each other's strengths and weaknesses after three years. Her agent knew Nicole wore her professionalism like a shield.

Denise slapped her full thigh in frustration, her cherry-red lips drawn tight. She turned away, running her hand through her close-cropped hair. The dangling globes she called *earrings* spun.

With a gusty sigh, Denise propped her hands on her well-rounded hips and turned back to Nicole. "Then how about fairness? I put six months into this deal. That's a lot of time and a lot of work. I deserve to know how you think I failed you."

"You didn't fail me," Nicole retorted instantly. "He did. He failed me four years ago." She bowed her head and rubbed her eyes with a thumb and two fingers, furious with herself for the sting of tears.

"Who did? Malcolm Bryant?"

"Yes," Nicole whispered.

"How?" Denise's tone was a perfect blend of confusion and frustration.

Nicole hid her face in her hands, unable to face her admission. "He left me." She lowered her hands and stared at the floor. "Four years ago, he walked out on me. The next thing I knew, I was being served with divorce papers."

The silence was deafening.

"Divorce papers?" Denise breathed.

Nicole lifted her gaze to Denise's wide eyes. "Malcolm Bryant is my ex-husband."

"That went badly," Tyrone remarked.

Malcolm noted his partner's bland tone and judged the other man had counted to ten a thousand times while they waited for the valet to retrieve his car. Now, as Tyrone inched the car south on the interstate toward their Inglewood office, he apparently considered himself calm enough to discuss the aborted meeting.

Malcolm sighed silently and prepared to relive his most recent failure. "We knew going in we had a fifty-fifty chance of pulling this off."

"We should have called her before she came to L.A.," Tyrone said, repeating his previous argument.

"She wouldn't have come," said Malcolm, restating his previous response.

"Well, she came, took one look at us—or rather you—and walked out. Now what?"

"I don't know."

In his mind, Malcolm imagined warm, laughing eyes growing cold and distant over the years. The Nicole he knew would have listened to him, if not today, then the next day. She had a temper like a summer storm. It rained briefly, and then the sun came out. The Nicole he had confronted today had frozen over. How was he going to get her to talk to him now when he hadn't been able to convince her in the past?

"You're going to have to think of something." Tyrone's voice grew terse. "When we get back to the office, send her flowers."

"I can't," Malcolm admitted.

"Why not?"

"Two reasons. First, flowers wouldn't work with Nicole. This is business." Malcolm paused. "Second, she's probably on her way to the airport by now. Or she will be by the time we get back to the office."

"What?" Tyrone snapped his gaze from the crawling traffic to stare at Malcolm. With his small, rimless glasses, he looked like an angry math professor. "She's supposed to stay through Friday."

"She dropped the deal, remember? Apparently, she doesn't think she has a reason to stay another two days."

"Great." Tyrone struck the steering wheel with his

broad palm. His dark face flushed. "That's just great." He sat glaring at the traffic. "You need to fix this, Mal. I don't care how. Just fix it."

"I will, Ty."

"We told the completion guarantor we would get the rights to *InterDimensions* and that we'd make a blockbuster out of it. I know we can do it. With my marketing ability and your creative skills, we can make a hit movie out of that book. But first we need the book."

"Don't worry," Malcolm assured him. "I want this at least as badly as you do."

"And how badly is that?"

Malcolm looked at the palm trees and the bright California sun. "Badly enough to go to New York in February," he said grimly.

He stood on the fringe of the lobby and savored his victory. It was indeed sweet. He'd followed the drama in the restaurant and taken heart from Ms. Collins's abrupt departure. But Malcolm had followed her. He allowed himself to relive his anxiety as he'd imagined Malcolm changing her mind.

He had decided against following them. It was too soon to show himself, and he had believed Ms. Collins still had time to prove her loyalty. He would have taken that opportunity away from her if he had revealed himself. He had made the right decision, hadn't he? She'd proven herself worthy of his family.

He sighed with deep relief as he gazed around the opulent lobby. It was well lit, nearly blinding with white stone walls and white-and-silver, marbled floors. He stood beside one of the half-dozen lush plants that added to the décor with their flamboyant accents.

The area was spacious and sparsely furnished, but still he felt hemmed in by the bodies congregating near him. He felt oppressed by their presence, contaminated by their smell. And the room was far too bright.

With the back of his hand, he dabbed at the sweat above his upper lip, then turned toward the hotel entrance. It was all right to leave now. He had fulfilled his duty to his family. He could return to their bosom, where he felt safe and accepted.

As he walked toward the surface lot where he'd parked his black Jeep, he thought again of his victory over Malcolm and Tyrone. He'd kept watch on Tyrone and Ms. Collins's friend, with an impatient eye on the time. He had begun to second-guess himself, reconsidering his decision to follow them, when Malcolm had returned. He had been too far away to hear what Malcolm had told Tyrone and the woman. However, triumph had filled him at the expression on Malcolm's face. Malcolm kept shaking his head. Tyrone had looked disappointed. Ms. Collins's friend had appeared stunned.

He'd wanted to cheer, pump his fist in the air. He still did as he almost danced to the surface parking lot. Ms. Collins had come to her senses. He wouldn't have to implement his plan after all. He was glad. He would hate to have to hurt her. But he would do whatever it took to protect his family.

# CHAPTER TWO

"That was a wasted effort," Nicole muttered to herself as she dumped her bags in the living room of her one-bedroom apartment, then strode back to the kitchen to call her younger brother.

"Hey, D. I'm back," she greeted him when he answered the phone, trying but failing to reach a jovial tone.

"You're back?" Derrick's smooth baritone carried his confusion. "You're a day early."

She paused, leaning against the kitchen counter. "Los Angeles didn't work out."

"Oh, Nicky," Derrick groaned, seeming to feel her disappointment as his own. "What happened?"

Nicole sighed. She really should be all cried out by now. After getting a list of today's flights back to New York, she'd spent Wednesday night crying herself to sleep. But she still felt an uncomfortable lump in her throat, making it hard for her to speak.

"Malcolm owns Celestial Productions."

"Malcolm?" Derrick repeated, baffled. Half a second later, Nicole almost heard his long-term memory click. "Malcolm Bryant?"

"The one and only." Nicole pulled a glass out of a cupboard and filled it with cold water from the tap.

"Wow," Derrick breathed. Then he paused. "Does he want *InterDimensions* for the story or because it's yours?"

"I don't know, and I don't care. I can't work with him." Nicole took a drink, then sighed. "But I don't know if I can afford to reject his offer. How's Simone?"

"She took a bad turn last night, Nicky." Worry for their cousin deepened her brother's voice. "She has an infection and a fever. Aunt Rose is with her now."

"Oh, D." A chill ran through Nicole at the news. "How's Aunt Rose?"

"She looks like she's aged ten years. I think she's starting to lose hope."

"Is anyone with her?" Nicole glanced at the clock.

It was early afternoon. She'd wanted to shower and change, and perhaps eat, before going to the hospital. But she didn't want her aunt to be alone at this frightening time. Someone needed to be there to take care of her. Rose wouldn't eat without prodding and had to be dragged from her daughter's bedside, even to sleep.

"Guy switched shifts with a co-worker so he could have the afternoon off," Derrick said, referring to Rose's son.

"I'll get to the hospital as soon as I can." Nicole paused, then smacked her kitchen counter. "If only Simone's company hadn't laid her off."

"If only she could have afforded to extend her medical insurance."

They shared a moment of silence that was thick with disbelief and heavy with sorrow.

"I can't believe the hospital won't put her on the organ-donor recipient list until they know she can pay for the operation." Nicole had lost count of the number of times she'd made that statement.

"Nicky, if you don't want to work with Malcolm, we can come up with another idea to get the money," Derrick proposed.

"How? We all pooled our resources, giving more than we could afford, and still we came up short. A movie contract is our last hope. It gives us more than enough to make up the difference."

"I know the divorce wasn't easy for you. Do you think you'll be able to work with him?"

Nicole clutched the cordless phone, channeling her desperation into her grip. "I don't think we have a choice."

"I'm sorry, Nicky."

"I'm sorry, too. Sorry Simone is in such pain, and sorry our family is experiencing another tragedy."

"A lot of years have passed. You and Malcolm aren't the same people you used to be."

"Maybe. Maybe not." Nicole rubbed her stomach, remembering the guilt that had pummeled her as she'd stood in the Los Angeles hotel room facing her past.

"I don't want you to do something you're not comfortable with," her brother said.

"Don't worry about me. We need to focus on Simone," Nicole said. But her mind still rebelled against letting Malcolm Bryant back into her life. *There must be another way.*

"I've checked into the motel," Malcolm told Tyrone over the phone. After giving his partner his room number and the motel's phone number, he assured him, "I'll call you daily."

"And you'll be back Monday?" Tyrone asked again.

"I should be," Malcolm replied, avoiding a commitment. "Listen, Ty, Nicole's not the same woman I knew. It's going to take a while to figure out the best way to approach her. But her agent's willing to talk to me. I'm hoping that, between the two of us, we can convince Nicole to sign the contract and get this project moving."

"I hope so, too." Tyrone sighed. "We really need this contract, Mal. We can do great things with the *InterDimensions* movie. And, if we do, great things will happen for us."

"I know," Malcolm agreed. "I'll check back with you

later today. I want to call Denise and make sure we're still on for tomorrow."

"Okay. Good luck."

"I'll need it."

Malcolm disconnected, then called Denise's office. He half-sat, half-reclined on the lumpy motel bed, listening to the agent's phone ring.

His gaze traveled his clean but cramped quarters. He could smell cigarette smoke in his nonsmoking room, which was several steps removed from the spacious executive suites in Los Angeles he'd reserved for Nicole and her agent. He'd been grateful Tyrone hadn't even raised an eyebrow when the usually thrifty Malcolm had approved the invoice for the expensive accommodations. He'd been trying to impress Nicole, he admitted to himself, feeling like a foolish schoolboy.

Denise's assistant answered the phone and explained the agent was on another line with a client. He left his name and his motel telephone number and room number, and asked that Denise call him back.

Malcolm moved to the windows. Back in New York. He and Nicole had met as students at New York University. Met and fallen in love. He had been a senior, she a junior. After her graduation, they'd moved to Los Angeles where they'd married, tried to start a family, and divorced.

New York had changed a lot in the eleven years since he'd left, he thought, studying the high-rises on top of high-rises and the human congestion in the City That Never Sleeps. How much had he and Nicole changed? Too much? Or not enough?

Nicole gripped the receiver, trying to hold back her nervousness. "Denise, there are hundreds of production companies in this country. There's got to be one out there that's still interested in the movie rights for my book."

"Yeah, and it's called Celestial Productions," Denise answered dryly.

"Okay. Two production companies interested in the movie rights," Nicole muttered.

"Face it, Nicky. We're crapping out here. It's time to wake up."

Nicole squeezed her eyes shut as images of spinning clocks and Simone floated across her mind. "Trust me, I'm wide awake."

"Then let's face facts. No other production company in this country is going to agree to your terms. You're a talented writer. Very successful. Highly acclaimed. But as an executive producer, you're nothing. Nobody."

"Thank you, Denise." Nicole laced her voice with heavy sarcasm.

"Girl, you know I only tell it like it is." Denise sounded unperturbed. "You don't have a track record. You're not Stephen King. And God knows they've changed King's stories so much, I wonder if *he* even recognizes them."

"But I'm willing to give up my request for executive producer privileges."

"Why should you when you can have both?"

Nicole cradled her forehead in the palm of her free hand. "You're right." She sighed. "I don't want to look up at the screen and not recognize my story. I understand some things may need to be changed. But I want the integrity of my characters and the story's suspense to remain intact."

"The only way I can guarantee that you'll have even a snowball's chance in Hollywood of recognizing your story is if you sign with Celestial Productions," Denise stated.

Nicole wandered to the window. An image of an hourglass superimposed itself on the harried, half-commercial, half-residential neighborhood outside. The sand drained quickly. "There's no other production company interested in the movie rights?"

"Well." Denise paused. "There is one company that's still interested."

"But you said—"

"But they don't want to give you executive producer

privileges," Denise continued. "I know the rights are important to you. That's why I didn't mention it before."

"You're right, Denise." Nicole sighed again. "I guess I've just run out of time."

"Maybe. Maybe not. Come in to my office tomorrow morning. Eleven-thirty. Give us a chance to talk about things."

"There's nothing to talk about."

"Come in to my office, Nicky."

Nicole paused. She didn't see the benefit of meeting with her agent. What more was there to talk about? But with a mental shrug, she capitulated. "All right, Denise. I'll see you at eleven-thirty tomorrow."

"Thanks."

Nicole hung up the phone, then returned to her bedroom and pulled her space-saver treadmill out from under her bed. As she jogged on the treadmill, she let her mind wander. She tried to concentrate on plotting her next *InterDimensions* story line, but Simone, Malcolm, and the movie rights kept slipping into her thoughts.

After loving each other so completely, she and Malcolm had been strangers by the end of their marriage. The thought of working with him after that emotionally wrenching experience made her stomach burn. Nicole prodded the treadmill to a faster setting, forcing herself to concentrate on breathing rather than on the memory of how much they'd disappointed each other on the way out of their marriage.

Malcolm prowled the threadbare carpet of his motel room, debating the merits of bypassing Nicole's agent and contacting his ex-wife directly. He had left the message for Denise more than an hour ago. He didn't want to harass the only ally he and Tyrone had, but he couldn't wait all day, either. Malcolm felt the tension bunching in his shoulders.

Should he call Nicole? Tyrone was expecting an update,

and his friend would strain a heart valve if he didn't hear something soon. He didn't want to call his partner just to tell him he hadn't heard from Nicole. That would tip Tyrone right over the edge. He would take that information and craft a tale of doom and disaster. Tyrone was probably breathing into a paper bag by now.

Malcolm paced the small, dingy room, casting measuring looks at the beige phone. He dropped to the queen-sized bed, his hand hovering above the receiver. Who should he call? Tyrone, to admit he hadn't heard from Nicole? Nicole, to talk to her personally? Or her agent, to have her ease the way? The room phone screamed, scattering his thoughts. Feeling both optimism and dread, he grabbed the smudged receiver. "Hello."

"I'm doing this for her." Denise skipped the pleasantries. "She needs this movie deal—for more reasons than you'll probably ever know. And a successful movie will be great for her career. You understand?"

"I understand," Malcolm said.

"Now, I don't know what happened between you and Nicole in the past, and I don't want to know," Denise continued. "It's your business. But whatever it was, she needs to close the door on it. I'm very fond of her, and I don't like to see her like this. You understand?"

"I understand," he repeated.

"Good. Now you know my motivation. What's yours?"

Caught off guard by the attack, Malcolm scrambled for footing. "Ty and I bid for the movie rights to *InterDimensions* because of the story. The series is written with a lot of visuals. *InterDimensions* will translate easily and very successfully to film."

"You've read all of the books?"

"We both have," Malcolm confirmed. "In addition, market research shows that similar movies targeted to the older-youth and single-adult audiences have netted strong profits."

Denise emitted a noncommittal hum. "That's a very

well-practiced response, Malcolm. I don't buy it, and I doubt Nicky will, either."

Malcolm also had his doubts. But he had no intention of admitting the opportunity to return to Nicole's life had played a large part in his willingness to accept her contract terms. He just hoped Nicole wouldn't challenge him as directly as her agent had.

"It may sound like a sales pitch, but it's the truth," he assured her.

Denise hummed again. "You know, Nicky has worked very hard to get where she is today. She wasn't an overnight success."

"I know. I've followed her career." Malcolm recalled the first *InterDimensions* book had been published three years ago, the same year he'd started Celestial Productions. He'd remembered her working on the series when they were together. She'd put her writing aside after the miscarriage, though.

He knew the first book hadn't become popular until the second installment had been released six months later. Now, all three books had a cult success with a loyal and growing following.

"I'm not going to do anything to undermine her work," Malcolm continued.

Denise's voice grew hard. "If you hurt her again, California won't be far enough for you to go. I'm from New York. Born and raised. I know people. You understand?"

"I understand."

"Good. Be at my office at eleven-forty-five tomorrow morning." Denise disconnected.

Nicole sat in one of the comfortably stuffed chairs in front of Denise's polished, mahogany desk. A big picture window behind her agent's amethyst leather executive chair provided a visual journal of the bustling community outside the office building.

The cozy office was decorated in warm mahogany wood

and accented in vibrant colors that reflected the owner's personality. A forest-green love seat with gold-and-red throw pillows sat against the right wall and was flanked by large, leafy plants. Across the room, a conversation table stood with two small chairs in the same forest green as the love seat. Although Nicole had never asked, she suspected the beige carpet was compliments of the management firm that owned the building in which Denise's company, The Maitland Agency, rented office space.

Nicole stared at the list of production houses Denise had approached on her behalf in the past nine months. She'd seen the chart before. It included the company name, address, and representative. The words *no longer interested* marched down the final column until she came to the Celestial Productions entry.

"The other company you referred to yesterday—" she began.

"Carter Enterprises. It's in L.A. as well," Denise filled in.

"Do you think they would reconsider my requests?" Nicole scanned the list again, pausing at Carter Enterprises's entry. "They're willing to pay ten percent more than what I'm asking. Surely it would be worth it to them to save that money and just let me approve the script, location, and cast."

"That's what I keep telling them," Denise replied. "But apparently they think it's worth the money to pay you to shut up."

"Hush money." Nicole snorted. "It makes you wonder what they want to do to my work."

"It certainly does."

"I should have accepted one of the offers tendered the first time Hollywood showed interest in my stories. I just couldn't trust someone else to interpret my characters. I still don't."

"Girl, I completely understand. You know I only take on work I believe in. And I fell in love with *InterDimensions*. Absolutely fell in love." Denise pressed a small, bejeweled hand to her ample bosom. "It's like you're their mother and I'm their doting aunt. You understand?"

"Yes, I do." Nicole smiled.

Denise was a terrier. She represented Nicole fiercely at the negotiating table and always looked out for her best interests. She had bullied Nicole's publisher into going back in print after the series' popularity had soared due to Nicole's modest marketing efforts and a frenzy of word-of-mouth recommendations. It had also helped that the series appealed to both genders and a large age group.

Nicole leaned forward to return the list to Denise. Propping her elbows on her knees, she hooked her thumbs under her chin and tapped her fingers together, her lips pursed in concentration.

"It looks like I don't have a choice," she mused. "I need the money, and I'm out of time. I'll have to accept Malcolm's offer."

Denise's intercom buzzed. "Excuse me." She picked up the red receiver. "Yes, Leslie? Thanks. Please send him in."

Nicole frowned. "Who is it?"

Denise ignored the question. "What you need is an opportunity to get used to the idea of Malcolm being back in your life."

Nicole looked over her shoulder as the door opened. And Malcolm Bryant walked in.

"Here's your opportunity," her agent announced.

At first, Nicole couldn't credit what she was seeing. Malcolm. Here in New York. Denise's office, to be exact. This couldn't be happening. She would have popped out of her seat if she thought her knees would support her.

She turned back to her agent. "What's going on?"

Denise held up both hands with their plum-colored fingernails. "Face it, the two of you need to talk. Clear the air, so to speak, so you can put the past behind you and work together."

"We don't need to rehash the past," Nicole contradicted. "We just need to make the movie."

Denise gave her a level stare. "I've never known you

not to try to make something work. I only asked him
here so you can talk. The final decision is still yours. But
you owe it to yourself to try."

"Denise, I don't need a reunion. All I need is a check."
Nicole felt ashamed when she saw the genuine concern
in Denise's eyes.

"Nicky, you'll never get a second chance to make your
first movie. I don't want this to be a bad experience for
you. And I don't think it has to be," Denise said.

"Denise—"

"Come on, Nicky. It's not going to kill you."

Malcolm shifted into her line of vision. "Just give me
an hour of your time. That's all I'm asking. We'll have
lunch. Please."

In the end, it was the "please" that made the difference.

"Fine." She picked up her purse and coat, then brushed
past him to pull open the door. "Separate checks."

Malcolm followed Nicole down the two flights of stairs
to the lobby. Her sneakered feet were almost silent on
the steps now. Malcolm decided it was a good sign that
she'd stopped stomping.

Her figure-distorting wardrobe for today consisted of
a nut-brown, knee-length coat over a teal-green, crew-
neck sweater and blue jeans. A clip at the nape of her
neck again secured her hair. Malcolm missed the sassy
little cut she used to wear.

"I'll drive," he said as they reached the lobby level.

"This is New York." Nicole zipped her coat. "You don't
drive, you walk. Follow me."

Malcolm put his hand on her forearm and felt Nicole
stiffen beneath his touch. "I'm not going to discuss a movie
deal with you at a McDonald's." He smiled to himself. Her
quick frown told him he could still—occasionally—read
her mind. Maybe she hadn't changed as much as he'd
feared. "There's a restaurant down the street. We'll walk.
Together."

"Fine." She tugged on her gloves. "It had better be a
good restaurant."

"I'm sure you won't be disappointed." Malcolm tried a smile, pulling on his own gloves. "It's a little Italian place. Do you still live for pasta?"

Nicole ignored his question, obviously not ready to stroll down memory lane.

"Okay. Let's go," Malcolm said. But when she turned toward him, he couldn't move away. Instead, he stood fossilized by Nicole's regard. He wondered what she was thinking as her gaze skimmed his slate-gray tweed overcoat hanging open over his pale gray suit and high-collared white shirt.

"What is it?" he asked as her gaze darted away from him.

She shrugged and looked up at him. "I'm surprised you have such a heavy winter coat. It must have been eleven years since you've needed one."

"I visit my family in Michigan a couple of times a year, including Christmas." He took her arm as they continued across the lobby. He was pleased she only eased away from his touch rather than shrugging him off. Progress.

Malcolm held the lobby door open for her, and they walked in silence to the restaurant. After being seated and placing their orders, Malcolm, taking advantage of the fact that Nicole looked everywhere but at him, studied her again.

Her bulky sweater masked her figure. His Nicole had worn clothes that had complemented her generous curves. The Nicole he'd known had worn makeup as well. This Nicole didn't. At least not on the occasions he'd seen her. But her delicate features were beautiful with or without makeup. Her slanted ebony eyes, brown skin, and dusky rose lips didn't need enhancements. His gaze followed her small, slim hands as they stirred her iced tea. No nail polish, no rings. He hadn't wanted to admit his relief, not even to himself, when he'd discovered she hadn't remarried.

She looked up and caught him staring at her. He saw the flash of irritation in her eyes before her lips parted.

Malcolm spoke to forestall the attack. "Your agent is very protective of you. How long have you worked with her?"

"Since I started shopping my manuscript. I signed as one of her first clients after she left the firm she worked for to start her own agency."

"It looks like the two of you make a good team."

"I think so." Nicole picked up her iced tea and sipped through her straw.

"She's a terrier," Malcolm teased.

Nicole blinked, a smile tipping her generous lips before she remembered to scowl again.

"How's your mother?" he asked, hoping to build on her softening mood. When she stiffened, he realized he had miscalculated.

"She died," Nicole murmured.

Malcolm felt his eyes widen with shock. He remembered the loving woman who had welcomed him into her family and treated him like her own. He reached across the table and gripped her hand. "Nicky, I'm so sorry. When?"

She tried to pull her hand away but stilled when his hold didn't break. "Two years ago." Her tone did not encourage questions, but Malcolm pressed on.

"What happened?"

"Cancer." Her tone was clipped. "Malcolm, I'm not going to answer any more questions. This is business, remember? Let's not get personal."

Malcolm saw pain and anger swirling in her eyes. He also saw wariness. *Why?* "What are you afraid of?"

Nicole made a visible effort to relax. He watched her look around the small, neighborhood restaurant. Its dark, scarred hardwood chairs. Its faded red-and-white-checked tablecloth. Italian music played softly in the background as he waited for her answer.

Nicole's gaze returned to his. "I'm afraid you'll quit before the project's over. That you'll leave in the middle of production or something."

Malcolm went cold. He'd never expected that response. "What makes you think I would do something like that?"

Nicole reached out and ran the tip of her index finger over the fake red bud in the plastic centerpiece on their table. "Despite your company's success with previous projects, you're not well-known in the film industry, and I'm not well-known, either. We're going to face a lot of challenges making and marketing this project, and I don't know how you'll react."

Malcolm leaned into the table. "You say that as though you don't know me. We knew each other for seven years. For five of those years, we lived together."

Nicole sipped her iced tea. "And during three of those years, we were married." She held his gaze. "And when things got tough, you left."

Malcolm clenched his teeth at the unfair accusation. If she hadn't pushed him away, he never would have left. But he steered the conversation back to business. Their more personal discussion would need to wait for another time and place.

"We would have a signed contract detailing all aspects of the project." He strove for a moderate tone, suppressing the anger beneath. "If my word that I won't abandon the project isn't good enough, we could add a clause to the contract to make you more comfortable."

Bitter humor gleamed in her eyes. "We had a signed contract before, Mal." She folded her hands on the table. "I think the clause read something like, 'Till death do us part.'"

Malcolm felt his face heat as the waiter arrived with their meals. He waited until the young man served their entrées and left them again.

"If you didn't want the divorce, why did you sign the papers?" Malcolm twirled the pasta onto his fork. The scents of tangy red sauce and seasonings wafted up to him.

Nicole lifted wide, ebony eyes to his and blinked with exaggerated innocence. "Oh, I'm sorry. Was I supposed to beg you to stay?" She held up a hand to stop Malcolm's frustrated response. "I must not have gotten that script revision."

Oh, she was enjoying herself. Malcolm made a concerted effort to relax his jaw before he wore the enamel from his teeth. "This isn't getting us anywhere."

"You've noticed."

Steam rose from her manicotti as Nicole sliced it into manageable portions. Malcolm sympathized with the entrée.

"Mistakes were made in the past."

"I'll say," she muttered, slipping a forkful of pasta into her mouth.

"On both sides," Malcolm added pointedly. "Can't we leave them there? This is about business."

"It's also about trust." Nicole sipped her iced tea. "You don't have a very good track record for sticking through the tough times, Malcolm."

"You're determined to react to this emotionally," he shot back, receiving visceral pleasure from the glare she aimed at him. "Rationally, you know this movie deal will benefit both of us."

Nicole put down her drink, staring at Malcolm in silence. He held her gaze—a bewildering mixture of anger and desperation. The anger never went away, but the desperation seemed to grow. And then she lowered her gaze. Moments felt like hours as he waited for her response.

"Yes, I know. And I accept your offer," she said softly.

Malcolm stared at her. "What did you say?"

"I said I accept your offer." Nicole lifted her gaze to his. "I'll sign the contract giving Celestial Productions the movie rights to the first *InterDimensions* book."

Malcolm couldn't believe she'd given in this soon. She had cut him down with finality in Los Angeles, and her reaction to him this morning had been hostile, to say the least. "What made you change your mind?"

"You don't need to worry about that. I've changed my mind. That's all that matters."

"You're right. I know. I'm just surprised." Malcolm leaned back in his chair. "Great. Well, once the contract is signed, we'll move you to L.A. to start pre-production."

"I'll need time to make some arrangements before the move." Nicole watched the server refill her glass.

"How much time?"

"I don't know." Nicole shrugged, playing with the rest of her manicotti. "I should have a better idea Monday."

"Is there anything I can help you with?"

She flicked a dismissive glance toward him. "Not a thing."

Malcolm wondered if he should press further. He decided against it. For now, he'd celebrate this first victory. He tried a smile. "Okay. We'll eat now, deal with the details later."

Conversation was stilted at best with Malcolm selecting innocuous subjects and Nicole reluctantly following his lead. They ate mechanically, and when lunch was over, Malcolm walked with Nicole to the subway station. She had rejected his offer to drive her home.

"Here's my cell phone number." Malcolm handed her his business card.

Nicole glanced at his contact information. "I don't think I'll need to discuss anything with you. You and Denise can decide what time we'll meet to sign the contract. Anytime Monday works for me. Denise will let me know what you've decided."

"Are you sure you don't want me to wait with you for the train?" he asked again.

"Positive." Nicole turned toward the subway entrance.

Malcolm halted her with a hand on her arm. "Will you call me to let me know you've gotten home safely?"

Nicole glanced at the hand restraining her. "Don't worry. I'll be careful. At least until I've signed your contract."

Malcolm's patience snapped. "I don't care about the contract."

Nicole arched a brow. "Then why are you in New York?"

Malcolm continued as though she hadn't spoken. "I care about you. About your safety."

32 *Patricia Sargeant*

"Sure you do," she tossed back before descending into the subway station.

"Be careful," Malcolm shouted.

"You, too," Nicole shouted back.

Malcolm watched until she disappeared underground. She was stubborn and antagonistic. He was better off keeping their contact to the bare minimum. But he knew he wouldn't, because he couldn't.


He slammed the door, letting it reverberate in the threshold, and stomped across the room. He had just found out Malcolm was in New York trying to convince Ms. Collins to change her mind about the movie rights. He knew Malcolm wanted control of his *InterDimensions* family, but he wouldn't allow that to happen. Rage flowed warm and thick in his veins. He turned and marched to the opposite wall.

He would not allow his family to be cheapened by another man's greed. He would do whatever was necessary to protect them from being misinterpreted by people who didn't understand them as well as he did.

He stalked back toward the window, pausing as he reached his desk to pick up the framed photo of his family. It was the cover of the first *InterDimensions* book. He gazed at the illustration of the honorable captain and his courageous second-in-command. His temper cooled, and he began to think more clearly. His family owed their lives to Ms. Collins. For that, he would be forever grateful, but she didn't have the right to exploit them.

"I'll protect you." He carefully returned the photograph to his desk.

He would have to put his plan into action. He couldn't trust that Ms. Collins would continue to deny Malcolm the movie rights. He knew from past experience that Malcolm was very persuasive. He couldn't remain in the shadows any longer. He just hoped no one would be hurt.

# CHAPTER THREE

"Well, Phoenix," Nicole addressed her spider plant. "What if we brought Senator O'Neill back to the *InterDimensions* space station?"

Nicole gave Phoenix a moment to absorb the story line while she poured water into the plant's soil. She had named all of her plants, and she thought Phoenix, the name of one of the X-Men's female heroines, the perfect name for her plotting partner. Like the Marvel Comics heroine, Nicole had lost her direction for a while, and then she'd started writing again.

But with Simone's illness, Nicole had identified her kryptonite. Her family's pain made her weak, and worry had brought on a hellacious case of writer's block. She stroked one of the spider plant's offsprings, then exchanged the watering can for the misting bottle. While she sprayed Phoenix's leaves, she combed her mind for a story idea for the fifth book in her science-fiction series.

"O'Neill hasn't made an appearance since book three. I think it's time to remind our readers of his goal to federalize the station. What should we make him do? What brings him to the station?" she asked her silent partner.

Nicole continued to roll the idea around in her mind as she moved on to her other babies, including a flourishing African violet named Isis and a rabbit-legged fern named Batgirl. She fed them all water as well as words of love and encouragement.

The ringing telephone burst the creative web she was trying to weave. Foiled, she glanced at the clock. It was a little after 8:00 A.M. Who would call this early on a Saturday morning? As she realized the call could be bad news about Simone, her heart thumped once, then seemed to stop. She rushed to the phone and grabbed the receiver.

"Hello."

"Leave my family alone," the caller demanded.

"Excuse me?" Nicole asked. The voice was so muffled, she couldn't be certain of the words.

"Just let them live their lives."

"I think you have the wrong number."

Nicole replaced the receiver and tried to shrug off the incident. At least it wasn't a call about Simone. But something about the distorted voice made her uneasy. The doorbell was a welcome distraction, at least until she checked the peephole and saw who stood on the other side. She opened the door.

"What are you doing here?" she demanded, experiencing an unpleasant sense of déjà vu.

"An unusual greeting you've adopted," Malcolm observed. "Do you use it with everyone or just me?"

"What are you doing here?"

"I brought you breakfast." He lifted a bagel bag and a drink carrier, which held two coffee containers. "You're welcome. May I come in? I hate to eat standing up."

Nicole debated whether to send Malcolm on his way or give in to the call of caffeine. Before she could decide, the apartment door across the hall opened and her elderly neighbor, Mrs. Velasquez, stepped out. Surprised pleasure spread across the woman's features. Nicole stifled a groan and forced herself not to run back into her apartment.

"Hello, sweetheart," the elderly meddler lilted in a heavy Puerto Rican accent. Her bright bird eyes darted between Nicole and Malcolm. "How are you doing today?"

"I'm fine, thank you, Mrs. Velasquez. How are you?"

"I'm fine, sweetheart. Just fine." She continued to glance between Nicole and Malcolm.

"Good." Nicole searched for a graceful way to end the stilted exchange. "I appreciate your taking care of my mail and plants while I was away."

"Oh, it was no problem, sweetheart. No problem at all." Her neighbor waved a hand dismissively, sending her bulky, purple purse on a downward slide from her plump shoulder.

Nicole knew her neighbor was dying for an introduction, but she didn't want to give Malcolm that much importance in her life. As though sensing her thoughts and wanting to thwart her, Malcolm stepped forward to do the honors himself.

He wrapped his long fingers around the woman's small hand. "Good morning, Mrs. Velasquez. I'm Malcolm Bryant, a friend of Nicole's."

"Oh," Mrs. Velasquez cooed, her round cheeks flushed with excitement. "I didn't know Nicky had such handsome friends."

Nicole cringed at the sly look Mrs. Velasquez slid her way. She envisioned her privacy being ripped to shreds right before her very eyes.

"Well, I can see you're on your way out—" Nicole began in a desperate attempt to stop the carnage.

"Do you know, Mr. Bryant—" Mrs. Velasquez's voice rolled over Nicole's words.

"Malcolm, please," her ex-husband encouraged as he towered over the tiny lady.

"Malcolm." Mrs. Velasquez smiled coyly. "Do you know that in the three years I've lived across this very hall from Nicky, I have not seen her with a single boyfriend?"

"No?" Malcolm asked.

Nicole shrank inside herself. In her peripheral vision, she saw Malcolm look toward her, but she was too embarrassed to meet his eyes.

"No," Mrs. Velasquez happily continued. "Not in three

years. And she's so lovely. Little and lovely. Don't you think so?"

"Yes, I do." Malcolm caught and held Nicole's gaze.

"Oh, she talks to some of the men in the building. The old men," Mrs. Velasquez emphasized. "The only young men I see her talk to are relatives. Her brother and her cousin. But you, you're not old. Right? And you're not related to her. Right?" Mrs. Velasquez smiled up at Malcolm. Obviously, she thought she had identified a romantic prospect.

Nicole had had enough. "Well," she tried again, raising her voice, "I can see you're on your way out, Mrs. Velasquez. I don't want to keep you." She stepped aside, signaling Malcolm to precede her into her apartment.

"Oh, it's no problem, sweetheart." Mrs. Velasquez watched as Malcolm crossed Nicole's threshold. "Will I see you at church tomorrow morning?"

"I'll probably attend the evening services tonight." Nicole smiled. "You know Sunday is my day to rest."

Gazing over Nicole's shoulder, Mrs. Velasquez winked. "You'll probably need it."

With a final cherubic smile, the incurable romantic walked away, leaving a gaping Nicole staring after her. After picking up her dropped jaw, she followed Malcolm into her apartment, pulling the door closed behind her.

"So, can I interest you in breakfast?" Malcolm asked again, lifting the bag and the drink carrier.

"I've already had breakfast." Nicole wanted to stand her ground, but her stubbornness wavered in the face of coffee.

"It's only eight o'clock," Malcolm said, walking past her kitchen into an area she magnanimously referred to as her dining room.

Nicole followed him, feeling slightly put out. "I've been up since six."

Malcolm paused in front of her dinette table, a furniture discount store triumph. "On a Saturday?"

Nicole smiled at his incredulous tone. "I'm a writer.

We don't restrict our work to eight-to-five weekdays. We write whenever the Muse strikes us."

"And this one struck at six? How rude." Malcolm put the bag and carrier on the table and shrugged out of his coat. His eyes widened as he gazed toward the window. "Wow. Are you zoned for this park land?" He stepped closer to the foliage.

"Very funny," she said.

Trailing after him, Nicole tried to view her plant menagerie through his eyes. She supposed it could be a bit overwhelming.

"Do you still name your plants after comic book heroes?" He turned toward her. The warmth of his brown gaze beckoned her into their shared memories.

She resisted the call. "No. I name them after heroines now. I don't have much experience with heroes."

Malcolm's gaze cooled, and he turned back to the plants. He nodded toward a ficus in the corner. "Isn't that Superman?"

"No," she replied, surprised he'd remembered she'd had a ficus. "That's Superwoman. The Man of Steel didn't survive the move." *I barely survived it myself*, she thought.

"And who are these beauties?" Amusement tinged Malcolm's voice as he pointed to a clique of potted plants on top of a waist-high bookcase.

Gesturing toward each plant in turn, Nicole identified them: "The dwarf nikita is Harley Quinn. She's the Joker's girlfriend, remember?" Nicole waited for Malcolm's nod before continuing. "The cactus is Catwoman. And the miniature dendrobium orchid is Poison Ivy."

Malcolm frowned. "Aren't those Batman's villains?"

Nicole flicked him a chiding glance. "They aren't bad," she explained, returning to the dining room. "They're misunderstood."

"Oh. I see." Amusement returned to Malcolm's voice.

Nicole examined the bagels. "How did you get my address?"

"Your agent gave it to me. And the directions," Malcolm said.

"How helpful of her." Nicole's tone contradicted her words.

"I thought so." Malcolm grinned, revealing the dimple she used to caress.

She looked away. "Are you trying to bribe me with food?"

"Would it work?"

"No." Her hands hovered above the bag, restless for some task. "Do you want your bagel toasted?"

"That would be great. Thanks."

She grabbed the bag and escaped toward the kitchen.

"Do you have any clothes that aren't baggy?" Malcolm called after her.

Nicole stopped, glancing first at her faded, oversized gray sweat suit, then back at Malcolm. "I have a piece of paper in my files that states you've signed away your rights to comment on my wardrobe."

Malcolm frowned. "Can we have one conversation in which you don't bring up the divorce?"

"Sure." She forced a grin. "Which one do you want?" Nicole continued into the kitchen.

The sink, counters, and overhead cupboards formed a call-through between the kitchen and the dining room. Nicole leaned her hips against the opposite countertops and used the call-through to study Malcolm as she waited for the bagels to toast.

"Why are you here, Malcolm? I told you I would sign the contract."

"I know." Malcolm wandered back to the dining room. "But since we're going to work together, we need to spend some time together."

Nicole frowned. "Why?" She took the bagels out of the toaster.

"Because I think your hostility is going to hurt the project."

Stung, Nicole stood away from the counter. "My hostility?"

Malcolm cocked an eyebrow at her. "Do you deny you've been hostile to me?"

"With good reason."

"Is the reason good enough to risk the project?"

Nicole opened the refrigerator. She thought it debatable whether her hostility was putting the project at risk. However, she'd consider his concern objectively, when he wasn't around. For now, she'd change the subject. "Do you want butter?"

Malcolm's sigh was impatient. "Sure."

"Orange juice?"

"Yes, please."

Nicole poured two glasses of orange juice. She turned to carry them to the table and almost spilled them onto the caramel sweater spanning Malcolm's broad chest. She hadn't heard him enter the kitchen.

"Here." She handed the glasses to him.

Malcolm carried the juice into the dining room. Nicole followed with the plates of toasted bagels and butter. She passed him the butter and sat across the table from him.

"So, what are you doing today?" He buttered his bagel.

"I'm working on the revisions for book four and the outline for book five," she answered, ignoring her writer's block.

"All day? Do you want some butter?"

"Pretty much. No, thanks."

"How 'bout going to the movies with me later?"

"I'm on a deadline," she reminded him.

"It's just a few hours," he coaxed. "It might help you get over your hostility toward me."

"Malcolm, this is not a joking matter."

"It's been four years, Nicky."

"Actually, Mal," she countered, "it's been two days."

"I'm going to get bored in that motel room all day."

"I'm not your entertainment." Nicole put down her coffee. "Stop pressuring me. I'll sign the contract Monday, and I'll work with you on the movie. I have no intention of jeopardizing this project. After all, it will have my name on it as well."

Malcolm paused, searching for the right words to persuade her. "We need to develop a working relationship. Or are you afraid of finding out how well we'll work together?"

Nicole's ebony eyes sparked, and Malcolm braced himself for the eruption. Instead, he heard a door squeak and a childlike voice called, "Momma?"

Malcolm looked toward the voice. He froze as a little girl weaved sleepily into the room. Her hair was gathered in two mussed braids. A pale yellow flannel gown hung to her ankles and billowed around her thin body. Malcolm couldn't breathe.

"Hi, baby. Did we wake you?"

Nicole greeted the child in a sweet, soft tone that made his heart weep. She pulled the little girl onto her lap and nuzzled the top of the child's head with her lips. Here was love, he thought, rubbing his chest. How much he had missed it.

"I had a dream. I thought I heard my momma," the child whispered. She rested her cheek on Nicole's chest and closed her eyes.

Nicole tucked the little girl closer into her, creating a warm cocoon around them that left him on the outside, yearning in.

"Was it the sad dream again?" Nicole whispered back. "Yes."

Nicole kissed the crown of the girl's head. "Do you want to talk about it?"

"Not yet." She wiggled closer still.

Nicole started to speak, then glanced at Malcolm and appeared to change her mind. "Okay. I'll be here when you're ready."

"Okay." The little girl sighed. When she opened her eyes, her gaze locked with Malcolm's. "Good morning."

Malcolm stared at her catlike ebony eyes like a deer caught in the headlights.

"Lynnie, this is Mr. Bryant. Mr. Bryant, my goddaughter, Lynnette. She's my cousin Simone's daughter."

Regret swept through Malcolm. What had he missed these past four years? What could he have had if pride and fear hadn't crippled him?

"Good morning, Lynnie," he said. "I hope our talking didn't wake you."

"No, you didn't wake me." She yawned wide before settling more comfortably into Nicole's lap.

Nicole tipped her wrist to check her watch. "Oops. We're running behind schedule, sweetie pie." She rubbed Lynnette's upper arms before sliding the little girl off her lap. Lynnette claimed the seat Nicole vacated, sitting sideways in the chair and swinging her legs.

"What would you like for breakfast?" Nicole called over her shoulder as she hurried into the kitchen. "Scrambled eggs, sausage, hash browns, panc—"

"Cereal," Lynnette interrupted in a singsong voice that suggested this was a rehearsed exchange. She slid a look toward Malcolm, her lips tipped shyly. Malcolm winked at her, and Lynnette ducked her head as her smile blossomed into a chubby-cheeked grin.

"Just cereal?" Nicole called incredulously, continuing the script.

"Just cereal," Lynnette affirmed. "Cereal and—"

"Juice," Nicole finished, carrying the requested meal on a tray. Once she'd placed the cereal, juice, and spoon on the table, she handed Lynnette a napkin, which the child crushed into the neck of her nightgown with pudgy, little hands.

"Thank you," Lynnette said, digging into the bowl.

"I'm going to get your clothes together, sweetie." Nicole stroked her goddaughter's hair. "Just call me if you need me."

"Okay," Lynnette answered, her attention on her cereal.

Nicole looked at Malcolm, and he understood her hesitancy. He gave her a reassuring smile to let her know he didn't mind watching Lynnette while Nicole was in the other room. Nicole hurried into what appeared to be her bedroom.

Malcolm returned his attention to his young companion, searching his brain for a conversational topic. He was accustomed to being around children. He visited with his nephews several times a year and spoke with them often on the phone. He was fluent in the language of Power Rangers, Transformers, and Dragonball Z. But somehow he didn't think those languages would interest this young-lady-in-training. He had steeled himself to ask about Blues Clues or even Barney, when she surprised him by opening her own dialogue.

"Are you a friend of my Aunt Nicky?"

"Yes, I am."

"How come I haven't seen you before?" she asked between spoonfuls of Apple Jacks.

"I live in California. This is my first trip back to New York in a long time," he added in an effort to extend the topic. Anything to avoid a discussion of Barney or Blues Clues.

"California?" Her eyes widened, and her spoon slipped from her fingers to clatter against the bowl. "Isn't that really far away?"

"Yes. It's about three thousand miles away."

"Wow," she breathed, concern coloring her tone. "How can you be friends with Aunty Nicky if you live so far away?"

"Well," Malcolm searched for a simple answer, "we aren't close friends."

Lynnette giggled at the unintended joke. She leaned forward eagerly, eyes sparkling in her small, brown face as she waited for his next comedic endeavor.

Malcolm laughed. "How old are you, Lynnie?"

"I'm four," she stated. "I'll be five on my next birthday."

With that, she launched into a discussion of her birthday plans: who she wanted to spend it with, where she wanted to go, and what she wanted to do. All the while, Malcolm wondered why the enthusiasm in the little girl's words wasn't reflected in her eyes.

YOU BELONG TO ME          43

Nicole reentered the room. "I'm sorry to break up the party, but it's time for you to hit the showers, sweetie pie."

"Okay." Lynnette hopped off the chair and dashed out of the room.

"Thank you for keeping her company," Nicole said.

Malcolm grinned. "It was my pleasure."

Pride and joy tinted her cheeks. "I'd better supervise her bath."

A knock sounded at the door as Nicole turned to leave the dining area. She tipped her wrist to check the time before answering it.

"You're early." Her words floated back to Malcolm as she greeted the new arrival. Although he couldn't see them, he could hear them, and Malcolm was concerned by the strain in Nicole's voice.

"How long does it take you to make cereal?" A male voice teased. Malcolm recognized the voice and prepared himself for the reunion with Nicole's overprotective younger brother.

"I have to do a bit more than make her cereal," Nicole said. "I can't send her out on the street naked."

"What's wrong?" Derrick asked.

"What makes you think something's wrong?"

"Well, for starters, you're blocking the door," her brother observed dryly.

"Oh. Sorry. Come in."

"Thank you." Sarcasm dripped playfully from the baritone voice.

The door closed, and Malcolm heard footsteps coming toward him.

"Derrick," Nicole said as she and her brother entered the room. "You remember Malcolm."

Derrick's eyes widened almost imperceptibly. "How could I forget?" he drawled.

Eyes that once had offered Malcolm friendship studied him coolly. Derrick took in the two place settings and the breakfast remains.

"Good to see you again, Derrick. How've you been?"

"Fine, thank you," Derrick replied. "And you?"

"Fine." Malcolm decided Derrick was probably waiting until Nicole was out of hearing range before delivering the retribution promised in his eyes.

"Aunty Nicky," Lynnette sang out, "I'm ready for my shower."

"I'll be right there, sweetie pie." Nicole considered the two large men taking each other's measure. "Do whatever you want, but don't bleed on my furniture." She turned in the direction of Lynnette's voice.

"What are you doing here?" Derrick asked.

The younger man's hostility triggered an answering antagonism in Malcolm. But Malcolm also had a sister. He understood Derrick's need to protect Nicole, so he decided against arguing and tried to reassure him.

"I wanted to discuss the movie project with Nicky," he explained.

Derrick nodded. His gaze slid back to the table settings, half-eaten bagels, and coffee containers. "What are you really doing here?"

The question poked at Malcolm's temper. "I told you the truth."

"Look." Derrick's tone hardened. "I'm not comfortable with the feeling that we're sacrificing Nicole for Simone. But I know we don't have any choice."

"What are you talking about?" Malcolm asked.

Derrick charged on, refusing to be sidetracked. "I'm warning you. If you hurt her again, you won't be able to hide this time."

Malcolm's temper jerked against its leash at the accusation he had hid after the divorce. He had a feeling rousing his temper was Derrick's goal. Malcolm further suspected Derrick's cool exterior belied a desire to punch him out.

They stood in silence, ignoring each other. The minutes dragged by until Nicole glided back into the room with a skipping Lynnette in tow.

"We're clean, clean, clean," Nicole sang. Her smile

faltered as though sensing the tension in her modest dining room.

Derrick's face glowed when he saw his young cousin. Malcolm blinked at the speed with which the younger man's earlier animosity disappeared.

"How's my best girl?" He hunkered down to allow Lynnette to fly into his open arms. The little lady was dressed in a pale pink sweater and dark green corduroy pants.

Sounds of helpless laughter whirled around Malcolm. Nicole grinned as she watched her small goddaughter struggle to plant a noisy kiss on Derrick's cheek while straining to evade a similar attack.

"Get your coat, sweetie pie." Nicole stroked Lynnette's neatly brushed hair. The little girl dashed out of the room.

Noting her brother scowling in Malcolm's direction, Nicole rubbed Derrick's upper arm. "We have more important things to worry about. Tell Aunt Rose that Lynnie had the sad dream again."

Derrick's scowl changed to a frown of concern. "Did she tell you about it this time?"

Nicole shook her head. "No, she didn't. She acts as though it doesn't bother her, but she's had it too often. Something must be troubling her."

Derrick nodded his agreement. "I'll tell Aunt Rose."

Malcolm sensed his reluctance. Apparently, Nicole did, too.

"I don't want to burden her, either," Nicole said. "But Lynnie needs us now, too."

The subject of their concern skipped back into the room. "I'm ready," she announced.

Nicole knelt and folded Lynnette into a bear hug. "Take care of Grandma."

"I will." Lynnette's thin, nut-brown arms wrapped just as desperately around Nicole.

Nicole drew back, allowing Derrick to take Lynnette's hand. "Be careful," she said as she followed them to the door.

"I'll see you later," Derrick answered.

"Bye, Mr. Bryant." Lynnette threw a wave over her shoulder.

Malcolm smiled. "Bye, Lynnie."

Derrick offered him a curt nod, then walked out.

Nicole sagged against the closed door. The need to comfort her propelled Malcolm forward. His protective instincts switched back on as though they'd never been apart, as though the divorce had never occurred. He'd always needed to keep her safe, even when she wouldn't let him.

He stopped just short of touching her, separated by a sigh, and spoke to her back. "What's wrong, Nicky?"

She flinched like a deer sensing danger. "Nothing."

She squared her shoulders and turned to face him. The animation had drained from her features, leaving behind a polite mask. She was shutting him out again. "You're worried about Lynnie," he pushed.

"She's having nightmares." Nicole walked past him.

Malcolm pivoted to keep her in sight and changed the direction of his questioning. "What did Derrick mean when he said they were sacrificing you for Simone?"

Nicole shrugged. "You should ask Derrick." She spoke over her shoulder, her gaze on the view outside.

"I did. He didn't tell me."

"I'm afraid I can't tell you, either."

"Can't or won't?" Malcolm envisioned a door closing between them.

Nicole turned to face him. "I've got a lot to take care of today, Malcolm. I'll see you Monday."

Malcolm hesitated, reluctant to let the door shut. "Do you want to see a movie?"

"No, thank you. I'm not in the mood for a movie."

"You could use a distraction, Nicky."

Nicole's mouth tipped in an ironic smile. "I don't need any more distractions. I just need some time to think."

"About what?" Malcolm changed gears again.

The half-smile returned. "Everything. Really, Malcolm, I'll see you Monday. Thanks for the coffee."

She led the way out and held open the door. Malcolm had no choice but to follow her. He covered the hand Nicole rested on the doorknob with his own.

"I'll see you Monday. If not before," he said.

Nicole arched a brow. "Monday."

Malcolm crossed the threshold and listened to the door close behind him.


Sunday was Nicole's day to pamper herself and clear her mind in preparation for the week ahead. Or at least Sunday used to be a pampering day. Over the past few months, she'd become almost overwhelmed with worry for her cousin, which had brought on her writer's block. Now she could add Malcolm Bryant to her list of concerns. He'd unwittingly awakened the insecurities that had lain dormant since the publication of her first book. Her inner critic was back, assuring her she was not good enough—for anything or anyone. Unless she silenced the voice soon, Nicole feared she would never be able to get rid of it.

She closed the magazine she'd been unable to read and got up from the sofa. The clock on the wall nudged the morning along. Derrick was coming over for brunch before they left to visit Simone. Nicole padded into the kitchen, thinking a cup of tea would comfort her. She didn't want Simone to pick up on her tension.

She was waiting for the water to boil and planning the brunch menu when the phone rang. In the past, Nicole would have ignored the summons. But she'd become wary of doing that while Simone was in the hospital.

"Hello," she answered.

"What's going on? Give me an update."

Denise's thousand-watt personality lifted Nicole's mood. She felt a grin spread across her face and couldn't resist the urge to tease.

"Hello, Denise," she drawled. "How are you?"

Forced to put a brake on her rapid-fire monologue,

Denise sighed into the phone. "I'm fine, thank you, Nicky. How are you?"

"Fine, thanks," she replied with perky good cheer.

"Good. Are you done now?" Denise forged ahead. "Why didn't you call me Friday to let me know how your lunch with Malcolm went?"

"There wasn't anything to report. We're meeting with you Monday. Tyrone will be waiting for us to fax the contract to him so he can sign it and fax it back."

"Yes, yes," Denise said. "I figured all of that. What I want to know is whether the two of you talked."

Nicole frowned. "About what?"

Denise's sigh conveyed exasperation this time. "About your divorce."

Nicole's bubble of good cheer burst. "No, we didn't. There's nothing to talk about, Denise."

"Well, that's too bad. If you don't discuss whatever it was that ruined your marriage, you'll never be able to let go of that man."

Nicole took a deep breath to ease the pain Denise's words unintentionally caused. "What do you mean?"

"Look at the way you reacted when you found out he co-owned Celestial Productions. And you didn't even want to have lunch with him Friday."

"I did have lunch with him Friday. And coffee with him yesterday." Nicole regretted the childish "nah-nah" tone of her voice.

"You did? What did you talk about?"

"Denise—"

"Okay. Never mind."

Nicole pictured her agent drumming her nails on her desk and absently wondered what nail polish color Denise had chosen for today.

"Thanks for telling him where I live, by the way."

"You're welcome," Denise replied, Nicole's sarcasm wasted on her. "I still can't believe you were married. You never even said anything."

Nicole rolled her neck to ease the gathering tension. "I don't like to dwell on unpleasant memories."

"They couldn't all be unpleasant; otherwise you wouldn't still be so upset about the divorce."

Nicole's heart clenched in an echo of the hurt. "No, they weren't all unpleasant."

"So, are you going to talk to him?"

"We don't need to talk." Nicole grew increasingly agitated with the conversation, but she couldn't think of a way to stop it. "I already know why he divorced me. He didn't want to be married to me anymore."

"I think you should ask him why he didn't want to be married to you anymore. I think you should tell him how it made you feel, and tell him how you feel now."

"There's no point to that." Nicole filled the kettle with cold tap water and set it on the stove to boil.

"Yes, there is," Denise insisted. "Talk to him. Yell at him. Sleep with him. But you need to do something with him so you can move on with your life."

"I am not. Going to sleep. With Malcolm Bryant," Nicole enunciated. "And I have moved on with my life."

"No, you haven't," Denise refuted. "That's why you're reacting so violently toward him. And that's why you haven't been able to form any other serious relationships."

"I'm perfectly happy with my life." Nicole took a mug out of a cupboard. She opened another cabinet and examined its contents. Perhaps she expended more energy than necessary in selecting an herbal tea.

"You mean your half-life," Denise clarified. "Why are you afraid to confront him?"

That question caught her full attention. Maybe it would be easier to talk about it over the phone. Her friend wouldn't see her pain, and she wouldn't see her friend's pity. Nicole carried the cordless phone to the dining room and dropped her trembling body into a chair.

"I don't have to ask him, Denise. I know why he left." Nicole sensed her friend grow still at her somber tone.

"Why'd he leave?" Denise finally asked.

Nicole drew a deep breath. "Because I had a miscarriage. I lost our baby."

Denise gasped. "Oh, Nicky. I'm so very sorry. When did this happen?"

Nicole steeled herself against the memory of pain, both physical and emotional. "About six years ago. A couple of years into our marriage."

The words were harder to say than she'd thought. She hadn't talked about the miscarriage in almost six years. She'd never forgotten, though. She'd wanted Malcolm's child so badly. Had her baby lived, she would have been a little older than Lynnie. Nicole rubbed the ache over her heart with her free hand.

"And the bastard just left you after that?" Denise seemed outraged.

Nicole hesitated, past images rolling through her mind. The blood. The frantic race to the hospital. Malcolm's empty eyes watching her silently. "No. But we weren't able to find our way back to where we'd been before our baby died."

"What happened?" her agent asked.

Nicole shrugged restlessly. "While I was pregnant, I continued to work full time." When the kettle began to whistle, she returned to the kitchen and turned off the stove. "Things got really hectic. The stress was too much. And then I lost our baby."

"He didn't blame you, did he?" Denise's voice crackled with righteous anger.

Nicole remembered the uncomfortable silences. The loneliness. The guilt. How many nights had she slept on the sofa—when she'd been able to sleep at all?

"He said he didn't. Every time I asked him, he said it wasn't my fault." She brewed her tea. "It wasn't anyone's fault."

Nicole heard Denise's pensive silence.

"But you blame yourself, don't you?" Her friend guessed correctly. When Nicole didn't answer, Denise continued. "Grief and guilt are normal reactions, but

Malcolm is right. A miscarriage isn't anyone's fault. Did you two talk at all afterward?"

"No," she whispered. "Not really."

Her agent hummed noncommittally. "Are you going to talk now?"

Nicole picked up her mug with restless hands and turned from the stove. "I don't want to go there, Denise. Our baby's gone. Our marriage is long over. What would be the point in bringing up the past?"

"What indeed?" Denise asked.

Malcolm stepped off the elevator and onto Nicole's floor. He carried takeout he'd purchased from an Italian restaurant a few blocks away. He hoped Nicole liked the place. Breakfast hadn't worked for him yesterday. He was hoping lunch would be a better bet. He balanced the meals on his left forearm before knocking on her door, then waited for what he hoped would be a warmer greeting today.

"She's not home," a lilting voice said behind him.

Malcolm turned, cradling his package in both arms. Mrs. Velasquez walked down the hall toward him, re-splendent in her Sunday finery. Her hat was tipped rak-ishly above her twinkling bird eyes. A knowing smile quivered, ready to burst free.

"Good morning, Mrs. Velasquez. How was mass today?" Malcolm eased into the role of romantic hero in which Nicole's neighbor apparently had cast him.

"It was beautiful. Just beautiful." Mrs. Velasquez beamed. "Nicky, she goes on Saturday so she can have a peaceful day on Sunday."

"So where is she this Sunday?" Malcolm asked.

"Her brother, he took her to the hospital," Mrs. Velasquez announced.

"What?" The bag almost slipped from his arms. He juggled it—tossing the containers of linguini and ziti— trying to reclaim his hold. "What hospital? Where is it?"

Mrs. Velasquez started to speak, then seemed to reconsider her words. "I will tell you where he took her and how
you can get there." She cocked an eyebrow. "You have a car?"


"Isn't that Malcolm Bryant?" her cousin Guy asked
incredulously.

Nicole looked up and saw Malcolm striding across the
parking lot toward them. His gray tweed winter coat
flapped in the breeze. He seemed impervious to the
cold that must have been weaving its way into his bulky
maroon sweater.

"Yes," Derrick replied. "What's he doing here?"

Nicole was aware of the men closing ranks around her
like the Symplegades, the rocks from Greek mythology
that smashed anything that tried to get past them. But
her attention was on Malcolm's chiseled features and his
long-legged stride that quickly closed the distance
between them.

Malcolm stopped before her, his features tense, the
look in his eyes urgent. "Are you all right?"

Nicole frowned. "Of course. Why?"

"Mrs. Velasquez told me Derrick had taken you to the
hospital." Malcolm nodded a greeting to her brother,
then glanced at Guy.

Nicole could just imagine how the matchmaking Mrs.
Velasquez had delivered that information. She sighed
inwardly and considered her options. Malcolm would
hound her until she confessed all about her hospital
visit. Still, she was reluctant to tell him about Simone.

"Do you remember my cousin Guy?" Nicole asked.

"Hello," Malcolm said.

"How're you doing?" Guy returned, clasping the hand
Malcolm extended in greeting.

From the almost relieved expression on Malcolm's
face, Nicole could tell he hadn't remembered Guy. She
wasn't surprised. They hadn't seen each other that often
when Malcolm had lived in New York. Guy probably rec-

ognized Malcolm from the wedding photos Aunt Rose refused to remove from her family album. Aunt Rose, a strict Catholic, didn't acknowledge Nicole's divorce.

"May I take you home?" Malcolm returned his attention to her.

She glanced at Derrick and Guy. Guy had offered to take them home before driving Aunt Rose to the hospital so she could sit with Simone while Guy took care of Lynnette. Nicole's going home with Malcolm would save Guy a trip, but was she ready to spend more time alone with the man tied to such painful memories of her past? Nicole already was drained emotionally from seeing Simone.

"Go ahead," Derrick encouraged. He leveled a steady gaze at Malcolm. "Take care of her."

"I will." Malcolm took Nicole's elbow to guide her back to his car. "Nice to see you again, Guy."

"Same here." Her cousin gave her a worried look.

She tossed him a reassuring smile that felt wobbly around the edges.

Malcolm held open the car door for Nicole to slide into the rented Ford Fiesta, then took the driver's seat. He drove out of the lot and merged into traffic before he opened the conversation.

"What were you doing at the hospital?" He glanced at her before returning his attention to the road.

"Visiting my cousin Simone."

Nicole thought she saw relief cross Malcolm's features. As they drove the short distance to her apartment, she explained to him about Simone's need for a kidney transplant.

"That's what finally convinced me to sell the movie rights to *InterDimensions*. Simone moved back in with Aunt Rose after her husband died." Nicole paused to clear the lump in her throat.

"Her husband must have been young," Malcolm commented.

"He was twenty-nine. He loved Simone and Lynnie a lot. Lynnie doesn't remember much about him. She was only two when he died."

"That's rough," Malcolm murmured.

"Things were hard for Simone. She couldn't manage all of the bills on her own. Moving in with her mother helped. Then Simone became ill." Nicole paused to survey the area. "Turn left at the next light."

"Thanks."

Nicole waited a moment more. "Anyway, the company she worked for started having financial problems. They laid off dozens of employees, including Simone. She couldn't afford to extend her medical care, even though she was sick."

"That's terrible."

"Yes." Nicole sighed. "Now, Aunt Rose, Guy, Derrick, and I are taking turns caring for Lynnie. I'm sure this instability and not understanding what's wrong with her mother are the causes for her nightmares."

Malcolm pulled into the underground parking garage of Nicole's apartment building. "Once we sign the contract tomorrow, the bank will release the check and we'll be able to pay you for the rights."

Malcolm found a parking space. He turned off the engine before facing Nicole. Shadows from the underground garage outlined his high cheekbones and darkened his brown eyes.

Nicole held his gaze. "That check will allow us to put Simone's name on the donor list. I'm very grateful. We all are."

"There's no need to be grateful. You earned that money."

"Despite my grand gesture of rejecting your offer, you can see I need this project a lot more than you do," Nicole remarked, ashamed at the memory.

Malcolm broke eye contact with her, and they sat in silence for several moments.

"The important thing is, we're going to make this movie," Malcolm said. "Working together, we're going to create a blockbuster."

"Yeah." She grinned. "It will be exciting."

# CHAPTER FOUR

Malcolm watched Nicole enter the terminal at the Los Angeles International Airport. The month he'd spent waiting for her to settle her affairs in New York before flying to L.A. had been painfully long. He stepped away from the wall that had supported him for the past hour this morning and took the first steps toward what he hoped would be his second chance.

He smiled into her gaze. "Hi. How was the flight?"

She didn't return his smile. Apparently, any strides he had made in New York were forgotten. "Fine, thanks. I appreciate your meeting me. I hope I didn't ruin any plans you had for your Sunday."

"No, you didn't." He extended his hand toward her. "Can I take your bag?"

"No, thanks. It's not heavy. I'm glad I sent all of my belongings ahead with the movers." She lifted the knapsack onto her shoulders, freeing her hands. She pulled her hair away from the bag, and the ebony cloud resettled around her shoulders. "Where are you parked?"

"This way. How's Simone?" Malcolm adjusted his long strides to accommodate Nicole's steps. He felt her stiffen as he cupped her elbow, but he held firm. He wanted Nicole to know he wouldn't let her ignore him or brush him aside as she had before.

"She's doing fine so far. The surgery went well. Now we're praying she doesn't develop any antibodies against the transplant."

"How long before you know?" Malcolm released her arm and walked onto the moving platform behind her.

With her long, slender legs encased in dark blue jeans, a stoplight-red parka, and black knapsack, she looked like the college student he'd fallen in love with eleven years ago.

"Most organ rejections occur within the first three months after surgery."

Nicole rattled off additional facts about kidney transplants. The wealth of information indicated the extensive research she'd done on her cousin's condition. Her nervous chatter revealed her family still had cause for concern.

"I'll add my prayers to yours," he said, and finally was rewarded with a smile.

"Thank you," she tossed over her shoulder. "I also appreciate your waiting until after the surgery for me to come to California. That meant a lot to me."

"I understand."

They stepped off the moving platform and continued toward the garage. Malcolm held open the door to the parking level, then escorted her to his Honda Accord. He deactivated the alarm, which automatically unlocked the doors. Before he could move to help her, Nicole had tossed her knapsack into the back and had slid onto the front passenger seat. Malcolm climbed into the driver's seat and started the car.

"How's Lynnie?" he asked as they fastened their seat belts.

"She's doing a bit better now that she knows when her mother's coming home. The sad dreams seemed to have gone away."

"I'm glad."

"So are we." Nicole turned toward him with another smile. "Lynnie's now planning for her birthday, which is more than three months away. You're invited, by the way. But I'm sure she'll understand if you're not able to attend."

Malcolm stared at Nicole, touched and pleased that her goddaughter would extend a party invitation to him. "I would be honored."

A myriad of expressions crossed her face. He could tell she hadn't expected him to accept Lynnie's invitation, and now she regretted extending it. He also identified the moment she realized she couldn't disinvite him. Smiling to himself, Malcolm shifted his Honda into reverse and pulled out of the parking garage.

"Your furniture arrived Thursday," he said, breaking the awkward silence. "You arranged everything really fast."

"I've been planning this for a while," Nicole said, speaking toward the window. "I've been hoping a company would want to buy the movie rights to *InterDimensions*. Once one did, I knew I'd have to relocate for the production. It was just a matter of when it would all come together."

"You didn't exactly make it an offer a company couldn't refuse." He pulled to a stop at a traffic light and turned to look at her. "You and your movie rights or nothing at all. That's a tough sell."

She arched a slim, winged eyebrow at him. "You took it."

"Yes, I did." He pushed down on the accelerator as traffic moved with the green light. Silence ensued again as they drove toward the apartment Malcolm had rented for her.

He wondered what Nicole was thinking as she studied L.A. and its beach communities through her passenger window. She should have been familiar with some of the sights. Like the smog that masked the mountains in the distance. And the palm trees that remained evergreen in early March, while the maples waited for April's nod before allowing their leaves to bud.

However, in the four years since she'd lived in L.A., there had been subtle changes in the area. And, though she must have noted some of those on her trip back last month, Nicole stared at the passing scenery as if viewing it for the first time. Or perhaps she was just lost in thought, which brought him back to his original question. What was she thinking as she gazed out the window?

"Are you hungry?" he asked. "Or did you eat on the plane?"

"I didn't eat on the plane, but I'm not hungry. Just tired. I want to get to the apartment and take a nap."

"All right. It's a good thing I stocked your fridge. If you do get hungry later, you can fix something to eat."

Nicole turned away from the world outside to spare him some attention. "You stocked my fridge?" Her tone held a mixture of humor and surprise. Malcolm wondered whether her reaction should offend him.

"Yes." He checked the lanes before exiting the freeway.

"But you hate to shop." Her voice was rich with suppressed laughter.

He smiled. "I still do. But I didn't think you should have to worry about groceries your first week here."

"Wow. I'm impressed. Thank you." She returned to studying the passing scenery, but not before Malcolm saw the ghost of a smile tilting her full lips.

"People change, Nicky."

"Forgive me if I don't believe that." Again she spoke to the window.

Malcolm stopped at a red light. "If you give me a chance, I can prove it to you."

"There's no need for you to go to the trouble."

He glanced her way, catching her gaze. "Oh, it wouldn't be any trouble."

Malcolm pulled into a quiet, residential neighborhood. Using an automatic opener he took off the dashboard, he activated the gate that led to the street-level parking garage of a homey apartment building. Once the gate had lifted, he pulled the car into a parking space near the entrance.

"I asked for this assigned space in case you wanted to

rent a car." He turned off the ignition. "But I'd be happy to chauffeur you around myself."

Again, before he could help her, Nicole climbed out of the car and took her knapsack from the backseat.

"Thank you, but I don't want to trouble you." She swung the knapsack onto one shoulder and waited for him to lead the way.

"It wouldn't be any trouble," he repeated.

Malcolm opened the door to the three-story building. "This key is for this parking lot door and for the security door in front of the building."

He gestured toward the door at the top of the staircase they were climbing. Handing her the key, he pointed toward the row of boxes affixed to the wall on the other side of the security door.

"Your mailbox is here," he said. "It has your apartment number on it but not your name."

Turning, Malcolm climbed two more stories to the top floor. "It's a small apartment building, as you can see. Just eight units, four to a floor. Some older people. A few young couples. It's a quiet neighborhood. Relatively safe. But you should still take precautions. This one's yours." He unlocked an apartment door at the top of the staircase and stepped aside to allow Nicole to precede him.

Light from the two arched windows on the front wall filled the apartment. Malcolm had directed the movers on how to place the furniture. The cream sofa was centered between the arched windows. The matching love seat stood against the wall to the left of the door. They tossed their coats across the arm of the love seat and wandered farther into the apartment. Leading off the living room was a wide, bright kitchen with walnut wood cabinets. Her dinette set was tucked into a cozy area between the living room and kitchen.

Nicole walked across the living room into the kitchen and opened the refrigerator. Malcolm watched as she studied its contents. He had chosen skim milk. He'd also bought her favorite fruits, vegetables, and diet soda. He waited impatiently for her reaction.

"Thank you for the groceries," she said. "How much do I owe you?"

"It's on me," he said, acknowledging his disappointment. He wasn't certain what kind of reaction he'd anticipated, but he knew it was something more than she had given.

Nicole glanced at him uncertainly. "That's very generous of you."

Malcolm followed her as she walked past her bookcase toward the door off the living room. The short hallway was covered in the same thick beige carpet as the rest of the apartment. On the left was a spacious bathroom complete with a vanity and combination shower/bathtub. To the right was a bedroom. Malcolm had reassembled and positioned her bed, dressing table, nightstands, and chest of drawers by himself yesterday.

Nicole looked toward the dressing table where Malcolm had placed a baby coleus. "Oh," she breathed, walking toward the table. "It's beautiful. Thank you."

Malcolm stepped forward, pleased with her reaction. "You're welcome. What will you name it?"

She lifted the plant to examine its maroon and yellow leaves more closely. "Firestar, I think." Nicole returned the coleus to the dressing table.

Malcolm imagined the Marvel Comics heroine with her flaming red hair and brilliant yellow costume. "Good choice."

Nicole shot him a teasing glance. "I'm glad you approve."

She turned to examine the walk-in closets and the view from the window to the left of her double bed. "Thank you for supervising the movers. You all did a great job. I thought I'd have to curl up on the sofa and worry about assembling the bed later."

"I wanted to make certain you were comfortable."

She turned away from the window but still avoided his gaze. "I'm sure I will be. For the few months I'm here."

"Maybe you'll change your mind and decide to give L.A. another chance."

Nicole frowned at him. "I don't have fond memories from the last time I lived in Los Angeles. I'm a New Yorker at heart. I always will be."

Malcolm stared at her in surprise. "I didn't know you didn't like L.A. You seemed happy here."

Nicole turned away from him. She sat on the side of her bed and checked the contents of her nightstand. Her movements seemed agitated.

"I wasn't. But you wanted to move here and"—she shrugged one shoulder—"I wanted to be with you."

Malcolm knew Nicole had missed her family, but he hadn't realized she had been unhappy in L.A. "Well, perhaps you could give L.A. another chance." He winced at his lame response.

Nicole closed her nightstand and stood to face him. "Why should I go to the trouble?"

Malcolm approached her with deliberate steps. "Because I want another chance, Nicky. I want to try again with you."

He paused before her, close enough to share her warmth and count the pulse beats that fluttered in her throat. When her ebony gaze evaded his, he bent his knees and dipped his head until he recaptured it. He eased back to his full height, drawing her gaze up with his own and searching for messages in her wary eyes. He found her questions, but he'd already given her his answers. Another chance. That's what he wanted.

With the backs of his fingers, Malcolm traced the curve of her cheek, marveling at the warm, soft texture of her brown skin. Just as he'd remembered. He brushed her full lips until they parted on a sigh that seeped between his fingers.

He caressed her pointed chin, trailing his fingers along the delicate structure. Her head tipped back, baring her long, slender neck to his hungry eyes. His body throbbed with the need to stroke his tongue along those supple lines. He clenched his teeth and forced back the urge. Instead, with infinite care, he cupped her head and laid his lips over hers.

He tasted her gasp, soft and sultry, and responded by gathering her close and nibbling her moist bottom lip. Nicole's tongue slid out to tease his upper lip, and he throbbed against her belly. A fresh gasp rose from her throat. He moaned and she swallowed it. But the sound shattered the passionate haze.

Nicole stumbled back, breaking free of Malcolm's loose, single-armed embrace. She locked her shaking knees and nervously licked her lips. A mistake, judging by the steam emanating from Malcolm's hot-chocolate eyes.

"What are you doing?" Her voice shook.

Malcolm's gaze darkened with unquenched desire. "Kissing you." His voice stroked her, connecting with every reawakened erogenous zone.

Nicole swallowed hard. "Why?"

Malcolm cocked an eyebrow. "Because I wanted to. As I said, Nicky, I want another chance with you."

"You really are big on second chances, aren't you? First, Los Angeles and now you. If you can't think of me as just your business partner, then perhaps we should reconsider our contract."

"It was just a kiss, Nicky. And I stopped as soon as you moved away."

Nicole didn't think what they'd shared could be described as "just a kiss." It was a phenomenon, one she instinctively knew she could never share with anyone else.

"I want you to leave." She touched her fingertips to her still-trembling lips. "Now."

"All right. I'm going."

Malcolm turned and left the bedroom. Nicole followed close behind him.

"I'm sorry I upset you," he continued, shrugging into his coat. He turned to face her. "But, Nicky, the passion wasn't all on my side."

Nicole funneled her reawakening desire into anger. She

marched past Malcolm to the front door, yanked it open, and waited for him to walk through. Her arm trembled with the effort not to slam the door behind him. She dropped onto the arm of the love seat and pulled at her hair.

Tyrone would kill him if he'd done anything to hurt this project, Malcolm thought as he drove away from Nicole's apartment. First, his partner would give one of his sermons on the evils of impetuosity and the gravity of business responsibilities. A lecture that would make him want to take his own life. Then Tyrone would quite simply choke him with his bare hands.

Malcolm didn't know what had come over him. His need for Nicole had suddenly overwhelmed him. When she'd slipped her tongue into his mouth and pressed her lithe body against him . . .

The ringing of his cell phone shattered the image and cooled his heated skin.

"Malcolm Bryant," he announced.

"Leave my family alone," the caller demanded.

"You have the wrong—" The line disconnected. "Number." Malcolm shrugged and ended the call.

The memory of the few nuisance calls, all hang ups, he'd received the past week crossed his mind. His cell phone was listed only on his business card. In the three years he'd owned this phone, he'd never experienced such a rash of misdirected calls. He wondered what had changed to cause this problem.

The next morning, a stranger sat in his car watching her as Nicole neared the end of her jog. His silver BMW stood at the curb in front of her apartment building, which served as her finish line. She tensed. Despite the chill in the early morning air, she prepared to do another lap around the block rather than let him see where she lived. Growing up in New York City had taught her to be ever ready for an attack. Her heart jumped as the man uncoiled from his car a few feet in front of her.

"Nicole Collins." His voice was California casual.

Nicole saw before her a self-assured black male displaying the trappings of his success. A tall, broad form with cover-model good looks. His smile revealed perfectly white teeth.

"You're even more attractive than your publicity photo." He pulled out his wallet and stepped toward her, extending his business card. Ever on the alert, Nicole shifted closer to the curb—casually, she hoped. "I'm Omar Carter of Carter Enterprises."

Nicole examined his card, relaxing slightly. "Your company bid on the movie rights to *InterDimensions*."

"And were very disappointed not to get them."

Nicole tried to return his business card, but Omar waved it away.

"How did you know where to find me?"

"Directory cross-reference online." Omar flashed another charming smile.

Nicole frowned. "Why did you go to this trouble?"

"To ask for just a moment of your time. Perhaps we could talk in your apartment."

Nicole regarded him skeptically. With her fingertips, she scraped her wet bangs back from her forehead. He couldn't actually think she would allow a strange man into her apartment?

"What do we have to discuss?" she asked.

"A new bid for your *InterDimensions* movie rights."

Nicole tilted her head to the side as she considered Omar's bold statement. She knew Denise had mailed letters to the production companies letting them know she had sold her movie rights and thanking them for their interest. In light of that, she wondered what game Omar Carter was playing.

"I've already sold those rights, Mr. Carter. Have a good day."

Nicole stepped around him, and Omar fell into step with her.

"I know. To Celestial Productions. I think you've made a mistake."

She paused to reevaluate Mr. Omar Carter. He wasn't just self-assured. He was cocky. Nicole's lips twitched with amusement. "What makes you think I've made a mistake?"

"Celestial Productions lacks the sophistication to do your story justice."

Nicole chuckled. "*InterDimensions* is a good story, but it's not meant to be sophisticated." She eyed his Rodeo Drive suit, visible under his Burberry of London wool overcoat. "At least not by your definition."

"What I mean is, Carter Enterprises can do a much better job for you. Better production quality, better marketing, better distribution."

"Celestial Productions owns the movie rights. I'm sorry, Mr. Carter, but I have too much to accomplish today to debate a moot point." Nicole turned to climb the stairs to the building's entrance.

"Please, call me Omar. According to the contract you have with Celestial Productions, if they choose to sell the movie rights, you have the option to buy it back first."

Nicole turned back toward him. "How did you know that?"

"Because it was one of the conditions of your sale. I assumed it would also be in your contract."

"What's your point?" Nicole braced her hands on her hips. She was becoming impatient to escape the persistent producer. Her body temperature was cooling, and her sweat-drenched clothes were giving her a chill.

"If we can convince Celestial Productions to sell the movie rights back to you, I can make you a very attractive offer for them," Omar promised her. "Even more attractive than my original offer."

"It's not about the money. It's about the creative control," Nicole insisted. "As I recall, you wouldn't agree to share that control with me, which is the reason I chose not to sell the rights to you."

"I don't believe the money isn't important to you,"

Omar scoffed. "You can't turn your back on that kind of money. Nobody can."

"Believe whatever you want to, Omar. I don't have the time to discuss this with you any further. Have a good day." She continued up the stairs.

"You drive a hard bargain, Ms. Collins," he called after her.

She did not look back.



Nicole stopped in front of the receptionist's desk. "I have a ten o'clock appointment with Malcolm Bryant."

A petite Mexican woman smiled with recognition in her eyes. Nicole felt at an uncomfortable disadvantage as she searched her memory for images of the voluptuous woman. Nothing came to mind.

The woman stood and circled the glass-topped counter, extending her hand. "Hello, Ms. Collins. I recognize you from your pictures on your books. I'm Rita Collozo."

Nicole shook the other woman's small hand, warming to her twinkling brown eyes and lyrical voice.

Rita continued. "I enjoy your books very much. Mr. Bryant and Mr. Austin are expecting you. We're all very much looking forward to working with you."

Nicole smiled, her nervousness easing. "Thank you."

"Please, follow me."

Celestial Productions made a good first impression. As she crossed the waiting area, Nicole enjoyed the soothing combination of emerald-green carpeting and eggshell-white walls. The baseboards were of polished ebony wood. The coffee table and matching end tables were made of glass and black metal. The sofa and armchairs were ivory twill.

The lobby exhibited framed posters of the company's films. She hadn't seen any of them at a theater. She rarely made it to the movies anymore. But, after signing the contract, she'd rented several of the videos and could well understand the praise the productions had received.

The films were high quality, technically as well as artistically. Nicole was impressed.

She followed Rita, who briskly crossed the length of the hall. The administrative assistant stopped outside a partially opened door and knocked before pushing it wide.

"Ms. Collins is here, Mal."

Nicole watched as Malcolm rose from the chair behind his oak desk. Khaki pants hugged his lean hips. A royal-blue sweater showcased his well-muscled shoulders.

"Thanks, Rita." He walked toward them. "Could you ask Ty to join us?"

"Yes." Rita turned toward Nicole. "It's a pleasure to meet you."

"The pleasure is mine." Nicole shook her hand again. Rita spun, setting her dark curls in motion as she charged back down the hall.

"May I take your coat?" Malcolm reached to assist her out of her wool jacket.

"Thank you."

Nicole relinquished her coat, smoothing her oversized ruby sweater, which hung to midthigh over her wide-legged, polyester-blend black pants. She saw the flash of disappointment in Malcolm's eyes as he viewed her latest figure-concealing ensemble.

"Have a seat." Malcolm gestured toward the two soft armchairs before his desk. "Did you sleep well?"

Nicole's gaze lifted as she sank into one of the seats. She wondered whether his question was an attempt to remind her of their kiss. If it was, her tripping pulse proved he'd succeeded.

"Very," she lied, crossing her legs.

"I envy you. I hardly slept at all." Malcolm gave her a final lingering look before returning to the black leather executive chair behind his desk.

Nicole narrowed her eyes. "Malcolm, what game are you playing?"

Footsteps approaching Malcolm's office interrupted them. Nicole turned toward the door.

"Ms. Collins. It's an honor to meet you."

Nicole hadn't taken a good look at Tyrone Austin when they'd first met. Studying him now, the writer in her decided he looked more like a studious college professor than a movie producer. His round face and close-cropped hair gave him an eternally youthful appearance. Dark brown eyes sparkled with pleasure behind wire-rimmed glasses. His build, taller and broader than Malcolm's, was clothed in a conservative suit that matched his eyes. Nicole smiled at the image of Marvin the Martian, the Warner Brothers space alien, marching across his tie.

"The pleasure's mine. But, please, call me Nicky." She stood and extended her hand to clasp his.

"And I'm Ty." He gave her hand a squeeze.

"Thank you, Ty. I apologize for the horrible first impression I gave you when we were first introduced."

"That was all Mal's fault," Tyrone said with careless good humor.

Nicole laughed. "I've enjoyed your movies."

Her smile widened at Tyrone's blush. He waited for Nicole to resume her seat before taking the chair beside her.

"They're my movies, too," Malcolm interrupted. Nicole and Tyrone ignored him.

"My fiancée, Joyce, and I have read every book in your *InterDimensions* series. We can't wait for the next one. Tell me, how many more books are you planning for the series?"

Nicole chuckled as Tyrone's words tripped over each other. "As many as I can sell."

"If the love fest is over, can we start the meeting now?" Malcolm grumbled.

Nicole turned toward Malcolm in surprise. She didn't understand his irritation. Was he upset she and Tyrone were getting along? Frankly, Tyrone's warm welcome was a salve on her frazzled nerves. Contrary to what she'd told Malcolm, she hadn't slept well. Not well at all. Their kiss had recalled too many memories and stirred too many dreams.

"You're right," Tyrone agreed, unaware of or unconcerned with Malcolm's annoyance. "We've scheduled a cocktail reception Friday night to welcome you to L.A. and to generate more interest in the project. The more interest we have in the movie, the more free publicity we'll get."

"A cocktail reception?" Nicole asked. "I didn't realize there would be social events."

"Just a few," Tyrone replied.

Nicole understood the importance of a good marketing campaign. It increased sales of books as well as movie tickets. But she wasn't comfortable in social situations. She pictured with dismay the upcoming reception. She wouldn't be able to blend into the background since she would be one of the guests of honor. She looked up into Malcolm's probing gaze.

"Is something wrong?" he asked.

"No. Nothing at all." It annoyed her that Malcolm could still read her so easily.

"Are you sure? You look a bit troubled," he observed.

"No, I'm fine." She noticed Tyrone also studying her with concern.

"Is it the reception?" Malcolm persisted.

"I'm fine," Nicole repeated. "Can we please talk about something else?"

"It will be a small reception," Tyrone said. "Just a few industry publication and broadcast journalists, and suppliers. We want to generate a buzz."

"You used to like socializing," Malcolm commented.

"People change, Mal." Nicole's lips quirked as she gave him back his words. "I haven't done much socializing lately." *As in the past six years,* she thought. "I'm a little out of practice, but I'm sure I'll be fine."

She held Malcolm's gaze with a challenging stare, daring him to probe further. He looked reluctant to let the topic drop but inclined his head and moved on. They spent the next two hours discussing the movie's production time line, casting agencies, and location scouts. Nicole had done her film production research and was familiar with these subjects and the terminology. Still, by the end of the meeting, she felt as though her brain had doubled in size.

She gathered her pages of notes. "I've finished reading the screenplay."

"Good," Malcolm said. "When do you want to get together to discuss it?"

Nicole turned to Tyrone. "Have you had a chance to review it?"

"I don't usually get involved on the creative end. I'm the business partner. I handle the bank, the license agreements and guarantors, the contracts, and the marketing and distribution. Malcolm takes care of the creative end: the scripts, locations, actors, pre-production, production, and post-production."

"So when do you want to get together?" Malcolm repeated.

Nicole wanted to get started on the production right away. But she couldn't think while her apartment was still unpacked. "How about first thing Wednesday morning?"

"Fine. Wednesday at eight A.M. We can talk about the screenplay and start scheduling the site surveys and casting." Malcolm punched the information into his Palm Pilot.

"And tonight, we can take you to dinner. A sort of welcome-to-L.A. celebration," Tyrone proposed.

"Oh, that's not necessary. I've been here before." Nicole gathered her purse and stood. Both men stood with her.

"Please?" Tyrone begged. "Joyce won't speak to me again if she doesn't get to meet you."

"Won't I meet her Friday night?"

"Yes, but it won't be the same. There'll be so many more people at the reception."

"I have a feeling you and Joyce will hit it off," Malcolm put in. "Come on, Nicky. You've got to eat."

Nicole tried to ignore the taunt in Malcolm's eyes as

he and Tyrone escorted her back to the lobby. She considered it childish and beneath her to react to his dare. Still, she found herself accepting the invitation. She never could resist a challenge.

"I would enjoy meeting Joyce." She directed her answer to Tyrone.

"Great." Triumph colored Malcolm's voice. "I'll pick you up at seven o'clock."

"There's no need for you to go to the trouble," she said. "I've rented a car."

The lobby was empty. Nicole glanced at the wall clock. The time had flown by. It was after noon; Rita must be at lunch.

"It's no trouble." Malcolm slipped his hands into his front pockets.

Reluctant to argue in front of Tyrone, Nicole once again allowed Malcolm to get his way. "I'll see you at seven, then." She turned to Tyrone. His bright brown eyes restored her good humor. "I'll see you tonight."

He grinned. "Joyce is going to be thrilled."

Nicole laughed. "Helping you keep the peace with your fiancée is the least I can do after my rudeness the last time we met."

"That was all Mal's fault," Tyrone repeated with a wink.

Nicole looked at Malcolm. "Yes, I suppose it was."

Malcolm watched Nicole walk out the door, then turned to his partner. "What are you grinning about?" he grumbled.

Knowing Tyrone wouldn't realize the question was rhetorical, Malcolm retreated toward his office. He inwardly groaned when he heard Tyrone following him. His partner wrapped an arm around Malcolm's shoulders and shook his head in sorrow.

"Mal, it pains me to say this, man, but you're an ass. You let a smart, classy—not to mention beautiful—woman like that get away from you? Dumb. Very dumb."

"Is that why you were being so friendly to her?" Malcolm asked. "Were you trying to show me what an ass I am?"

"I was just trying to make Nicky feel more comfortable." The weight of Tyrone's arm slid off Malcolm's shoulders. "I could feel the tension between you two all the way down the hall."

Malcolm grunted. Tyrone trailed him into his office.

"Besides, I figured you already knew you'd been an ass," Tyrone continued, easing himself uninvited into a chair. "That's why you're trying to get her back."

Malcolm paused. "What makes you think I'm trying to get her back?"

Tyrone smiled pityingly. "I don't know. Maybe it was the way you kept trying to regain her attention every time she looked at me."

Malcolm grunted again, then took his seat.

Tyrone propped his right ankle on his left knee. "I think my first clue was when you booked her and her agent into a four-star hotel and paid for it out of your own pocket."

Malcolm held Tyrone's laughing gaze. "Don't you have work to do?"

"It won't be easy, you know," his friend warned. "To get her back. A successful, independent woman like that. She doesn't need you."

Malcolm caught the teasing tone in Tyrone's voice, but his partner's comment still resurrected old insecurities. Had Nicole ever needed him? She hadn't seemed to need him after the miscarriage. Why would she need him now?

Tyrone continued. "Why did you let her go in the first place?"

Malcolm hesitated. "I didn't let her go. She let go of me."

Tyrone's brows shot up. "What did you do?"

Malcolm glared at his friend. But, since Tyrone's question was too close to the truth, becoming defensive would be a waste of time.

"Two years into our marriage, we became pregnant." Malcolm watched surprise, then confusion, cross his partner's face. "We didn't have a lot of money, so Nicky kept working. The stress was too much. The baby died. She almost did, too."

"Oh, man, Mal. I'm really sorry," Tyrone said.

"Yeah. Our marriage never recovered." Malcolm leaned back in his chair, facing away from his friend's intent gaze. "If I'd had a better job, she wouldn't have had to work so hard. Things might have been different."

"Is that why you were so determined to get this project?" Tyrone asked. "You want another chance with your ex-wife? Maybe try for an alternate ending?"

Malcolm surveyed the candid photos that hung on his wall and rested on his bookshelves. The pictures were taken on the sets of commercials, music videos, and movies Celestial Productions had produced.

"I want her to see me as a success," he answered. "As someone who can take care of her."

Tyrone's eyebrows rose. "Then let's hope she doesn't get a close look at our finances."

Nicole paced the length of the phone's cord and back in her apartment's living room. "What are they going to ask me? What am I supposed to say?"

"It's not as though you've never done this kind of thing before." Denise's voice carried across the phone line, dismissing Nicole's concern.

Nicole listened to the clicking of a computer keyboard as Denise continued to work. She idly wondered what color her agent's nails were today.

"I've never attended a cocktail party to promote my movie before," Nicole corrected.

"So? What's the big deal? They're going to want to know about *InterDimensions.* You know you can talk people deaf about your books. The problem is getting you to stop talking about them," Denise teased.

"You're not helping, Denise." Nicole continued pacing.

"Nicky, you whine every time you have to make a personal appearance. But you always do a great job. You'll be fine at the cocktail party. Suck it up and get on with it. I love you like a second cousin twice removed, but I don't have time to deal with your neuroses," Denise said. A printer whirred on in the background.

"Ah, one of your famous pep talks. You should have been a motivational speaker."

Nicole chuckled at her own joke. But she had to admit, she always felt better after one of Denise's unique pep talks. She knew her agent understood her trepidation about public appearances. And somehow Denise knew coddling her would make it worse. Nicole didn't want to be taken care of. She needed to be challenged.

"Whatever," Denise said. "Enough about you. I need to fill you in on my news now. Eileen's lining up interviews for you."

"Where?" Nicole asked, aware that Eileen Lane, her publisher's publicist, worked hard to get her as much media coverage as possible.

"Newspapers, magazines," Denise answered vaguely. "They're to promote the release of book four as well as the movie."

"Great." Nicole relaxed. She was more comfortable with print interviews.

"Hold on. I'm switching to speakerphone." After a brief pause, Denise returned to the line sounding as though she were speaking into a jar. "We might as well take advantage of your being in L.A."

"That's a good point," Nicole agreed.

"We're also looking into radio and TV." Denise's voice grew faint as though she'd moved away from the phone. "Eileen's talking to some people over at *A.M. L.A.*"

"I don't know about doing TV." Nicole rubbed at the pulse jumping at the base of her neck.

"It'll be great. I've got to go. Let me know how the cocktail party turns out. Remember," she added bracingly, "it's your party."

"I can cry if I want to," Nicole quoted an old love song.

"No, you can't." Denise disconnected.

Nicole recradled the phone, muttering fondly about bossy agents.

She sorted through her mail, mostly junk, thinking about the odds and ends left to put away and a couple of items she needed to pick up during the week. Her hands paused over a letter forwarded from her New York post office box. There wasn't a return address, but the original postmark was Los Angeles. She didn't usually open mail without a return address, but she was curious to see what was in this envelope.

She went cold as she read the letter. The back of her neck prickled as though someone were watching her. And, according to the letter, someone was.

# CHAPTER FIVE

Nicole's hand trembled as she returned the glass of iced tea to the table. She picked at her chicken Caesar salad, avoiding Malcolm's prying scrutiny. Every time their gazes met, she saw the question in his eyes. She resented his ability to read her like a book after all these years when, during the last two years of their marriage, she'd wished for a decoder ring to decipher his feelings.

She tried to ignore Malcolm by focusing on Tyrone and his fiancée, Joyce Allen, a certified public accountant. That wasn't hard to do. The couple had a myriad of stories to share. They almost made her forget about the threatening letter waiting for her at home.

"How did you two meet?" she asked Joyce.

The vivacious CPA swallowed a forkful of blackened chicken before answering. "Ty asked my firm to do his business taxes, and I got to work with Celestial Productions. He kept calling to talk about his account, even after tax season."

Joyce set down her fork and entwined her fingers with Tyrone's. Nicole envied the connection the couple seemed to share, the balance in their give-and-take.

"She's the sexiest woman I've ever met." Tyrone kissed Joyce's knuckles. "Smart and beautiful. But, at first, I couldn't find the guts to ask her out."

Malcolm cut into his steak. "Watching them fumble their way into a relationship was painful."

Tyrone smiled and smoothed his tie, a vivid red nylon featuring the Space Ghost cartoon character reclining behind his talk show desk. "Don't be a hater." He stabbed a slice of his steak and tucked it into his mouth.

"Don't mind them," Joyce said. "They enjoy trash talking. They're both such little boys at heart. It's amazing they were able to build, much less maintain, a successful business."

Nicole envied Joyce her history with Malcolm and Tyrone. If Malcolm hadn't walked out of her life, she could have been there with him while he and Tyrone built Celestial Productions. Perhaps she could even have helped them. And she could have watched the bond develop between these two men who were now as close as brothers.

"How were you able to build your business, Malcolm?" Nicole asked.

"With a lot of tenacity, determination, and sacrifice," he said.

Nicole read the pride of accomplishment in his eyes.

"Tell her about the apartment you two shared," Joyce prompted.

Nicole felt a stab of hurt at this additional reminder that Joyce had shared experiences with Malcolm and Tyrone.

Tyrone smiled with fond remembrance. "It had only one bedroom. We had bunk beds."

"He's a slob," Malcolm muttered.

Tyrone grinned. "And you're moody as hell."

"But when it comes to business," Joyce interrupted, "they're in perfect sync."

"Ty must share a lot of information about his work with you," Nicole noted.

Joyce leaned against her fiancé. "We do talk a lot about our work."

"It must be nice to have someone to share that part of your life with," Nicole murmured.

"Yes, it is," Joyce agreed.

"When is your wedding?" Nicole changed the subject.

Joyce smiled. "June."

"I'm sure you'll be very happy."

Tyrone stroked a finger down Joyce's hair, his gaze locked with hers. "I know we will be. I've been happier with her than I've ever been in my life."


"Invite me in," Malcolm said as they pulled up in front of Nicole's apartment building. The drive back from the restaurant had been strained.

"Not tonight." Nicole slid out of the car.

She was annoyed, but not surprised, to hear the driver's door open, then slam shut. She turned to face Malcolm over the roof of the car. "I'm not letting you in. So you can get back into your car and take yourself home."

"I want to know what's bothering you," Malcolm said. "Now, we can talk out here and freeze our butts off, or you can invite me in."

Nicole remembered the outcome of a similar ultimatum. "Nothing's wrong, Malcolm. Go home."

Malcolm circled the car until he stood in front of her. Puffs of steam streamed from his mouth as his words hit the cold evening air. "After we talk." He claimed her elbow and escorted her into the building.

Nicole considered shrugging away from him but decided against the childish reaction. Instead, she clenched her teeth and bore his high-handed behavior in silence.

"What's wrong?" he asked as they entered her apartment.

"Nothing." Nicole bristled as Malcolm followed her and hung his coat next to hers in the hall closet. He apparently intended to stay a while.

"You've been tense and distracted all night." He shadowed her back to the living room.

Nicole spun to face him in front of her writing desk. "I told you I didn't want to go to dinner with you tonight."

Malcolm crossed his arms over his broad chest. "That's not why you were tense tonight. What's wrong?"

"It has nothing to do with you." She moved away from him, distancing herself from her writing desk and the threatening letter.

He turned, keeping Nicole in his sight. "Then there is something wrong."

"Leave it alone, Malcolm. I don't want to talk about it."

Malcolm's expression softened. "Talking about it might help."

Nicole laughed in surprise. "You, the king of the sphinx, are going to tout the benefits of discussing one's feelings? You can't be serious."

But Malcolm was right. She did need someone to talk to. But not him. She hadn't been able to talk to him in more than four years. She'd considered calling her brother, but she didn't want to worry Derrick when he was three-thousand miles and three time zones away.

Nicole's eyes widened as Malcolm leaned against her writing desk. A foolish reaction, she knew, since he wouldn't take it upon himself to go through her belongings.

"We were friends once, Nicky," he said. "I'd like to be friends again."

Nicole arched a brow. "Why?"

"Because I miss it."

"Sunday, you asked for more than friendship."

Malcolm crossed his arms over his chest. "And you threw me out. So now that's all I'm asking for."

"Malcolm, I don't think we were ever friends." Nicole turned and paced farther away from him. "Friends support each other during the hard times. After our baby died, we couldn't help each other."

"I tried to help you, but you wouldn't let me." His voice was tired.

Nicole hunched her shoulders, scrubbing her face with both palms. "I tried to lean on you, but I'm not going to do that anymore. It gets lonely when the other person won't lean back."

"Please, Nicky, let's just try again." Malcolm sounded closer to her. "One step at a time. Tell me what's been eating at you all night."

Nicole turned toward him, debating her answer. Should she show him the door? She didn't believe he'd settle for friendship. Malcolm was biding his time, tearing down the wall between them one brick at a time. The question was, did she want him to? She was honest enough with herself to admit she didn't know what she wanted for the long term. For the short term, she knew she needed a friend, and Malcolm would do for tonight.

Nicole walked past Malcolm to the writing desk. He followed her. She took the letter from the drawer and handed it to him.

He studied the envelope, glanced at her, then pulled out the letter. It didn't take long for his reaction. After all, it was a short letter that simply read, *I'll do whatever it takes to protect what's mine. This is your last warning.*

Malcolm's jaw tightened, his arched brows flattening as they drew closer in a frown. The predator just under his calm surface had returned.

"Who sent this to you?" He examined both sides of the letter as though searching for the writer's identity.

"I don't know."

Malcolm looked up at her, his gaze sharp, his face tense. "Do you have any idea what he's warning you about?"

Nicole shook her head. "No."

He paced away from her. "The letter says this is your last warning. Have you received others?"

She shook her head, baffled. "No."

Malcolm rubbed the back of his neck. "Have you contacted the police?"

"Not yet." Nicole walked back to sit on the sofa. Her knees would no longer support her.

Malcolm shot her an incredulous look. "Why not?"

"I wanted to make a copy of the letter first in case the police want to keep the original."

"Why do you want a copy of this?" Malcolm shook the letter as he resumed his pacing.

"I don't know." She shrugged restlessly. "I just know I want a copy."

Watching Malcolm was like seeing her own reaction to the letter. He paced the same floor she had and asked the same questions that had flooded into her mind. She knew he needed to work through the initial shock. So she waited as patiently as she could as he paced and questioned more. Once he wound down, she would try to soothe him and herself again.

"Are you sure you haven't received anything else that could be construed as a threat? Other strange messages? Weird phone calls?"

"Yes. In New York, it wasn't unusual for me to get wrong numbers or hang-ups. But I don't think they were threats, just nuisance calls."

"This letter originated in L.A.," Malcolm murmured.

"I noticed that."

"It probably means the person who wants to hurt you is in L.A."

Nicole shivered. That thought had occurred to her. "I made a copy of the letter before you picked me up for dinner. I'll go to the police station tomorrow morning."

"I'll go with you," Malcolm said.

"That's not necessary."

"It is to me." He shot her his warrior's look. Nicole took shameful pleasure in it.

"All right."

"And you're coming home with me tonight."

Her jaw dropped. "No, I'm not."

"I'm not planning to seduce you. I just think we'll both feel better if you're not alone tonight. Pack an overnight bag, and we'll get going."

"That isn't necessary, Malcolm."

"It is to me," he repeated. "I can't drive away and

leave you alone tonight after finding out someone is threatening you."

She followed him into her bathroom. He collected her toothbrush.

"What else do you need?" he asked.

"Pajamas," she replied in a daze.

"Fine. Let's get packed." He moved past her and strode into her bedroom.

"Shouldn't I be objecting or something?" Nicole trailed him around her apartment.

"No. You should be packing."

A little less than an hour later, they were pulling into his garage. The connecting door led to the hallway of his two-story home. The open floor plan and soothing tones of his southwest decor intrigued her. The Malcolm she remembered had been a restless man, preferring contemporary furniture in edgy colors. Would the real Malcolm Bryant please wake her up?

"This way," he said.

She followed Malcolm and her tote bag upstairs.

"This is the guest room." He put her bag on the bed. He stepped back into the hallway to point out the linen closet and spare bathroom before escorting her back to the guest room. "Let me know if there's anything you need."

"Thank you."

He held her gaze. She saw her forgotten passion in his hot-cocoa eyes and knew he was inviting her to remember it. But she'd already learned that lesson. Passion alone couldn't hold a marriage together. She wouldn't repeat that mistake.

"Good night," she murmured, stepping back into the guest room and closing the door.

Later, lying between the chilled bedsheets, she strained to hear sounds of Malcolm in the house. *Weird,* she thought, curling onto her side. *I'm spending the night with my ex-husband. Hell must have frozen over.*

\* \* \*

"I absolutely love your ties." Nicole studied Tyrone's latest neckwear.

"Thank you." He smoothed the polyester-blend tie with its *Star Wars* robots R2-D2 and C-3PO. It may not have suited the formality of the cocktail party, but it suited Tyrone perfectly.

"Please don't encourage him." Joyce linked an arm with one of Tyrone's. "I'm really into sci-fi, too, but those ties are a bit much."

Nicole laughed and accepted a glass of diet soda from a passing server. The cocktail party had drawn quite a crowd. She studied the guests as they interacted with one another. Nicole could smell the money and power, and that made her nervous. She feared she would say or do something that would have a negative impact on the movie project.

If it were up to her, she would stay right here beside the buffet, sampling its fruit, vegetable, and cheese plates, and hot and cold hors d'oeuvres. But her persistent companions would never allow that. They insisted she mingle with every industry and media contact invited to the party.

She took a fortifying sip of the diet soda. "All right. Who's next?"

She scanned the crowd, seeking a nonthreatening target. They'd been at the mixer for a little over two hours, but to Nicole it felt like half the night. With a nervous hand, she smoothed the black rayon material of her long-sleeved, scooped-neck evening dress.

"You didn't used to be this uncomfortable around crowds," Malcolm noted.

She turned to study him. He looked even more compelling in his fashionably cut black evening suit. His snowy-white shirt had a pewter button high on his neck, negating the need for a tie.

He hadn't said much to her since picking her up for the reception. In fact, he hadn't said much to her in the four days since she'd spent the night in his home.

"A lot happens in four years," Nicole drawled.

"Production company executive at nine o'clock," Tyrone whispered, moving closer to her side.

Malcolm's partner had been giving her advance notices like that one every time they were about to approach or be approached by someone of influence in the industry. Nicole put on her game face and turned toward their latest target, an older gentleman with steel-gray hair and a comfortably bulky body.

Tyrone gripped the older man's hand and returned his warm smile. "Hi, Leo. We weren't sure you'd make it."

"Wouldn't miss it, Ty. Wouldn't miss it for the world. I have a feeling this will be your best project ever."

Malcolm laughed and stepped forward to shake Leo's hand. "You say that about every project."

"And I'm right every time." Leo chuckled heartily, slapping Malcolm's upper arm. "Joyce, it's good to see you again."

Joyce took Leo's offered hand. "It's good to see you, too. How have you been?"

Leo rocked on his heels and shoved his hands in the pants pockets of his conservative, blue Ralph Lauren suit. "Can't complain. I mean, I'd like to, but no one would listen." Leo winked a twinkling blue eye and brushed a recalcitrant lock of hair off his forehead. "And you?"

"Fine, thank you." Joyce glowed, and Nicole smiled at the understatement.

"I see Ty's still holding on to you. Literally." Leo nodded toward Joyce and Tyrone's joined hands. "Smart man."

"Very smart. I've asked her to marry me," Tyrone elaborated.

Leo's face lit up like a Christmas tree. "That's marvelous news," he exclaimed, then paused, pinning Joyce with a probing stare. "Did you say yes?"

Joyce laughed. She thrust her hand forward so Leo could view her ring, a one-carat princess cut. "Yes, I did. We're getting married in June. We hope you and Ava will come."

Leo beamed. "I look forward to it. Thank you."

Malcolm palmed Nicole's back, nudging her forward into the group.

"Leo, I'd like you to meet Nicole Collins," he said. "Nicky, our good friend Leo DeCaprio."

"No relation to the popular young film star." Leo winked and grinned as though he used the line often and enjoyed it every time.

Nicole chuckled. "How do you do, Mr. DeCaprio?" She shook Leo's hand, wondering whether Malcolm realized his palm still rested on her back.

"Leo, please. And I do fine, thank you. I enjoy your books. Your mysteries, I mean. Haven't read your science-fiction series."

Nicole was surprised Leo knew of her mystery novels. He was the first person she'd met tonight who'd read any of her books.

"I'm flattered, Leo. Thank you."

Leo waved away her words. "My son, Frank, is hooked on your *InterDimensions* series." He broke off to look around the room. "Frank's around here somewhere. Expect he'll join us shortly. He's excited to meet you. His name is actually Francis, but he goes by Frank." Leo shrugged and rolled on his heels. "His mother loved the name, and after nine months and eighteen hours, I wasn't going to argue with her."

Nicole smiled, entertained by Leo's running commentary.

"How is Ava?" Malcolm asked.

"She's fine, thanks. She's visiting her sister this weekend, or she would have been here with me. Miss her when she's gone. You know what I'm talking about." He beamed at Joyce and Tyrone. Then he turned toward Nicole. "Are you married?"

"No," she murmured, feeling her face heat.

"It's a wonderful institution," he declared, swaying on his heels. "Highly recommend it."

Nicole's face went up in flames. Leo continued to stare at her, so she felt compelled to offer some type of response. She managed a noncommittal "Mmm," and avoided Malcolm's gaze.

"Ah, here's Frank. Ms. Collins—"

"Nicole, please," Nicole interrupted.

Leo beamed. "Nicole, I'd like you to meet my son, Frank. He's a senior at USC and a big fan of yours." The proud father put his hand on Frank's shoulder.

The resemblance between father and son could not be denied, despite a few notable differences. Frank was long and lean, at least four inches taller and fifty pounds lighter than his father. Instead of twinkling blue, Frank's bedroom eyes were violet. Returning his gaze, Nicole imagined she could hear coed hearts breaking all over the University of Southern California's campus. And maybe some older women's hearts as well.

Nicole grasped Frank's outstretched hand. "I'm glad to meet you."

Frank smiled shyly. "Your books are great. You've created strong characters that readers can identify with."

"Thank you." Nicole thought she'd float away from the compliment.

Leo slapped Frank on the back. "My son's studying English at the university. He wants to be a novelist like you."

Frank's smile looked a bit pained around the edges, as though Leo hadn't quite interpreted his son's life goals accurately.

"Are you concerned the *InterDimensions* characters won't translate well to the screen?" Frank asked.

"I chose Celestial Productions for this project because I want to protect the integrity of my story and characters. Malcolm and Ty will help me do that because they also enjoy the series."

"Don't be so modest, Nicky," Tyrone said. "We're big fans of *InterDimensions.*"

"Frank has all of your *InterDimensions* books," Leo said.

This time, Frank ignored his father's interruption. "Will there be other *InterDimensions* movies?"

"We don't have plans to make others at this time." Nicole didn't want to tell Frank she wouldn't have sold the movie rights to any of her books if Simone hadn't become ill.

"How do you think other people will react to the movie?" the young man asked.

"Based on research on similar movies—" Tyrone began.

Frank interrupted. "No, I mean, how do you think your fans will react to *InterDimensions* being made into a movie?"

Nicole frowned over the question. "I hope they'll be excited about it. How do you feel?"

Frank paused as though considering his answer. Then he smiled. "I'm really not sure. Usually, movies based on books aren't faithful to the story or the characters. It's almost as though the author cared more about their paycheck than the people they created."

Frank's words didn't offend Nicole because they shared a similar concern. That was the reason she'd insisted on some creative control over the *InterDimensions* movie.

"You don't have anything to worry about there," she assured him. "I care very much about my work."

"Do you have any actors in mind for specific characters?" Frank asked.

"No." Nicole angled her head quizzically. "As an avid reader of the series, do you have anyone in mind for a particular role?"

Frank shook his head. "No. I can't really see anyone in those roles."

"Well, we don't want to hold you up," Leo said. "A pleasure to meet you, Nicole."

Nicole shook their hands. "The pleasure was mine, Leo. Frank."

Leo clasped Malcolm's hand and then Tyrone's. "Good luck with the project. Let me know if I can help in any way."

Once father and son had disappeared into the crowd, Joyce surveyed the room. "Okay, Nicky, let's start mingling again."

Nicole groaned and checked her watch. "How much longer?"

Joyce looked at her. "You really do hate these events, don't you?"

"Yes, I do."

"Well, don't think of this as an event." Joyce linked her arm with Nicole's. "Think of this as a small group of friends paying you a visit."

Nicole slid her an amused glance. "When can I ask them to leave?"


Although he was friendly enough, when compared to Leo DeCaprio, Nathan Rutherford seemed bland. The tall, lean, blond reporter had scrutinized Nicole from head to foot. Then he made her wince with his first words.

"I've never read any of your books," he stated. "What are they about?"

Nicole chuckled. "In a nutshell, *InterDimensions* takes place on a space station charged with protecting a wormhole that brings travelers to different worlds and different times."

"Hmm. Interesting," Nathan said, sounding bored. "Can this wormhole take you to different times in different worlds?"

"Yes." She wondered whether this surfer-in-a-suit had any interest in science-fiction books and movies.

"What makes you think it would make a good movie?"

"We know it will," Malcolm interjected. "The book has a lot of action and visual elements that will translate very well into film."

Malcolm went on to draw comparisons between scenes in her book and scenes from successful science-fiction movies. He had hard numbers on budgets from those movies and their returns on investments, as well as their similar audience demographics. Listening to his impromptu presentation, Nicole felt a rush of excitement and something very much like pride in her ex-husband.

"How much will this cost?" Nathan asked. "And how much will it make?"

"We've run some preliminary numbers," Tyrone told the growing crowd. He began to outline the numbers Malcolm and he had been working with, and the various costs and return scenarios.

"It sounds as though even the low-end example would net a decent income," Nathan noted.

"Wow," Nicole whispered to Malcolm as they moved on to speak with other guests. "You guys are really impressive."

Malcolm smiled. "It's a good night."

An uncomfortable silence sat between them during the drive back to her apartment. Malcolm had been charming to the guests at the cocktail party but now seemed distant. Nicole slanted him a glance as they pulled up outside her apartment building. She prepared to interrupt his contemplative mood.

"Malcolm, what's wrong?"

He paused. "Nothing."

The sphinx had returned. Nicole shifted in the passenger seat to face him. "Oh, no. You're not going to get away with trying to dismiss me after your performance Monday night. You badgered me until I told you what was bothering me. Tonight, I'm going to return the favor. Turn off the engine and come upstairs with me."

Malcolm's lips twitched. "Your tone of voice removes any doubt you want to do anything other than talk."

"That's because I don't want to do anything other than talk."

Malcolm's eyes scorched her. "Pity."

"Stop it, Malcolm." Nicole ignored the nerve endings leaping to life all over her body. She suspected he was trying to distract her. The tactic might have worked four years ago, but it wasn't going to work tonight. "Turn off the engine and come upstairs."

Apparently, her voice still wasn't firm enough.

Malcolm hesitated, erasing all expression from his face and pulling a curtain to shield his eyes.

"Whatever you want." He pulled the key from the ignition.

Preparing for battle, Nicole led the way to her apartment.

"What's wrong?" she repeated. She took off her coat and held out her hand for Malcolm's. She hung them in the hall closet as she waited for him to begin.

"Why didn't you want me to go to the police station with you Tuesday?" he asked as she returned to the living room. His voice sounded tight, as though he'd forced the words out.

Nicole stared at him, surprised by the question and the fact he'd asked it. "That happened three days ago. And we've been through this. I can file a police report by myself. I told you they took down my information and kept the original letter, as I suspected they would."

"There's more to it than that."

Nicole frowned. "More to it than what?"

Malcolm shoved his hands into his pants pockets. "There's more to your reason for insisting on going to the police station by yourself."

"What are you talking about?" Nicole strode to the love seat beside the front door, putting some space between them. "You didn't miss anything. I told you everything that happened. I have no idea who could have sent that letter or what the letter is referring to, so there's nothing more the police can do right now."

Malcolm followed her. "I'm not talking about what I might have missed by not being at the police station. I'm talking about the point you were trying to make to me and to yourself by leaving me behind."

"And what would that point be?" Nicole felt trapped. Malcolm was too close. She could feel the strength of his determination pushing past her defenses, barriers that kept the truth hidden even from herself.

"You went to the station alone to prove you don't need me," he stated.

"That's—"

"By going alone, you threw my offer of friendship back in my face."

"I—"

"The same way you threw it back in my face when I offered to sleep on your couch Tuesday night."

"All right," Nicole snapped, pushing past him. She marched to the other side of the room before spinning to face him. "I was trying to prove I don't need you. That I can manage on my own just as well as you can."

Malcolm closed the gap between them. "But I'm here, and I want to help you."

Nicole held her ground. "I'm fine on my own."

"Really?" He grabbed her. The curtains lifted from his eyes, allowing her to see the impatience and frustration swirling in their chocolate depths before he fused his hungry lips to hers.

Nicole shoved against his chest. Malcolm banded his arms around her and crushed her closer against him. When her lips stayed firm against his tongue, he switched from using ineffective pressure to irresistible persuasion. As he nuzzled her ear, she feared their years together as lovers gave him unfair insider information. Her body reacted from memory, despite her resolve. He nipped at her neck, and she pressed against him. He caressed her with his body, and her body trembled back. He stroked the seam of her lips with his tongue. Lightly. Once. Twice. She moaned in surrender. His tongue stroked her mouth, and she melted down his body.

He followed her onto the floor, she in her formal dress, he in his suit. The hunger was more intense on this reawakening. It became an emptiness begging to be filled. He lay above her, tempting and teasing with kisses and caresses, preludes to a joining while their lower bodies strained toward each other. She reached around him to bring him closer still. He responded with a kiss so deep, it pulled her desires to the surface.

And then he was gone, rolling off her and pushing himself unsteadily to his feet.

"Mal?" she asked, dazed.

"There's obviously something still between us," he said in a graveled voice. "Let me know when you're ready to stop lying to yourself and accept it. And me."

He left without his coat.


Nicole settled in to watch the Sunday morning pregame show before her beloved New York Knicks basketball team faced off against the Miami Heat. She didn't feel her customary excitement before the game, though. Her mood was dampened by resentment over the fact she hadn't heard from Malcolm in two days, not since the evening of the cocktail party. She didn't expect to hear from him today, either.

Thinking about Friday night's kiss and subsequent unfulfillment lowered her mood even more. After a fitful night, she'd been tempted to call him Saturday to blister his ears. But she'd decided against doing that.

Why had Malcolm kissed her so passionately, then walked away? From her reaction, he must have known he could have stayed if he'd wanted to. And she could tell that from his response to their heated kiss he had wanted to stay.

What had he meant when he'd told her to let him know when she was ready to accept what was still between them? If he'd wanted sex, they would have had sex. What more did he think was between them?

The phone rang, breaking her train of thought. Nicole debated answering it. If it was Malcolm, she didn't know what to say to him. With a shrug, she picked up the receiver. If it was Malcolm, she'd wing it.

"Hello."

"Ms. Collins? It's Rita Collozo from Celestial Productions. Ms. Collins, there's been an accident."

# CHAPTER SIX

Nicole was too late. By the time she arrived at the hospital, Malcolm was holding Tyrone's fiancée. Joyce was crying hysterically, her face buried in his chest.

Nicole's heart stuttered. She noticed Rita crying quietly on a sofa across from Malcolm and Joyce. Nicole approached her, laying a tentative hand on her shoulder.

"Rita?"

The small, heart-shaped face tipped up. Her soft, brown eyes were red and swollen from tears.

"What happened?" Nicole asked. "You said there'd been an accident."

"Ty didn't make it." Tears deepened her lilting accent. "He lost control of his car. He was on his way home from his morning run along the beach, and he just lost control of his car." Rita choked on a sob.

Nicole dropped onto the sofa before her knees gave out. Dazed, she wrapped her arm around Rita's shoulder, automatically pulling her closer as misery shook the woman's small body. She was glad the four of them were alone in the small, sterile waiting room.

"The doctor said he died instantly." Rita's voice trembled as she tried to gather control.

"Were you able to contact his family?"

Rita nodded. "I got their answering machine. I left a

message for them to call Mal." Rita heaved a teary sigh.
"He was such a good man. He and Mal are the best
bosses I've ever had."

Snapshot images of Tyrone clipped through Nicole's
mind. The way he'd brushed aside her embarrassment
over their first meeting, his boyish byplay with Malcolm,
his ties that paid homage to the sci-fi genre. How could
someone so alive, with so much to look forward to, die
so suddenly?

"Rita," Nicole said. "You don't have to hold back. It's
okay to let go and cry. Ty was a wonderful man. He deserves your tears."

"I know. I know." Rita sniffed. "But I have to try to be
strong for Mal and Joyce."

"They have each other right now. Take a moment for
yourself. If they need anything, I can help them."

Rita sat stiffly a moment more, then relaxed and allowed the tears to fall. Nicole stroked her arm and offered what she could in the way of comfort.

She looked over to where Malcolm sat with Joyce in
his arms. *I've been happier with her than I've ever been in my
life,* Tyrone had said. She was so happy they'd shared a
love that strong.

Nicole watched Malcolm as he allowed Joyce to weep
her heart out onto his sweater. His eyes were red and
blinked frequently as though he fought to keep his own
tears from falling. People always leaned on Malcolm. Yet,
when he was hurting, he'd never allowed himself the
comfort of resting in someone else's care. Malcolm knew
how to give, but he didn't know how to receive. That had
been a problem between them, because she was also a
nurturer. The one time in their relationship they had
needed to support each other, he had pulled away from
her. Now, it broke her heart to watch him once again
struggle to be strong at a time that made people weak.

Nicole saw him help Joyce up and, with an arm supporting her, lead her from the room. They paused in
front of Nicole and Rita. She looked past his composed

expression to the grief in his eyes. Nicole wanted to stand, to touch them both in a gesture of sympathy, but she didn't want to let go of Rita.

"Mal, Joyce, I'm so sorry," she said.

"Thank you for coming." Malcolm inclined his head, then led Joyce from the room.

Nicole watched them leave before returning her attention to Rita. "Let me take you home. Is there anyone who can stay with you now?"

With a shuddering breath, Rita lifted her face from her hands and looked toward the now-empty sofa. "Where are Mal and Joyce?"

Nicole continued to rub the other woman's arm. "They've left."

"Oh." She blinked. "I didn't notice." She pulled another tissue from her purse.

"Do you want me to take you home?" Nicole repeated, understanding that in Rita's distraught condition, she would have trouble focusing on what people were saying to her.

"No, thank you. I have my car."

"Rita, you're in no condition to drive. Your car will be safe in the hospital parking lot overnight. We can get it in the morning."

Rita took time to absorb Nicole's suggestion. Finally, she nodded. "Okay."

Nicole helped Rita stand. "You shouldn't be alone now. Is there anyone at your house, or do you want to come home with me?"

Rita looked up at her. "Could you take me to my sister's house?"

"Of course, I will." Nicole waited while Rita gathered her purse and coat. She matched the other woman's steps as they left the waiting room. Rita's usual pace was an aerobic workout. Now her steps dragged with sorrow. Nicole held the exit door open for her.

"I can't imagine what Mal will do now." Rita brushed

away a tear. "With Ty gone, what will happen to the company?"


Malcolm walked into Joyce's house and followed her to the living room. He hadn't seen her in the week since Tyrone's funeral, and he regretted that. But he thought they'd both needed some time alone to grieve.

As Malcolm entered the living room, he was surprised by its darkness. One of the things Tyrone and Joyce had liked about the room was the amount of natural light it offered. Today, Joyce had the curtains drawn. Only one corner light was left to battle the gloom.

"How are you?"

Malcolm thought it a stupid question even as he asked it. The room's condition alone indicated she was grieving hard. Not only was it dark and stuffy, but it was also in an unusual state of disorder. Blankets and pillows were tucked into a corner of the sofa as though she'd taken to sleeping on it.

"Some moments are better than others," Joyce replied. "How are you?"

"The same."

Joyce sank into a straight-backed armchair across from the sofa she had offered to Malcolm. She gazed around the room as though searching for memories.

"I hadn't been sure I wanted to move in with him," she remembered. "It was such a big commitment for me. But he kept after me and after me. It took him more than eight months to convince me to move into this house with him. Then, when we'd unpacked my last box, he took me to dinner and asked me to marry him. Talk about commitment." She ended with a watery laugh.

Malcolm's lips curved. That was Tyrone all over. Press every advantage, take advantage of every opportunity. He'd loved strategizing, which was why he'd loved the business aspect of Celestial Productions.

"I'm sorry." Another inadequate statement, Malcolm thought.

"I don't regret that we didn't have a wedding ceremony," she said, playing with the engagement ring she still wore. "I felt married to him. He made me feel like a very important part of his life. But I do regret that we won't have any children now. Although sometimes he was like a really big kid himself, with his toys and silly jokes."

Joyce gave another watery laugh. It tugged at Malcolm's heart.

"He was a kid at heart." Malcolm chuckled. "One minute he was the consummate businessman, working deals and making the impossible possible. The next minute he was singing theme songs from cartoons or quoting movie lines."

In the silence that followed his words, Malcolm took stock of Joyce's appearance. She was wearing one of Tyrone's sweaters. Even in the dim light, strain showed clearly on her unpainted face. Her hair was disheveled, and her eyes were tired and tear-swollen above dark circles.

"I also regret that he won't see the *InterDimensions* movie." Joyce pulled a well-used tissue from her sweatpants pocket to dry her eyes. "This project was his personal dream and his professional goal."

"I regret that, too," Malcolm admitted. "He and I felt the same way about this project."

"That's why I asked you to come over. I want to make sure that nothing prevents this movie from being made."

"Don't worry," Malcolm assured her. "Nothing will get in the way of this project."

"I know the completion guarantors are getting nervous with Ty gone. They just don't understand that you're just as capable of handling the business side as Ty is—was."

Malcolm tensed. "How did you know about the guarantors?"

"I called Rita."

Malcolm shook his head with a sigh. "I really wish she hadn't told you."

"I want to be kept informed."

"Well, don't worry. The guarantors will come around."

"Mal, you've got a lot on your plate doing your work and Ty's. If there's anything I can do to take some of the load off of you, just let me know. This project is very important to me, too."

Malcolm told himself an offer of help was not a criticism of his business abilities. It didn't mean Joyce thought he couldn't make the movie project a success on his own. He stood and paced to the bookcase where Tyrone's sci-fi movie action figures played hide-and-seek with Joyce's self-help books.

"Thanks, Joyce." He turned back to her, trying to think of something comforting to say. "Do you want me to get you another tissue?" He gestured toward the tattered one in her hand.

"No. I'll be right back." She rose from the armchair and shuffled down the hall. She returned with a nearly empty box of tissues. She rested the box at her feet and clung to the tattered one still in her hand.

"Is there anything I can do for you?" Malcolm asked, unable to think of anything else to say.

Joyce shook her head, staring into the distance. "It shouldn't have happened like this." Her breath quivered on a sob. "It shouldn't have happened at all, but it definitely shouldn't have happened like this. We had so much left to do. Is that the way it goes? Do people leave you when you still have so much left to do?"

Malcolm crumpled the phone message in one fist and hurled it across the office. Another message from a contractor canceling an appointment had been waiting for him when he'd returned from visiting Joyce. *Damn it.* He restrained the urge to pound his desk and instead shoved out of his chair to pace his office.

He had to keep his wits about him. He couldn't let Rita see how frustrated he was becoming. He couldn't let anyone see how the industry's lack of faith in his business ability affected him. Malcolm massaged the back of his neck. What would Tyrone do in this situation? he asked himself again. The answer was never easy, because he and Tyrone had handled the hard parts together. Now, at this very moment, he felt so alone. He hadn't felt this alone since he'd seen Nicole's signature on the divorce decree.

His intercom buzzed. Pulling himself together, he returned to his desk.

"Yes, Rita?"

"There's a Mr. Nathan Rutherford here to see you, Mr. Bryant. He knows he's not on your calendar," she said with wonderful censorship. "But he wonders if you might be able to spare some time for him. He wants to discuss a possible interview with you for a feature he's working on for *Silver Screen Preview.*"

*When it rains, it pours,* Malcolm thought.

Nathan Rutherford never gave Celestial Productions favorable press. It wasn't a secret: he and Omar Carter were friends, and Nathan wasn't opposed to using the power of his pen to hurt Omar's rivals. Unfortunately for Malcolm, it would do more damage to Celestial Productions if he refused an interview with the industry's leading publication.

"Sure, Rita. Could you escort him back, please?"

"Of course, Mr. Bryant." Rita disconnected.

Malcolm's brow quirked at Rita's formality. She must be in full overprotective mode. He put down the phone and turned back to his computer. His gaze was on the memo he was composing, but his mind searched for angles Nathan might take for his article. The possible headline, CELESTIAL PRODUCTIONS FLOUNDERING UNDER BRYANT'S CONTROL, flashed before his eyes.

The knock on his door signaled he'd run out of time.

Rita pushed open the door. "Excuse me, Mr. Bryant. I know you're very busy. Mr. Rutherford is here."

"Thank you, Rita." Malcolm approached them. He shook Nathan's hand. "It's good to see you, Nathan. Have a seat."

Malcolm walked back to his desk, leaving his office door open after Rita left. He didn't want Nathan to get too comfortable. He sat down and waited for the reporter to start the unscheduled meeting.

"I was sorry to hear about Tyrone," Nathan began. "That's quite a blow for your company."

Malcolm stiffened. "Ty was a very good friend."

"Yes. Well, I hear he was the brains behind the company."

A slow boil began. He forced a casual tone. "Where did you hear that?"

If Nathan noticed the gathering storm, he didn't indicate it. The reporter slipped into his bored persona. "You hear things on the industry's grapevine, especially when you're in the media. The consensus is, you don't have what it takes to succeed on your own."

The slow boil bubbled and erupted. He wasn't certain whether it was the aspersions against his abilities, Nathan's insensitivity toward Tyrone's death, or Nathan himself. But suddenly the idea of ripping into someone was irresistibly appealing. He opened his mouth to voice his anger, frustration, and grief, but another voice cut in before his.

"As a former reporter myself, I would suggest you check your sources. They don't sound very reliable."

Malcolm looked up to see Nicole standing in his doorway, her face a study of cold contempt. She cradled bags from a nearby Mexican restaurant.

"Ty and Mal shared their preliminary figures with you." Nicole repeated the numbers she'd heard during the cocktail party eons ago. "And those are conservative estimates."

"But how do we know he can pull it off without Tyrone?" Nathan asked, jerking a thumb toward Malcolm.

"What makes you think he can't?" Nicole countered.

"Well . . . because . . . that's what people are saying," the reporter finished. His chinless face flushed under Nicole's cool gaze.

Malcolm wondered if the "people" Nathan referred to meant Omar. Initiating slanderous gossip sounded like a tactic Omar would use to discredit him.

"People are wrong," Nicole stated.

Malcolm grew tired of having them act as though he weren't there. "If people don't believe I can pull this off on my own, then I suggest they watch and learn."

Nathan turned to Malcolm and appeared to rally his composure. His gray eyes narrowed. "I hear vendors aren't taking your contract because they're afraid you can't pay them."

"Your sources are wrong," Malcolm said flatly.

"I also hear the completion guarantors aren't returning your calls."

Malcolm stood. "Why don't you go back to your office and check your facts? We're through here."

Nathan rose. "Are you going to give me a quote for my article?"

Malcolm clenched his teeth. He wanted to wipe the smug look off Nathan's face. Nicole's presence and the knowledge Nathan wasn't the main cause of his anger were the only things keeping his hands in his pockets.

"I already have," Malcolm replied. "Now get out."

Malcolm watched Nathan swagger from his office. He still wanted to punch something. Instead, he turned away and practiced the breathing technique Tyrone had taught him. Breathe in to the count of seven, hold for the count of eight, breathe out for the count of seven. Afterward, you were supposed to feel more relaxed. It didn't work.

Nicole broke the silence. "Now I understand what

Rita meant when she said you were the victim of a surprise attack."

Malcolm turned back to her. "Where is Rita?"

"She's at lunch." Nicole's eyes narrowed in concern. "Are you okay?"

Malcolm sighed. "Not really. I'm a grown man who just had to be protected by a woman like a ten-year-old boy watched over by his mother." Malcolm knew his comment wasn't fair. He watched with regret as hurt replaced the concern in her eyes.

Nicole set the restaurant bags on the conversation table in the corner of his office. "I'm sorry. I didn't mean to make you feel that way."

Her apologetic tone made Malcolm feel like a bully. He rubbed the back of his neck. "I suppose I should thank you. You saved me from saying something to him I'm sure I would have regretted. Eventually."

Nicole arched a brow. "You're welcome, I think." She turned to unpack the contents of the bags.

"So, why are you here? Did you stop by to save me from myself?"

"No. I'm here for a working lunch. I have a feeling you haven't been eating. And we need to find a way to convince the vendors to work with us."

She pulled an industry magazine out of her knapsack and laid it on the table. It spread open to an article titled, CELESTIAL PRODUCTIONS ON SHAKY GROUND. Despite himself, Malcolm felt defensive. Old guilts and insecurities floated to the surface.

He scanned the article. "It makes you wonder what it is about me that doesn't inspire confidence."

"Stop it. People who know you know you're a capable businessman."

From the fierce light in her eyes, Malcolm believed she meant what she said.

"How do you know what kind of businessman I am? You don't know anything about Celestial Productions."

Again, he saw hurt darken her eyes before she looked away.

She served the food. "I know what kind of businessman you are because I know you."

He waited, but she didn't seem inclined to say any more. Malcolm refolded the magazine and laid it on the table. "I'm handling the situation."

"But you shouldn't have to do this alone. You told me yourself this project is important to all of us—you, me, and Ty."

Malcolm grew colder. "And you don't trust me to protect our interests? Although I helped build this company from scratch?"

"I believe you can protect our interests, if you try. My question is whether you're going to try."

He battled his temper. "What makes you think I won't?"

"A little piece of paper in my personal file titled, 'Divorce Decree.' I think you also have one of those." She folded her arms across her chest. "After our baby died, our marriage needed work. Instead of sticking around, you took the easy way out by ending it."

He glared at her. It was a toss-up as to which bothered him more: her lack of faith in his work ethic or her misconception about his intent regarding their divorce. "You returned those signed divorce papers pretty quickly. What does that say about your interest in working on our marriage?"

Nicole jerked as though slapped. He watched her eyes cloud before she turned to arrange the food on the table.

Malcolm frowned. Did she think she was the only one who'd had her heart torn out? He sighed. Now they were acting like children trying to outdo the other's pain.

"Nicky—"

"You're right." Her voice was high and sharp. "Maybe we both gave up too soon."

"I'm not going to back out of this project, Nicky."

She turned to face him. "Good. What can I do to help?"

Malcolm paced away from her, trying to distance himself from the pressure he felt to accept her offer and the pressure he felt to stand on his own. "I can manage this on my own."

He heard her walk toward him, felt her presence just behind him.

"But you don't have to." She gripped his upper arm, and he let her turn him around. "You keep asking me to try again with you, to go back to being friends. Well, friends lean on each other."

He gently removed her hand from his arm. "I didn't ask you to come to L.A. to bail me out of a jam."

Nicole crossed her arms over her chest. "No, you didn't. But I'm here for you, anyway."

# CHAPTER SEVEN

The black sport utility vehicle sat at the curb across the street again. Locating the vehicle had become like a game. Nicole's gaze dropped to the license plate to confirm the SUV's identity: KZY-2525. Several other SUVs were parked on the street, but this one stuck out because it never stayed long in the neighborhood. She saw it in the morning before her jog; then it vanished after breakfast. She'd wondered at the owner's story. Was he or she having an illicit affair with one of Nicole's neighbors?

Nicole grinned to herself as she trudged up to her apartment. She tossed her keys on the bookcase, then grabbed her bottled water. She wandered over to her window to spy on the SUV. The vehicle's tinted windows were too dark to tell whether someone was in it. She moved away from the view and used the remote control to turn on the television. She toed off her running shoes in preparation for her cooldown stretches.

The phone rang, and she pushed herself back up to her feet. "Hello."

"Hi. What are you doing for breakfast?" Malcolm asked.

Nicole smiled. "Eating. What about you?" She propped herself against the wall and pulled off her socks.

Malcolm's pause seemed uncertain. "Are you eating right now?"

"No. I'm getting ready to take a shower." She stuffed her socks into her running shoes.

"Why don't I come by and pick you up? I could take you out to breakfast."

"You're asking this time? You usually just show up," Nicole teased, using the remote to turn off the television.

"I need to talk to you."

"What about?" She went back to leaning against the wall.

Malcolm paused. "I'd prefer to talk with you over breakfast."

"All right. But I don't want to go out. I'll cook here."

"Okay. What time?"

Nicole consulted her sports watch. "Give me an hour. I don't want to rush through my shower."

Malcolm's soft laughter echoed in her abdomen. "Fair enough. I'll see you in an hour. Thanks, Nicky."

"Bye." She rang off.

She turned toward the hallway leading to the bathroom, then paused. She crossed back to the living room window. The black SUV was gone.


She looked like a cat burglar.

Malcolm clenched his jaw to keep his mouth from dropping open when Nicole let him into her apartment. Her hair was unbound, floating like a thick, dark cloud around her shoulders. The baggy clothes had been replaced by a ribbed black sweater that hugged her torso and cupped her butt. Black leggings stroked every curve of her legs from thigh to calf to ankle. He wondered about her choice of clothing. It was the most form-fitting outfit she'd worn since he'd found her again. Malcolm smiled when his gaze reached the fluffy orange-and-blue New York Knicks socks.

"What would you prefer?" she called as he carried his jacket to the hall closet. "Scrambled eggs? Poached eggs? Or boiled eggs? And I have bacon."

Malcolm couldn't think about breakfast. His mind was still on the curves Nicole's outfit revealed. "Just coffee will be fine."

She turned to face him. "Have you been living on coffee since Ty's funeral?" When he looked at her blankly, she continued. "When was the last time you had a meal?"

"We had lunch together yesterday."

"And you didn't eat much. What did you have for dinner?"

Malcolm considered her question. "I don't remember." He hadn't thought much about food since the day he had driven Joyce home from the hospital. The realization surprised him.

Nicole's expression softened in sympathy. "Mal, I understand food's not a big priority right now. But you've got to keep your strength up. We'll start with eggs and toast. How do you want it?"

"Whatever's easiest for you." He followed her into the kitchen.

"They're all easy."

"Then I'd like scrambled eggs, please." He had fond memories of her scrambled eggs.

She pulled the egg carton and bread from the fridge and turned to take the spices from her cupboard. Watching her move around the kitchen preparing their meal carried Malcolm back in time. She swayed from the cupboards to the stove, to the fridge and back. He settled comfortably into the memories of meals they'd prepared and eaten together.

"What are you doing?" she asked.

He glanced down, surprised to find mugs and dishes in his hands. "Setting the table."

Nicole's gaze grew uncertain and drifted away. She continued cooking breakfast while he set the table, made coffee, and poured orange juice.

"This brings back memories." His comment was deliberate.

Nicole kept her eyes on the eggs. "Let's not go back

there. If you're serious about this friendship, we need to move forward."

Malcolm was eager to accept her offer. "All right. What are your plans for today?"

She brought the filled plates to the table Malcolm had set. "Work on my manuscripts. I have a couple of publicity interviews. Why? Is there something you need, friend?"

Malcolm returned her smile. "No. Just curious." He sipped his orange juice. "You told Ty you'll write as many sequels as you can sell for *InterDimensions*."

"That's right." Nicole bit into her toast. "I really enjoy the series and the characters. We go through so many things together. Like a family."

Nicole's words triggered a memory in Malcolm's mind of the caller who'd dialed his cell phone in error more than two weeks ago. *Leave my family alone,* the caller had said. Malcolm didn't know why he'd remembered that misdialed call at this time. He shrugged the memory away.

"Do you enjoy the series as much as you enjoy writing mysteries?" he asked.

Nicole picked up her coffee cup. "I have a feeling you aren't here to talk about my writing, Mal. What's on your mind?"

Malcolm finished his coffee, using the time to gather his thoughts. He didn't want to have this discussion but knew he had to.

"We didn't finish our conversation yesterday. About the project," he started.

Nicole stilled, then returned her forkful of eggs to her plate. "You didn't seem to want to continue, and I thought I'd pushed as far as I could."

He looked at the table as he rubbed the back of his neck. "It's not easy for me to talk about the way that I feel. Half the time, I don't even know."

Nicole's smile was rueful. "That's not a news flash."

He chuckled. "Okay." He looked up and tried to keep

his gaze steady on her eyes. "One of the reasons I wanted to work on this project with you is that I wanted you to see me as a success, as someone who could take care of you."

"What do you mean?"

"Four years ago, I had a job barely making minimum wage. You had to work too hard to help pay the bills. Now I have my own company. We're not doing great, but we have enough that I can afford a house."

Nicole rose to get the coffeepot. In pensive silence, she refilled their coffee cups, replaced the carafe, then reclaimed her seat. "It's times like this I wonder whether you ever knew me at all."

Malcolm frowned, surprised. "What do you mean?"

She sipped her coffee. "I didn't marry you for your money. As you said, you didn't have any."

Malcolm scowled at his fresh cup of coffee. The deeper into the conversation they traveled, the harder it became for him. "I wanted to be able to take care of you."

That sentiment seemed to annoy her. "I didn't want someone to take care of me. I wanted someone who would be my partner. Someone I could lean on and who would lean on me." She paused. "You still won't lean on me, Mal."

He wouldn't pretend not to notice she'd changed the subject. "It's my company, Nicky. I can deal with the vendors on my own."

Nicole put down her mug. "But our contract states we're partners on this project."

Malcolm shook his head. "Creative partners. The business side is my responsibility."

"Didn't Ty help you?"

"That's different. Celestial Productions was Ty's company, too."

Nicole gave him a long, frustrated stare. Then a reluctant chuckle escaped her. "You are such a stubborn man. My offer of help still stands. It always will."

Looking into her laughing ebony eyes, Malcolm remembered all the reasons he loved her and wondered how he could have been foolish enough to let her go. She stood to clear the table, and he rose to help her.

Once the dishwasher was loaded, he checked his watch. "I'd better get going."

Nicole trailed after him as he collected his coat from the hall closet. "I hope you have a better day today."

He paused in the living room as she came to walk him out. On impulse, he reached for her arms and pulled her up on her toes. She looked startled as she braced her hands on his shoulders.

"For luck," he whispered before touching his lips to hers.

Nicole pulled back and touched her fingers to her mouth. "I don't think we should have kissing in this friendship. I don't think we know how to handle it."

Malcolm's hands slid down her body, and he pressed his fingers into her lithe waist. His eyes twinkled into hers. "I know how to handle it," he murmured, his lips a breath away from hers.

He closed the distance and drank from her mouth. His hands moved up from her waist, his thumbs stroked the undercurve of her breasts. Nicole sighed and leaned into him. The humming in his blood increased in volume. He wanted so badly to slip her out of her sweater and pull off her form-fitting leggings. But when they came together again after four years, he wanted the loving to last. And right now, he knew the timing wasn't right.

His hands shook as he pulled them away from her breasts. Her moan of protest almost lured him back. But the image of a long, leisurely loving in the future—the very near future—gave him the strength he needed to stay his course. He wrapped his arms around her and tried to soothe them both with long, gentle strokes up and down her back.

"I hate to leave you now," he whispered. "I really do."

"I think it's for the best." Her voice was muffled against

his chest. "You may be able to handle this, but I don't think I can."

"All right." He sighed, still stroking them back from the edge.

She stirred and pulled away from him, her hands braced against his upper arms. He linked his fingers behind her back, unwilling to let her go yet. He felt her fingers flex against his biceps.

"Don't skip lunch," she said.

He smiled, his gaze dropping to her kiss-swollen lips. "Thanks for the luck."


When Rita called him to announce Leo's arrival, Malcolm was surprised at how quickly the day had passed. He went to the reception area to greet his mentor, then escorted Leo back to his office.

"I'm glad you could see me on such short notice, Mal."

"You don't need to make an appointment to see me, Leo." Malcolm stood aside to let his friend precede him into his office.

"I don't like to drop by unannounced."

"You're always welcome." Malcolm gestured to one of the chairs at the conversation table in the corner.

"I haven't spoken to you since Ty's funeral. I'm sorry for that." Leo eased into the seat.

"That's all right. Ty's family, Joyce, and I appreciated your attending the service." Malcolm sat, stretching his long legs and crossing his ankles.

"How is Joyce?"

"She's doing her best. She's taken a leave of absence from her job."

"That's an excellent idea." Leo paused, then asked, "And how are you?"

Malcolm's hesitation was brief. "I'm doing my best as well."

"I knew you would."

Malcolm waited a moment, but Leo slipped into silence. "What's on your mind, Leo?"

Leo folded his hands on the table. "I don't want to add to your stress, but as your friend, there's something I feel we need to discuss."

Malcolm scanned Leo's grave expression. The habitual twinkle was missing from the warm blue eyes. Malcolm braced himself for bad news. "What would that be?"

"I know several vendors aren't returning your bid requests and have expressed their concern about the project now that Ty is gone."

Malcolm felt the tension crawl along his shoulder and climb up his neck. "Word spreads."

"The rumor is that you don't believe you can continue with this project, either."

Malcolm kept his expression neutral. "Do you believe that rumor?"

"No, I don't." Leo shook his head. "I have confidence in you. Ty had confidence in you. You need to show the industry that you have confidence in yourself."

"What would you suggest I do?"

"First, you need to stop the bad press. This movie is going to be another Celestial Productions success. I can feel it. Make them feel it, too."

Malcolm thought of the vendetta Nathan Rutherford had for him. "I think that's easier said than done."

"If there's any way I can help you, let me know. Although, Frank won't be pleased." Leo gave a tight smile.

Malcolm was surprised. "Why not?"

The older man leaned back in his chair. "He thinks the movie will hurt the *InterDimensions* series."

Malcolm recalled the cocktail party. "Does he think Nicole is more interested in getting paid than in protecting her story?"

"I think that's part of it. He also doesn't trust Hollywood."

Malcolm arched a brow. "You're a successful film producer. Does he consider you 'Hollywood'?"

Leo sighed. "I'm afraid so. And now with the *InterDimensions* movie going into production, he resents me more than ever."

Malcolm frowned. "But you don't have anything to do with this project."

Leo shook his head, then lifted a hand to smooth locks of graying hair off his forehead. "That doesn't matter. He puts us all in the same category."

Leo was silent for a while, lost in thought, before he continued. "I didn't spend a lot of time with my family when we were younger. I was too busy climbing the corporate ladder so I could get them things—a bigger house, fancy cars, whatever they may have wanted."

Malcolm thought of the times during his marriage when he'd told Nicole how much he regretted not being able to buy her expensive things. *You're all I need,* she had replied. But she hadn't seemed to need him after the miscarriage. She had turned to her family and shut him out. Malcolm put those memories behind him as Leo continued his story.

"Then one day, I woke up and realized I didn't know my wife and son anymore. They had developed a bond between them that shut me out of their lives. I'm still trying to find my way back in. But it's strange. I think Ava resents my efforts. She even threatened to leave me."

"Ava was going to leave you?" Malcolm found that idea hard to believe. The older couple always seemed so affectionate toward each other whenever he saw them together.

Malcolm could sense Leo's pain beneath his smiles.

"Oh, yes," his mentor said. "I was so wrapped up in my work, I hadn't realized how bad the situation had become. Ava said she and Frank had been managing just fine on their own all these years. That I was just an interference."

Malcolm winced. "That must have hurt."

"Those words hurt enough to sink in. I had to find a way to connect with my son. That's when I started reading for pleasure again. Frank really loves to read. And he loves Nicole's *InterDimensions* series."

"They're great stories."

Leo's brows rose. "I'd forgotten you've read her series."

"Yes. And her other titles." Malcolm almost groaned when his comment brought the twinkle back to Leo's eyes.

"Nicole is a very attractive woman."

"Yes, she is."

Leo watched Malcolm intently. "Much more attractive than her book jacket leads one to believe."

"I agree. But before you start getting any ideas, I want you to know our relationship is strictly business."

Leo laughed. "Ah, Mal, my friend. Your best years aren't behind you until the pretty ladies stop noticing you. And this one is definitely noticing you."

"Oh?"

"Definitely. She was checking you out." Leo struggled with a grin.

Malcolm frowned. He was glad to see Leo's spirits lifting, but he wished it wasn't at his expense.

"Strictly business, Leo," he reminded his friend.

"All work and no play makes for a very dull and lonely life, Mal. Take it from someone who knows."

"Do you have any other clichés for me?"

Leo threw back his head and roared with laughter. "Is there anything I can do to help you with the *InterDimensions* movie project?" he asked when he regained his composure.

Malcolm's reflexive reaction was to deny any need for help. It was hard to go against the do-it-yourself attitude with which he had grown up. But, with an effort, he choked back his refusal and took a moment to consider Leo's offer.

"Perhaps there's something you can do."

Later, Malcolm sat alone in his office. He missed Tyrone. He needed to speak with him about his plan to move forward with the project and ignore his critics' doubts. He closed his eyes and concentrated. In the stillness, he imagined he could hear Tyrone's voice: "The company's in good hands, Mal. Your love life needs help."

Startled, Malcolm's eyes flew open. That wasn't the response he'd expected. But he'd heard Tyrone's voice as clearly as though his friend stood right next to him.

Malcolm picked up his telephone and dialed Nicole's number before he could reconsider his decision.

"Hello."

Malcolm ignored her sharp greeting. "Have dinner with me tonight."

"Mal?" she asked after a brief pause.

"Who else would it be?"

"Did you call me a second ago?"

"No. Why?"

"Someone called and just breathed into the phone. I thought perhaps it was you and we had a bad connection."

Concerned, Malcolm sat straighter in his chair. "You sound upset. Are you sure the caller didn't say anything?"

"There were no sounds on the other end of the line except breathing. I think that's what unnerved me. That and the note I received the other day."

Malcolm frowned. "Do you think they're connected?"

"I don't know. All I know is, they were both disturbing."

Malcolm glanced at his watch. It was after five o'clock. "Do you want me to come over?"

"I'll be okay in a minute. How did your day go?"

Malcolm reluctantly accepted the change of subject. Maybe he was overreacting. Perhaps it was just a nuisance call and nothing more. "I'll tell you all about it over dinner tonight."

"Just tell me now."

He smiled at her impatience. "No. Over dinner."

"Don't keep me in suspense. That's mean. At least tell me if it went well."

"It went very well."

"Oh, Mal, I'm so pleased."

He heard the smile in her voice. "Great. Have dinner with me."

"Mal, I don't like going out to eat."

"I'm getting that impression. I'll cook." He leaned back in his chair, swinging it from side to side.

Nicole's silence hummed with disbelief. "This ought to be interesting."

He sat up again, offended. "I can cook."

She chuckled. "Since when?"

He ignored her disbelieving snort. "I'll pick you up at seven o'clock."

"I can find my way to your house."

"I'll pick you up, and I'll feed you," he insisted.

"Mal, I'm going to drive to your house," Nicole repeated with a laugh. "There's no point in your picking me up just to drive us back to your house."

Malcolm gave in. He didn't want to argue with Nicole before asking for her help. "I'll see you at seven, then."

Malcolm replaced the receiver. He vowed to cook her a meal that would have her taste buds singing for months and would win her cooperation for the plan he and Leo had decided on. He knew Nicole was going to be annoyed, to put it mildly. He'd have to do some fast talking to convince her to work with him on this plan.

# CHAPTER EIGHT

Nicole hoped she'd misunderstood Malcolm. "I'm sorry. What did you say?"

"You heard me. Leo offered to host a dinner party for the *InterDimensions* project," he repeated.

Nicole sensed Malcolm's tension. He seemed to be bracing himself for a fight. She couldn't blame him after her reaction to the last *InterDimensions* social event. She looked down at the remains of the deliciously spicy pasta dish he'd served for dinner. The man had told the truth, she thought with a sigh. He really could cook. She wondered if he'd intended the meal to make her more amenable to his plan. She smothered a smile at that idea.

She returned her attention to Malcolm, keeping her gaze above his chest-sculpting black sweater. "How would the dinner party help us?"

"Leo is a well-respected veteran of the film industry. He has a lot of clout. By hosting the dinner party, he'll be showing his support for the project. It would go a long way toward countering the bad press I've been receiving."

"*We've* been receiving," Nicole corrected.

Malcolm nodded absently. "After Ty's death, the project stalled. But now we're regrouping, and the party will help give us positive exposure. Publicists, trade press, and agents will be there."

Nicole sipped her fruit punch, considering the strategy. "It sounds like a good idea."

Malcolm's brows shot toward his hairline. Then a cautious look entered his eyes. Nicole felt her lips curve in amusement.

"It would really help to have you there to show a united front," he said. "Everyone knows how important you are to this project."

"I agree." She smiled as Malcolm's eyes narrowed in suspicion. "You seem surprised," she teased.

He shared her smile. "I am. We had to practically drag you to the last cocktail party. And you started asking when you could leave almost as soon as we arrived."

"I'm not comfortable at social events."

"You used to enjoy parties and socializing. What happened?"

Tension gathered in Nicole's shoulders. Her gaze dropped from his. "Over the years, I seem to have lost my self-confidence."

"Nicky—"

Nicole looked up into Malcolm's stricken expression. "Mal, I'm not telling you this to upset you. I'm giving you the answer to a question you keep asking. I'm sure the miscarriage and divorce weren't easy for you, either. Don't worry, I'm dealing with it. And I'll have you there to help me through it, friend," she added, forcing a smile.

Malcolm still looked concerned, but he managed to return her smile. "I'll do my best. But I'd better warn you. Leo's son isn't happy about this project."

Nicole winced. "I got that feeling during the cocktail party. Do you think he'll be there?"

"Probably." Understanding softened Malcolm's gaze.

"Well, I survived my last encounter with him."

"You handled him very well."

"Mal, you don't have to sweet-talk me. I've already agreed to go. When will it be?"

"Leo needs to talk with his wife, Ava. But we were planning on the first or second Saturday in April. We want to do it as soon as possible so we can move forward with the production. We've had the auditions and site surveys on hold long enough."

"A Saturday evening?" Nicole was incredulous.

"Yes. Why?"

"Well, the NBA play-offs are going on now. Suppose the Knicks are playing?"

Malcolm looked amused. "Can't you tape the game and watch it later?"

Nicole squeezed her eyes shut and sighed. Her eyes popped open. "You've never liked the Knicks," she accused.

"I don't dislike the Knicks," he prevaricated.

"You have 'Los Angeles Lakers fan' written all over you."

"Which is convenient, since I live in L.A." Malcolm stood to clear the table.

She laughed. "You're from Michigan. You should support the Detroit Pistons."

"They suck this season." Malcolm waved a hand dismissively.

Nicole smiled at Malcolm's snort of disgust. "True." She rose to help clear the table. "Fine. I'll tape the game."

"Thank you, Nicky. I appreciate the sacrifice."

"You'd better," she warned teasingly.

"Don't worry. I'll make a few for you in return."

Malcolm grinned, and in a flash, the atmosphere between them changed as a new element entered the room. Sexual hunger. She saw it in his eyes and felt it in her gut. She took a step back, even as she realized there wasn't enough distance in the world to ease her need to touch him.

"I don't need you to make sacrifices for me, Mal." She turned and stacked her dishes in the dishwasher, then started from the room. "I think it's time for me to go home."

"What *did* you need me for, Nicky?"

She turned and frowned at him. "What are you talking about?"

"You didn't need me for money. You had your own. You didn't even need me to help you through the miscarriage. You had your family for that." He stepped toward her with each accusation, but she refused to give ground. They ended up with barely an arm's length between them. "So, what *did* you need me for?"

"I did need you to help me through our baby's death. You're the one who didn't need me." She forced the words past the air clogging her throat.

"Yes, I did."

"Then why did you keep pushing me away?"

"I'm not pushing you away now." He gripped her forearms and pulled her against him. His lips locked over hers, and the need that had been stoked and restrained several times in the past weeks was resurrected with a growl that reverberated in her core. The desire had been building since he'd kissed her the day she'd returned to Los Angeles. Now, reawakened, it was so much more than a need. It was a hunger. A wild thing clawing its way out of her to mate with him.

He slanted his lips—his warm, firm lips—across hers and deepened the kiss, adding a dimension that melted her bones and made her muscles quiver. Her arms, which had pressed against his chest, slid over his shoulders and linked behind his neck. A warning voice buzzed in her ear, but the hunger slapped it away and urged her to press her body along the length of his. He groaned and she shivered.

"I want you," he growled into her mouth.

"I know. I want you, too," she breathed back.

"Thank God."

She gasped as her feet left the ground, and he carried her up the stairs to his bedroom.

"I'm—" Her words caught in her throat when his lips returned to pull her back into the vortex of need. Her pulse pounded in her ears; her body trembled and burned.

She felt Malcolm lower her body against his until her feet touched the ground. His large, firm hands slid under her sweater. His fingertips stroked against her ribs, all the while scrambling her mind with a kiss so deep and dark it pulled at the wild thing straining within her.

Nicole dragged her hands over his form-fitting sweater before pulling it up and off him. His skin was smooth, firm, and hot. Her hands curved over his pectorals. She pulled her lips away from his and dipped her head to lick his collarbone. He shivered beneath her hands, tempting her to further explore his bare skin with her tongue and fingertips. But as she dipped her head toward his nipple, he held her back, stripped off her sweater, and fell with her onto the bed.

"Later," Malcolm murmured. "We'll play later. I need you now."

They continued to undress each other. When their clothes were piled on the floor, he ran both hands over her from heel to head, then eased his body onto her. He caressed and licked and nipped her until she was writhing beneath him.

"Take me. Take me now, dammit, before I go insane," Nicole panted.

"Yes, baby. I'll take you now. Now and forever."

Malcolm pressed into her long and hard. Nicole gasped as her body adjusted to the long-missed pleasure of having him inside her. His hot breath blew into her neck, adding to her arousal. The pressure built, and she bit her lip to keep from screaming in ecstasy.

She dug her fingertips into his broad back as he moved above her. Tighter and tighter the coil pulled within her, the ache building until she thought she'd snap. Until she did snap. Wave after wave of pounding pleasure rushed through her. She felt his body stiffen, and the force of his release intensified her own. It was too much. She threw her head back and screamed.


Nicole's body purred. She felt . . . languid. Yes. That was a good word to describe it. She hadn't felt so languid in years. Now why would that be?

Her eyes snapped open with total recall. She squinted against the morning light, and her gaze locked with Malcolm's. Her body tensed, and the feeling disappeared without a trace. His gaze was watchful, shuttered. She resisted the urge to squirm. The silence held long after they took each other's measure.

"I'll make coffee," he finally said before rolling naked out of bed. He took a pair of sweatpants from his closet, pulled them on, and walked out the door.

Now temper joined Nicole's tension and unease. She'd had mind-blowing sex with the man. They'd spent the night naked in each other's arms, but he couldn't even say to her, "Good morning." She threw off the sheet and bedspread, snatched up her clothes and underwear, and marched with stiff, irritated movements into the adjoining master bathroom.

The shower called to her. She just couldn't stomach the idea of putting her clothes back on without washing first. Nicole cracked open the bathroom door. After making sure Malcolm hadn't returned, she moved quickly but stealthily out of the bedroom and toward the linen closet at the end of the hall. She crossed her arms over her breasts to minimize the bounce. She'd almost reached the closet when Malcolm climbed the stairs next to it.

They froze. Nicole saw a slow simmer begin in his hot-cocoa gaze as it caressed her face, then lower to the arms clasped over her breasts and across her quivering abdomen. When his gaze lingered between her legs, she lowered her left arm to cover her breasts and used her right hand to shield her privacy. His attention didn't move immediately. She felt herself grow warmer, and moisture gathered between her thighs. Still, she couldn't move or speak to break this spell. She wasn't certain she wanted to.

"What are you doing?" Malcolm's voice was a husky whisper. She felt a pulse begin to beat within her.

"I . . . I wanted . . . I came to get a towel. To shower."

Malcolm's gaze lifted slowly to her face. Then, as though in a daze, he turned, pulled a towel from the closet, and handed it to her. Nicole hesitated, reluctant to move her arms and bare herself. But, with no other choice, she reached for the towel and stepped back to wrap it around her body. As she walked away on her spaghetti legs, she thought she heard a muffled groan.

Nicole locked the bathroom door, dropped onto the rim of the combination shower/bathtub, and waited for her muscles to stop shaking. *Distance.* She needed to put some distance between this situation and herself.

*You never needed me for anything,* Malcolm had said to her. Nicole frowned. He'd said that before. What made him think that? She'd needed him for everything. And then he'd left. She'd thought perhaps he'd blamed her for losing the baby. But maybe that wasn't true.

She turned on the water and adjusted the temperature, then stepped under the shower spray. Flashes of the previous night seduced her as she lathered herself with Malcolm's no-nonsense soap. The things he'd done to her. The sounds he'd made. The way he'd made her feel. The way he'd made her scream. After the thunderous release she'd had last night, she thought her hunger would be sated. But a new hunger built as the heated water and Malcolm's soap worked to stir memories. And not just the new memories from last night, but memories of a young Nicole being loved by a young Malcolm who had pledged to stay with her forever.

This was wrong, her mind screamed, even as her body ached. Malcolm may be a caring, fulfilling lover who pleased her as she knew no one else ever could, but they weren't compatible for a long-term relationship. She'd learned that years ago. She was a nurturer. She needed to take care of people. He needed to stand on his own. She couldn't go against her nature, and she wouldn't ask him to change his.

Nicole quickly dressed, opting not to put on her underpants and cringing as she pulled on her socks. She couldn't find her hairpins, so she braided her hair and secured the end with a rubber band she found in the medicine cabinet.

Malcolm looked up as she entered the kitchen. "Have a seat," he invited as he rose to pour her a cup of coffee. "Eggs?"

"Just toast and jelly, if you have it, please."

He smiled briefly, a sexy tilting of his lips that served as foreplay to her senses. He pulled a loaf of wheat bread and a jar of grape jelly from the fridge. Nicole sipped her coffee and tried to keep her eyes from straying to the shoulders she'd scratched and the waist she'd squeezed between her thighs last night. He put the toast on the place mat in front of her.

"Thank you." She felt nostalgic when she saw he'd cut the two slices of toast into triangles.

"You're welcome." He resumed his seat and sipped his coffee. "Nicky, about last night—"

"Last night was a mistake," she interrupted, undaunted by the shuttered look he gave her. "I want us to be friends, Mal, like we were before we got married. But you want more. And, frankly, you're too much of a temptation for me. I lose my focus around you. So I think it's best if we don't blur the lines anymore."

Malcolm regarded her closely, heat simmering in his eyes. "Are you sure?"

Nicole frowned. "Absolutely."

Malcolm smiled at her tone, but Nicole held his gaze.

"All right. I guess it's on to business, then." He picked up his coffee cup. "I'm going to schedule casting and location appointments for this week and next. As I mentioned yesterday, we need to get this project back on schedule. Or on a new schedule. The next couple of weeks will be hectic."

Nicole was caught off guard by Malcolm's quick and easy acceptance of her decision. Her mind hurried to catch up with him. "Okay. Will the director join us for the casting and location visits?" Nicole bit into a slice of toast.

Malcolm set down his cup. "I'm the director."

Nicole froze midchew, then hastily swallowed. "As well as the producer? That's going to be hard on you, won't it?"

"It won't be easy. There's a lot to do. But I can handle it. And Joyce has offered to help with the books and billings."

"Oh? She never mentioned that."

Malcolm looked surprised. "You've spoken to her?"

Nicole shrugged a shoulder. "I've stopped by her house a couple of times to bring her something to eat. She's lost quite a bit of weight."

Malcolm regarded her strangely. Again, Nicole couldn't hold his gaze. "That was very nice of you, Nicky."

Nicole shrugged again. Feeling uncomfortable, she rushed to change the subject. "She didn't mention she would be helping with the accounting."

"Joyce has always done our books, ever since we hired her firm to handle our accounting."

It hurt Nicole to learn Malcolm would accept help with the project from Leo and Joyce, but all he'd allow her to do was attend parties with him. He would lean on anyone but her. Making that realization after sharing her body and a part of her soul with him last night made her almost physically ill. She needed to escape, to leave before she said something embarrassing.

Nicole glanced at her watch, feigning surprise. "Oh, look at the time. I'd better get going."

"What's the rush?" Malcolm stood with her.

She looked up, and the sensuality emanating from him shoved the breath back into her throat. For a brief time, he'd been hers again. And during that time, it was as though he had never left her.

"I need to go." She carried her dishes to his dishwasher.

"Shouldn't we discuss the schedule for the casting and site surveys?" Malcolm followed closely behind her, prompting Nicole to move more quickly.

"There's no need to. There's nothing on my schedule I can't move to accommodate those appointments." She scooted around him and out of the kitchen.

"Just don't schedule anything for evenings or weekends, if possible," Nicole continued, retrieving her jacket from his coat closet.

"The NBA play-offs. Okay." He helped her slip her hand into the second sleeve. "Evenings and weekends are out."

"That's right." She avoided his gaze as she zipped her coat.

Nicole strode to the front door with Malcolm strolling beside her.

"Well." She forced a smile. "Have a nice day."

Malcolm's eyes sparkled with humor. The idiocy of her statement made Nicole want to groan from embarrassment. Instead, she gritted her teeth to keep her smile in place.

"Have a nice day," he returned.

Her cheeks flaming, Nicole yanked open the door and fled down the steps toward her car. She cast surreptitious glances up and down both sides of the street, trying to determine whether anyone saw her leaving Malcolm's house so early.

She rounded her car and opened the driver's door. Before sliding into the vehicle, she glanced up and saw Malcolm studying her from his porch. She froze, torn between desire and a need to protect her heart. Just get into the car, she ordered herself. *Distance,* she thought. *I need distance.*

She forced another smile and tried a jaunty wave. He

lifted a hand in response, but his expression remained inscrutable. She ducked into her car and made herself drive away.

Nicole wandered into the mall bookstore. After leaving Malcolm this morning, she'd been restless at home, staring sightlessly at her computer. She'd tried jogging, cleaning, and even channel-surfing. Nothing had eased her troubled thoughts. In desperation, she'd climbed back into her car and pointed it in the direction of the closest bookstore.

She meandered over to the sci-fi section, disappointed to find that none of her *InterDimensions* books were on the shelves. Nicole scanned the rows for titles by her favorite sci-fi authors and found she'd read all of their latest releases.

Shrugging, she wandered over to the mystery section. A few of her books were on the shelves, and one was being perused by a prospective buyer. Nicole selected another writer's novel to use as a cover while she waited for the young woman's final decision. After reading the back cover and the preview scene, the shopper flipped the book over to look at the front cover again. Finally, when Nicole didn't think she could take the suspense any longer, the woman carried the book to the cash register. Nicole did a happy dance in her mind.

She picked up a couple of new books by her favorite mystery authors, then turned toward the romance section.

"I thought I recognized you."

Nicole looked up and saw Leo DeCaprio's son.

"Frank!" Nicole exclaimed in surprise.

His face brightened at her recognition. A slow smile eased over his lips. "You remember me."

Nicole chuckled. "Of course I do. How are you?"

"I'm fine. And you?"

"Fine, thanks." She pointed toward the paperback

clasped in his hand, eager to talk about books with another voracious reader. "What are you getting?"

He glanced at the book, then lifted the cover for her to see. "Christopher Gilliard's latest release."

"Oh. I enjoyed that one. He created a really exciting world and a lot of plot twists."

Frank used his fingers to comb back an errant lock of hair from his forehead. "He's my second favorite sci-fi writer, after you."

Nicole felt her eyes widen in surprise. Her cheeks warmed. "That's a very great compliment."

"And what are you getting?"

Nicole lifted the paperback. "Cam McCloud's *Gray Lines*."

"A mystery?"

Nicole smiled at his dubious tone. "Yes. A mystery."

"Why aren't you getting a science-fiction book?"

"I read other genres besides science fiction."

"Even romances?"

Nicole tipped her head toward the section behind her. "Actually, I was on my way to the romance section when I saw you."

His eyes widened briefly before he seemed to catch himself. His lips quirked again in a promise of humor. "Well, I'm glad I saw you—"

"So you could save me from buying a romance novel?" Nicole teased.

He returned her smile. "For that reason. And because I'd like a chance to talk to you."

"About what?" Nicole asked, concerned he wanted to try to change her mind about the movie.

"About your books and writing. I've read quite a few of your interviews, but they all ask the same questions, and there are other things I'd like to know. Would you like to get something to eat?"

Nicole hesitated, checking her watch. She was behind schedule with her rewrites.

"Please? I promise I won't take up a lot of your time."

Nicole capitulated. She had time to spare for an aspiring writer. She could always make up the time tonight, if she had to. "Okay. But I've already eaten, so I'll just get something to drink."

"Great." Pleasure shone in Frank's violet eyes. It transformed his face, and again Nicole thought she could hear the sighs of young coeds.

Nicole followed Frank to a little sandwich shop in the mall. After they received their orders, she led them to a table toward the front of the shop. She claimed the chair facing the pedestrian traffic in the main mall.

"So, what's your favorite genre?" Frank asked, trailing his fries through a pool of ketchup.

Nicole stirred her straw around her jumbo diet cola. The ice cubes crashed into one another.

"I can't think of any genres I don't like. I read pretty much everything. What about you? Do you read only science fiction?"

"Yep. Is there any other genre?" Frank treated her to another mischievous smile.

Nicole chuckled. "What do you think about fantasy?"

"I don't like fantasy. I prefer pure sci-fi."

"What do you find so appealing about it?"

Frank bit into his burger and chewed thoughtfully. He swallowed before answering. "I love the imagination of it. Creating new worlds, new technology, new beings all based on probabilities as opposed to improbabilities. That's very exciting to me."

"So sci-fi is the ultimate escape for you. It doesn't just take you out of the moment. It takes you away from reality." Nicole was intrigued, even more so as she felt Frank's withdrawal.

"I don't lose touch with reality." He spoke stiffly.

"I didn't mean to imply you did. But for some people, books are an escape," Nicole explained. "They're a way of taking a break from their lives and moving into someone else's. And science fiction is more of a break from reality than most genres."

"I don't live in a fantasy." He shoved a lock of curly, dark hair back from his forehead.

"No. But you escape into one."

"I know what's real."

"I know you do," Nicole assured him, concerned she had unintentionally offended him. She liked Frank. He appeared to be an interesting, intelligent person. She'd never meant to insult him. She tried to change the subject. "Your father said you wanted to be a writer. Tell me about your stories."

For the next several minutes, they discussed the sci-fi short stories he'd written and was hoping to sell. Nicole drew him out, providing writing tips for the problem areas he confided to her.

Frank slid her a bashful glance before turning his attention to his fries. "Maybe one day I could show you some of my work."

Nicole smiled. "I'd like that. Your stories sound fascinating."

Frank beamed at her before taking another bite of his burger. A comfortable silence settled between them as he chewed. Nicole poked her straw around her plastic cup. By now there was more ice than cola in the container.

"You refer to your books as your babies," he stated, changing the subject. "That's an indication that you have a really strong connection to them."

"You have read my interviews." Nicole played with her straw. She'd finished her diet soda and was contemplating getting another.

"Yes, I have. At what point do your characters become real to you? At what point do your stories or your characters become your 'babies'?"

She looked into Frank's intense gaze. "They're always real to me. If they weren't real to me, I couldn't tell their stories."

"Then why are you doing a movie about them? Was it for the money?"

Nicole sat straighter, vaguely noting that Frank's fries

lay forgotten on his plate. She didn't know how to answer his question, especially since it was so close to the truth. But she didn't want to tell him the only reason she'd sold her movie rights was to raise money for her cousin's kidney transplant. That information about Simone was too personal to share with a virtual stranger.

"I wanted to share my stories." That was as close to the truth as Nicole could get.

"But people who want to go to the movies to experience your stories don't deserve to know your characters. If they want to get to know them, they should read your books."

"Frank, you and I will never agree on this issue." Nicole glanced at her watch. "I'd better go. I still have a lot to get done today."

Frank stood with her. "I'm sorry if I've upset you."

"I'm not upset," she lied. "I just need to get back to work."

"Maybe we can get together again sometime. And talk about books. Not movies." His lips curved in an inviting smile.

"Maybe." Nicole returned his smile to show there were no hard feelings.

"Great. Well, I look forward to your next book. It's due out in July, right?"

"That's right."

Frank groaned good-naturedly, raking the recalcitrant curls from his forehead. "That's a long time to wait."

Nicole smiled. "Just a little more than three months." She pushed her chair back under the table. "Take care, Frank."

"See you soon."


The female newscaster's voice was pleasant, and the information she shared was interesting, but Malcolm wasn't really listening to her. The television news served only as a background distraction as he suffered through the time splits on the fitness club's treadmill.

As he huffed his way through his workout, he mentally reviewed his task list. After Nicole had left that morning, he had spent the day scheduling casting appointments and site surveys. The next two weeks were booked solid. He needed to give Nicole a copy of the schedule. Things would be hectic for the next couple of weeks, but at least she wouldn't be able to avoid him. So far, he felt as though he'd taken two steps backward for each step forward.

Malcolm sighed as the training program ended with a slow walk. He climbed off the machine and wiped it down with his towel. A movement in his peripheral vision prompted him to glance up. Malcolm saw Omar Carter moving around the fitness room. He swung the towel around his neck, hoping to disappear unnoticed.

"Mal."

He groaned mentally before turning to face his business rival. "Omar."

His competition paused before Malcolm, his stance awkward. Omar's hesitancy made Malcolm impatient. He'd started to make some excuse to leave when Omar found his voice.

"Mal, I'm really sorry about Ty. He's—was—one of the best," Omar said, his tone sincere. "I have good memories of him. You two were a great team."

Grief settled like a cloak over Malcolm. In the years he, Tyrone, and Omar had grown from production co-workers to industry rivals, they hadn't said much to one another. Time had built a wall between them, reinforced by Omar's penchant for pursuing the same projects as Malcolm and Tyrone. Omar's family's wealth allowed him to outbid them more often than not. But, with those unexpected words from this unexpected source, gratitude replaced resentment.

"Thank you," Malcolm said.

"How are his family and Joyce?"

"They're getting by."

"I'd heard he and Joyce were getting married."

Malcolm nodded.

"What a tragedy." Omar sighed heavily. "How are you?"

Malcolm shifted, becoming uncomfortable with the unusual camaraderie between them. "Getting by. How are you?"

"Fine, thanks. Keeping busy."

"What are you working on?" Malcolm asked automatically.

Omar smiled. "Nothing right now. But I've got my eye on a project."

Malcolm returned the smile. "Anything I've heard of?"

"The *InterDimensions* project."

Malcolm's smile vanished. "Excuse me?"

"I'm hoping to get another shot at *InterDimensions*."

Malcolm's spine stiffened. "And how do you intend to do that? *InterDimensions* is mine."

"For now," Omar returned smoothly.

"Forever."

"Come on, Mal. Your distributors are running scared. The only thing that matters to them is money. If Ty had survived the accident, they know they would have made a return on their investment, even if the product had suffered. But, with you, the product may be good, but will they make any money?"

Malcolm made the effort to keep his voice calm even as his pulse pounded as though he were back on the treadmill. "The distributors know Celestial Productions will deliver a high-quality product and a solid return on their investment."

"That's not what I've heard."

"Not what you've heard? Or not what you've said? I know you're not above spreading rumors about my company, Omar. You've done it before."

"The fact is, the money's drying up, Mal. The writing's on the wall. Even Nicole's read the signs."

"Nicky?" Malcolm's skin chilled. He knew it was more than his sweat starting to cool him off.

"She knows you won't be able to make her movie."

Malcolm struggled through the shock. "She told you that?"

"We spoke. She knows I'll pay her well for her movie rights."

Malcolm fought a losing battle with his temper. "Unfortunately for you, they aren't hers anymore. They're mine."

"I can give you a good price for those rights, Mal. More than enough to recoup your losses."

"I don't have any losses on this project—and I won't." Malcolm turned. He wouldn't allow anyone to take this project away from him. Not a backstabbing business rival or a faithless ex-wife.

# CHAPTER NINE

"Hold on a minute, Denise. Someone's ringing my security buzzer." Nicole lowered the telephone receiver to her shoulder and activated the intercom for the front lobby. "Yes?"

"It's Mal." His deep voice responded with more than a hint of tension.

"Come on up." She pressed the button to release the security lock to allow him into the building before she returned to the telephone. "Denise?"

"Still here," her agent said.

"I'll call you back. Mal's on his way up. But, please, ask Eileen to give me more time to think about that talk show."

"*A.M. L.A.* is a golden opportunity for you to promote your books and the movie. Just ask Malcolm. You'd be stupid not to take it."

"I don't want to look stupid if I take it. I've never been on TV before. I don't want to make a fool of myself."

"Oh, go irritate Malcolm. Eileen and I will be in touch."

"Denise?"

When only the dial tone responded, Nicole recradled the phone, muttering about agents who never listen. Her thoughts were interrupted by a brusque knock on her door. Malcolm. She checked the peephole. He didn't appear to be in a good mood. Great, she thought, just want she needed—another argument. She opened the door with resignation, and Malcolm brushed past her.

"Come in," she muttered after the fact.

"I will make a success of the *InterDimensions* project," he stated. "Everything is a little off-balance now because of the shock of Ty's death. The distributors are cautious, but I'll bring them around. I may have been known as the creative partner, but I have just as much business savvy as Ty had. We worked together to build Celestial Productions. We both contributed to the creative and business sides of the company. I will succeed with this project. And I want you to believe in me."

Nicole stared at him, her heart nearly bursting with warmth and pride. "That's wonderful, Mal. That's exactly what you should tell the distributors and the guests at Leo's party."

Malcolm blinked. "I'm telling you."

Nicole frowned. "Why? I do believe in you."

"Then why did you meet with Omar Carter?"

She felt her eyes stretch with shock. "I never met with Omar Carter."

"He said you did."

"He ambushed me outside the apartment building," Nicole said, walking past Malcolm and into the living room.

Malcolm turned to face her back. "Why didn't you tell me you spoke to him?"

"I didn't see any point in that. I told him I didn't own the movie rights anymore. I told him, if he still wanted them, he had to talk to you."

"He said you didn't think I could handle this project without Ty."

Nicole turned to face him, offended beyond belief. "And I told you, you can make this movie a success—if you want to."

Malcolm turned from her. He propped one hand on his

hip and used the other to massage the back of his neck. "It hurt to hear someone say you didn't believe in me."

She crossed her arms over her chest. "Why would you listen to someone who doesn't even know me?"

"Because you have good reason to believe I can't succeed."

Nicole wanted to grab his hair and shake him. "I've always known you would be a success. I just wish I had been there with you. Like Joyce was for Ty."

Malcolm turned to face her. "You can be with me now."

She narrowed her gaze. "What are you talking about?"

"We've been given a second chance, Nicky. Don't you think we should take it?"

Nicole shook her head, amazed at how quickly her anger with him could turn to yearning. She saw the wariness beneath his earnest expression and knew he wanted this more than he was willing to admit, maybe even to himself. But she needed answers and reassurances before she could ever return to such a high level of vulnerability. "We can't pretend nothing happened; otherwise, how do we know we won't make the same mistakes again?"

"Because we're older now and more mature." Need thickened his voice.

She had to ask the question, although for four long years, she'd feared the answer. "Is that why you left, Mal? Because you thought I was immature?" She flashed back six years to a time she thought she could have it all: marriage, family, career. But meeting the demands of her career had taken a toll on her health and perhaps caused her miscarriage. "Did you think I was too selfish?" That was the closest she could bring herself to asking if he blamed her for their baby's death.

Malcolm stepped up to her, taking her upper arms to draw her closer. "No, Nicky."

"Then what happened?"

"You stopped talking to me."

Nicole pulled out of his embrace. "We stopped talking

to each other. You said you wanted to take care of me, but I wanted us to take care of each other."

"Can't we start over and try again?"

"What would be the point if neither of us is willing to change? This would just be a second chance to make a mistake. I don't want to get my heart broken a second time."

"I won't—" he began.

"Maybe you won't mean to." She walked to the door as pain tore her up inside. "If we've cleared up the misunderstanding about what I did and didn't say to Omar, I'd like you to leave now. I'm willing to work with you, Mal. But once this project is over, I'm going home."

Slowly he walked toward her. His cocoa eyes were soft and vulnerable, tearing at her.

"Is that the way you want it?" His deep-sea voice eased into her, calling to the part of her that still believed Malcolm could give her the happily-ever-after she'd once believed in.

"That's the way it has to be." Her voice was weak, though her words were strong.

He nodded and left, thankfully without looking back. A final look from him might have been all she needed to let her heart triumph over her mind.

*It's all in a day's—or night's—work,* Nicole mentally chanted two weeks later as she circulated among investors, potential investors, industry heavies, and friends and family at Leo DeCaprio's dinner party. Malcolm had been by her side the entire time, looking mouthwatering in a formal black evening suit. His long, lean form made the clean, simple lines appear spectacular.

At first, being with him after she had rejected his offer of a reconciliation had been awkward. But the casting appointments, site surveys, and interviews with prospective production crew members had kept them focused on the *InterDimensions* project. They had been able to slip back into a comfortable working relationship and tentative friendship.

Several times she had caught him looking at her, though. Intense, searching looks that had itched at her hunger and called to her heart. But she had found the strength not to scratch the itch or answer the call. It had taken her too long to start living again after he'd left her the first time. But the hunger was growing.

For tonight, she was grateful for his close proximity. His support was helping her get through this event in which she could sense dozens of strangers staring at her. With Malcolm next to her, she didn't feel so alone and exposed.

"Are you enjoying yourselves?"

Nicole turned to find Ava DeCaprio twinkling at her. Leo's arm was wrapped around his wife's shoulders, holding her comfortably close.

"Very much." Nicole smiled back at the petite woman who had enough energy and humor to match her jovial husband.

Watching the couple together, she realized Frank was a perfect blend of them both. However, his above-average height was still a mystery since he had two such petite parents.

Leo rocked once on the balls of his feet. "Our guests were impressed by your presentation, Mal."

Before dinner, Malcolm had announced that, after a period of mourning for Tyrone's passing, Celestial Productions was moving forward with the *InterDimensions* project. It had been an impressive speech, similar to what he had told Nicole the day he'd thought she hadn't believed in him.

"I'm glad," Malcolm said. "Let's just hope they're impressed enough to want to support the project."

"I think several of them are." Leo beamed at Nicole. "And I'm hearing very complimentary comments about you, my dear."

She smiled, wondering how much longer they had to

stay now that dinner was over and everyone was saying nice things about them. She looked around at the Tinsel Town heavyweights, film critics, and movie insiders. These were the people who set the vision for an industry.

"Thank you again for hosting the dinner party," she said. "This is very generous of you."

"It's our pleasure, dear," Ava replied. "Now that we've met, we hope you won't be a stranger. It doesn't always have to be about business, you know." She winked before moving on with Leo.

"Not much longer now," Malcolm murmured.

"Do you promise?" Nicole whispered back.

"Promise." Malcolm's grin froze as he looked over Nicole's shoulder. "Uh, oh. Don't look now, but here come Omar and his date for the evening. I wonder if they're really dating or if she was his ticket here tonight."

"Cynic."

"Hello, Mal." Omar nodded. "Nicole, it's nice to see you again. I'd like you to meet Janet Greene."

Nicole extended her hand. "It's nice to meet you, Janet."

The golden-skinned vamp swayed forward to clasp Nicole's hand. "Nice to meet you, too." She slanted a look toward Malcolm, licking her lips. "How've you been, Malcolm?"

"Oh, that's right," Omar commented. "You two know each other."

Something in Omar's tone prompted Nicole to reevaluate his companion. The taller woman wore a snug, blood-red dress that hugged her ample curves. Her glossy, dark hair was a riot of curls around her skillfully made-up face.

Nicole's gaze skipped away when she caught Omar watching her. She didn't want him to see the hurt she wouldn't explain. She and Malcolm were just friends.

"I've been fine, Janet. Thank you." Malcolm's smile appeared stiff around the edges.

"I don't think you're familiar with Nicole's work, are you, Janet?" Omar's question brought Nicole back to her surroundings.

"No, I'm afraid I'm not." Janet smiled an apology.

Nicole returned her smile. "Don't worry. It's not as though I've been on the *New York Times* best-seller list."

"Yet," Omar inserted. "But you will be. They're great stories, and they'll make even better movies. I just hope the project will be completed."

"It will be," Malcolm stated.

"Omar, I believe there was a misunderstanding with a previous conversation we had," Nicole began.

"Oh?" A wary look entered Omar's eyes.

"Yes, I'm afraid I must not have made myself clear when I explained Celestial Productions has the *InterDimensions* movie rights. I have absolute faith Mal's company will do an excellent job interpreting the story, and the project will be a success. In fact, I don't believe any other company could do justice to my story."

"I'm sorry that you feel that way," Omar murmured.

Nicole inclined her head. "I'm sorry for the misunderstanding."

"Perhaps you'll change your mind in the near future."

"I don't think so." Nicole shook her head to emphasize her point.

Omar smiled smoothly. "Never say never. Have a good evening." He escorted Janet away.

"I can't believe you thought I would sell my movie rights to that man," Nicole muttered. "I think I'm offended."

"I'm sorry," Malcolm apologized.

"You should be." Nicole shook her head at a passing server who offered her a tray of drinks.

"I'll make it up to you." Malcolm also refused the server's offer.

"It would take a lot." Nicole sniffed, determined to be stubborn.

"Let's mingle one last time and then leave."

Nicole looked up at him in surprise, her determination melting under an offer she couldn't refuse. "All is forgiven," she said, then started forward.

"Nicole. Malcolm." Frank's voice stopped them.

With a smile, Nicole turned toward the young man. "Hello, Frank. How are you?"

"Fine. Thanks. Are you enjoying the evening?" Frank linked his hands behind his back and rocked on his heels, causing a lock of hair to bounce against his forehead.

"Yes, we are," Nicole responded. The writer in her was fascinated to see Leo's mannerisms reflected in his son.

"Is it everything you'd hoped it would be?" he continued, raking back his unruly curls.

Nicole tilted her head, contemplating the question. "I guess that remains to be seen. What are your impressions of the evening?"

Frank accepted a glass of wine from a passing server. He sipped the drink, eyeing her. "People seem interested. What do you think, Malcolm?"

Malcolm smiled wryly. "As Nicky said, the final results aren't in yet."

"How long do you think it will take to count the final votes?"

"Hopefully we'll know in a week or two," Malcolm responded. "When we see the media coverage."

"Good. Nicole, Christopher Gilliard is giving a talk at USC next Tuesday." Frank paused to pull a folded flyer from his inner jacket pocket. "Would you like to go?" He passed the flyer to her.

Nicole skimmed over the information. "No, thank you. I've attended his presentation on this topic before. It's very interesting, and he's a good speaker. You should get a lot out of it." Nicole tried to return the flyer to Frank.

"Keep it," Frank said. "If you change your mind and decide to go, let me know. His presentation starts at seven. I can pick you up at five, and we can get dinner first."

Nicole decided not to argue the chance of her changing her mind. "All right. I'll let you know."

Frank gave Nicole his lady-killer-in-training smile. "Okay. Sure." He turned toward Malcolm. "You're welcome to join us, of course."

"Thank you. I think Nicky and I will mingle a bit more now. It's good to see you, Frank." Malcolm extended his hand. Frank shook it, then reached for Nicole's outstretched hand.

"It's good to see both of you," Frank said, then lifted the empty wineglass in a toast. "Take care."

Less than an hour later, Nicole's legs felt as though she'd been walking the entire evening. She leaned against a wall, waiting for Malcolm to return from the restroom.

"I'm glad to finally find you alone, dear. I thought Malcolm would never leave your side." Ava DeCaprio's voice interrupted Nicole's thoughts.

She stepped away from the wall she'd been leaning against and turned to face her hostess. "We'll be leaving shortly. It's been a lovely evening. We appreciate all the trouble you went through."

"It was our pleasure, dear," Ava replied. She looked around at the guests, who were still mingling and mixing, before turning her dark blue gaze back to Nicole. "I noticed you talking with my son earlier."

Nicole smiled. "Yes, he's a very nice young man."

Ava stared at her intently. "Yes, isn't he?"

Nicole frowned, wondering what subtle message she might be missing.

"Oh, there's no need to be coy, dear." The older woman waved a negligent hand. "I understand. Having a handsome, young man enthralled with her helps a woman feel young and desirable. Doesn't it?"

Nicole arched a brow. "I wouldn't know."

Ava smiled, the expression not reaching her eyes. "There's no need to pretend, dear. I understand that some women need that boost. They don't feel adequate on their own. But I don't want any woman playing with my son's feelings. Call me overprotective, but mothers don't like people hurting their families."

Nicole wondered at the woman's sanity. "Ms. DeCaprio, your concerns are not warranted. I don't have any designs on your son, and I don't believe your son has any interest in me."

"I hope you're right. In any event, it's probably best if you don't lead him on." Ava regarded Nicole thoughtfully. "You and Malcolm make a handsome couple."

Nicole took a calming breath. "Mal and I are just friends."

"Well, certainly, dear. If you say so." Ava turned and disappeared.

Nicole convinced Malcolm to leave the party shortly after her exchange with Ava. She was uncomfortable during their good-byes to their hosts. Now, as she stared through Malcolm's car window at the night embracing the city streets, she wondered how anyone could imagine Frank would be attracted to her. Ava must be crazy.

"Is Frank developing a crush on you?" Malcolm's voice startled Nicole from her brooding.

She turned to look at him, wondering if the whole world had gone mad or only those people involved in the Los Angeles film industry. "No."

"Are you sure?" Malcolm's gaze remained glued to the road and its sparse traffic.

"Of course I'm sure. He's what? Twenty-one? Twenty-two? I'm thirty-three. What would a young white man want with a much older black woman?"

"A very attractive woman," Malcolm clarified.

Nicole snorted and returned her attention to the Los Angeles streets.

"If he's not getting a crush on you, why did he ask you out?" Malcolm persisted.

Nicole shifted to face him. "He didn't ask me out. He

told me about an upcoming presentation by an author
we both like."

"What about his invitation to dinner?"

"What about your relationship with Janet Greene?"
Nicole's irritation made her reckless enough to ask the
question she'd promised herself to avoid. She felt Malcolm's sudden tension and braced herself for his answer.

"We dated briefly," he admitted. "It was a long time ago."

"How long? Four years? Or longer?"

Malcolm pulled the car up to the curb in front of her
apartment building and shut off the engine. He turned
to her and impaled her with a hard look. "What are you
implying?"

Nicole tilted her chin, determined not to be intimidated. "Is she the reason you left me?" She forced herself to ask the question despite the pain.

Malcolm's gaze narrowed. "No. I was faithful to our
vows."

Nicole searched his eyes and knew he spoke the truth.
She nodded, then unfastened her seat belt and opened
the car door. "Good night, Mal."

"I'll walk up with you."

"That's not necessary," she said, but he joined her on
the curb.

"It is to me." He cupped her elbow and escorted her
to the building.

Nicole felt inexplicably awkward leading the way to
her apartment. She searched her mind for something to
say. Inspiration didn't hit until she stood before her
apartment door.

"Thank you for driving tonight." She unlocked her
door, then turned to smile at him. "Good night, Mal."

"Good night, Nicky. Pleasant dreams." He offered her
a slight smile, then turned to descend the stairway.

She slipped into the apartment and, without turning
on the lights, locked her door. She rushed to the picture
windows overlooking the street in front of her building.

As she watched, Malcolm approached his car and climbed into the driver's seat.

*Pleasant dreams,* she thought.

"So, what's the progress report on the project?" Denise asked.

Nicole sat on the couch, the phone cord stretching across the room. She'd already told her agent about the dinner party the DeCaprios had hosted the previous weekend.

"Mal and I finished the casting calls last week. They were pretty intense and exhausting. We're narrowing down our choices. I think we have a good mixture of unknowns and well-known actors. I'd rather go with a cast of unknowns so moviegoers won't attribute traits of the actors' past roles to my *InterDimensions* characters. But Mal said we should cast at least a couple of known actors for marketing purposes and to benefit from their fan base."

"He's right."

"I know. I agree with him. It's just that I hope the actors' images don't detract from the characters they'll play." Nicole shifted to stretch out on the sofa.

"Just make sure they're cast in roles they'll be compatible with." Denise's no-nonsense comment made Nicole smile. "How are the site surveys going?"

Nicole slouched farther into the couch, trying to get more comfortable. "We've chosen a couple of locations and agreed on our preferences. Now we're just waiting to see which one works best on paper."

"Good. And how's the budget?"

"We're coming in at just a little under our initial estimates."

"Even better news. Now for my update. Marketing for book four begins next week."

"Great." Nicole felt her pulse thump with excitement.

"I thought you'd be pleased. How are things going

with you and Malcolm?" Denise's tone seemed a bit too casual.

"They're going well. We have a comfortable working relationship."

"You've been in L.A. for more than a month now. Have you discussed the divorce with him?"

"Yes, I have."

From across the phone line, Nicole noticed a slight clicking noise. It sounded like Denise drumming her nails on the desk. Nicole's lips quirked with humor. She wondered whether her agent had polished her nails purple like she had last year in honor of Easter Sunday, which was six days away.

"And?" Denise's impatience crackled through the receiver.

Nicole swung her legs off her sofa and rose to pace. "He doesn't want to talk about the past. He just wants to start over."

"And you want to discuss it?"

Nicole paused and stared across the dining area into the kitchen. She wished the phone cord was long enough to extend to the sink so she could pour herself a glass of water. Instead, she licked her dry lips and continued pacing. Each step seemed to take her further back in time until that final day appeared before her like a tarnished wedding photo.

"After our baby died, I thought the pain from the loss would kill us," she began. "Everyone told us, 'Time heals all wounds.' But the days turned into weeks, and the weeks turned into months, and we just felt worse. Mal and I went into a deep depression. We weren't talking to each other." She laughed without humor. "We took turns sleeping on the sofa."

"Did you try counseling?"

Nicole shrugged to relieve the tension in her shoulders. "Yes. We attended sessions for months. But Mal's never been good at expressing his feelings. Talking to him was like talking to a wall."

She wandered over to the picture window and stared across the street. A silver luxury car was parked in the space where the black SUV often sat. She hadn't noticed the SUV during her jog this morning.

"So then what happened?" Denise asked.

Nicole turned away from the window and gauged the distance to the sink. She decided against asking Denise to hold on while she filled a glass with water. Instead, she continued with her story. "And then we ran out of time. I came home late one day, and he picked a fight."

"A fight?" Denise's tone rose in alarm.

"A verbal argument." Nicole made the clarification quickly. "A very ugly verbal argument, full of blame and accusations."

"I thought you said he didn't blame you."

Nicole strained to see through the clouds of memories. She stopped pacing and ran a hand through her unbound hair. "I told you he never came right out and said the words. He never accused me, but I felt as though he blamed me."

"It's not too late for you to clear the air."

"I've tried, but he won't talk about the past. He just wants to start over."

"And what do you want?"

Denise's question faced a long silence as Nicole had a realization about herself.

"I want answers," she said. "I want to know whether he blames me. And if he's telling the truth, if he doesn't blame me, then I want to know why he left."

"I understand, and I think you're right. This foolishness needs to stop," Denise said, warming to her subject. "You've been letting him get away with ducking the issue for far too long."

"But, Denise," Nicole said, troubled by her own thoughts. "There's a part of me that's tempted to let him get away with avoiding the issue. What does that make me?"

"Very confused."

\* \* \*

Nicole stepped out of the shower muttering to herself about agents and ex-husbands.

The steam followed her out of the bathroom and down the hall to her bedroom. A shower often helped to clear her mind and give her ideas for the next scene or the next chapter, but it wasn't working tonight. As she slipped into her nightgown, she decided to shut down her computer and go to bed early with a book.

Nicole padded back down the hall, this time branching off to her dining area where she'd set up her laptop. After shutting off her computer, she turned to go back to her bedroom. A piece of paper near her front door snagged her peripheral vision. She crossed her living room, wondering who would have slipped a note under her door.

As she read the note, fear turned her blood to ice.

*Time is not a luxury for you. It is not on your side. I'm watching you and waiting.*

Working late again, Malcolm stared at the flashing cursor on his computer screen, reviewing the e-mail he was about to send to the completion guarantor. The message was firm and positive without being effusive. He wanted to minimize his usual marketing voice and mimic Tyrone's standard business tone. His dry business tone. Malcolm smiled to himself, remembering the way he'd teased his partner about his business memos.

"My tone is not dry," Tyrone would protest. "It's direct, to the point."

"It's dry, Ty," Malcolm would tell him. "It's as dry as the desert heat."

And that was fine, Malcolm thought. Besides, Tyrone's business memos always achieved the results they needed. Conversely, when Tyrone wrote a screenplay, his dialogue brought the characters to life and allowed the readers to feel all the characters' emotions.

"You had a lot of talent, buddy," Malcolm murmured.

"*So do you.*" Tyrone's voice whispered through Malcolm's mind, recalling past conversations he'd had with his partner.

"*We were a great team. I wouldn't have been able to build this company on my own,*" Malcolm thought.

"*I don't know about that,*" Tyrone's response replayed in Malcolm's memory. "*You have a lot of talent and a lot of guts. You're going to need guts to finish this project.*"

"*I know,*" Malcolm thought. "InterDimensions *is turning out to be our riskiest venture ever.*"

Tyrone agreed. "*Riskier than you know. But you can't give up. I need you to make this work.*"

"*I'll try.*" Malcolm sighed.

"*There is no 'try.' There is only 'do' or 'do not.'*" Tyrone quoted a line from one of the *Star Wars* movies, making Malcolm smile. The phone rang, interrupting their conversation.

"Hello," Malcolm answered, reluctant to let go of his memories of Tyrone.

"Mal, it's Joyce." The strain in her voice forced Malcolm to focus his attention on the call. He checked his watch. It was a little after 10:00 P.M.

"What's wrong?" he asked. Joyce burst into tears. "Joyce, what is it?" Malcolm's grip tightened on the receiver, and his heart thundered with dread.

"Mal." Joyce gasped to a stop. "Mal, Ty's father just called me. He said . . . he said . . . The police just called him and told him . . ."

"Joyce, what is it?" Malcolm repeated, anxiety sharpening his tone.

"The police said Ty's accident wasn't an accident."

"What?" Malcolm grew cold from the inside out. His hand began to shake. As if from a distance, he heard Joyce sobbing on the other end of the phone. Her breathing was ragged.

"They said it looks like another car forced him off the road. Oh, Mal," Joyce sobbed. "Someone killed my Tyrone."

# CHAPTER TEN

A piercing shriek bounced off her bedroom walls and jerked Nicole from a dead sleep. She snapped on the bedside light and huddled against the headboard, her heart lodged in her throat. Half-blind from the remnants of sleep, she moved on instinct. Her gaze darted to every dark corner of her bedroom. Alone. She was alone. Then what was that noise?

The shriek sped through her apartment again, and, with a mixture of chagrin and irritation, she identified the sound as her security buzzer. She'd never realized what an ugly, threatening sound it was until she heard it in the middle of the night.

She started to throw off her comforter, then paused to check the time. The radio alarm clock on her bedside table read minutes after one in the morning. Who would be visiting her now? The fear returned.

*I'm watching you and waiting.*

The security buzzer shrieked again. Nicole sat fossilized with fear. Would a stalker who slipped notes under her door ring the security buzzer?

She shook herself impatiently. *This is ridiculous. I'm not going to allow myself to be a prisoner in my own apartment.*

Drawing strength from manufactured anger, Nicole threw off the comforter and marched down the hall. She hesitated as she passed the phone. She considered dialing 911 but regrouped and continued to the door. She wasn't certain this was an emergency, and she didn't want to risk calling the police on a false alarm.

She snatched the security phone off its cradle and tried for a firm, tough tone. She grimaced when her, "Who is it?" wavered and croaked in her fresh-from-sleep voice.

"It's Mal. Can I come up?" His deep-sea baritone washed over her, turning her fear and anger into concern.

"Sure." She pressed the button that released the security lock.

Nicole unchained and unlocked her door. She leaned across the doorframe and waited a long time before she saw Malcolm climbing the stairwell. Her concern deepened when she observed his rounded shoulders and dragging gait.

As he climbed the final staircase to her floor, he lifted his head and caught her gaze. The pain in his eyes ripped a hole in her heart. If possible, his expression was even more wrenching than it had been in the hospital after he'd learned Tyrone had died. She wanted to wrap her arms around him but remembered he didn't respond well to comforting gestures. She stepped back so Malcolm could enter her apartment. Without breaking eye contact, Nicole locked her door. She held out her hand for his coat, then tossed it on the love seat.

"What's happened, Mal?" she asked.

Malcolm closed his eyes and rubbed his forehead with his fingertips. He had to pull himself together. He was here because Nicole had a right to know what was happening. Celestial Productions was working with her on the *InterDimensions* project. She had a right to be informed of events that impacted the company. Granted, it was one o'clock in the morning. But he didn't think this could wait. He wanted her to hear the news from him and not from the media. *The media.* Malcolm sighed. He couldn't stand to think what they might do with this news.

"Maybe you should sit down." His tone was raw. He cleared his throat and tried again. "There's something I need to tell you."

Nicole hesitated, searching his face. His gaze wavered beneath the concern he saw in her ebony eyes. He wouldn't be able to keep it together if she kept looking at him like that. Malcolm jumped when he felt Nicole take his hand and lead him to her sofa. He stumbled a bit and was embarrassed when she shot him a look of surprise. She pulled him down to sit beside her. They turned toward each other, their knees almost touching, and she appeared to brace herself for whatever he might say.

Malcolm cleared his throat again and began. "Joyce called me tonight. She was very upset by some disturbing news she'd received from Ty's family."

He paused. He couldn't sit still to tell her this. The pain was compressing his chest. He stood and began to pace. In a controlled voice, he continued. "The police think Ty may have been murdered."

Malcolm turned as he heard Nicole gasp. Her hand covered her mouth, and her eyes stretched wide. She looked as frozen as he had felt before the shock had worn off and left him with this incredible pain. He wished the shock had lasted just a little longer. Long enough for him to talk with Nicole. He didn't want to feel right now; he didn't want to appear weak in front of her.

"Oh, God, Mal. I can't believe . . . Oh, my God." Her catlike eyes filled with tears.

Malcolm turned away before he got caught in an emotional chain reaction. He took deep breaths and prayed for the strength to get through this conversation.

"I'm so sorry," Nicole said.

"Yeah." Malcolm gritted his teeth against the emotions battering his heart.

"Don't do this, Mal." Nicole's voice was a soft plea behind him.

"Do what?" His tone was sharper than he'd intended.

"Don't push away and pretend you're not feeling. You always do that. But Ty was a warm and generous person. He deserves more than stoicism. Your friendship with him was too valuable for you to pretend you're not hurting now."

"What do you want me to do? Bawl like a baby?" Malcolm's eyes began to burn. He kept his rigid back to her even as he heard her rise from the sofa and walk toward him.

"Yes, if that's what you're feeling."

"And what good will that do? It won't bring Ty back." His voice rose as he began to lose control. My God, she was unmanning him. Again. "This isn't what I came here for." He scrubbed his hand across his eyes. Then, his face averted, he maneuvered around her and headed for the door. "I came to tell you about Ty, not to be psychoanalyzed. I didn't intend for you to try to convince me to get in touch with my feminine side."

"Feelings don't make you less of a man, Mal." Her gentle response reached the part of him that wanted her to keep him from spinning out of control.

"What do you want me to do, Nicky?" He stopped, still keeping his back to her. "Curl up in the fetal position and cry my heart out? Will that make you feel better?"

"Only if it will make you feel better. I can tell you're hurting. I can see it in your body language. I can hear it in your voice. It's nothing to be ashamed of."

She was pleading with him to acknowledge emotions he didn't want to have. He was afraid of the feelings beneath his anger.

"Why won't you leave it alone?" He spun toward her. "Why won't you let me deal with it my way?"

Malcolm watched as Nicole approached him, undaunted by his anger. She reached up to cup his cheek. "Because your way is tearing you apart," she whispered.

"Do you think I care? Do you think I care if I die from this pain? He was my brother." Malcolm couldn't believe

the words coming out of his mouth. He turned away
from her again.

Nicole was making him crazy. He had come to update
her on the situation, and she was turning him into a day-
time soap opera. He covered his face with his hands,
squeezed his eyes shut, and struggled to regain control.

"I see him." His words emerged unbidden, muffled by
his hands. "In my mind. Driving that road. Planning his
day. Out of nowhere, a car slams into him. Tries to shove
him off the road. His eyes widen behind his glasses. He
never would wear contacts. He tries to control his car.
He's scared. I can see him. Feel his confusion, his fear.
But I wonder, when he realized he was going to die, what
were his last thoughts?"

Malcolm lowered his hands and stared at the damp-
ness on his palms. He felt the dreaded tears flowing
down his cheeks. His body shook. He was falling apart.
Nicole's arms wrapped around his waist from behind.
She placed a soft kiss on his spine. Through his sweater,
he felt the gentle weight of her head come to rest between his shoulder blades.

Her hands splayed over his chest. He covered her
hands and pressed them tighter against him, hoping
their combined contact would heal his heart. Her
breasts trembled against his back with her silent sobs. He
wrapped his other hand around her forearm and held
on tight as the storm tore him apart and her caring put
him back together.

He watched Nicole through the tinted windshield of
the black SUV as she jogged toward him. He'd waited for
her all morning. She was later than usual.

The author of the *InterDimensions* series was a beautiful woman with a long, athletic figure. Her stride was
strong and sure, carrying her effortlessly down the city
block. Her thick, dark ponytail danced behind her. She

glanced toward the SUV as she usually did. A short, dismissive glance from sultry, catlike eyes.

The bitch.

He'd been so wrong about her. He had thought she'd cared about the family she'd created and the home she'd provided for them. But all she cared about was what they could do for her. She had lied when she'd said they mattered to her because she'd sold her rights to them. She'd given control over their well-being to a stranger. Now it was up to him to protect the people she'd invited him to share with her. He was up to the challenge. He was capable of protecting himself and those he cared about.

Nicole drew closer, her attention no longer drawn to the SUV. He watched her, the anger growing. She'd betrayed her family—their family. She would pay. He would make sure of it.

Malcolm stretched as far as he could in his makeshift bed on Nicole's sofa. They'd fallen asleep, spooned together on the cushions. He vaguely remembered Nicole leaving earlier for her morning run. He'd been half-awake, listening to her getting dressed. Probably thinking he was still fast asleep, she'd kissed his bare back, just below his shoulder blade, before she'd left. Just as she had when they had been married. He smiled at the too-distant memories. He looked around her living room, noting the sun was much brighter now. She was probably on her way back. He'd better get dressed.

Malcolm tossed off the blanket and stood stretching his arms above his head. He'd better borrow Nicole's iron, he decided, glancing down at his wrinkled pants. He scratched his bare chest and padded barefoot into the bathroom. He wasn't certain how he'd face her after his emotional display last night. Part of him was angry and embarrassed. But another part had to admit she had been right. He did feel much better after talking to her and releasing some of his emotions.

When Nicole returned from her run, he was standing in her bedroom pulling on his newly ironed pants. He looked up as she halted in the threshold of her bedroom door, staring at his half-naked body.

"Oh. Sorry." She started to back away.

"Come in," he said. "It's your room."

She moved farther into the room. "How are you feeling this morning?"

He avoided her searching gaze. "Fine. And you?"

"Okay." She shrugged.

Malcolm zipped his pants, then recaptured her gaze. "How was your run?"

"Good, thanks. Natural endorphins help lift the spirits, I suppose." Her smile appeared forced. "If you give me twenty minutes to shower and change, I'll cook breakfast for you."

"How about if I give you twenty minutes to shower and change while I cook breakfast for you?"

Nicole's smile eased as she moved toward the bathroom. "Deal."

While Nicole showered, Malcolm used his cell phone to check his voice mail and to leave a message for Rita that he wouldn't be in until later in the morning. He'd have to tell Rita about Tyrone, but he didn't want to think about that right now.

Malcolm waited until he heard Nicole complete her shower before he started breakfast. French toast, he decided after surveying the contents of her refrigerator and cupboards. He was setting the table when he brushed against her computer desk, knocking some of the papers to the floor. He picked up the fallen papers and started to put them back on her desk when a note captured his attention.

"Something smells good," Nicole announced as she strode into the dining area. Confronted by Malcolm's hard gaze, her smile retreated.

"When did you get this?" He shook the sheet of paper in his hand.

Nicole glanced at it, recognizing the note that had disturbed her sleep last night.

"Yesterday," she answered reluctantly.

Malcolm's expression went from anger to incredulity. "When were you going to tell me about it?"

Nicole sighed. "Today."

"Why didn't you tell me yesterday?"

Nicole moved farther into the room. "Mal, I got that note late last night. I left a message for the police officer I've been talking to; then I went to bed. I promise I was going to tell you today."

"You got this message before you went to bed?" he asked. Nicole nodded. Malcolm groaned. "Then I came over and told you about Ty."

"I'm glad you did." Nicole shifted her feet as Malcolm continued to study the message.

"This is the worst one yet," he concluded. "Where did you find it?"

Nicole claimed a chair. Thinking about the message made her knees a little shaky. "Someone had slipped it under my door sometime after ten P.M."

Malcolm's eyebrows stretched upward. "Someone got through your security door?"

Nicole smiled. "I hate to disillusion you, Mal, but that security door isn't all that secure. I've seen my friendly neighbors, as they come and go from the building, holding that door open for strangers."

Nicole's smile widened as Malcolm cursed.

"Some security," he said. "How can you be so sure about the time?"

"It wasn't there before I took a shower at ten o'clock."

"You were in the shower? Dammit." He studied the note again, then read aloud, "'Time is not a luxury for you. It is not on your side. I'm watching you and waiting.'"

Nicole shivered. "I've read it, Mal."

"The notes are getting more threatening." Malcolm paced the length of the combined dining/living area, still studying the note.

"I noticed."

Malcolm's gaze sharpened on her face. "You always get sarcastic when you're nervous. I don't mean to frighten you, but we've got to figure out who is sending these messages to you, why, and what they mean. I don't want anything to happen to you."

"You're right. I'm sorry. I don't mean to be rude, but I am scared, and, as you noticed, sarcasm is an unconscious defense."

Nicole's legs felt steadier now. She stood and walked into the kitchen. "Listen, I left a message for that police officer. In the meantime, let's eat breakfast so we can get you off to work before noon."

"I've got a better idea. Let's get you packed and moved into my house." Malcolm followed her into the kitchen. He almost walked right into her back as she stopped midstride.

"Why?" She turned to face him.

"Why?" He seemed stunned. "Weren't we just agreeing these messages are getting worse? I don't want you here by yourself. It could be dangerous, especially with your building's antisecurity security system."

"Let's not get carried away over a couple of creepy letters."

"Nicky, this psycho knows where you live. He slipped his latest threat directly under your door. I'd categorize that as more than creepy." Malcolm opened the fridge and pulled out the orange juice.

Nicole was doing her best to forget the panic the message had induced in her. Now, in addition to the panicky feeling, her stomach fluttered at the image of living with Malcolm again. Saying "Good night" to him at the end of the day; saying "Good morning" to him at the start of a new one. Eating breakfast with him again, just like a married couple. She shook off the mental pictures that superimposed the past onto the present. In her current emotional state, she thought she could handle a threatening stranger a lot more easily than she could handle her ex-husband.

Nicole took down plates for the French toast. She passed the toast to Malcolm, then poured coffee.

"I have several sturdy locks on my door." Nicole sat down, thanking Malcolm for the glass of juice he placed before her.

"What about when you're not in your apartment? He could wait for you to leave your apartment and follow you."

Nicole paused, with a forkful of French toast halfway to her mouth. Her appetite was quickly deserting her. "Even if I moved in with you, he could still to do that. You can't be with me twenty-four/seven, Mal. You're working."

"You can come with me to work. We can set you up in Ty's office." Malcolm took a gulp of coffee. His gaze was compelling above the rim of his cup.

Nicole's gaze wavered beneath his force. "I'll be fine."

"How can I be sure?"

"I can't give you guarantees. But if it makes you feel better, I'll consider your offer."

Malcolm sighed. "Do you promise?"

"I promise."

Malcolm considered her for a long moment. "All right. That's something at least."


Every drop of color drained from Rita's face. Her large, mink-brown eyes filled with tears.

"Who would do this?" she asked. "Why? Ty never hurt anyone."

Malcolm's grip tightened on her hands. He'd asked Rita to join him in his office as soon as he'd arrived. He'd invited her to take one of the chairs in front of his desk, and he'd taken the other. It hadn't been easy repeating the information. Each time he shared the news, he imagined the attack.

"I have no idea," he said. "But the police have already started investigating. Hopefully we'll find out soon."

"Is it possible the driver wasn't deliberately trying to hurt him? Maybe it really was an accident."

"No." Malcolm was reluctant to dim the hopeful light in Rita's eyes. It was difficult enough to accept a loved one dying unexpectedly without learning someone had deliberately taken him away from you. "Ty's family asked the police the same question. The police said, based on the pattern of the skid marks and the damage to Ty's car, the attack was deliberate."

Rita slumped in the chair. "How is Joyce?"

"Devastated." Malcolm stood and walked to the window. "It took me more than two hours to help her settle down last night."

"Perhaps I should call her."

"That might be a good idea," Malcolm agreed, more to escape the conversation. He'd talked to Joyce this morning on his drive into work. She seemed tired, but much calmer.

"Thank you for telling me, Mal." Rita stood. "Please let me know if there's anything I can do."

"Of course, Rita. Thank you."

He was tempted to ask her to call Leo DeCaprio, but that was his responsibility. Leo had been a good friend to him and Tyrone. He owed it to that friendship to call Leo himself. Afterward, he'd try to get some work done. With so much on his mind, *try* would be the operative term.


Tyrone and Joyce's house reflected their personalities. It was neat and trim with touches of whimsy in the bird feeder and tiny clay chipmunks and squirrels that posed in and around the front garden. It was shown to advantage in the late-morning sunlight.

Nicole climbed out of her car, reaching back to pick up the basket of fruit she'd bought at a produce store.

The purchase was an impulse, just like her decision to visit Joyce. Now she wished she had called first to ask whether Joyce wanted company. She hesitated at the curb. The few occasions she'd stopped by in the weeks following Tyrone's funeral, she'd called first and had been welcomed. But that was before Joyce had learned Tyrone's death wasn't an accident. Under the circumstances, she may not want to see anyone.

Taking a deep breath of air scented by the nearby spring flowers, Nicole mounted the stairs and rang the doorbell. If Joyce wasn't up for company, Nicole would give her the basket and leave.

The door opened. Nicole offered Joyce a tentative smile, despite her concern over the other woman's puffy, red eyes.

Joyce stepped onto the porch and wrapped her arms around Nicole's shoulders, the basket of fruit squeezed between them. "I'm so glad you're here," she whispered. "The police just left."

Nicole followed Joyce into her house. She wandered into the living room while Joyce took the fruit basket to the kitchen and prepared tea. The room was as disheveled as it had been the last time Nicole had visited. Now it was stuffy, too, as though the thermostat had been set for a much cooler day. Nicole found this curious, considering Joyce was wearing a sapphire sweater, which obviously had belonged to Tyrone. She settled onto an overstuffed armchair and resisted the urge to open the curtains.

"Here you go," Joyce announced as she rejoined Nicole. She put the tray of tea, sugar, fruit, cheese, and crackers on the table between the straight-backed chair and the sofa.

"Thank you." Nicole stood, stepping forward to accept the cup Joyce had poured for her.

"You must have read my mind." Joyce crowded into a corner of the sofa. Her movements were very slow, as though she was still half-asleep.

"What do you mean?" Nicole sipped her tea.

"I wanted to talk to someone, but most of my friends and family are at work, and I didn't want to disturb them."

"The meeting with the police unsettled you."

"To say the least," Joyce murmured.

"Do you want to talk about it?"

"Yes. I'm just not certain where to begin."

"I'm not in any rush. I'm here to see you. Start at the beginning, if you'd like, and take your time."

Joyce took another sip of tea, then sighed brokenly. "I really didn't want to believe it. When Ty's family called me last night, I thought I was having a nightmare. It was like hearing he'd died all over again. I was sure I'd wake up and find out it was just a bad dream. Then the police showed up at my door this morning. This is like a nightmare."

"I'm so sorry, Joyce." Nicole fought back her own tears.

"I can't believe that someone hated the man I love so much that they would kill him." Joyce's voice grew thick with tears. She drank more tea, then paused.

"I can't believe it, either," Nicole broke the silence. "Ty was such a nice man."

"The best." Joyce smiled sadly. "Even my father liked him. And you know how fathers can be. But Ty impressed him." Joyce paused again, lost in thought.

Nicole glanced around the room, picking out touches of Joyce mingling with traces of Tyrone. Warner Brothers's Marvin the Martian waved from the cockpit of his spaceship positioned between two delicately curving candlesticks on the mantle. In a corner of the room, *Star Wars* storm troopers scaled a pewter wine rack. She smiled and Joyce followed her gaze.

"He loved his toys," Joyce said.

"And you loved that about him," Nicole added. "I can tell by this room. Only a woman in love would allow a man to compromise her home decor."

"I don't think the police share your insight." Joyce chuckled bitterly. "I guess everyone is a suspect, so I really shouldn't feel so violated. But they made me feel as though I were at the top of their list. They asked whether Ty and I were having any problems. They wanted to know if I would get a part of his company. They asked if I had any alibis to verify that I was home alone when Ty was out running. Of course I didn't. Ty usually went running while I was still asleep."

"The usual suspects are family and friends," Nicole said, trying to console Joyce. "So they would ask you questions like that."

Joyce scowled. "But running him off the road. Someone must have really hated him to terrorize him like that."

"Who could do that?"

"I don't know anyone who disliked Ty." Joyce's voice was strained. "He had a lot of business contacts, but he didn't have a lot of friends. Just me, Mal, Rita."

Nicole stared blindly at the snack tray. "Maybe we need to try another angle. What were his hobbies?"

"Besides cartoons and science fiction? And when you combined a cartoon with science fiction, he was in heaven." Joyce smiled. "He didn't have time for hobbies, though. He exercised to keep in shape. It also helped him think. But the company takes—took—up a lot of his time. He and Mal were still building it. The company isn't financially stable."

"How can that be?" Nicole asked, surprised by this revelation. "All of their movies have been successful, according to what I've read."

"They do have a great track record, but that's on smaller independent films. One financially unsuccessful movie would ruin them. They were hoping *InterDimensions* would show the film community that they could make a profit even on bigger films."

Why hadn't Malcolm told her? She had told him about her mother and about Simone. Dammit, the confidences shared can't only be hers.

Joyce got up and poured herself more tea from the pot, but she still didn't eat any of the snacks she'd brought to the living room. Nicole wondered when Joyce had last eaten.

"Can I refresh your cup?" Joyce gestured with the pot.

"No, thank you."

Joyce settled back into her chair and sipped her tea. They shared a moment of pensive silence. "The police will probably consider Mal a suspect, too," Joyce commented in a flat tone. "Which is completely absurd. They were like brothers."

"Mal really misses him," Nicole said.

"They were the perfect partners. They balanced each other. Ty was contemplative and deliberate. Mal is impetuous. Ty was cautious. Mal takes risks. Mal has a tendency to push a project as far as he can, but Ty would make sure Mal didn't push it too far. They called it taking considered risks. Sort of like the risk they took when they contacted you."

Nicole stiffened. "What do you mean?"

Joyce paused. "I know you and Mal used to be married. Ty told me."

Nicole felt her cheeks begin to burn. How many other people knew? Her imagination ran back to those cocktail parties and the crowd of investors. Did they all know she and Malcolm were divorced?

"Don't worry," Joyce continued as though reading Nicole's mind. "Ty asked me not to tell anyone else. He was concerned that you would be uncomfortable if other people knew about your former relationship."

Nicole sighed, grateful for Tyrone's consideration. Then she frowned, remembering the rest of what Joyce had said. "How was contacting me a risk?"

"Mal was afraid that, if you found out he co-owned Celestial Productions, you wouldn't even consider their offer," Joyce explained. "Ty suggested a couple of ways they could submit offers for the *InterDimensions* movie rights without revealing Mal's name. But Mal didn't want to do anything to mislead you."

Nicole dropped her gaze to stare absently at the thick,

rose carpet. Joyce's explanation had painted such a clear picture of the man she had fallen in love with in her past life. A man of integrity. Malcolm had never played games. He didn't believe in subterfuge. If he wanted something, he asked for it.

*I want another chance, Nicky. I want to try again with you.* The memory of his words caused her to soften. If only it was that easy for her. Nicole thrust that thought aside. She was here for Joyce, who was staring quizzically at her.

"How is Ty's family?"

"I spoke with them this morning before the police arrived. They're doing as well as can be expected." Joyce stared at her empty teacup.

"May I pour you some more tea?" Nicole asked, already stepping forward to take Joyce's cup.

"Thank you."

Nicole returned Joyce's cup to her before refilling her own. She slipped back into the chair.

"The police told Ty's parents they don't have any new information on 'the case.'" Joyce emphasized the impersonal term. "They're not very forthcoming with the information they do have. I understand that they don't want to compromise their investigation, but can't they give us something?"

Joyce's voice broke. Nicole set her cup on the table and hurried over to sit beside the other woman. She covered Joyce's trembling fingers with one hand and curved her arm around Joyce's shoulders. Nicole's mind searched for comforting words, but what could she say? *Don't cry?* Why not? *Everything will be okay?* How did she know? Nothing suitable came to mind. Instead, Nicole pulled Joyce closer into her embrace, as though comforting Lynnette, and said nothing.

Shortly after one in the afternoon, Malcolm led two homicide detectives back to his office. He was anxious to speak with the police directly about the investigation rather than hearing about it second- or thirdhand.

"Please, have a seat." He gestured to the two chairs in front of his desk.

Malcolm felt too anxious to use the conversation table in the corner of his office. The solid oak executive desk would offer him more support. As he settled behind the desk, he noticed the detectives taking in the knickknacks and memorabilia decorating his office: photos of him and Tyrone on shoots and celebrating company milestones, civic certificates, and movie props. He wondered what message his office conveyed to these trained observers.

"We appreciate your taking the time to meet with us on such short notice, Mr. Bryant," said the detective who had introduced himself as Jim Miller.

He had a friendly, if fleshy, face under dark, unkempt hair. His flushed complexion tagged him as a heart attack waiting to happen. Under his ill-fitting clothes, he appeared to be carrying an extra thirty or forty pounds on his average frame.

Malcolm folded his hands on the desktop and leaned forward. "It's not a problem. I'm anxious to find the person who killed my partner. Were there any witnesses to the crash? Someone who could identify the car?"

"No one has come forward yet," Miller answered. "How long were you and Mr. Austin partners?"

"About three years," Malcolm answered. "We shared all of the responsibilities for running the company, but technically, he handled the business end and I handled the creative end." Malcolm switched gears again. "Have you heard reports of any similar attacks anywhere else in the city or the county?"

"No, we haven't heard of other attacks," Miller answered.

Detective Ethan Fairway shifted in his chair. He was taller and slimmer than his partner. "Mr. Bryant, if you don't mind, we'd like to get through our questions first.

Afterward, you can ask us your questions, and if it doesn't compromise the investigation, we'll be happy to answer them for you."

"Of course. I apologize," Malcolm murmured. He tamped down his impatience and prepared to ride out the interview.

"Don't worry about it," Miller said, giving him an absent-minded smile. "You and Mr. Austin were partners for three years, you said. How did you two meet?"

"We were production assistants at Leo DeCaprio's company. We worked together there for about five years before deciding to strike out on our own." Malcolm leaned back into his chair, trying to get more comfortable.

"What can you tell us about Mr. Austin—as a business partner?" Fairway asked. "Did he work hard? Was he dedicated to the company?"

"Definitely." Malcolm didn't hesitate. "Very dedicated. The business takes up every spare moment we have."

"You spent a lot of time together, then?" Fairway continued his line of questioning.

"Yes. We were business partners. We were also roommates for a while to help save on expenses when we started the company," Malcolm elaborated.

"You worked together and you lived together? Didn't all that time together drive you guys nuts?" Miller interrupted.

Malcolm smiled. "I can understand why you would think so, but it didn't. Ty and I are"—Malcolm hesitated—"were very good friends. We were like brothers."

"Did you have a good working relationship?" Fairway asked.

"Yes." Malcolm wondered whether he imagined the detective's hostility. "We wouldn't have gotten as far as we have without one."

"I suppose that's true," Fairway acknowledged. "How's your company doing?"

"Very well," Malcolm answered, hoping his growing defensiveness wasn't reflected in his voice.

"Were you both satisfied with the company's performance?"

Malcolm hesitated, not certain he was comfortable with the direction the questions were taking. "The company is on the track we plotted for our five-year plan. We agreed we were ready to take on bigger projects."

Miller stepped in, seeking clarification. "So you're saying you both agreed to change the company's direction?"

Malcolm began to suspect Miller was either hiding a tape recorder or he was hard of hearing. Either would explain why the detective repeated everything Malcolm said.

"This isn't a new direction," Malcolm corrected. "We cut our teeth on commercials, music videos, and smaller movies. We're now ready for the bigger projects."

"I see," Miller murmured with an absent nod.

"What happens to Mr. Austin's share of the partnership now?" Fairway asked.

"The partnership agreement provides that, on the death of a partner, his share of the company would go to his immediate family members," Malcolm explained.

"So you're saying you would have to buy out his family in order to gain sole ownership of Celestial Productions?" Miller asked.

"Yes." Malcolm would have been amused by Miller's constant repetition if the conversation wasn't a police interrogation.

"And how much is Mr. Austin's share of the business worth?" Fairway's close scrutiny belied his casual pose.

Malcolm named the figure and Fairway whistled.

"I don't suppose you have that sort of cash handy?" he asked.

Malcolm cocked a brow. "No, I don't." He returned the detectives' somber stare, waiting for their next question.

"Where were you that morning?" Fairway asked.

The tension in Malcolm's shoulders eased. Apparently

the detectives had tired of the cat-and-mouse game, much to his relief. He preferred the direct approach to dealing with accusations.

"I was at home asleep," he answered.

"Were you with anyone?" Fairway followed up.

"No." Malcolm returned Fairway's steady stare. "Am I under suspicion, detectives?"

Miller looked up from his notepad. "At this point, Mr. Bryant, everyone is under suspicion."

Patricia Sargeant

# CHAPTER ELEVEN

Night never really fell in Los Angeles. Neon lights cast a near midday brightness until dawn. Malcolm stared down at the street through his office window, fighting the melancholy that allowed such thoughts to take root. It was hard to cope with a friend's death. But being suspected of his murder ripped open wounds before they'd even had a chance to heal. Disgusted with his self-pity, Malcolm turned away from the window.

Since the detectives' interrogation that morning, he hadn't been able to get much work done. Between his concern for Nicole's safety, which was compromised by a stalker who'd found access into her security building, and the news he was suspected of his friend's murder, Malcolm had found it hard to focus on work. He felt overwhelmed by the emotions churning in his soul, of which anger, sorrow, and fear were the most recognizable.

Someone had killed his best friend. Who? Why? Was it a random act of violence? Was it road rage?

Someone was stalking the woman he loved. Was it a secret admirer? Could it be a case of mistaken identity?

These questions had plagued him all day, driving him insane. Yet all he'd been able to accomplish was wasting time. He glanced at his watch, surprised to find it was after eight o'clock. He might as well call it a day.

Malcolm wandered to the door, pausing to take his jacket from the coat tree. Then he glanced at the phone. *Should I call Nicky?* He'd already called her several times during the day. Each time, she'd been a bit less tolerant of his concern. She said he was making her more tense than the stalker was. Still, maybe he should check in with her one more time before heading home.

"*No. You should go see her.*" Tyrone's voice ran across his mind.

*No,* Malcolm thought, feeling unsure of himself. *I don't want her to see me like this again.*

"*She's already seen you cry.*" Tyrone's reminder was not appreciated. "*As a matter of fact, I think you could say she made you cry. And that didn't seem to disgust her.*"

"She didn't make me cry," Malcolm snapped aloud, rising to the bait as readily as he would have when Tyrone was alive. He imagined the suppressed laughter in his partner's voice as snippets of remembered conversations merged to make him feel as though he were actually talking to his friend.

"*Yes, she did. But don't worry about it. Go see her. You know you want to.*"

Malcolm made the restless trip down the four flights of stairs to the lobby. "*No, Ty,*" Malcolm replied. "*I don't want her to see me upset again. That's not the image of me I want her to have.*"

"*Why not? Don't you want someone who can accept you in good times and in bad?*"

Malcolm deactivated his car alarm as he approached the driver's side door. "*Of course. I just wish she didn't always have to see the bad. It kind of undermines the image of success I was trying to cultivate.*"

"*Forget the image, player,*" Tyrone's voice teased. "*I think she wants to know the real you this time.*"

Malcolm slid behind the wheel and started his car. "What do you mean, 'this time'?" Alone in his car, he felt comfortable enough to talk out loud.

*"You didn't really let her get to know the whole you last time,
did you?"*

"Of course, I did," Malcolm argued. "We were together
for five years."

*"Time is relative,"* Tyrone noted. *"What are you afraid of?"*

Malcolm pondered the question. "My company is in
trouble, and I'm a suspect in your murder. My life is spinning out of control. I feel as incompetent as I did six
years ago when our baby died and I couldn't reach Nicky
emotionally."

*"Go see her. You know you want to,"* Tyrone repeated.

But his friend's words weren't necessary. Malcolm
realized his car was traveling the road his heart had
already taken.


The phone rang just as the heroine was fighting for
her life against the villain.

Nicole slipped the bookmark into the romantic suspense novel to save her place.

"Drat. Right at the good part," she muttered as she
tossed aside the afghan and swung her bare legs over the
side of the sofa. She crossed the room and picked up the
wall phone on the third ring.

"Hello."

"Hello, Nicole," a formal voice responded. "This is
Frank DeCaprio."

"Hi, Frank," she greeted.

"I hope I'm not disturbing you?" he asked.

"Not at all." She dropped cross-legged onto the carpet.
"I was just reading."

"What were you reading?"

"A romantic suspense." Nicole knew that with that response she'd gone down another notch in his estimation.

"How can you read those things?" Frank sounded
more curious than condemning.

"A good story is a good story," Nicole said mildly. She

could almost feel him considering her words. "So, what are you up to?"

"I was hoping you'd changed your mind about going to Christopher Gilliard's presentation with me tomorrow night."

The hopeful lilt to Frank's voice reminded Nicole of Malcolm's warning. Was the young sci-fi enthusiast developing a crush on her? No, she discounted. That was ridiculous. Wasn't it? Nicole remembered Frank's mother's reaction to her conversation with her son. She mentally shook her head. The thought was too absurd for consideration.

"No, I haven't changed my mind. Thank you for asking, but as I mentioned, I've already heard that particular presentation. It's very good, though. I'm sure you'll enjoy it."

"Are you sure you don't want to hear it again?" Frank's chuckle sounded awkward and forced.

Nicole knew she'd made the right decision. She'd have to be careful around Frank in the future. She didn't want to do anything to inadvertently encourage him.

"I'm sure." She stared at the view from the window across the room. "Besides, I have a feeling I'm going to need Saturday afternoon to get through a difficult plot point in my manuscript."

"Oh?" Frank's curiosity was apparently piqued. "What plot point is that? Perhaps I can help you."

Nicole's eyebrows shot up in surprise. The idea of brainstorming, with a reader, the plot of her unfinished manuscript seemed strange to her. "I appreciate your offer, Frank, but I'd hate to give away anything at this stage of the manuscript."

"Are you sure?"

"I'm sure. Besides, it would ruin the suspense for you."

"I don't mind, and I'm sure I can help," Frank insisted. "I know the characters."

Nicole was amused by his persistence. "Frank, I appreciate your offer, but I'll work it out." She shifted to find a more comfortable position on the carpet.

"All right." Frank hesitated before continuing. "I've written a couple of stories based on the *InterDimensions* characters."

"You have?" The revelation startled Nicole. Although many fans had written to her with suggested story lines, the idea of her characters living other lives without input from her didn't sit well. "Tell me about them," she invited.

"Well, they're not nearly as good as what you've done," Frank qualified before launching into a description of some of his story lines. Although unpolished, they hinted at a talent waiting to be developed.

"Those are good ideas, Frank. What are you going to do with them?"

"Just keep working at them."

"Good. I think you should. You have talent," Nicole encouraged. "But perhaps you'll want to create your own characters."

"Perhaps." Frank paused. "What are you going to do about the captain and the lieutenant commander?" he asked, referring to two of the *InterDimensions* heroes. "Some people on your fan loop are guessing that you're going to make them fall in love. At first, I was sure they were wrong. Commander Albright and Captain Mallory are too career-focused to fall in love. But now that I know you read romances, I'm not too sure what you'll have them do."

Nicole rubbed her forehead, wondering at the censor coloring the edges of Frank's tone. Was she being hypersensitive, or was Frank rather obsessive about her series? "Readers have sent me letters asking about a possible romance between Albright and Mallory as well. I'm on book four of the series. I don't know if a relationship between those characters will develop. I've always let the characters guide me as to what they might want to do."

"Fair enough, since it is their lives." Frank sounded satisfied.

Nicole frowned. "I'm glad you approve," she said dryly. The security phone buzzed, claiming her attention. "Hold on a second. Someone's at my door."

Nicole glanced at the clock on the wall as she set the phone down. It was shortly before 9:00 P.M. She uncrossed her bare legs and walked to the security phone.

"Yes?" she prompted.

"It's Mal. May I come up?"

She frowned at the tension in his voice. "Of course."

Nicole pressed the security button to let Malcolm into the building. She then hurried back to the phone. "Frank, I have company. I'm afraid I have to go now. But thank you for calling."

"Who is it?" Frank asked.

"It's Mal," Nicole answered, distracted. She glanced toward the door, knowing the phone cord wouldn't stretch the distance. She was anxious to get off the phone to greet Malcolm. *What put that tone in his voice?* Nicole realized she still held the phone. "I'm sorry, Frank. I have to go now."

"I understand," he said. "I'll talk to you again."

"Yes. Good-bye, Frank." She recradled the phone, then opened the door seconds after Malcolm knocked. She grew wary at the look in his eyes.

"What's happened?" She led him into the room.

Malcolm shook his head. "Did the stalker contact you today?"

Nicole sighed. "For the umpteenth time, no. I didn't receive any strange calls or threatening notes. Nothing. Now tell me what's wrong."

Malcolm dropped onto her sofa. "The police came to see me today."

"What did they say?" She sat beside him, their knees inches apart.

Malcolm rested his head on the back of the sofa and stared at the ceiling. "They asked questions about Ty.

About the company. About Ty and the company. And about Ty, the company, and me."

Nicole stiffened. "What did they want to know?"

"Whether Ty and I got along personally and professionally. How well the company is doing. What happens to Ty's share of the company now. In other words, did I kill him?"

Nicole gasped as though someone had thrown ice-cold water in her face. "You're a suspect?"

Malcolm looked at her. "According to the police, everyone's a suspect." He turned away and closed his eyes again.

Nicole heard the pain in his voice. She knew he said the words not because he believed them, but rather to make them both feel better. She looked at his hand lying beside his thigh. Her gaze continued up his arm where the once-crisp sleeves of his white shirt were rolled up to his elbows. Her gaze curved over his shoulder.

Malcolm's tension telegraphed itself in the taut lines of his neck. His eyes were closed, allowing her to study him without his knowing. Nicole hurt for him, anxious to find a way to provide comfort. But, in the past, he'd pushed her away whenever she'd offered support. She didn't want him to turn from her today. She had to find a way to be with him while he grieved.

"It bothers me that they think I was involved in Ty's death." Malcolm seemed to force the words past his lips.

Nicole's fingers itched to grasp his hand. "I understand. It would bother me, too. But I'm certain it was routine questioning. They talked to Joyce today also."

"I know," he murmured. "I called her. She really didn't need to go through something like that." Malcolm opened his eyes and caught her staring at him. "She told me you visited her this morning. That was nice of you."

Nicole shrugged a shoulder. "I'm concerned about her."

Malcolm gave her a faint smile, then turned away and

closed his eyes again. Nicole searched her mind for something encouraging to say.

Malcolm could feel Nicole's scrutiny. It seemed to test his emotional barrier, trying to weaken his ability to remain detached and controlled. He didn't know how to handle this trauma. But he did know that after Nicole had made him face his grief, then wrapped her arms around him to share his pain, he'd gained a measure of peace, at least temporarily. It shamed him how much he wanted to experience that peace again. Even as he fought against the need, he could feel his subconscious reaching for her.

"I hear him sometimes," he admitted.

"Pardon me?"

"Ty. Sometimes he talks to me," Malcolm clarified. "I hear his voice in my mind."

"What does he say?" Nicole asked, with more than curiosity in her tone.

Malcolm shrugged. He didn't see any need to discuss Tyrone's attempts to play matchmaker. "I don't know if he's actually speaking or if I'm losing my mind."

He flinched when Nicole clasped his hand, which lay between them on the sofa. His eyes popped open, his gaze caught by her soft regard. Her smile further ensnared him.

"You're not losing your mind," she said. "That's what people mean when they say our dearly departed never really depart from us. It's a sign of how strong your bond is with him."

Malcolm considered her response. He slid his hand free of her grasp, afraid the physical connection would further undermine his control. But he regretted the flash of pain in her eyes.

"Is that what happened to you after your mother died?" he asked.

A sad smile tugged at a corner of her lips. "Yes. And when my father passed away. Sometimes I still hear them both. They encourage me when I wonder if I have what it takes to be successful. Or scold me when I'm not getting enough sleep. In my mind, they repeat words or phrases they used to say when they were alive."

"That's what it's like for me," Malcolm admitted. "They're parts of conversations Ty and I have had in the past, cut together." He paused, lost in thought. "I remember when your father died," he murmured, recalling her depression and insomnia.

"You were my rock. I can't tell you how much your support meant to me." Nicole's response brought back memories of all the times he'd held her as she'd cried. How he'd worried about her.

Nicole lifted her hand. Then, as though rethinking her impulsive act, she lowered it back to the sofa. "I hope you'll let me return the favor."

"You have." Malcolm shifted to see her better. "It helps to just be here talking to you like this."

A quizzical expression drifted across Nicole's face.

"What is it?" Malcolm asked.

"Nothing." Nicole stood, turning toward the kitchen. "Do you want something to drink? Some water?"

Malcolm followed her. "Nicky, don't change the subject. Tell me what you're thinking."

Nicole put ice in two glasses, then filled them with water from the tap. She avoided his eyes as she responded to his question. "I've never seen this side of you before."

Malcolm stiffened. He cursed the weakness that had allowed him to give in to the need to see her when he wasn't ready, when he wasn't himself. He hated craving her comfort. Malcolm hurried to resurrect his barriers as Nicole turned to offer him the glass of ice water.

"I've always wanted you to feel comfortable coming to me when you were troubled, but you never did," she continued. "I don't know what made you finally change your mind, but I'm glad you did. I'm happy to be able to help you the way you had always helped me."

Caught off guard, Malcolm stared at her. Her response left him scrambling for footing behind his

semireconstructed barrier. Under his fixed stare,
Nicole's gaze slid away. As she moved to brush past him,
Malcolm reached out and wrapped his hand around
her slender bicep.

"What is it?" he asked again. "What are you thinking?"

He didn't think she would answer this time. Her
reply was so long in coming. Then he had to strain to
hear her words.

"I never thought you would need me for anything,"
she whispered.

A half-dozen needs swept through him with her words.
The need to comfort and be comforted. The need to
cherish and be cherished. The need to be wanted, loved,
respected, and needed by this woman who meant so
much to him. He stood dumbly in the eye of the storm.

Nicole turned to face him, her eyes brilliant with
unshed tears. She lifted her hand to cup his jaw.

"Don't be afraid of the pain, Mal. It takes a long time
to function past it. And, even then, you'll still feel the
echo of it. But that's normal. It hurts when you lose
someone you love."

He looked at her, thinking not only of Tyrone but also
of what he'd had with her and had thrown away.

"I know," he said, drinking in more of her comfort.
"I know."


The battle on the *InterDimensions* space station raged.
The invading forces overwhelmed the station's soldiers.
Captain Mallory had been badly wounded in the laser
fight. Lieutenant Commander Albright—the woman
behind the man charged with protecting the galaxy—
prepared to drag her captain farther behind battle
lines as she reluctantly shouted orders for her officers
to retreat.

As the lieutenant commander, Nicole's alter ego,
started to make one of her trademark dry comments, the
security buzzer of Nicole's apartment summoned the

author abruptly back to planet Earth. Nicole finished her thought before it was forever forgotten, then, still caught between two worlds, walked to her security phone.

Images from the space station battle still played in her head. She could hear the explosions, smell the smoke, see the blood as it spread over the captain's tunic. How was she going to get her characters out of this one?

"Yes?" she snapped.

"Detectives Miller and Fairway to see Ms. Collins." The gruff male voice claimed Nicole's full attention.

The *InterDimensions* images cleared, and Nicole landed back on twenty-first-century Earth. "Just a moment."

She hurried into her bedroom and pulled on her sneakers before jogging downstairs to the security door. A woman living alone couldn't be too careful. Nicole would examine their police badges before letting these strange men into her apartment. When she caught her first sight of them through the glass security door, she smiled. One partner resembled a taller Detective Columbo; the other looked like a heavyset Sonny Crockett, a detective from the 1980s series *Miami Vice*. She could use these characters in one of her mystery novels.

The detectives held up their badges without her having to ask for the identification. Still smiling, Nicole opened the door and stepped back.

"Good morning, detectives. Please follow me."

Nicole trotted back up the stairs, then waited outside her open apartment door for the two men to catch up.

"You have a lot of energy for this time of the morning," puffed Jim "Columbo" Miller.

Frowning, Nicole glanced at the clock above her entertainment center. It was almost eleven o'clock. Not that early.

"I've been up for a while," she explained as he and Ethan "Sonny Crockett" Fairway walked past her into the apartment.

Miller grunted as he pulled a crisp white handkerchief from his pocket and rubbed it under his jaw and across his throat. His pink cheeks were even more flushed than they had been when she'd first seen him at the security entrance. Nicole felt a twinge of guilt. She shouldn't have set such a brisk pace back to her apartment. The detective wasn't in a condition for it.

She looked at Ethan Fairway. He wasn't saying anything, but from the quick rise and fall of his chest, he also was trying to catch his breath. Nicole's guilt increased.

"May I get you gentlemen anything? Perhaps some water?"

"That would be terrific," Miller said.

"Yeah. Thanks," Fairway agreed.

"Please, have a seat." She walked toward the kitchen.

She filled three tall glasses with ice and cold water and put the glasses on a tray. She returned to find the detectives seated on her sofa visually cataloging everything in her living room and dining area.

"Here you are." After the detectives each took a glass, she set the tray on the coffee table, claimed a glass for herself, then settled onto the love seat.

Miller gulped half the glass of water. "Thank you."

"Yeah. Thanks," Fairway echoed. "And thank you for agreeing to see us."

"I'm happy to help however I can with the investigation, although I didn't know Tyrone Austin well. He was a very nice person."

Miller set down his empty glass and pulled out his notepad. "When did you first meet Mr. Austin?"

"January thirty-first." Nicole still mentally cringed when she thought of the bad first impression she must have made. "I came to Los Angeles to discuss Celestial Productions's bid for the movie rights to my sci-fi books."

"How did that meeting go?" Fairway asked.

Nicole paused at his curt tone. Apparently, Fairway wanted to play good cop/bad cop and had cast himself as the bad cop. His rapid-fire delivery probably was designed to catch her off balance. Fair enough, she decided, determined not to let him rattle her. She hadn't done anything wrong. Her objective was to help the police find Tyrone's killer.

"That meeting was inconclusive." Nicole smiled. "I wasn't certain I wanted to sell the movie rights."

"What made you change your mind?" Fairway persisted.

Nicole hesitated, reluctant to reveal personal family information. "Celestial Productions's offer was very generous, and they agreed to my contract terms."

"You didn't feel any pressure to sign?" Miller's measured delivery contrasted with Fairway's brusque tone.

"Not from Ty or Mal, no."

Fairway's gaze sharpened as though sensing a vulnerable spot. "If not from Mr. Austin or Mr. Bryant, who did you feel pressure from?"

Nicole shrugged. "Myself," she answered honestly.

Fairway's eyes narrowed as though he doubted her answer. He finished his drink before resuming his questions. "Did you know Celestial Productions is having financial problems?"

"Yes, I did." Nicole mentally thanked Joyce for sharing that information with her. She would have hated being caught off guard by Sonny Crockett's evil twin.

Fairway frowned. "And you agreed to the deal anyway?"

Nicole sipped her water. "I didn't see a need for a financial disclosure, Detective Fairway. The contract was in order, and my check didn't bounce."

Miller shifted on the sofa before redirecting the questioning. "Did you sense any tension between Mr. Austin and Mr. Bryant?"

"No. They seemed like good friends as well as good partners." Nicole drank more water.

"Can you think of anyone who showed signs of hostility toward Mr. Austin?" Miller followed up.

"No. No one at all. That's what makes this situation so strange to me," Nicole confided. "I would think you'd have to really hate someone to force him or her off the

road. But Ty didn't seem like the kind of person to inspire such a strong, negative emotion."

"In cases like these, Ms. Collins, nothing and no one
are the way they seem," Miller warned.


Malcolm hadn't slept well on Nicole's couch the night
before. The second sleepover in a row, counting his
emotional breakdown. The sofa didn't make a comfortable bed, and he'd had a lot on his mind, including
coming up with an airtight argument for her to move
into his house. The intercom interrupted another yawn.

"Eunice Gannon is on the line for you."

Rita spoke in a subdued, preoccupied tone. They both
carried much heavier loads now that they were picking
up Tyrone's tasks. Neither minded the extra work. It was
the reason for the responsibilities that caused the
burden. Someone out there—perhaps someone they
knew—had murdered a good friend.

Malcolm tapped the computer's mouse to save the
production schedule he was altering in preparation for
his meeting with the completion guarantor. He then
pressed the button on the telephone to take the casting
director's call.

"Hello, Eunice," he greeted. "How are you?"

"I'm fine, Malcolm. And you?" The casting director
briskly exchanged the perfunctory greeting.

"Good, thanks. What can I do for you?"

"Malcolm, I've had to make a difficult decision, and I
hope you'll understand. This is business."

Dread settled over him. "What's that, Eunice?"

"I'm pulling out of the *InterDimensions* project."

Malcolm took a steadying breath. "Can I ask why?"

"My company can't handle the negative publicity right
now." Eunice's tone was unapologetic.

Malcolm's anger built. "I think of Ty's death as a
tragedy, not negative publicity."

"Tyrone didn't just die. He was murdered. And,

YOU BELONG TO ME

according to the film-industry rumor mill, the police suspect you."

Malcolm had his suspicions about the identity of the film-industry rumor mill. Bracing himself for her answer, Malcolm leaned back in his chair. "You've known me for more than four years, Eunice. Do you suspect me?"

Her hesitation was answer enough.

"All right. I admit I'm disappointed, but I don't want you involved in a project you aren't comfortable with. Thanks for the call." Malcolm recradled the receiver.

It hurt that a longtime associate would think him capable of killing his best friend. But Malcolm couldn't allow that pain to distract him. He rubbed the back of his neck.

Tyrone's death. Nicole's stalker. The problems with the *InterDimensions* movie. They were all coming to a breaking point at the same time. Malcolm was tempted to put the project on hold. But he knew if he did, the film-industry rumor mill would announce he couldn't handle the movie without Tyrone. No, he had to keep moving forward. He also had to bring Tyrone's killer to justice and find Nicole's stalker before she was hurt.


"What kind of threats?" Derrick's voice, as it carried over the phone, was remarkably calm under the circumstances. Rigid and forced perhaps, but otherwise calm. For that Nicole was grateful.

"The latest letter implies bodily harm."

From her position on the love seat, Nicole studied the cloudless blue sky through the arches of her living room window. It was an odd juxtaposition to the conversation she and Derrick were having. She'd debated telling her younger brother about the letters. She didn't want to worry him. But on the other hand, she didn't want to keep such an important thing from him. Putting herself in his position, she would be very agitated if he kept similar information from her.

"Why is someone threatening you?" Tension increased in Derrick's voice.

"I don't know. The letters demand I leave the person's family alone. But I don't know who he or she is talking about. I haven't interfered with anyone's family." Nicole stretched her legs on the love seat, crossing them at the ankles. Its tweed material lightly scratched the backs of her thighs.

"Have you told the police?"

"Yes. They have the letters, but I've kept copies." Nicole swung her legs over the side of the love seat and propped her elbows on her knees.

Derrick's questions started picking up speed. "What are they doing about it?"

"There isn't much they can do right now. There aren't any prints. The letters are typed. But the postmark is Los Angeles."

"Well, that narrows it down to about four million people," Derrick noted with sharp sarcasm.

"I have a feeling he lives nearby." Silence met Nicole's comment.

"Why do you think that?"

"Because one of the letters was slipped under my door late one night." Nicole braced for Derrick's reaction.

"I thought you lived in a security building." Derrick sounded startled.

"I do," Nicole replied ironically.

"And you're still living there?"

Nicole stood and paced the length of the phone cord. "Yes."

"Nicky, I think you should come home." Her little brother's voice was inflexible.

"D, I can't leave now. I found out a couple of days ago Ty's death wasn't an accident."

"What do you mean?"

Nicole rubbed her forehead with her free hand. "The police believe Ty was forced off the road." She explained everything she knew about the case so far, including Malcolm, and Joyce's accounts of their police interviews.

"Oh, man." Derrick groaned. "That's bad. That's really bad."

"I know. I just can't leave Mal right now."

"Okay. I understand," Derrick said. "But you should at least leave that building. The stalker knows where you live. He knows which apartment is yours. He probably knows you live alone. Is Mal aware of these threats?"

"Yes." Nicole dropped back onto the sofa and crossed her legs.

"And what is he doing to protect you?" Derrick demanded.

Nicole combed back her hair with her fingers. This cross-examination made her feel cornered. "He slept on my couch last night."

"He can't continue to do that. It's not fair to him."

Nicole tried again to rub the tension from her forehead. "I know. He wants me to move in to his house."

"And you're still in your apartment?" Derrick's voice rose with incredulity.

Nicole fought against a feeling of idiocy. "D, if the stalker wanted to hurt me, he could have done it by now. Like you said, he knows where I live."

"That theory doesn't comfort me. Let's not tempt him any more. Nicky, you're my sister. I want to make sure you're safe."

"I know."

"I think you should move in with Mal."

"I'll think about it." Nicole thought she could hear Derrick grinding his teeth.

"Think really fast."


The coffee-shop midmorning scents weren't pleasing any longer. Instead, the muffins, bagels, mocha, and latte combined to make Malcolm nauseous.

He frowned at the article in the industry weekly, one

of the *Silver Screen Previews*'s competitors. It updated readers on the police investigation into Tyrone's death. The article explained that police had found evidence indicating the young, up-and-coming movie producer had been murdered. This wasn't the way he wanted Tyrone to be remembered. His partner's accomplishments and successes would be overshadowed by the media's sensationalizing his murder. He folded the magazine, covering the gossip on his friend's death, and left the restaurant.

As he walked toward the parking meters where he'd left his car, Malcolm saw a familiar figure come out of the novelty store farther up the block. Frank DeCaprio clutched a brown bag, his head tilted downward as he walked an intersecting path toward Malcolm.

"Hi, Frank. How are you?" Malcolm called.

Frank's head jerked upward as though he were coming out of a daydream. He stopped an arm's span from Malcolm. "Oh, hi, Malcolm. I didn't see you there."

"I could tell. What brings you to this neck of the woods?" Malcolm asked, surprised to find the Beverly Hills resident in Inglewood.

Frank nodded back in the direction of the sci-fi/fantasy novelty store. "Oh, I wanted to pick up a few things. Have you talked to Nicole recently?"

"Yes. I spoke with her yesterday."

Frank flushed pink. Malcolm's concern that his friend's son may have a crush on Nicole returned. He was on the verge of telling the college student he was too young for Nicole. However, he had a feeling his ex-wife wouldn't appreciate his belaboring that point. Besides, he was certain she could deal with Frank and the awkward situation. Malcolm's involvement probably would only serve to embarrass Frank.

He glanced at the store Frank had just left. "A Different World," he read. "I haven't been inside that store in years."

He and Tyrone had satisfied their inner children with

frequent trips to the novelty shop. It was a treasure trove of specialty items, including comic books, graphic novels, posters, model kits, and collectible toys. They'd invested a lot of time in that store. But their trips had become less frequent as their company had grown. Then Tyrone had fallen in love with Joyce, and he'd spent the little free time he'd had with her. Now Malcolm couldn't conceive of going to the store by himself. At least not for a very long time. Too many memories.

"My mother introduced me to A Different World when I was a kid," Frank was saying.

"Does she like sci-fi memorabilia?"

"Oh, no." Frank's smile softened his features. "But she knows how much I like anything to do with science fiction. She used to take me there just to spend time with me doing something I enjoy."

"Your mother's a very special lady."

"Yes, she is." Frank's obvious devotion to his mother touched a cord in Malcolm. He felt the same way about his mother.

"But somehow I can't imagine Leo in A Different World." Malcolm smiled at the imagery.

"No. My father isn't big on science fiction." Frank's voice cooled just a bit, taking Malcolm off guard. "That's one of the reasons I was so surprised by his enthusiasm for the *InterDimensions* movie."

Malcolm felt an automatic need to defend the father to his son. "Perhaps he's changing. Perhaps he wants to share this interest with you."

"Then he's going about it the wrong way. He's never even read an *InterDimensions* book. I've tried to get him to read one, but he won't do it. Supporting the project doesn't make you a fan."

"That's true. On the other hand, I've read the books, and I am a fan."

"I'm not denigrating your skills as a movie producer, Malcolm. I'm just saying that my father and I have different interests. And that's fine."

Malcolm had a feeling it wasn't fine with Frank. Somehow he couldn't shake the image of a disappointed little boy. But he didn't want to get involved any further. This was a family matter, something father and son would have to work out themselves.

"I'd better head into the office." Malcolm took a step back and turned toward his car.

"But it's Saturday."

"I've got a lot to keep up with." Malcolm was used to the long hours, which were made even longer now without Tyrone's help.

"Oh. Well, it was good to see you again."

"It was good to see you, too. Give Leo and Ava my best."

"I will." Frank gestured toward the meter next to Malcolm's car. "I'm parked next to you, so I'll wait for you to pull out."

Malcolm looked at the black Lexus SUV, glancing briefly at the license plate. "That's some vehicle."

"It's my mother's. She lets me drive it sometimes."

"I thought Leo bought you a car last year."

Frank walked toward the SUV. "Yes, but I like Mother's."

"Who wouldn't?" Malcolm climbed into his Honda. He drove away thinking about fathers and sons and unrealistic expectations.


Eight hours later, Malcolm sat in Tyrone's office thinking about budgets, production schedules, and unrealistic expectations. They were almost a month behind schedule, and each day cost more money. He didn't know how to make up that lost time.

He pushed the chair away from the desk and rose to pace the office. The business accounts were kept on Tyrone's system, the financial papers filed in Tyrone's cabinets. It only made sense he reviewed the accounts in his partner's office.

What would Ty have done? They'd had trouble with

scheduling before and talked it through to come up with a solution together. He really needed someone to talk it through with now.

Malcolm circled Tyrone's office, pacing off the circumference. Accounting books and marketing texts shared shelf space with *Lord of the Rings* action figures. Community-service certificates and project awards hung side by side with movie posters. Each item brought memories to the forefront. Some memories stung his eyes; some made him smile. It had been almost five weeks since Tyrone's death, but Malcolm and Joyce weren't in any hurry to pack up his office.

He returned to Tyrone's desk. What would Ty do? How could he make up the time? Restlessly, he pulled open the center drawer and caught a whiff of mint from the open roll of original-flavor Certs. Writing pads, spare change, and individual packets of salt joined the Certs. The top-corner drawer yielded rubber bands, paper clips, and an extra box of staples.

Malcolm rifled through the notepads and napkins and came across an envelope. The postmark was Los Angeles, less than a week before Tyrone's death. It was directed to Tyrone, but it didn't carry a return address. The hairs on the back of his neck stirred in an uncomfortable foreboding. He opened the envelope and pulled out a single sheet of paper.

*Leave my family alone,* the typewritten note read. *This is your one and only warning.*

"Shit," Malcolm breathed.

Ice tumbled in his gut. He stared at the note, seeing in his mind's eye the notes Nicole had received and hearing what he thought had been a misdialed phone call on his cell phone. What in God's name did this mean?

He snatched the phone from its cradle and dialed Tyrone's home phone number. Joyce answered on the third ring.

"Hello?"

"Joyce, it's Mal. Did Ty ever tell you about receiving any strange letters?"

"Strange in what way?"

Malcolm forced himself to slow down and reconsider his question. "Before his death, did Ty mention receiving a letter warning him away from someone's family?"

Malcolm waited through Joyce's thoughtful silence.

"A letter about a family?" Joyce murmured; then her voice sharpened. "A couple of days before he was killed, he told me he'd received a weird message. He said it said something like, 'Stay away from my family' or, 'Leave my family alone.' But he thought he'd gotten it by accident. Why are you asking?"

Malcolm stared at the letter. "I found that letter in his desk and was wondering what it meant. Is that all he said about it?"

"Yes. Do you think it's important?"

Malcolm heard her anxiety. He knew Joyce needed answers. She deserved answers. But until he understood the implications of these messages, he didn't want to worry her.

"I don't know, Joyce. I'll call you later."

Malcolm hung up. His heart thumped in his throat. He clenched his fist to hold back the panic.

*Dear God, Ty. What does this mean?*

# CHAPTER TWELVE

"What's going on?" Nicole stood back to let Malcolm enter her apartment. Her anxiety had been building ever since his cryptic call more than half an hour ago. She didn't understand why he couldn't tell her what was so urgent over the phone.

"I need to see the copies of the letters you've received."

Nicole studied him. He seemed so tense, she feared he would pop right out of his skin. Squelching the questions trembling on her lips, Nicole hurried to her credenza and pulled out the folder containing copies of the three messages she'd received. She spun around and almost trod over him. She hadn't realized Malcolm had followed her so closely. She took a step back and handed the folder to him.

Malcolm scanned the letters. "Have you heard from him today?"

"No."

Nicole followed Malcolm back into the living room. He read the letters again as he walked. Then he collapsed onto the sofa and pulled a folded sheet of paper from his inner coat pocket. He studied the four sheets of paper, then leaned back against the sofa and closed his eyes.

"What's wrong?" Nicole's patience was at an end.

Malcolm opened his eyes and handed her the paper he'd pulled from his coat. She read the single, typed sheet.

"Oh, my God," she breathed, collapsing onto the sofa next to him. "Was this sent to you?"

"No. I found it in one of Ty's desk drawers."

"It was sent to Ty? Why didn't you tell me?"

"Ty never told me. Apparently, he didn't take it seriously."

"Did he tell Joyce about it?"

Malcolm stood and began to pace. "He mentioned it to her. He told her he thought he'd received it by accident."

"And now he's dead." Nicole was having a hard time taking in this turn of events. She studied the sheet of paper again. "These threats are all connected, and they're all from the person stalking me."

"I don't think there's any doubt about that." Malcolm's voice was grim. "The messages are too similar."

Nicole shivered. The shock running through her made her fingers numb. "But what family is this person referring to? Ty and I had only just met. Our only common acquaintance is you."

Malcolm turned and paced to the opposite wall, his head bent in concentration. He didn't seem to notice he'd never taken off his coat.

"I received a similar message," he said.

Nicole gasped. "You received a letter? You never told me."

"It wasn't a letter. It was a call on my cell phone." Malcolm stopped pacing. He stood staring across the room, his profile to her.

Nicole frowned. "Did you list your cell phone number in the phone book?"

Malcolm shook his head. "It's only listed on my business card."

Nicole felt her eyes widen. "The stalker has your business card? Do you think he's a business acquaintance?"

Malcolm sighed and resumed his prowling. "That's the most likely scenario."

Nicole started to tremble and wrapped her arms around herself. Then a thought occurred to her. "I received a call, too, when I was in New York. The caller said the same thing about his family, but I assumed he'd dialed the wrong number."

"So it started in New York. And you've had several letters and nuisance calls since you arrived in L.A." Malcolm stopped to stare at the wall again.

Nicole leaned forward, rubbing her arms to ward off the cold. "This is a family known to the three of us and probably related to one of your business associates."

Malcolm resumed his silent prowl. "That pretty much sums it up."

"We need to take this information to the police."

"I agree." He stopped and met her gaze. "I'll call Detective Miller and ask him to meet with us as soon as possible. Will that work for you?"

"Yes, of course." Nicole shivered again.

Malcolm glanced at his watch. "It's getting late. I should go." But he didn't move.

Nicole stood and nodded toward the door. "I don't like the idea of you going back out there tonight."

Malcolm shook his head. "I'll be fine. But have you given any more thought to moving in with me? There's strength in numbers. And neither of us likes the idea of the other being alone under these circumstances."

Nicole made up her mind on the spot. Knowing he'd received similar threats made her almost frantic with fear.

"I've decided to accept your offer. I'll pack an overnight bag and get the rest of my stuff tomorrow."

"Good." Malcolm followed Nicole into her bedroom. "We'll call Miller in the morning."

"Tomorrow's Easter Sunday," Nicole reminded him as she pulled a bag from her closet.

"We'll leave a message if we don't reach him."

Nicole stuffed everything she could think of into the

overnight bag, then packed her laptop and notes. She still had reservations about moving in with Malcolm, but overall she believed she'd made the right decision. The nurturer in her needed to help protect him.

Nicole surveyed the small, dim police meeting room. From the smell permeating the furniture and walls, she suspected smokers gathered here in inclement weather. What a way to spend Easter Sunday.

She and Malcolm had been surprised when Detective Miller had returned their message and asked them to meet him and Detective Fairway this morning.

Stiff with tension, Nicole took the seat Detective Miller held for her. She didn't understand why the detectives had decided to continue questioning Malcolm and her separately about the anonymous note Malcolm had found in Tyrone's office. She wondered whether they both were under suspicion. Of course, they had nothing to hide, so she shouldn't be nervous. And she wouldn't have been, if she hadn't noticed the detectives exchange a silent nod before Fairway left the room with Malcolm.

Miller lowered his bulk into the chair opposite Nicole. "Ms. Collins, have you reported receiving these letters to the department?"

"Yes. I've been talking to an Officer Strahan."

"Ah, Deirdre Strahan."

"That's right." Nicole folded her hands together to keep from fidgeting. These were questions Miller could have asked in front of Malcolm. Her suspicions grew.

"And when did you start getting these letters?"

Nicole took a moment before answering. "As I explained earlier, I received the first letter shortly after I moved to Los Angeles."

"But you got the first call in New York?"

Nicole nodded. "That's right."

"Was this before or after you signed with Celestial Productions?"

Nicole paused warily. Where was Detective Miller going with this?

"You say you found this note in Austin's desk drawer last night?" Fairway fired the question at him before Malcolm could sit down.

"Yes." Malcolm sat straight and alert. The look Nicole had given him before they had been taken to separate rooms told him she wasn't any more comfortable with this setup than was he.

"Was anyone with you?" Fairway rested his right ankle on his left knee.

"No."

Fairway nodded. "What were you doing alone in Austin's office?"

Malcolm knew he needed to watch his temper. He couldn't afford to lose control. "As I told you before, all of the account information and contracts are on Ty's computer. I needed to review them and update the office expenses."

"If the files are on his computer, why were you going through his desk?"

"I was just looking around." Malcolm didn't like Fairway's "I've-got-you" smile, especially since he agreed with the sentiment.

"Too bad no one was with you," Fairway said.

"It was after I agreed to sign the contract but before I actually signed it," Nicole said.

Miller leaned toward her from the other side of the table. "I don't follow you."

Nicole reviewed the chain of events. "I agreed to sign with Celestial Productions that Friday. I received the prank call the next day, which was Saturday. Mal and I met with my agent to sign the paperwork that Monday. We faxed the contract to Ty for his signature the same day."

Miller leaned back in his seat. "So Bryant was in New York when you got the call."

"Yes," Nicole answered cautiously.

She knew Malcolm was a suspect in the investigation. She had no doubt her ex-husband was innocent, and she didn't want to give the police anything they could use against him.

"Did he have your number in New York?"

"I'm in the book. But, detective, I know Mal didn't make that call," Nicole added with a flash of memory.

Miller frowned. "How do you know that?"

She arched an eyebrow. "Because he showed up at my apartment the minute I hung up the phone."

Miller smiled with pity. "So Bryant could have had someone make the call for him."

The tension in the car wrapped itself around Nicole like a sweater. Malcolm hadn't said a word since he'd asked whether she was ready to leave the station. Nicole hadn't pushed him. Instead she sat, trying to collect her thoughts as they tumbled over and around each other.

"Do you think I had anything to do with Ty's death?" Malcolm's quiet question scattered her thoughts again.

Nicole's head snapped in his direction. "No," she almost shouted.

"Not even a little bit?"

"Not. At. All."

"They tried to make you believe I was involved, though, didn't they?"

Nicole sighed. "Yes, they did. They're looking for an easy answer to this case, Mal. But I think we both know there isn't one."

"To clear my name, I'm going to have to find the killer." Malcolm sounded as though he were thinking aloud.

"I came to that conclusion as well."

"There's a connection between the three of us."

Malcolm worked his way through the stop-and-go traffic. "We have to find it."

"I can't think what it might be. Until February, I didn't even know who Ty was. The only thing we have in common is the movie project."

"There must be something else. Or something the stalker thinks is there."

Nicole turned away to stare out the window again. After a moment of silence, she asked, "Why didn't you tell me Celestial Productions was having financial trouble?"

Malcolm didn't answer right away. "I didn't think it was important. Who told you that?"

"Joyce. And I'm glad she did because the detectives asked me about it. If she hadn't told me, I would have been caught off guard. I think the detectives consider it one of your motives. They said Ty was considering dissolving the company. Is that true?"

"Yes."

She turned back to him. "Why didn't you tell me?"

Malcolm took one hand off the steering wheel to massage the back of his neck. "I was tired of you seeing me as a failure."

His answer took Nicole's breath away. "I've never seen you as a failure."

"I don't know why not." Malcolm returned his hand to the steering wheel and concentrated on the traffic for a time. When he spoke again, his tone was hesitant.

"The entry-level production assistant job I took after we moved to L.A. barely paid enough to help with the bills."

Nicole shook her head, shifting in the passenger seat to face Malcolm. "Most entry-level jobs don't pay much. That's one of the reasons they're called *entry-level*. But that's not your fault. It doesn't make you a failure."

Malcolm pulled his car into a space in front of Nicole's building. He shut off the engine, then turned to face her.

"Well, it certainly doesn't make me a success. Maybe I was being foolish, but I wanted you to see me as a success. I was afraid you would think I was still a loser if you knew about the trouble I was having with my company."

"You're not a loser," she snapped. "Don't ever say that." Nicole gave him her harshest glare, angry beyond words that he could think she viewed him that way.

Malcolm looked surprised at her fierce defense of him. "All right," he agreed. "But just so you know, I didn't argue with Ty about closing the company if we couldn't make a profit from this project. I'd hoped it wouldn't come to that, though."

Nicole unlocked the passenger door. "Fine," she said, still annoyed. "I just wish you had told me."

Malcolm nodded. "I'm sorry."

Nicole shrugged, then stepped out of the car. "I appreciate your offering to help me pack my apartment. I know how busy you are. We don't have to get everything today."

They walked up the stairs in silence. She was digging around in her purse for her keys when she realized she wouldn't need them. Someone had broken into her apartment. She jumped back from the door in disbelief. Malcolm swept her behind him.

"What are you doing?" she hissed as close to his ear as she could get. He ignored her and reached toward the door. Nicole snatched his arm back. "We should call the police. Where's your cell phone?"

Malcolm pried her grip from his arm and pushed open the door.

Nicole swallowed back a scream. Her apartment looked as though a tornado had torn through it. Bags of food had been ripped open and spilled all over her kitchen, dining area, and living room. Their sticky, gritty, and powdery contents coated her countertops, floor, and carpet. Her cabinets had been emptied of dishes, mugs, and glasses, and the items had been smashed and ground into her linoleum.

Dazed, Nicole followed Malcolm into the destruction. She could feel the vibrations of hate clinging to the air.

Who? Why? When? The questions ricocheted through her mind.

To her left, the entire contents of her bookcase had been tossed. Books and magazines had been ripped. The intruder had used one of her shoes to shatter her television set. The shoe was lodged in what remained of the screen. Nicole winced, her stomach muscles clenched at the thought of what the rest of her apartment must look like.

She turned her head and saw the butcher's knife embedded dead center in her discount kitchen table. Her knees shaking, Nicole stumbled as she approached the table, lured to it by the obvious strength used by the person who had wielded the knife. As Nicole approached the scene, she saw the knife pinned a note to the table. The message read, *Time is a luxury, but not for you. Leave my family alone.*

A memory switched on, and the horror of its implication pushed her away from the table. She stumbled over a book on the floor. Nicole glanced down and extended a trembling hand to pick up a cover that had been ripped from *InterDimensions* book two.

"Don't touch anything." Malcolm's firm tone reached out and grabbed her from the edge of hysteria. "I'm going to call the police."

Nicole nodded, the lump in her throat too big to allow words to escape.

He sat slumped in the SUV across the street from Nicole's apartment. He was several buildings down from his usual parking space, but still close enough to observe the activities taking place around the building. He'd seen Nicole and Malcolm arrive. He'd watched them get out of Malcolm's car and enter the building. He'd stared at the building's façade, breathing deeply as he imagined them climbing the stairs to her apartment. The same stairs he'd mounted earlier.

He'd ripped and shredded and shattered her belongings,

allowing the anger to flow through him and express itself in the destruction. Yet, barely an hour later, his hands still trembled with rage. Why wouldn't she listen to him? Why couldn't she understand?

Two police cruisers pulled up in front of Nicole's building, breaking his concentration. Minutes later, two men joined them. The younger man was dressed in jeans and a leather jacket. His companion wore khaki pants and a rumpled trench coat over a white shirt and tie. He judged them to be plainclothes detectives. They scanned the street as they spoke with the patrol officers. Crime-scene investigators joined the group.

Why were they here? Had Nicole called them, or were they going to talk to someone else? Why would Nicole involve the police? All she had to do was leave his family alone.

Although he sat shielded by the SUV's tinted windows, caution prompted him to slide lower in his seat. He believed his actions were completely understandable and acceptable. After all, a man had to protect his family. But he knew not everyone would view it that way.

He watched as the officers and investigators strode to Nicole's building with the detectives ambling a stride or so behind.

An hour passed. He grew hungry and cold but ignored the discomfort. He was doing this for his family. He would wait as long as necessary.

The uniformed officers left first. He frowned as he saw them carrying envelopes. Had they collected items from Nicole's apartment? But he couldn't be certain they'd gone to her apartment. They climbed into their separate cruisers and drove away. Shortly afterward, the detectives emerged from the building, got into their vehicle, and left. Only Malcolm, Nicole, and the crime-scene investigators remained.

Still he waited. He wanted to see Malcolm leave. He wanted to make sure Nicole understood his message. He didn't want to repeat himself.

He started to shiver. His stomach growled. And still,

YOU BELONG TO ME            203

he waited. He fought to remain focused and was rewarded when Malcolm and Nicole appeared. His gaze
shot to the suitcases Malcolm carried. Could it be? Was
it possible? Had she finally understood?

He watched as Malcolm stored the suitcases in his
trunk, then assisted Nicole into the car. He had won.
Nicole was leaving. He had protected his family. The
crisis was over.

With relief, he watched them drive away before starting his car and heading home.

At work the next morning, Malcolm stared at his computer monitor in his office, seeing instead the shattered,
disbelieving expression in Nicole's eyes. She'd barely ut-
tered five words since they'd arrived at his home yesterday. He'd led her to his guest room, helped her get
settled, then left her to sleep. He'd checked on her twice
during the night. She'd seemed so still, too still. He'd
wondered if she was pretending to sleep so he would
leave her alone with her thoughts.

The violence reflected in the attack on her apartment
had shaken him as well. He didn't doubt the stalker had
committed the destruction. That someone so violent
and insane was following Nicole scared him witless. The
stranger had somehow gotten into her security building and through the locks on her door. What if she had
been home? Had his purpose been to frighten her, or
had he intended to hurt her? Would he try to get to her
again? Malcolm wondered whether Nicole would be
safer back in New York.

The intercom buzzed. Malcolm leaned forward and
pressed the hands-free button for the speaker.

"Yes, Rita?"

"Mr. Bryant." His assistant's cool, censorious tone
warned him he had an unwanted visitor. "Nathan
Rutherford of the *Silver Screen Preview* is here without
an appointment. Again."

Malcolm sighed and rubbed his neck. Now what? He should have stayed home, but there was too much to do in the office.

"Give me fifteen minutes before sending him back, would you, please?"

"Of course, Mr. Bryant," Rita agreed before disconnecting.

Malcolm finished revising the *InterDimensions* production schedule. He was saving the document when Rita knocked on his office door. Malcolm shook off his irritation at the unscheduled appointment and stood to greet the reporter. Alienating the press would only hurt the *InterDimensions* project more. He approached the threshold, his hand outstretched.

"Nathan," he greeted, shaking the younger man's hand. "What can I do for you?"

Nathan's smile didn't mask his calculating gaze. "Thank you for seeing me, Malcolm. I'd like to talk with you about the progress you're making on the *InterDimensions* project."

Malcolm smothered a sigh and prepared to do some fast talking. He gestured toward the chairs facing his desk.

"Have a seat."

"Thank you." Nathan sank into one of the straight-backed chairs and pulled his steno pad from his briefcase. He wore baggy, gray denim pants. His ill-fitting black blazer fell open over his white shirt. He crossed his legs and placed his notebook on his knee. "So, how's the project going?"

Malcolm came around to take his seat behind the desk. "We've adjusted the time frame. The original schedule had some cushion built in so the revised delivery date isn't that far off the original completion date."

The reporter nodded and jotted down a few notes. After a moment of silence, he snared Malcolm's gaze. "How's the murder investigation going?"

Malcolm froze. He should have realized Nathan had planned this unscheduled visit with the intent of a surprise attack. The reporter was well known for his sensationalism. He could have called Malcolm if all he'd wanted was a project update. For a status on the investigation into Tyrone's death, he would have to interview Malcolm in person, where it would be much harder to evade questions.

Malcolm forced himself to lean back in his executive chair. "You'll have to call the police department for that information. I'm not the one conducting the investigation."

"I know the police questioned you. Twice," the reporter continued.

Malcolm narrowed his gaze. "That's right."

Nathan's piercing gray gaze scanned Malcolm's expression. "What did they ask you?"

"I'm not going to discuss that with you. I don't want to jeopardize the investigation into my best friend's murder."

Nathan wrote hasty notes. Malcolm's gut burned with anger that this questionable reporter was quoting him for an article he hadn't agreed to do.

"Is it true you're a suspect?" Nathan persisted.

Malcolm's patience began to unravel. "Do you have any questions about the movie production?"

"All of these questions are in connection with the production," Nathan insisted. "After all, the production has been affected by your partner's death. How is Ms. Collins reacting to this scandal?"

Malcolm stood. "That's the end of this interview," he announced, striding to the door.

Nathan turned in his chair to keep Malcolm in his sights. "What is your relationship with Ms. Collins? Why is she staying with you when everyone else has left?"

Malcolm ignored the question and held open his office door. "Make an appointment if you want to speak with me in the future."

Nathan rose, a taunting smile twisting his lips. "I had hoped to get your side of the story. If I don't get the answers from you, I'll just have to get them from another source."

"Your implication being you don't care whether your story is accurate."

Nathan's smile wavered. "That's not what I said. I want—"

"But it's what you meant," Malcolm interrupted. "You do whatever you think you need to, and I'll do the same."

The reporter's cockiness faded under Malcolm's implacable gaze. "Are you sure you don't have anything you want to say to me?"

Malcolm shoved his hands into the front pockets of his pleated Dockers. "Nothing that can be printed. Now get out."

The reporter closed his steno pad, picked up his briefcase, then brushed past Malcolm on his way out.

Malcolm resisted the urge to slam the door.


The words kept coming back to her. *Time is a luxury, but not for you.* Nicole knew those words. This was the second time the stalker had included them in a message to her. Their use obviously was deliberate. And he knew she would recognize them. But Nicole needed to be sure.

She couldn't go back to her apartment to verify her memory, though. The thought of seeing that hate and violence again made her shudder. Besides, the police had sealed her apartment as a crime scene. Even if she could gather the fortitude, she wouldn't be able to get in. She'd have to go to a bookstore. She'd have to leave the relative security of Malcolm's house and risk the wide-open spaces.

Nicole peeked through the window blinds. Was he out there waiting to get her alone? She jerked her hand away from the blinds and turned from the window. *This is ridiculous.* She wouldn't stay locked in this house like some kind of prisoner. She was free to come and go as she pleased.

As long as she was careful.

Now, how was she going to get to a bookstore? She'd

call a cab and have the driver take her to the mall. There was a large bookstore in the nearby fashion mall. Decision made, she checked her watch. If she hurried, she'd be back before Malcolm returned home.

"Nicole."

She started at the unexpected sound of a man's voice drawling her name in the mall. Clutching the plastic bag that carried her purchase, she turned to confront the voice's owner.

Omar leaned against the bookstore display window, looking for all the world as though he'd been waiting for her. Under his moss-colored leather jacket, a wine-red shirt skimmed his well-muscled torso before disappearing into the waistband of his designer jeans. With his forearms flexed over his chest and his ankles crossed, he looked like an advertisement for casually elegant clothes.

Nicole's gaze settled on his smiling eyes. The skin at the nape of her neck tingled with unease. "Hello, Omar. Strange running into you like this, isn't it?"

Omar pushed away from the display window. "It's quite a coincidence, but it's a popular mall."

Nicole locked her knees and stood her ground as Omar approached her. "It's a large mall. A person would have to work hard to find a familiar face in a mall this size. Or he'd have to follow her."

Omar chuckled, his Hollywood charm never faltering. "No," he denied, stopping several paces from her. "Just lucky, I guess."

*Lucky my eye.* Her suspicions in no way easing, she clutched her purchase closer. If he was the one stalking her, what would he think if he saw what her bag contained?

She controlled her legs' desire to sidle away. "I would think you'd be at work."

"I gave myself the day off. Have coffee with me."

Nicole made a show of checking her watch, although

she wasn't able to focus on the numbers. "I'm afraid I don't have time. I'm meeting Mal tonight about the *InterDimensions* project." Nicole stilled as she remembered Omar was one of Malcolm's business associates, albeit a competitor. Did he have Malcolm's cell phone number?

Omar's expression sobered, and he slid his thumbs into his front pockets. "That's what I wanted to talk to you about. I don't think it's safe for you to be around Mal. He may have already killed one person—"

"That's enough." Nicole trembled with outrage. In her peripheral vision, she saw a group of people look her way in surprise. She slowed her breathing in an effort to control her temper and her tone. "Mal has not killed anyone."

"He's a suspect in Ty's murder." Omar regarded her earnestly.

"But he's not guilty." Nicole turned to leave. Omar's grip on her arm stopped her.

"Don't let Mal's charm fool you," he cautioned. "I've known him for five years. You've only just met him. He's ruthless."

Nicole stared at Omar in surprise. Malcolm? Ruthless? She could agree with his being obstinate and driven. But ruthless? She almost laughed.

"If you can believe Malcolm is capable of killing anyone, then you're the one who doesn't know him." She pulled her arm from Omar's grip and forced herself to walk away calmly.

Nicole raised her hand to insert the spare key into Malcolm's front door. The door flew open without her assistance, and strong hands grabbed her waist to lift her through the threshold.

Malcolm stood her in the hallway before he locked the front door. His hard gaze pinned her in place and swept her from head to toe.

"You're home early," she managed stupidly.

His hot-cocoa eyes simmered. His movements were stiff and jerky. Nicole squared her shoulders and cautioned herself to tread carefully.

Malcolm took two strides away from her; then he turned to blast her with his gaze. "Where have you been?"

"The mall. I thought I would be home before you."

Malcolm glanced at the plastic bag she clutched to her chest. "You went shopping?" he asked incredulously. "When there's someone out there intent on hurting you, you went to the mall? Do you have any idea what you've done to me? I've been going out of my mind. And you went shopping?"

Nicole flushed, embarrassed and contrite. "Mal, I'm sorry I worried you. I should have called to let you know where I was going, but I truly thought I would be back before you."

Malcolm rubbed the back of his neck. Lowering his hand, he took several deep breaths and spoke with deliberate patience. "You're missing the point. It's not safe for you to go around alone. After what happened in your apartment, there's no question that someone is trying to hurt you."

"But I was at the mall. It's a public place."

Malcolm stared at her for long silent moments. His anger was palpable. "What were you doing at the mall?"

"I'll show you."

Nicole took his arm and led him down the hall to his family room. They sat next to each other on the sofa. With slightly shaking fingers, she reached into the bag and pulled out her purchase, the second book in her *InterDimensions* series. She sat for a moment trying to figure out how to start. "Do you remember the message left in my apartment last night?"

"How could I forget? 'Time is a luxury, but not for you. Leave my family alone.'"

Nicole nodded. He'd quoted the message exactly. "I recognized those words."

Malcolm's eyebrows arched in surprise. "How?"

She opened the book to the dog-eared page. "I wrote them." She handed him the book.

He accepted the paperback from her. But it took him a few moments to wrest his surprised gaze from her face to read the page. He skimmed the words, then stiffened as he apparently came to the passage in which one of the alien ambassadors to the InterDimensions Space Station chastised the captain for human beings' lack of appreciation for time. Nicole wondered if he was experiencing the same eerie chill she'd had when she'd realized someone had used her own words to threaten her.

"I remember this scene," Malcolm murmured. "Ambassador Ore criticizes humans for trying to control time rather than enjoying the time we have. 'Time is a luxury, but not for you.'"

"Yes. The scene is significant to the plot." Nicole shrugged out of her coat without standing up, and laid it across the arm of the sofa.

"What does this mean?" The question seemed pulled from him. "Why is he quoting from your *InterDimensions* books?"

"I think we've found our link. The connection between Ty, you, and me. The stalker—our stalker—is an *InterDimensions* fan." She paused as Malcolm looked at her. "I'm the reason Ty was killed."

# Chapter Thirteen

"That's ridiculous." Malcolm wrapped his long, lean fingers around Nicole's slender upper arms and turned her to face him. "You had nothing to do with Ty's death. It was this maniac who broke into your apartment who killed him."

Nicole eased away. The room had grown cold suddenly. She rose and shrugged back into her coat, pulling it close around her. She walked to the windows. Through the blinds she saw storm clouds rolling across the Southern California sky.

She spoke with her back to him as she watched the clouds advance. "I hate the idea that someone is so enthralled with my stories, they would kill because of them."

"I still don't understand." Malcolm's frustration came through loud and clear. "What does the reference to his family have to do with Ty or your books?"

Silence settled over the room while they each considered the question. Why would someone reference his family while quoting from the *InterDimensions* books?

"I don't know," Nicole said after a while. "I can't get my mind around that one. I think I used up all its resources trying to comprehend that someone knows my books well enough to threaten me with my own words. What kind of fans has my work attracted?"

Nicole burrowed farther into her coat. She started as Malcolm rested his hands on her shoulders and began to massage her tense muscles. She reached behind her and covered his right hand with her left.

"We should tell the detectives about our theory," she said.

"I know. I should probably also tell them I've read all your books. They're going to ask me, anyway."

"I'm so sorry, Mal."

"Don't be." He slid his hand free of hers and turned away.

Nicole felt his rebuff like a cold wind breaching the defenses of her coat. His message was clear. He didn't want her empathy or support. Too bad. He had them, anyway. She spun toward him.

"How can I not be?" she demanded. "I can't imagine how much it would hurt to have anyone believe I could kill my best friend."

Malcolm kneaded the back of his neck, apparently trying to find the relief he had offered her. Nicole started to approach him, hoping he would allow her to provide him this ease. But he turned and she stilled.

"That's not my main concern right now." He dropped his arms. "For now, I need to make sure you're safe."

"That we're both safe," Nicole corrected. "We've both received threats."

"He called me only once, whereas he's become your personal pen pal," Malcolm pointed out, his dry sense of humor making what was a rare appearance these days.

Nicole winced. "I promise I won't go out again without letting you know first." She wasn't comfortable with this arrangement, but she knew she couldn't add to his worries.

Malcolm approached her. "That's not what I'm talking about." He rested his hands on her shoulders. "I think you should return to New York. It's not safe for you here right now."

Her eyes widened. "I'm not going to leave you to deal with this alone."

"You have to. That maniac broke into your apartment yesterday. In broad daylight. He's getting bolder. You've got to leave."

Nicole searched his eyes, a horrible feeling taking root. The situation had become unbearable. His best friend was murdered. The police appeared to have him as their top suspect. His company was in jeopardy of defaulting on its completion guarantor. Was he using the threats as an excuse to get out of the *InterDimensions* project? Had he reached his point of running?

"And what will you do?" She kept her voice steady, without a hint of the disappointment burning a hole in her soul.

Malcolm released her shoulders and rubbed his stubbled chin. "I'm going to find the person who killed Ty."

Nicole blinked. This wasn't the answer she had been expecting. "How?"

He shook his head. "I'm not sure yet."

Nicole smiled. He looked frustrated, baffled—but determined. She saw the warrior in him. Had he been like this when he and Tyrone were building Celestial Productions?

"Why are you going to do this?"

He looked at her as though she'd addressed him in a different language. "I'm not going to allow this psycho to skip free or to threaten you."

Nicole stepped forward. "But the police are investigating."

"And they're looking in the wrong direction. Meanwhile, this maniac is getting closer to you. Trashing your apartment was a wake-up call. You've got to go back to New York, and I've got to find this guy and stop him."

Nicole's gaze challenged his. They locked in a battle of wills from which neither was going to turn away.

She set her hands on her hips. "I'm not leaving you to deal with this alone. Ty was your best friend, but my work caused his death. I want to find his killer as well."

Malcolm began shaking his head before Nicole had finished speaking. "No. It's too dangerous for you."

"But it's not too dangerous for you?" Her voice rose in incredulity.

"Nicky, I can't search for a killer while I'm worrying about you."

"Then we'll both search for the killer while we're worrying about each other. I can't help thinking, if I hadn't agreed to make this movie, Ty would still be alive."

Malcolm approached her. "If you hadn't agreed to make this movie, your cousin might not be alive today."

Nicole turned away, caught by the truth of his statement. She'd been in a cosmic catch-22 without even realizing it. No matter what decision she'd made, she would have lost someone. Still, she was the cause of this tragedy. She wasn't hiding from that responsibility. "I'm not leaving, Mal."

Malcolm exhaled in exasperation. "Fine. For now. But I don't want you going anywhere without me."

Nicole didn't like the idea of restricting her movements. But, from the steel in Malcolm's eyes, she knew if she didn't agree to his terms, he'd try to strap her into an airplane seat. "Fine."

"And if we have any more stalking incidents, we put you on the first plane to New York."

Nicole showed some of her own steel. "We'll discuss that if the time comes."

Malcolm grunted.

Nicole sat on the sofa arm, exhausted from the negotiations. "I saw Omar Carter at the mall today."

Malcolm shoved his hands into the front pockets of his pleated gray Dockers and scowled. "Great. What did he have to say?"

"I'm telling you this because I know you'd want to know. Omar doesn't think I should spend any more time with you. He thinks you were involved with Ty's death. And he's probably telling other people that as well."

A flash of anger crossed Malcolm's features. "He probably is. I'm certain he's behind the vendors' sudden lack of confidence in me. I have to stop him. But the only way to do that is to find the person who killed Ty."

The next morning, Nicole repeated Malcolm's number from memory and waited while Denise wrote it down.

She'd called her agent after she'd showered and eaten breakfast. She had agreed with Malcolm—reluctantly—that she should take a hiatus from jogging outside until the police caught the homicidal maniac who was stalking her. Instead, she'd exercised with an hour-long weights-and-aerobics program that aired on one of the cable television stations. The toothy exercise instructor was one more reason she hoped the police caught the stalker soon.

"So, what are the cops saying about the break-in?" Denise demanded.

Nicole stretched out her calves. "Not much."

"Did they get any prints?"

"No. I guess the maniac isn't completely crazy. He knew to wear gloves." She leaned forward, stretching her quadriceps.

"This is terrible. I should never have forced you into this contract."

Nicole paused midstretch, shocked at her agent's conclusion. "You didn't force me. I chose to accept the contract."

"First, that nice Tyrone Austin is murdered, and now some crazy breaks into your apartment and trashes it."

Nicole sank onto the floor and folded into additional stretches. She debated how much she should tell Denise. She didn't want to worry her agent and friend, but she didn't think Denise could get much more worried than she was now. "We think the two situations are connected."

A startled silence met her announcement. "What?"

"Mal and I think the same person who's stalking me murdered Ty."

Nicole explained about the note left behind in her apartment and the dialogue in the second *InterDimensions* book.

"Oh, my goodness," Denise breathed. "He took the words right out of your book. Girl, this is really bad. Do you think you should still be there? Maybe you should come home."

"Mal and I believe I'll be safe here."

It was only a small fib, Nicole told herself. She and Malcolm did agree she could stay in Los Angeles. But Nicole wasn't about to tell Denise her ex-husband insisted on serving as her personal bodyguard. She didn't think that information would reassure Denise about her safety.

"What did Malcolm really say?" Denise's voice was thick with suspicion.

Nicole sighed. She should have known better than to try to put something over on Denise. "He suggested I return to New York."

"Uh-huh. And does Derrick know about this latest attack?"

Nicole leaned into her final stretch, becoming exasperated with the conversation's direction. She knew Denise was gathering support against her decision to remain in Los Angeles.

"Yes." Nicole sat cross-legged on the floor. "I called him last night."

"I'm sure he was in a really good mood after your talk, too." Denise snorted.

Nicole could hear her agent drumming her nails on her desktop. "He wasn't very happy," she said, remembering her brother's arguments for her to return home.

"I'm sure your overprotective baby brother freaked out. And he's right. It's three for three. This is not a good situation for you, girl."

"Denise, this isn't a vote. This is my choice. I've decided to stay here with Mal and find the murderer. Surely you can understand why I can't run away and allow this maniac to go unpunished?"

It was Denise's turn to hesitate. "But, Nicky, it's not safe. I don't want anything to happen to you."

"I know, and I appreciate that. I care about you, too. But would you choose any differently if the situation were reversed, and you were in my position?"

Nicole could sense Denise trying to find a way to wiggle off the hook. But she knew Denise too well. Her friend's sense of fairness was at least as strong as her own, as was her sense of loyalty and commitment.

"No," Denise admitted. "I wouldn't make another choice. I'd do the same thing you're doing."

"I know. And that's only one of the reasons I love you. Besides, you know I can't leave with the *A.M. L.A.* interview coming up," Nicole teased, trying to lighten the moment.

"Girl, they can always interview you from a safe house in New Zealand via satellite," Denise grumbled.

Nicole burst into laughter. "I'll be fine here, Denise. Really. Please don't worry. I promise to be careful."

Her promise did little to comfort her agent. Nicole could hear Denise's nails continuing the impatient beat in the background.

"So, what are the police saying about the murder investigation?" Denise asked. "Anything new?"

Nicole was becoming chilled from her damp exercise clothes. She pulled her knees up to her chest and wrapped her arms around her calves to warm herself while she updated Denise on the investigation.

"We talked to the detectives about the connection between the stalker and *InterDimensions*," she explained.

"And what was their reaction?"

Nicole shrugged. "They were interested. Providing a motive helps create a list of suspects. Unfortunately, it's a motive they can apply to Mal."

"What?" Denise screeched. "Mal may not be the same man he was when you all first married, but he couldn't have changed that much. And I know you'd never marry a murderer."

Nicole surprised herself with a chuckle. "Thanks. But the police don't know that. And I don't think they would consider as substantial evidence my opinion of someone's character."

Denise snorted. "How is Mal holding up?"

Nicole thought of the wall he'd erected to block his feelings from her. "Stoically, as usual."

"Does he look like he's going to bolt?"

"No. He seems determined to find Ty's killer, clear his name, and move on with the movie."

"Well, that's good. Maybe in the four years you've been apart, he found his courage."

"Or maybe this is something he thinks is worth fighting for." Nicole pushed herself up to a standing position.

"Well, I don't know about that." Denise sounded flustered. "It's not really an apples-to-apples comparison."

"I know. Intellectually, I realize proving you didn't kill your best friend is not the same as saving your marriage. It's just that . . ." Nicole hesitated. "My heart can't stop making the comparison. When I needed him to fight for us, he wasn't there."

"Nicky, there are always at least three sides to every story. Your side, his side, and the truth," Denise said. "You believe one thing. He believes something else. The truth is somewhere in the middle."


Two days later, Malcolm looked up from the proposals spread across his desk, surprised to see Rita standing in his doorway. Usually, he heard her purposeful march to his office. His gaze bounced down to the stack of envelopes and papers cradled in her arms, then lifted to study her eyes. "Is something wrong, Rita?"

"I've sorted the mail."

His gaze returned to the items she carried. He glanced at his in-box, where she usually set his mail. Granted, the tray was full, but its condition shouldn't prevent her from depositing his mail. "All right," he prompted.

She continued fidgeting in his doorway. "The *Silver Screen Preview* arrived today."

Malcolm cocked his head questioningly. They received the publication every Wednesday. He glanced again at the envelopes and papers in her arms. Then he remembered his aborted interview with the *Silver Screen Preview* reporter, Nathan Rutherford.

He squeezed his eyes shut. "I suppose there's an article about us in this issue?"

"Yes."

He opened his eyes and extended a hand for the mail. "Is it more bad news?"

Rita laid the mail in his in-box, then handed him the publication. "I don't think you'll like the way Mr. Rutherford has invaded your privacy."

Malcolm put the publication on his desk and looked down at the front cover. The headline of the second cover article read *INTERDIMENSIONS* AUTHOR STANDS BY HER MAN: THE SECRET MARRIAGE OF COLLINS AND CELESTIAL PRODUCTIONS OWNER, BRYANT."

Malcolm clenched his teeth. "Shit."

"I didn't know you and Nicole were married," Rita said.

"We're divorced." Malcolm skimmed the article to find out how much of his personal life would be entertaining his industry associates during their morning coffee.

"I don't think Mr. Rutherford got to that part." Rita's tone was dry.

"Shit." Malcolm leaned back in his chair and closed his eyes.

"How angry are you?"

"Very." Malcolm spoke without opening his eyes. He concentrated on the breathing exercise Tyrone had told him about. It still wasn't working.

"I thought you would be. I'm sorry to be the one to tell you."

Malcolm opened his eyes and leaned forward. "Don't worry about it. I appreciate your trying to prepare me."

He skimmed the article again, turning the page when the article continued inside the magazine.

"How did he find out about this? How did he even know to look for it?" Malcolm muttered.

He paused as he remembered Nathan's words: *"What is your relationship with Ms. Collins? Why is she staying with you when everyone else has left?"*

Sow a seed and the plant will grow. Then Nathan Rutherford will write an article about it.

Rita leaned over the desk and looked down at the page. "Are you going to call Mr. Rutherford?"

"No." Malcolm's tone was short. "I'm not going to give him a reaction."

He closed the publication and tossed it into his growing in-box. He eyed the tray's contents. It would take another long day and perhaps this weekend to get through all that mail. He glanced at his in-box again. Definitely the weekend.

Rita nodded. "I thought you'd say that." She straightened. "How do you want me to respond to any media calls?"

Malcolm groaned. Of course this article was going to generate a lot of interest. Something more for him to deal with. Or not. "We don't have any comments. We won't deny or confirm the story."

Rita frowned. "Are you sure? Maybe if you tell them you and Nicole are no longer married, the media will go away."

Malcolm twirled his pen between his index and middle fingers. His gaze remained on the magazine balanced on top of his in-box. "No. If you answer one question, you'll invite more. Don't give them anything. Just say, 'No comment.' Hopefully they'll go away."

Rita nodded. "Okay." She pivoted on her heel, then paused and turned back. "Nicole seems like a very nice lady."

Malcolm looked up. Rita's eyes shone with curiosity. "She is very nice."

"And you're a very nice man."

"Thank you." Malcolm set down his pen.

Rita leaned against the doorframe. "It's too bad the two of you couldn't work things out before. But, perhaps you've been given a second chance."

Malcolm smiled, surprised Rita's thoughts mirrored his own. He knew she meant well, but he didn't want people speculating on his social life—or lack thereof. "Nicky and I are working together. This project isn't about our past," he lied.

"Oh, well." Rita sighed. "Is there anything else you need right now?"

"No, but thanks again for the heads-up on the article."

"You're welcome." Rita pushed away from the doorframe and charged down the hall.

Malcolm watched until she disappeared, then pulled the trade magazine from his in-box to finish reading the article. Just as Rita had noted, information on their divorce was conspicuously absent, making it seem as though they were still married. What would people think about Nicole living on the opposite coast for the past four years?

Nicole. She was going to be pretty ticked off—at least as much as he was—to have their personal lives revealed so publicly without her approval. He checked his watch. He had a lot of work to get through. He would wait until he got home tonight to tell Nicole about the article. He glanced at the papers strewn across his desk. Late tonight. He'd better call to let her know when she could expect him home.

Malcolm felt his lips tip in a small smile. It had been years—four, actually—since he'd wanted to check in with someone about his schedule. Since there had been anyone who cared. He warned himself against becoming addicted to the high.

He sat alone on the plywood bench, watching the waves crash against the shore and thinking about his

*InterDimensions* family. It was early spring, and the beach was practically empty this Wednesday afternoon. With the roar of the waves dampening whatever sounds intruded, he felt isolated from the rest of the world. He loved the feeling. The only thing marring his enjoyment was the article in the *Silver Screen Preview*.

He glanced at the cover of the magazine lying beside him on the bench. So Malcolm and Nicole were married. How strange. In all the interviews he'd read about her, she'd never mentioned a husband. She'd mentioned other family members, though. And she lived in New York.

*Well, never mind that.* He shrugged the mystery aside. The point was, he'd figured out why Nicole had betrayed his family. Malcolm. The producer could be very convincing when he wanted something. He'd witnessed Malcolm's powers of persuasion. He could understand Nicole's defection. But she never should have allowed Malcolm to come between her and the family. Loyalty was vital, but in a moment of weakness, Nicole had forgotten that.

He'd felt pressured to take extreme action to remove the threat to his family. But he had been reluctant to hurt Nicole. After all, she had created the family. She had established their dynamics. She'd nurtured them and helped them grow. For those reasons, she deserved to be judged with more leniency than he otherwise would have afforded her. She was their mother, and mothers were to be placed on pedestals. That's why he'd released his rage and disillusionment on her apartment instead of on her. He'd wanted to make it clear she could no longer ignore him.

He watched the waves roar toward the beach and explode against the sand. Seagulls circled above, struggling against the same wind that beat against the ocean. Their screams bounced around him.

He glanced again at the *Silver Screen Preview*. Nicole had understood his message, and she had left L.A.

Or had she?

He stiffened as a horrible thought occurred to him. Suppose Malcolm had persuaded her to stay? Malcolm was committed to making the *InterDimensions* movie. Nicole was weak. How could he be sure she hadn't allowed Malcolm to turn her against the family again? How could he be sure she had gone back to New York?

He would have to follow Malcolm. Malcolm would know where Nicole was. He stood and picked up the *Silver Screen Preview*, rolling the magazine into a tube. Brisk strides carried him back to the street.

And if Nicole were still in L.A.?

If she were still in L.A., he would have to try harder to convince her to leave.

# CHAPTER FOURTEEN

Nicole turned down the oven's temperature, setting the ground-turkey enchiladas on WARM. She gave the garden salad a final toss before putting it in the refrigerator. Malcolm would be home soon.

She walked to the threshold of the dining room, and her critical gaze surveyed the table one final time. Candles. Fresh flowers. Linen napkins. Formal place mats. It looked warm and inviting. Perhaps too inviting. Bordering on seductive.

Nicole gathered the place settings and transferred them onto the kitchen table. Her intent was to help Malcolm unwind, not to give him ideas or seduce him. She tripped over that thought. Of course she wasn't trying to seduce him. She was just cooking him—them—a meal. Just because it was one of his favorite dishes didn't signify anything. She wanted to help him relax with a hot, healthy meal after a long, hard day.

When he'd called earlier, he had sounded tense, as though he were measuring his words with her. If she had been a suspicious wife, she would have suspected him of hiding something. But she wasn't any kind of wife, so she didn't have the right to be suspicious of him or hurt that he wasn't taking her into his confidence. Malcolm hadn't taken her into his confidence even when they had been married.

The sound of the garage door rising brought Nicole back to the present. She pulled the plates out of the cupboard and set them on the counter near the stove. She placed the salad and dressing on the kitchen table and was taking the enchiladas out of the oven when she heard Malcolm's footsteps approaching the room.

"What smells so good?" His voice sounded much more relaxed. She wanted to think the spicy aromas of her cooking put that smile in his voice.

"It's the enchiladas." She turned and saw his boyish grin.

"You made enchiladas?" Pleased surprise lightened his tone. He studied the place settings, salad, and pitcher of lemonade on the kitchen table.

"Yes. Do you want to change before we eat?"

Malcolm returned his attention to her, their gazes locking for a moment. Then his regard dropped to her bright lilac jersey tucked into form-fitting black jeans. Nicole forced herself to remain still under his intense scrutiny.

"Everything looks and smells great, Nicky. Thank you." His voice caressed her from across the room. "I think I'll take your suggestion and change first. I'll be right back."

In less than fifteen minutes, he'd changed and joined her for dinner.

"This is fantastic." Malcolm forked up more of his enchilada.

"That's the second time you've said that." Nicole chuckled, pleased but embarrassed by his compliments. "I'm beginning to think you either haven't eaten in days or you're trying to convince yourself the meal is edible."

Malcolm laughed, topping off their glasses from the pitcher of lemonade. "Do you remember the first time you made enchiladas for me?"

Nicole's fork stilled on her plate. Of course she did. It was the first and last time she'd made them. "It was your birthday." *Six years ago.*

Nicole fought the instinct to shy away from memories of Malcolm—good and bad. They all reminded her of their divorce and her inability to come to terms with that failure.

But now, sitting at the kitchen table enjoying dinner with her ex-husband, it was difficult to separate old memories from the ones they were creating tonight. Past and present were blending, allowing her to view both without bitterness or self-castigation. They'd made a lot of happy memories together, and Nicole had to admit she didn't like the person she'd become without them.

Her heart softened. "I didn't have enough money to take you to a restaurant, so I made a special dinner at home instead. Enchiladas were one of your favorite foods."

"They still are," Malcolm added, drinking the lemonade.

Nicole returned to her meal. "I got the recipe from a co-worker. They didn't turn out too badly, either."

"They were fantastic."

Nicole's smile spread. "Do you ever make them for yourself?"

Malcolm's smile dimmed. "No."

Nicole fought not to fall into his gaze. "But you claim to be able to cook."

Malcolm chuckled and returned his attention to his plate. "You've tasted my cooking. You know it's more than a claim."

She felt a smile tickle her lips. "Anyone can open a can of spaghetti."

"Hey! That wasn't from a can," he said, feigning outrage.

Nicole gave him a cheeky look before changing the subject. "I've been wondering why you were so willing to let me act as co-producer on the *InterDimensions* project. Were you that anxious to sweeten the pot for me?"

"If I had wanted to sweeten the pot, I would have done what everyone else did and offered you more money. I wouldn't have jeopardized the project and my company's reputation by agreeing to work with someone whose talent I didn't believe in."

Nicole swallowed her laughter. "You wouldn't risk your company's reputation for me?"

Malcolm's smile curled her toes. "No, sweetheart. I'm sorry, but I wouldn't."

Nicole ducked her head, carrying on with the game. "That's not very romantic."

Malcolm chuckled, low and deep. "I've never been accused of being romantic."

She arched a brow, even as her heart softened with more memories. "That's not strictly true. You had your moments."

"I remember those, too," he murmured.

Nicole ended the teasing before she spontaneously combusted. "Thank you for saying you believe in my abilities."

"I'm not just saying that. I mean it."

His cocoa-colored eyes warmed to a simmer. For Nicole, the line between past and present blurred even more. She stepped back before they erased the line entirely.

"How about some dessert?" she blurted.

Malcolm continued to study her, and for a moment, Nicole was afraid he would ignore her attempt to redraw the line. Then he blinked, and curiosity replaced heat.

"You made dessert?"

Nicole smiled. "Not made, bought. It's ice cream."

Malcolm patted his flat stomach. "That's tempting, but I'm stuffed. I think I'll pass."

She shrugged. "I'm pretty full myself."

Malcolm pushed away from the table, gathering dishes. "In that case, I'll clear the table."

"I'll help." Nicole stood, collecting items as well.

"No, I can manage this alone. You cooked dinner."

She shook her head. "If the two of us work together, we'll get the cleaning done more quickly."

The table was cleared and the dishes set to wash. There was nothing else keeping Nicole in the kitchen— except the hunger growing between her and her ex-husband. She continued to rub her dry hands with a hand towel while she considered her next move.

"Well, thank you for dinner," Malcolm said. "It was—"

"Fantastic," she finished for him with a smile.

"Yes." Malcolm paused.

Nicole saw a question in his eyes. Then he blinked, and the question disappeared.

"You're welcome," Nicole replied, searching his gaze.

"I brought some work home." He glanced at his wrist-watch. "I'm going to get through as much of it as I can and then turn in."

Disappointment warred with relief. He'd offered her an out. However, she sensed a hesitation in him that made her think he would be willing to change his plans for the evening—if she was interested. Was she?

Nicole reached over to put the hand towel back on its peg. The task gave her a moment to regroup. She turned back to Malcolm, tucking her hands into her jeans pockets. "I'm going to read before I go to sleep, so I'll say good night now."

"Okay." Malcolm hesitated again. "Good night."

Nicole dragged her gaze from his. She walked around him and left the kitchen with a deliberate pace. Each step drew her farther away from Malcolm. But this time she wasn't certain it was the direction in which she wanted to go.

Malcolm sat at the desk in his home office. Piled in front of him was information on casting companies he could contact to replace Eunice Gannon. He flipped through the paperwork, but his mind was down the hall in the guest bedroom with Nicole. Their shared dinner had sent Malcolm into a time warp, making him feel as though they were still married. But that wasn't the only reason he believed Nicole should be in his bed rather than in the guest room. He'd been having those thoughts on and off for the past four years. Unfortunately, it seemed those images were destined to remain in his dreams—with the exception of that one interlude he would treasure forever.

"Mal?"

Nicole's voice teased his fantasy, sounding just within his reach. When she called again, he looked up and caught her hovering in the doorway.

"I'm sorry to disturb you," she said, clasping her hands. "You seem busy."

Malcolm shook his head. This wasn't a fantasy. She was really there. He wondered what she wanted. He didn't dare hope the evening had affected her in the same way it had touched him. "No, I'm not busy. Is there something you need?"

Nicole shrugged, walking into the room. "I'm having trouble concentrating. I thought I'd see how you were doing. Are you having trouble concentrating?"

Malcolm swallowed at the smoky question in her ebony eyes. He swiveled his chair to face her as she came around his desk. "A little."

Nicole's soft smile made Malcolm's pulse race. She came to a stop an arm's length from him. "Do you think we're having the same problem?" she whispered.

"I don't know," Malcolm whispered back. "What's your problem?"

Nicole tilted her head, humor and desire swirling in her eyes. "This." She placed her hands on his shoulders and leaned in to draw her tongue across the seam of his lips.

Malcolm's lips answered her call immediately. They opened, and Nicole's tongue swept inside, stroking the roof of Malcolm's mouth and swirling a pattern on his tongue. Malcolm's stomach muscles quivered. His hands rose, traveling over her firm, smooth hips to clasp her taut waist. He pulled her onto his lap, and she flowed into him.

She smelled warm and womanly. A remembered scent

that filled his dreams. He molded her closer; her soft
weight on his lap filled his mind with wild possibilities
and wicked options. Nicole moaned into his mouth,
straining closer. She shifted until she straddled him, and
Malcolm realized their minds entertained the same
images. This Nicole moved like a woman ready to claim
what she wanted. The experience sharpened the feelings
he still had for her.

"Wait," he growled. "Your pants."

Nicole mumbled a response, then pulled away from
him. As he watched, she stripped off her jeans, underpants, and socks in one movement. Grace and urgency.
Malcolm stood to fumble out of his own clothes, then
whisked her jersey over her head. He brought her close,
wrapping her warm body into his. When he stepped
back, her breasts bounced free as her black, lace bra
floated to the ground.

Nicole chuckled breathlessly. "You haven't lost your
touch."

Malcolm smiled despite the painful throbbing
between his legs.

Nicole pressed Malcolm back into his chair, grateful
when he surrendered to her lead. She wanted to savor
the foreplay. His touch had become even more confident, more assured than it had been years before. *A re-
flection of the man.* Confident in what he wanted and in
what he could give in return.

But the hunger clawed in her, demanding to be fed.
She straddled his lap, ducking her head to claim his lips.
As she sucked his tongue deeper into her mouth, she
lowered herself onto his hot, pulsing manhood. Inch by
solid, demanding inch. She drove them both frantic with
the contrast between her patience and their need.

Nicole tightened her grip on his shoulders, massag-
ing the muscles there. She felt Malcolm tremble beneath her hands and pulse between her thighs. Nicole
threw her head back and undulated her torso against
him, crazed by the exquisite torture of her soft breasts

grazing his furred chest. She felt him working her hips, increasing the friction of their movements. She moaned and pleaded, gasped and screamed. His body urged her on, encouraging her to take that final leap. She arched her back, and he claimed her nipples. Sucking, nipping, tugging at them.

And the hunger went wild.

She shattered against him, her body rocked and jerked, tossed by the powerful release. She felt Malcolm slam her hips against his lap one last time as he flowed into her, his thighs stiffening beneath her hips.

And the hunger quieted, satisfied for the moment.

Early morning sunlight tickled Nicole's eyes. She squeezed them tight, but the call of a new day would not be silenced. She cracked her eyes open. As her gaze locked with Malcolm's, she had a discomforting sense of déjà vu.

He lay on his side, the sheet pulled only to his hips, leaving his well-sculpted chest bare to her fascinated gaze. His head was propped on his arm. He extended his other hand to cover her lips with his index finger.

"Let's try revising the script," Malcolm suggested in a husky morning voice. His smile contrasted with the wary look in his cocoa eyes. "I think our last morning-after scene left a bit to be desired. Let's try another take. How 'bout you start the scene with, 'Good morning, Mal.' And maybe add, 'You were fantastic last night.'"

Malcolm's wicked chuckle held a hint of uncertainty that relaxed the tension Nicole hadn't realized she held. Knowing he was as nervous about this morning as she had been upon awakening put her at ease and appealed to the imp in her.

Nicole licked the finger Malcolm had rested on her lips. Heat flared in his eyes as he moved his finger away.

"Good morning, Mal," she parroted obediently. Then

she grinned. "I was fantastic last night. And you were pretty okay, too."

Malcolm's eyebrows arched. "Pretty okay?"

Nicole shrugged, struggling to hold back her laughter. "Yeah."

Malcolm's eyes glinted, and his lips curved. He rolled on top of Nicole and pressed his hips into hers. His morning arousal melted her.

"Will you give me a chance to try again?" he murmured into her neck.

Nicole shivered. "You're always welcome to try."


Later that morning, Nicole parked a couple of blocks away from the beach. The thought of running in circles around Malcolm's neighborhood hadn't appealed to her. She'd run enough circles in her mind: Could she reconcile with her ex-husband? Would the second time around be any better? Or should they just be friends? Their on-again, off-again relationship was driving Nicole crazy. She needed a straight path on which to travel from point A to point B. The jogging trail leading from Manhattan Beach to Hermosa Beach seemed the perfect solution.

At least it had seemed a perfect solution to her. Malcolm had not been happy with the idea. But he'd reluctantly accepted her decision after she pointed out that the trail paralleled a residential neighborhood and was visible from the streets on either side. It also had a lot of foot traffic from walkers and joggers. He'd admitted none of that had changed in the past four years.

She locked her rental car and set a brisk pace for the trail. She had fond memories of the path. She and Malcolm had run there often when they'd first moved to Los Angeles. The packed earth and wood chips were easy on the knees. Trees and evergreen bushes bordered the trail and scented the air.

She looked forward to the run, to the distance she could put between herself and the feelings that had assailed her last night and earlier this morning. She'd felt as though she'd been jettisoned back to the time when she and Malcolm were still happily married. It was a disturbing feeling, but what had troubled her the most was her wish that it could be that easy. That she could just cook a meal and save her marriage.

Nicole snorted at the thought. She looked around, embarrassed to realize she had made the noise aloud. Luckily, no one was near enough to hear her. Pedestrian traffic was minimal at this time on a Thursday morning.

Although, there was one person a few yards ahead of her. With baggy sweats and an oversized hooded jacket, it was difficult to tell the person's gender. She thought the stranger might be a young man. In any event, he hadn't reacted to her snort of disgust.

The stranger was stretching next to his silver BMW as though he were also preparing to go jogging. In his worn, torn sweats, he looked incongruous next to the expensive luxury vehicle. For a fleeting moment, Nicole wondered if he were stealing the car. She glanced at him again. Surely he wouldn't be so casual about committing grand theft of an auto in broad daylight.

Deciding caution was the better part of valor, Nicole glued her attention to the sidewalk and maintained a steady pace as she walked past the young man. If he were a car thief, she didn't want him to think she was a witness to his crime. The trail was just one block away. Once she reached it, she would put this incident behind her.

Arriving at the trail, Nicole set the timer on her athletic watch. She paused, an uncomfortable sensation stirring the hairs on the back of her neck. She turned and saw the stranger across the street from her. With his head bent, the hood of his jacket covered the top part of his face and cast the rest in shadows. It gave him a sinister anonymity. Nicole forced herself to shrug off her discomfort. She activated her stopwatch and started jogging at an easy pace.

After several strides, Nicole glanced over her shoulder

and saw the stranger jogging a couple of yards behind her. She faced forward and continued on, but her concern grew.

Normally while jogging, Nicole allowed her mind to wander. She plotted her books or made to-do lists. But today, the scent of the pines around her and the cushion of the wood chips beneath her were overshadowed by the sound of the man behind her.

She was alerted instantly when his footfalls grew closer. Maintaining her stride, Nicole risked another peek over her shoulder. She tensed when she realized he was gaining on her. But he hadn't moved to the side to pass her. Instead, he kept his position as though he intended to run right over her.

Nicole increased her speed, passing two well-toned, middle-aged women on her way. She grabbed her courage and checked behind her again. The stranger had increased his speed as well, maintaining a standard distance behind her.

Teetering on the fine line between concern and fear, she assessed her options. She could stop and confront him, but she had no idea if he would become violent. The only thing she had that resembled a weapon was her car key. Very small comfort. At least they weren't alone on the trail. She'd passed two women and was gaining on another couple, a man and a woman. And farther ahead were four men. Nicole could only hope the stranger wouldn't harm her in front of all these people.

But if he stayed with her for her entire jog, what would she do when she came to the end of the trail?

She could still hear the man behind her. He seemed to be having trouble controlling his breathing. Her pace appeared to be a bit too fast for him. Her panicky thoughts stuttered to a stop at that point.

As she caught up with the next couple, she nodded good morning, then passed them—hard. She strained to filter out every sound but that of the stranger stalking her. His breathing was more labored. With desperate hope, Nicole increased her speed until she was running flat out. She channeled everything she had into her legs and pumped her arms for more leverage. She concentrated on her breathing, taking deep, controlled breaths. Four counts in, hold, four counts out. She had to stay strong. She had to stay focused. She had to get herself out of this situation—on her own terms.

Ahead of her were the four well-muscled young men she'd noticed at the start of her run. She came to the end of the trail less than a minute after them. They were walking in circles, shaking out their legs, but they paused when she sped up to them. She stopped and looked around. The stranger wasn't in sight.

"You shouldn't stop so suddenly," one of the men said with the camaraderie of a fellow runner. "You should walk it out."

"Yes," Nicole panted, forcing her quaking legs to keep moving. "You're right. Thank you."

"No problem." The young man grinned. "That was some finish."

"Thank you. You guys had a great run, too." Her smile was strained, her breathing labored.

The young men beamed with the pleasure of a good run and hard-worked muscles.

Nicole looked around again, shaking out her legs. Still no sign of the stranger. Her breath was coming back, but her pulse still galloped with warning.

"I wonder if I could ask a favor," she began. "Could you walk with me to my car? It's not far. I'm just a little concerned because there was a young man parked near me, and he made me uncomfortable."

They agreed as though embracing a new member of their running club and joined her on the short walk to her car. Nicole divided her attention between their discussion of time splits and personal records, and her curiosity about the stranger. Where had he disappeared to? Had he indeed been a threat to her?

When they passed the spot where Nicole had first seen the stranger, the silver BMW was gone.

"The doctor is impressed by how well my rehabilitation is going," Simone said.

Nicole had called to check on her cousin. She was thrilled by the improvement she could hear in Simone's voice. She sounded stronger, even stronger than the last time they'd spoken, which was the week before Nicole had moved in with Malcolm.

Simone was still in the hospital, but if she continued to improve at her current pace, she would return home shortly.

"Just make certain you don't overdo things," Nicole cautioned. "You don't want to wear yourself out and have to start therapy all over again."

"I know. I'll pace myself." Simone's singsong tone gave the impression her cousin had made this promise several times to other family members.

"Good. How's Lynnie?" Nicole asked, although Derrick had assured her that as Simone's health improved, so did Lynnie's sleep patterns. Her cousin's daughter hadn't had the sad dream in weeks.

"She misses you," Simone said. "So do I."

Nicole experienced a yearning to be two places at the same time. "I miss you, too."

"How's the movie coming along?"

"It's coming along just fine." Nicole winced at her non-committal response.

Nicole, Derrick, and Simone's brother, Guy, had agreed not to tell anyone else about the threats or Tyrone's death. They didn't want to worry Aunt Rose, Simone, or especially Lynnie. They needed to focus on getting Simone well and bringing her home.

But Simone must have heard something in Nicole's tone that caused her concern. "Is everything going okay with you and Malcolm?" her cousin asked.

YOU BELONG TO ME 237

"Yes." Nicole was relieved she could tell the truth this time. "Our working relationship is improving every day."

"Then what aren't you telling me?"

"What makes you think I'm not telling you something?" Nicole asked out of curiosity and in an attempt to stall.

"I can hear it in your voice. You're measuring your words. You never do that unless you're trying really hard not to tell me something."

"Everything's fine, Si. Please don't worry." Nicole toyed with the phone cord.

Simone's sigh was filled with frustration. "Guy and D are measuring their words, too."

Nicole chuckled. "What? Could it be some kind of conspiracy?"

"Yes. A conspiracy of silence." Simone's sassiness was returning. Another good sign. "Now, tell me about this *A.M. L.A.* interview. Can you send me a tape?"

They bantered back and forth for a while. Then, before saying good-bye, Nicole urged her cousin to get some rest.

She hated lying to Simone. They'd grown up like sisters. Nicole knew she would be terribly hurt if the situation were reversed, and Simone didn't tell her she was being threatened. But she couldn't risk causing her cousin anxiety and jeopardizing her recovery. Simone already felt guilty for bringing Malcolm back into Nicole's life, although Nicole had insisted Simone wasn't responsible for that twist of fate. That debate had dominated their conversation the last time they'd spoken.

Nicole sighed, shook her head, and rose to pour herself another cup of coffee. The steam wafted up, carrying the beans' rich, strong scent. She stirred in the milk and sweetener, then leaned against the kitchen counter for the first sip of her second cup.

She certainly wasn't going to tell Simone about her experience at the trail that morning. When she'd returned home, she'd been able to get into the shower without seeing Malcolm. He'd knocked on the bathroom door, asked if she'd had a good run, and told her he'd see her later.

Nicole had allowed the hot water to pelt out the tension and soothe her frayed nerves. Then she'd spent an hour trying to convince herself she'd overreacted. That the strange young man on the path hadn't been some weirdo plotting to hurt her. However, she couldn't shake the feeling he had meant her harm. But what could she do about it? Call the police and tell them some guy who hadn't spoken to her and hadn't touched her had scared her? Oh, and, no, she hadn't seen his face. She could just imagine their reaction to that.

Nicole turned her attention to a more productive project. She curled both hands around the warm coffee cup and padded barefoot to the sofa. She picked up the printout of the companies interested in the *InterDimensions* movie rights. Everything pointed to the movie project being at the heart of this nightmare. The list Denise had e-mailed her included the names of the production companies' contact people, phone numbers, and addresses. The list had only eight entries, but she wasn't trying to feed her ego. She was trying to find a killer.

The trick would be to identify the killer from this list of strangers. How would she do that? She couldn't call and ask them how disappointed they were not to have the movie rights. Nor could she ask to what lengths they would be willing to go to acquire the rights from Celestial Productions. Would they kill for it? Definitely a direct approach, but probably not a productive one. She needed to consult with someone who knew the industry and its players.

Nicole checked her watch. It was minutes away from 11:00 A.M. She didn't want to discuss this with Malcolm while he was at work. He was very busy and may not have a full hour to spare for lunch. She should wait until he got home and could give her his undivided attention.

But impatience gnawed at her. Who could she talk to in the meantime?

Nicole wondered if Joyce knew any of the names on the list. She dialed the woman's phone number from memory. Joyce picked up the call on the third ring. "Hello?"

Nicole was pleasantly surprised to hear Joyce sounding more alert. The few times she'd seen the other woman since Tyrone's funeral, Joyce had been listless and distracted.

"Hi, Joyce. It's Nicky." Nicole shifted forward on the sofa to lay the list on Malcolm's coffee table. "What are you up to?"

"I'm just tidying up some things." Joyce's voice lost some of its enthusiasm.

"Can you use a break?" Nicole asked, thinking perhaps they could both benefit from her visit. She could get some information, and Joyce would have a distraction.

Apparently, Joyce agreed. "You know, I think I could. Do you want to come over?"

"Yes, if you have the time. I wanted to ask if you recognized any of the people on the list of companies that bid for the *InterDimensions* movie rights."

"Sure, I'll take a look. But why do you want to know that?"

Nicole hesitated but decided to prepare Joyce before her visit. "I think Ty's death might have something to do with the movie project." Nicole heard Joyce's indrawn breath.

"I'll be waiting for you," the other woman said.

"I'll leave right now."

It was a short drive to the house Joyce had shared with Tyrone. On the way over, Nicole reviewed the questions she would ask about the people on Denise's list. Lost in thought, she almost missed the final turn onto Joyce's street.

Joyce opened the door to let Nicole in.

"Hi. I'm sorry my call upset you." Nicole crossed the threshold and stepped aside so Joyce could lock them in.

"Don't worry about it. I'm getting better. I don't feel quite as weepy as I used to." Still, Joyce's smile didn't make it to her eyes. She led the way into the living room and gestured to Nicole to choose a seat. "Can I get you something to drink?"

"I'd love a glass of water."

"Sure. I'll be right back." Nicole listened as Joyce's footsteps faded toward the kitchen.

She gazed around the room, surprised and pleased by the changes she saw. The drapes were drawn back, allowing strong, natural light to penetrate the white sheers beneath. The room was tidier and felt as though it had been aired out. The blankets and pillows were still in evidence but were folded and neatly stacked aside. Nicole felt a twinge of empathy. Some adjustments, such as sleeping alone in a bed full of memories, took longer.

Nicole was smiling at the *Star Wars* storm troopers scaling the drapes when Joyce returned with coasters and two glasses of ice water.

"I'm very curious about this list you were telling me about. The police seem to have stalled on the investigation since they can't find any concrete evidence against Mal and me."

Nicole looked up. "They still think you're a suspect?"

"It seems that way. Every now and then they call to ask me strange follow-up questions like, 'Have you read the *InterDimensions* books?'"

Cringing inside, Nicole forced herself to hold Joyce's gaze. "I told the police I think there may be a link between my books and Ty's murder."

Joyce froze with the glass of water at her lips. She slowly lowered her arm. "You think Ty's murderer is an *InterDimensions* fan?"

Nicole nodded. "Did Mal tell you about the letter he found in Ty's desk?"

"Yes, he did." Joyce's tone was subdued. "I wish I had asked Ty more about the letter when he first told me about it, but he believed he'd received it by mistake."

"Did Mal tell you I've received similar messages?"

Joyce's dark-brown eyes grew to the size of saucers. "No."

"The messages I've received are virtually identical to the letter Mal found in Ty's desk. But we couldn't identify a connection until the recent break-in at my apartment."

"Wait. Someone broke into your apartment?" Joyce's voice rose several octaves.

"Yes." Nicole paused to arrange her thoughts. "I'm going too fast. Let me start from the beginning."

Nicole described the phone calls and letters she'd received, including the note that had been slipped under her door. She admitted at first she'd thought the calls were misdials. She explained about reporting the letters to the police, knowing they wouldn't be able to do anything other than start a file. Still, she explained to Joyce, she'd kept copies of all the letters. Nicole told her everything she could think of, bringing her up-to-date with the vandalism in her apartment. She deliberately left out her panic at the trail this morning. She thought perhaps stress was making her paranoid.

"The message the stalker left in my apartment included a quote from one of my books," Nicole concluded.

Joyce leaned forward. "What quote?"

"One of Ambassador Ore's lines from book two: 'Time is a luxury, but not for you.'"

Joyce's eyes were troubled. "I can only imagine how frightened you must have been."

Nicole shook her head. "This is a frightening time for all of us."

Joyce turned her attention to the list of independent production companies Nicole had given her. "I've read about a couple of these producers in Ty's industry magazines."

"You read the industry magazines?"

"I'm really into movies. I enjoy reading the behind-the-scenes stuff—who's planning what, what projects are coming in over budget, and why. That kind of thing."

Nicole nodded her understanding. She'd felt the same way when she and Malcolm had been married. She still watched the entertainment programs and read the trade magazines that gave glimpses into the industry's backstage happenings. She shook off the nostalgia as Joyce's attention returned to the list.

"I've met most of these people at events Ty, Mal, and I attended—trade shows and stuff," Joyce continued.

"What can you tell me about them?"

"I don't know any of these people well, but they seemed okay to me." Joyce looked up at Nicole. "What sort of things are you looking for?"

"I'm not really certain." Nicole finished her glass of water. She allowed her mind to wander as she created a character profile—similar to the ones she wrote for her fictional characters—that fit the role. "The kind of person who would threaten people anonymously. A non-confrontational personality. Someone who exhibited a potential for violent behavior. Someone who would do anything to win."

Joyce frowned as though trying to dig deeper into her memories. "I can't really see any of these people doing those things. Although, as I said, I don't know them very well. The only one I'm sort of familiar with is Omar Carter, and that's only from what Ty and Mal have told me."

Nicole remembered the nervousness she had experienced when Omar had appeared unexpectedly before her at the mall. "What have they told you?"

"Ty, Mal, and Omar used to work for Leo."

Nicole felt her lips part in surprise. Why hadn't Malcolm mentioned that? "That must have been interesting."

Joyce smiled. "'Interesting' is one way of putting it. Omar comes from a very wealthy family whose connections were often very helpful. He liked to name-drop. That's one of his many habits that would drive Ty and Mal nuts. Another one was taking credit for work he didn't do."

Nicole shook her head as she imagined Malcolm's reaction to that. She knew she would feel the same way. "I can see where that would be a problem."

"So can I. When the guys were ready to go out on their own, Omar wanted to join them. As I said, he comes from money and was willing to bring some of that money with him. But the guys knew they wouldn't be able to work with Omar, so they said no."

Nicole was proud of Malcolm and Tyrone for making what must have been a difficult decision. She was certain they could have used the extra capital, but they hadn't been willing to compromise themselves for it.

"That must have come as a surprise to Omar." Nicole leaned forward to place her empty glass on a coaster.

"Yes, it did." Joyce chuckled. "For months, he kept trying to change their minds, but the guys wouldn't budge. Finally, Omar decided to start his own company."

"How did Mal and Ty feel about the competition?"

Joyce frowned. "At first they didn't care. They were very busy building their own company. But then Omar started going after the same projects they were bidding on. That's when they started paying attention."

A cold feeling grew in Nicole's gut. She remembered Omar introducing himself outside her apartment and badgering her about the *InterDimensions* movie rights. She also thought about the conversation Malcolm had had with Omar at his fitness club. Her encounter at the mall with the rival producer took on another dimension. "How did Omar find out about the projects?"

Joyce shook her head. "He has amazing contacts. I know he's very friendly with the *Silver Screen Preview* reporter Nathan Rutherford. I think he gets some of his information from Nathan. They seem to be using each other."

"Why do you think that?"

Joyce rolled her eyes. "I've met Nathan. I can't believe he has any real friends. He wants to start his own publication, and he's hoping Omar will bankroll him."

Nicole smiled. "Is this all conjecture, or are you basing your speculation on hearsay?"

Joyce chuckled again. "Some of it is conjecture, but some of it I've heard myself. Nathan told the guys and me that he doesn't want to be a reporter all of his life. He told us he wanted to start his own magazine publishing company."

Nicole nodded, understanding Joyce's reasoning better. But Nathan didn't concern her right now; Omar did. "So would you describe Omar as obsessively competitive?"

Joyce seemed to consider the question and her answer. Nicole didn't rush her. She didn't want an easy answer; she wanted a truthful one.

"Yes, I think I would," Joyce said. "But he seems to wait for other people to do the research and determine the profit margin. Then, if the profits are attractive enough, he'll put in a bid. And with his family's money, he can afford to outbid most people."

It was Nicole's turn to be quiet as she considered Joyce's words in relation to her theory about the movie project. She was beginning to doubt her idea had substance. Nicole found it hard to believe another producer would embark on a campaign of terror to obtain the *InterDimensions* movie rights. She looked around Joyce's living room, taking in Tyrone's sci-fi accents. *Star Wars. Aliens. The Terminator.* Those were blockbuster movies. In comparison, a movie based on her book would not have nearly as much of a draw.

"The *InterDimensions* project is the only thing I could see connecting Mal, Ty, and me," Nicole mused. "I was sure it was the reason Ty received the letter, Mal received the phone call, and my apartment was trashed."

"Mal got a phone call?" Joyce sounded startled. "He didn't tell me. What did the caller say?"

"The message is always basically the same whether it's in a letter or in a phone call: 'Leave my family alone.' That's how we knew the calls and the letters were from the same person."

"Who is the family this person keeps referring to?" Frustration coated Joyce's words.

Nicole shrugged a shoulder. "I don't know. It might be some kind of code."

The women sat in a long, pensive silence. Nicole felt a tension headache coming on.

Joyce broke the silence with a whisper. "I don't think Omar killed my Tyrone. I don't think he's a murderer." She smiled fleetingly. "He may inspire violence, but I don't think he would kill anyone."

"I guess I agree with you. He doesn't sound like he's unstable. But now I'm stumped. Why would anyone kill for the movie rights to *InterDimensions*? It's not a guaranteed success. I don't have the sales figures of Stephen King or Anne Rice or John Grisham. The book didn't inspire a bidding frenzy."

Joyce crossed her right leg over her left knee. "Are you sure *InterDimensions* is the only thing the three of you have in common?"

"Yes." Nicole stood to pace the room. "I didn't know anything about Ty until I accepted Celestial Productions's offer. Mal and I have been apart for four years."

Joyce swung her right foot back and forth. "Well, they both had you in common."

Nicole turned toward her. "What do you mean?"

"You were working with them on the project. They had you in common."

Nicole considered that. "And I received most of the letters and phone calls. Mal only mentioned one call. And he found only one letter in Ty's desk." She looked at Joyce. "Ty didn't mention any other letters, did he?"

"No, he didn't."

Nicole turned away. "Me and *InterDimensions*. The common denominators.

"Don't forget the references to someone's family."

Nicole frowned. "That's right. Now we just need to figure out how this all adds up."

# CHAPTER FIFTEEN

"I should get going." Nicole turned back to Joyce. "Thanks for talking this through with me."

Joyce stood and walked toward Nicole, pulling her deep-rose cardigan sweater closer around her. "I appreciate your help finding the person who killed Ty. I wouldn't know where to start."

Nicole hid her anxiety behind a comforting smile. "You're not alone in this. Mal and I won't give up until we find the person responsible for Ty's death." Her smile faded, and her gaze dropped. "The idea that my books may have played a part in this insanity horrifies me."

Nicole bent to collect her purse from the armchair. Joyce stopped her with a hand on her arm. The expression in her dark eyes was fierce.

"It isn't your books. It's some crazy person with an evil heart. If he is referring to your stories, he's using them as an excuse. So just don't even think your books had anything to do with Ty's death."

Joyce's fierce expression didn't mask the pain in her voice or the tears welling in her eyes.

Nicole turned toward Tyrone's fiancée and wrapped her in a hug, close and tight. "Call me if you ever need to talk. Mal and I are here for you," she whispered.

"I know. Thanks." Joyce's voice was thick with emotion.

Nicole stood back and picked up her purse. "I'd better get going."

Joyce followed her. "Are you going to show the list to the detectives?"

Nicole stopped beside the front door. "Not yet. You don't think the people on the list are killers, and I can't see anyone killing for the movie rights."

Joyce looked doubtful. "Suppose I'm wrong, though?"

Nicole pulled her purse onto her shoulder. "I don't think your instincts are wrong."

Joyce frowned, tugging her cardigan tighter. "I just don't want to risk withholding information the detectives could use to find Ty's murderer. What if one of those people is guilty?"

Nicole reached out to touch Joyce's arm. "Then we'll get them. But if we rush forward with a theory neither of us is comfortable with, we could cause trouble for innocent people. You saw what happened when Mal's name was released in connection with Ty's death. The press is having a field day creating a scandal. I don't want to put anyone else through that."

Joyce looked down as though weighing Nicole's words. Finally, she gave a reluctant nod. "All right. I suppose you have a point."

Nicole squeezed Joyce's arm. "We'll find him, Joyce. We won't give up."

"I just can't wait much longer, Nicky. I want to find the guy. Every day Ty's murderer walks free is another rip in my heart." Joyce's voice trembled with her final words.

Tears stung Nicole's eyes. She blinked to hold them back. "I understand," she said, hoping the words didn't sound as trite as they felt. Nicole stepped aside as Joyce unlocked the door.

"It's getting warmer." Joyce followed her onto the porch.

Nicole smiled, hoping to lighten Joyce's mood. "You Southern Californians are spoiled by your balmy winters."

Joyce returned her smile, though sorrow remained in her eyes. "Thanks for coming by."

Nicole descended the stairs. "Thanks for having me."

"Drive carefully," Joyce called after her.

"I will." Nicole waved but didn't turn.

At the curb, she glanced both ways, making sure traffic was clear before crossing the street. Certain there weren't any vehicles moving, she took two long strides toward her car.

"Nicky!" Joyce's scream shattered the silence.

Nicole spun in the direction of Joyce's voice. A car shot past her, a flash of silver in her peripheral vision. She jumped back, lost her footing, and teetered for a long second before falling. Her head bounced once on the concrete sidewalk. Stars flashed before her eyes in the late afternoon. Then everything went black.

"Mal, Joyce is on the line for you. She's frantic." Rita's tension carried over the intercom.

Malcolm pressed the blinking light that would connect him to the caller. "Joyce, what's wrong?" he demanded, clutching the receiver.

"Mal, Nicky's at L.A. County General. I had to call an ambulance to take her there after the accident."

Joyce's words tumbled over each other. Malcolm held his breath, hoping he'd misunderstood her. "What accident? Joyce, what's happened?"

"Oh, Mal. I don't have time to explain," Joyce fretted. "Please just meet us at the hospital."

Joyce disconnected the phone, leaving Malcolm frustrated and afraid. He concentrated on the frustration. Malcolm shot away from his desk. He grabbed his coat from the rack as he sprinted toward the door.

"I'm leaving for the day," he called to Rita. "Nicky's in the hospital. I'll call as soon as I know more."

Malcolm opted to run down the stairs instead of

waiting for the elevator. He was too anxious to stand still even for a moment.

What felt like an eternity passed before he burst into the hospital. He paused, uncertain of where to go. Luckily, Joyce was waiting for him. The scene was too reminiscent of the night Tyrone had died. Malcolm struggled to pull himself together. History wasn't repeating itself, he mentally chanted.

"What's happened?" he demanded as Joyce rushed toward him.

"Nicky came to visit me," Joyce explained, breathing as though she'd just sprinted up a long staircase. "As she was crossing the street to get to her car, another car pulled away from the curb and sped toward her. It looked as though the driver wanted to hit her."

Malcolm felt the blood drain from his face. "Did he?"

"No, no." Joyce shook her head, sending her curls flying around her tear-streaked face. "I screamed her name, and she turned around. That's when she fell. She hit her head on the sidewalk, but the car didn't touch her."

Malcolm cupped Joyce's arm, leading her away from the hectic hospital activity. "Is she going to be okay?"

Joyce looked over her shoulder as though searching for a hospital official she recognized. "They're checking her now. I was afraid to move her myself, so I called the ambulance."

Malcolm scrubbed the back of his neck. "Thank you." He looked up and captured Joyce's gaze. "I'm glad you were there for her."

"So am I."

Joyce returned his look. Malcolm knew they were both thinking of Tyrone.

Joyce squared her shoulders. "I called Detective Miller. I think we need to report this. The driver's behavior was just too suspicious."

"He deliberately aimed his car at Nicky?"

"Yes. I'm certain of it. I couldn't believe it." Joyce's voice rose several notches.

"All right. We'll tell them." Malcolm looked up as a nurse approached them.

"Ms. Allen?" the nurse asked.

Joyce turned around. "Yes."

"Ms. Collins is asking for you." The nurse glanced toward Malcolm. "You can go, too, if you'd like. She's in room 812. The elevators are down the hall on your left."

"How is she?" Malcolm asked.

"She has a concussion and a few scratches. Her right arm was bruised in the fall. She's lucky she didn't break it. We're going to keep her overnight to monitor the concussion, then examine her again in the morning." With a nod, the nurse disappeared into the crowd of bodies farther down the hall.

Malcolm and Joyce rode the elevator to the eighth floor. As they entered Nicole's room, Malcolm saw a nurse fussing around her bed. Nicole lay very still, studying the woman's movements through slitted eyes. She turned her pain-narrowed gaze toward them without moving her head.

"Hi. How are you feeling?" Malcolm spoke quietly as he approached her bed.

"Like I was almost hit by a car," Nicole responded in a soft, tired voice.

His eyes found thin, light scratches below her right temple and a bruise on her right cheekbone. His gaze traveled to her arms, which lay on top of the crisp white sheet. There were several shallow scratches on the back of her right hand and a fist-sized bruise on her right arm.

Rage pooled hot in Malcolm's chest like lava rising in a volcano. Someone had hurt the woman he loved. He wanted to find that person and bounce *him* against a sidewalk. Then he looked at Nicole, lying eerily still and looking heart-achingly vulnerable in the sterile hospital bed. He wanted to protect her. He wanted to take her out of the stalker's equation so he could find Tyrone's killer and make their movie without jeopardizing her safety. Surely after this experience, she'd reconsider returning to New York.

Nicole shifted her attention from him to Joyce. "Thank you for calling to me. You saved my life."

"You're welcome," Joyce whispered. "How are you really?"

"Okay. Just a headache. Soreness."

Nicole spoke in breathless, chopped sentences. Malcolm knew it was a result of the headache.

"I'll get you something for the pain," the nurse interjected.

"New head?" Nicole responded with a weak attempt at humor.

The nurse smiled. "I'll see what I can do."

"Maybe return without your instruments of torture." Nicole closed her eyes and breathed deeply.

The nurse quirked a brow and smiled at Nicole before leaving the room.

"Nicky!" Joyce struggled to smother her laughter.

Nicole opened her eyes and squinted at Joyce. "The nurse is nice. Just doing her job. But if she pokes me once more, I won't be responsible for reflexive actions."

Malcolm forced a chuckle. "I see you still get cranky when you're in pain."

Nicole's narrowed gaze slid to him. "You're no barrel of laughs when hurt, either." She carefully raised her left hand to massage her temple. "I'm a little cold. Could you pull the blanket over me?"

"Sure." Malcolm moved to the foot of her bed, grateful for something to do. He pulled the blanket up and adjusted it to cover her. He moved to the bed's other side, intent on pulling the blanket over her right arm.

"Arms above blanket. Don't want to feel like a mummy," Nicole joked.

"Okay." But when he started to lift her arm, he noticed Nicole's grimace and cautiously laid it back down.

"No, I'm okay," Nicole gasped. "Little stiff."

Malcolm lifted her arm, avoiding her bruises and

scratches. He was moving to the bed's left side to repeat the procedure with her other arm when he heard footsteps approaching the bed.

"Excuse us, Ms. Collins."

Malcolm looked up to see Detectives Miller and Fairway.

"Afternoon, detectives," Nicole greeted in her pain-modulated voice. "How did you know I was here?"

Miller flicked a glance toward Joyce. "Ms. Allen called us."

Nicole looked at the other woman. Joyce moved to stand on the other side of the bed beside Malcolm. "I think we should tell them what happened. That driver meant to hit you."

"So, what happened?" Fairway pulled a notebook from his pocket.

Joyce described the afternoon's events. Nicole was grateful she didn't mention the list of independent producers, although she wasn't comfortable keeping secrets from the detectives. She would discuss the list, as well as her theory and concerns, with Malcolm later.

"Can you ladies describe the car?" Miller asked.

"Didn't see it." Nicole spoke carefully. Every syllable caused her pain. "Just a silver blur. In my peripheral vision."

"It was a silver Beemer," Joyce said.

Nicole turned her head toward Joyce, signaling the percussion section in concert in her head. "A silver BMW?" she asked, her voice breathless from the renewed pain.

"Yes. It was a four-year-old model." Joyce gave them an apologetic smile. "I'm really into cars."

Nicole groaned soundlessly. She couldn't believe this was happening. First, the silver BMW at the jogging trail and now a silver BMW outside of Joyce's house when she's visiting the other woman. That couldn't be a coincidence. She started to shiver.

"Do you want me to get you another blanket?" Malcolm whispered to her.

"No. Thanks," she murmured.

The nurse returned with a packet of Tylenol tablets.

"Thank you," Nicole whispered, almost in tears from the pain. Malcolm propped her up so she could put the pills in her mouth and swallow them with the water the nurse handed her.

As silently as she entered, the nurse left.

"Did you see the license plate number?" Fairway asked, his pen poised to record new information.

"No," Joyce said. "The car was moving so fast."

"Even a partial plate would help," Miller pressed, his pen also at the ready.

Joyce shook her head. "I'm sorry. I didn't see it."

"Do you think this attempted hit-and-run is connected in any way to Mr. Austin's murder?" Miller asked them.

"I don't know." Joyce gave Nicole a startled look.

"Detectives," Nicole called for their attention. "I saw a silver BMW this morning when I went jogging."

"What?" Malcolm turned to face her.

"Driver was male. Faded, baggy sweatpants. Baggy, hooded sweat jacket. Hood covered his face. Tall. Thin. Maybe six feet, a hundred sixty-five or hundred seventy pounds."

"You have a good description of him." The jaded Fairway sounded impressed.

"Was a reporter. Trained myself to observe people," Nicole explained. Talking was increasing the pounding in her head, making her voice breathless again. She waited a moment before continuing. "I noticed him because he followed me to the jogging trail."

As she described the encounter to them, she felt Malcolm's growing tension beside her. She regretted having to tell him this way. She knew the incident would upset him enough without his having to hear it in front of an audience.

"When the other runners and I arrived at my car, the BMW was gone," Nicole concluded.

"And then a silver Beemer showed up outside my door as you were leaving," Joyce added. "You're right. That's too much of a coincidence."

Nicole looked at the detectives, who were still taking notes.

"You said this was about eight A.M.?" Miller asked.

"Closer to seven-thirty," Nicole corrected, wondering if Miller were testing her to make sure she wasn't making up the encounter. She'd told them the time. She couldn't see him misunderstanding 7:30 for 8:00 A.M.

"Did you get the license plate?" Fairway asked.

"No," Nicole admitted.

"Anything else?" Miller's pen hovered over his notebook.

"No." Nicole sighed, trying to control the pain.

Fairway pocketed his notebook. "We'll run a report on four-year-old silver Beemers owned by men ages eighteen to thirty-five. See what we come up with. Call us if you think of anything else." He paused and looked at Nicole. "You're very lucky, Ms. Collins. Speedy recovery."

Without waiting for a response to his uncharacteristic sympathy, he turned and left. Miller nodded at the three of them, then followed his partner out of the room.

"Why didn't you tell me?" Malcolm demanded as soon as the detectives were gone. His voice was low but harsh.

"I think I'll step outside for a while." Joyce looked at Malcolm. "Remember, she's not feeling well." Then she left them alone.

Nicole turned to face Malcolm, bracing for the throbbing she knew would increase. "Was going to tonight."

"You should have told me when you got back from your run this morning," he countered, beginning to pace.

"Wasn't ready." Nicole looked away from him. She wasn't up to monitoring his travels.

"Why not?" Malcolm turned to pace in the opposite direction.

"Thought I was being paranoid. Other joggers have paced with me during runs. Thought that's what he was doing." She paused often to manage the throbbing in her head.

"Well, you were wrong." Malcolm's tone was short, his anger growing. "Dammit, Nicky, something could have happened to you on that run. Have you forgotten someone broke into your apartment and trashed your stuff? Not to mention leaving behind messages threatening your life?"

Nicole winced as his raised voice cued the snare drummers in her head. She pressed her left hand against her pounding head and tried to catch her breath. "Mal, I hear just fine. And, no, haven't forgotten."

"I'm sorry." Malcolm lowered his voice. "I'm just angry with myself."

Nicole frowned. "Yourself? Why?"

"I should have gone with you this morning."

Nicole sighed and lowered her hand. "Those quiet words make me feel more guilty than your yelling."

"I wasn't trying to make you feel guilty." Malcolm sounded surprised.

"None of this is your fault," Nicole continued. "I promise I won't run alone again until the stalker is found."

Malcolm arched a brow. "How about you join my gym and run on the treadmills there?"

"A gym?" Nicole sighed in disgust. "We'll discuss it when I get home. When can I come home?"

"I'm hoping to bust you out of here tomorrow afternoon. And I'm going to hold you to your promise to discuss joining my gym."

"Fine," Nicole huffed.

Malcolm regarded her in silence for a long while. Nicole grew wary of the serious look in his warm brown eyes. When he spoke, he sounded almost resigned. "Will you reconsider your decision not to return to New York?"

Nicole met his gaze. "No."

Malcolm's chest rose and fell as he took deep breaths. "I was afraid you'd say that." He pulled his hand through his close-cropped hair. "Nicky, someone tried to kill you today. Perhaps twice today."

"I know," she whispered, wondering how long it would take for her to stop being afraid.

"This isn't a movie," Malcolm pressed on. "If the bad guy gets too close, I can't yell, 'Cut!' so I can rush in to save you."

"And what about you, Mal?"

Malcolm jammed his hands into his pants pockets. "I'm not in danger."

Nicole turned away to stare at the ceiling. She spoke quietly, in part because she was on the verge of tears. She blamed her sappiness on the pain and the fear. "I'm not going to run away, Mal. I'm not going to lock myself in some safe house while you become this psycho killer's target." She turned to capture his gaze. "We're in this together."

Malcolm stared at her, his jaw set. "Your safety is important to me."

"You're important to me," she returned. She was desperate for him to see the truth of her words reflected in her eyes. She needed him to accept how much it meant to her to stand with him during this crisis. She wanted to be with him always, in good times and in bad.

"It's your decision." Malcolm's tone left no doubt he wasn't happy with the outcome. He walked around her bed to leave the room. "I'll be right back. I'm going to call Rita and tell her you're all right. For now."

Nicole closed her eyes and tried to relax. Their contest of wills had aggravated her headache. She was counting each pulsing throb in her head when her tally was interrupted by a discreet cough. She opened her eyes just enough to see a young, burly, blond man standing awkwardly beside her bed. He was wearing an orderly's uniform.

"Excuse me, Ms. Collins." He spoke in a soft voice, his cheeks growing pinker by the moment.

Nicole glanced toward the door, wondering if anyone would come if she screamed. "Yes?"

The young man glanced nervously over his shoulder. Nicole could hear the orderly's rapid breathing and wondered if he was going to faint.

"I really shouldn't be doing this, but I wonder if you wouldn't mind, if it's not asking too much, could I ask you to autograph my book?"

Nicole spied the book in question. It was almost swallowed in his meaty grasp. She smiled up at him. "I would love to. Do you have a pen?"

A dazzling grin spread across his face, banishing the almost-painful shyness. He passed her the book and handed over the pen he'd pulled from his pocket.

"Scott," Nicole said, reading his name tag.

Scott's grin grew brighter, causing an answering curve to lift Nicole's lips. She looked down at the cover and saw he'd given her the third book in her series. She noticed the blank patient record form peeking from the pages and realized Scott was using the form to mark his place. He was more than halfway through the story.

"I'm rereading it," Scott offered. "I can't wait for the next one."

"I'm very flattered. Book four is scheduled for release in the summer."

"Oh." Scott's smile dimmed. "Well, I'll have to slow down with book three, then."

Nicole chuckled, then regretted the action because it increased the pounding in her head. "Thank you for the compliment."

She finished signing his book and handed it back to him, moving gingerly because of the stiffness in her right arm. The wattage of his smile increased again as he read her message. *Scott, thank you for taking care of me in Los Angeles County General Hospital. Warm regards, Nicole Collins.*

"Gee, thanks," he gushed.

"It's my pleasure." She returned his pen.

"Wait until I tell everyone in the chat room about this," he said, almost bouncing in his excitement. In that moment, he reminded her of a lovable St. Bernard.

"What chat room?"

"There's a chat room set up in cyberspace where people go to discuss your books. It's not a big group, and we haven't been up for very long. But people in the group are huge fans."

"I didn't realize I had a chat room," Nicole said. "That's amazing. What kinds of things do you discuss?"

As soon as she'd asked the question, Nicole wondered if she really wanted to hear the answer. It was gratifying to know people enjoyed your work. It also could be a little hurtful when people picked your stories apart. She thought it would be similar to the way parents felt when someone criticized their children.

Something about that comparison gave Nicole pause. It poked at a memory that should be closer to the surface of her thoughts. But the connection was disrupted by the throbbing in her head and the sound of Scott's voice.

"We talk about our favorite characters. My favorite is the Nguin ambassador's attaché," Scott said. "I love to hate that guy."

Nicole chuckled softly. "So do I."

Scott smiled. "Way cool," he declared. "We also try to figure out what's going to happen next with certain story lines. Like some people are trying to figure out Senator O'Neill's next move."

"Really?" Nicole mentally patted herself on the back. It seemed as though she'd captured some interest with her secondary plots. Way cool, as Scott would say.

"Yeah." He cocked his head and charmed her with a boyish smile. "I don't suppose you'll give me a hint?"

Nicole forced back a laugh. She didn't think her headache would handle the action. "Sorry."

"Okay." His smile didn't fade. "Some people are also wondering if the commander and the captain are going to get together."

Nicole wanted to shake her head in amused exasperation. She couldn't imagine why that question was getting so much attention. There wasn't any sexual tension between the self-contained captain and the fearless commander.

Scott regarded her closely. "I don't suppose you'll give me a hint on that one?"

Nicole hesitated, reluctant to commit herself. "I won't rule anything out."

Scott nodded. "Okay. I can appreciate that. There's a lot of discussion about the movie, too."

Nicole stiffened. "Really? What are people saying?"

"Some people are looking forward to it. They think you'll do a good job making sure the producers stay true to the story. Some people are pretty upset. They don't think you should have sold the movie rights because they think the producers will do whatever they want with the story."

*Are any of those people upset enough to kill me?* The thought made her headache throb even faster. "The producer is also an *InterDimensions* fan. He'll do an excellent job with the movie."

"Thanks for the vote of confidence."

Nicole looked up at the sound of Malcolm's voice. She felt more relaxed with his return. She watched with appreciation as his loose-limbed stride carried him into the room. He extended his hand toward Scott and offered a smile. "Malcolm Bryant. I'm the producer who's going to do an excellent job with the *InterDimensions* movie."

"Wow," Scott exclaimed, grabbing Malcolm's hand. "I'm Scott Gannon. I'm a big *InterDimensions* fan. And I've seen some of your movies. Great stuff."

"Thank you."

Nicole noted the twinkle in Malcolm's eyes. She wondered if he had noticed the young orderly's resemblance to an exuberant St. Bernard.

"Scott, how many chat members are upset about the movie?" she asked.

Scott cocked his head and squinted his eyes. "Only about four or five." He looked directly at her. "They said you betrayed the series by agreeing to do the movie. A couple of them got really carried away, and I had to block them from the loop. I'm the list moderator." He smiled proudly.

"List moderator. That's great." Nicole smiled weakly, wondering what he meant by "carried away."

Scott's cheeks were growing pink again. "Hey, maybe you guys can stop by the chat room and answer some questions for us about the movie. What do you think?"

"I think that's a great idea." Nicole looked at Malcolm, willing him to agree. "What do you think?"

"I agree. Maybe we can convince your members I'm not going to shut down the space station."

Scott looked uncertain, then returned Malcolm's smile. "Oh, I get it. That was a joke."

"That's a matter of opinion," Nicole said dryly.

Malcolm shot her a wounded glance, then turned back to Scott. "How do we sign in to your chat room?"

Scott provided detailed instructions on entering the chat room, as well as a history of the group and their dynamics. He also provided his e-mail address. Nicole and Malcolm listened patiently to Scott's well-meaning ramblings.

"Well, Ms. Collins, thank you for the autograph and everything," Scott said. "When do you think you guys will visit the chat room?"

"Perhaps next week," Malcolm offered. "Once Nicole's feeling better, we'll e-mail you to work out a date that's convenient for everyone."

"I'm sure I'll be up to visiting the chat room early next week. I'd like to attend as soon as possible." Nicole met Malcolm's curious look with a wide smile, despite the pain chipping away at her skull.

Scott looked stricken. "I'm sorry, Ms. Collins. I didn't even think. Of course, we'll wait until you're one hundred percent. Take your time. How are you feeling?"

"Call me Nicole."

Scott blushed. "Okay. Thank you, Nicole."

Nicole smiled. "I'm anxious to visit the chat room. I'll e-mail you when I get home tomorrow."

"Sure thing, Ms. . . . Nicole. Thank you." Scott started to back away toward the door. "It was nice meeting you, Mr. Bryant."

Malcolm took his puzzled gaze off Nicole. "Call me Malcolm. It was nice meeting you, too, Scott."

Scott beamed. "Way cool. Thanks, Malcolm. See you around." And he disappeared.

"Interesting guy," Malcolm remarked, turning back toward Nicole. "How's your head?"

Now that she didn't have to use complete sentences in consideration of her fan, Nicole could relax. She leaned back and closed her eyes. "Tylenol not working yet. Where's Joyce?"

"Out in the hall talking to Rita on my cell phone." Malcolm settled into a chair next to Nicole's bed. "Rita sends her best, by the way."

Nicole opened her eyes. "Tell her I said hi."

"I will," Malcolm promised. "So why were you sending me silent signals about Scott's chat room?"

Nicole wanted to discuss her suspicions about the chat room only once. "Let's wait for Joyce."

On cue, they heard Joyce's heels clicking back to Nicole's bedside.

"Here's your cell phone, Mal." Joyce rounded Nicole's bed to return the device, then circled back to stand on the opposite side.

"New development, Joyce," Nicole began. She recapped her conversation with Scott Gannon, much of which Malcolm had heard. "The stalker has some connection with the *InterDimensions* series. Chances are slim, but we might find someone who's a member of Scott's list and is also on the list of production companies that bid for the movie rights."

Malcolm rubbed his jaw, a pensive expression in his eyes. "It's a long shot but worth the try."

"Definitely." Joyce sounded more hopeful. "But how will we get the list of members?"

Nicole leaned back against the pillows. She was

exhausted. "I'll ask for it when I e-mail Scott. I'll make up some reason, like wanting to add their names to an *InterDimensions* e-mail newsletter."

Malcolm nodded. "That's a good idea. The worst that could happen is that he says no."

"I agree." Joyce looked between Malcolm, who was comfortably settled in the chair, and Nicole, lying drowsily against the pillows. "Well, Nicky, I think I'll head on home now so you can get some rest."

"Okay. Thanks again for saving me, Joyce. I owe you." Nicole tried to keep her voice firm, but fatigue made her words slur. She wondered if the pain tablets contained a sleep agent.

Joyce leaned over and cupped Nicole's hand. "No, you don't. Now try to get some rest." She turned toward Malcolm. "You, too, Mal."

Malcolm inclined his head. "I'll see you soon, Joyce."

Joyce pulled her purse higher up on her shoulder and left them alone.

Nicole continued to fight against her growing fatigue. Someone had tried to kill her. It was no longer anonymous threats in letters and phone calls. It had escalated to physical attempts against her life. She thought she had lost the young man at the running trail, but a silver BMW had shown up at Joyce's house, which meant the stalker knew she was staying with Malcolm.

She glanced at Malcolm and found him studying her. Was he in danger also? "I don't want anything to happen to you."

His gaze was steady. "It's you I'm worried about."

"Promise me you'll be careful," she demanded, fighting to keep her sleepy gaze focused on him.

"I promise."

Nicole's eyes slid shut. She could feel herself losing the battle to stay awake. She forced her eyes back open and caught Malcolm's gaze. "Could you stay with me? Just for a while longer?"

He answered without hesitation. "I'll stay all night."

She smiled, sliding down onto the thin hospital mattress, and closed her eyes. Still, her mind kept searching for the link between her, Tyrone, and Malcolm. What was that link? Or perhaps, who was the link?

"Mal?" Her sleep-slurred voice reached for him.

"Yes, Nicky?"

"What kind of car does Omar drive?"

She heard his answer as she fell inexorably into sleep. "A silver BMW."

# CHAPTER SIXTEEN

Winded, Malcolm pushed open the door from the stairwell. Walking up the eight flights to Omar's office may have taken his breath, but it had left his temper intact. He was just as furious today as he had been yesterday when he'd remembered Omar drove a silver BMW. Having to wait until Carter Enterprises opened this morning for business to confront his rival chafed. He'd barely slept in the hospital visitor's chair last night.

Now, as he stood with his back against the stairwell door catching his breath and mastering his emotions, he acknowledged that pounding Omar to dust was the only thing that would exorcise his temper. He'd almost lost control when he'd seen the silver BMW in the parking lot with the CARTER O personalized plates. He squared his shoulders and marched down the hall to Carter Enterprises's glass entrance.

A young woman looked up from behind a receptionist's station. A six-inch-high marble wall wrapped the desk behind which she sat. From the doorway, all Malcolm could see of the receptionist were her head and shoulders, making her appear like a pretty, redheaded desk ornament.

"Good morning," she chirped. "Welcome to Carter Enterprises. May I help you?"

Malcolm paced to the desk as he spoke. "Good morning. Malcolm Bryant to see Omar Carter."

"Do you have an appointment, Mr. Bryant?" She folded her hands on her desk, cocked her head, and regarded him smugly.

Malcolm had the impression she already knew the answer to that question. He looked down at her with cool determination. "No."

The receptionist blinked and lowered her gaze. "Well, Mr. Carter is a very busy man." Her birdlike voice faltered. She peeked up, and Malcolm held her uncertain gaze. "I'll see if he can spare a few minutes for you." She lifted her chin in shaky defiance and reached for the intercom.

"Thank you," Malcolm murmured.

He stuffed his fists into the pockets of his jeans and breathed deeply to ease his impatience. He understood the receptionist was only doing her job, arranging her employer's appointments. She was like Rita in that respect. But Malcolm didn't give a damn about Omar's daily planner. He had tried to kill Nicole. He probably had something to do with Tyrone's death as well. When Malcolm was done with his rival, he was going to hand over whatever was left of Omar, his schedule, and his Hugo Boss suits to the LAPD.

"A Mr. Bryant is here to see you, Mr. Carter. He doesn't have an appointment." The receptionist's voice was at once sulky and spiteful. She paused, sliding a speculative look in Malcolm's direction.

"Yes, Mr. Carter." She was back to chirping. "Right away." She replaced the phone and smiled at Malcolm. "Mr. Carter has a few minutes to spare for you. His office is at the end of the hall." She pointed behind her.

Malcolm nodded, his shoulders tense with anger. His shoes tapped against the tile, echoing his deliberate steps. He passed pale gold walls and vibrant paintings. Without knocking, Malcolm entered the tastefully decorated office, pulling the door closed behind him.

"Mal." Omar came around his desk, his hand outstretched and a grin spread across his face. "I was hoping you'd reconsider."

Malcolm's fists remained in his pockets. His anger strained against a short leash. "Reconsider what?"

Omar chuckled, dropping his hand. "The *InterDimensions* deal, of course."

Malcolm's hands exploded from his pockets to grab Omar's shirtfront. Through the hazy, red borders of his vision, Malcolm registered the other man's surprise.

"You bastard." Malcolm ground the words between clenched teeth.

Omar tried but failed to knock Malcolm's arms away. "What the hell is your problem?"

"Did you kill Ty, too?" Malcolm demanded, struggling against the urge to punch the shocked expression off his adversary's face.

"What?" Omar exclaimed.

Malcolm gave him one, hard shake. "Was that your intention all along? To kill everyone who matters to me until I reconsidered your offer?"

Omar struggled against Malcolm's hold. "Have you lost your damn mind?"

Malcolm released Omar with a shove. His temper spiked when the other man didn't stumble.

"Did you think I wouldn't remember you drove a silver BMW?"

Omar smoothed his shirtfront, fury and bafflement burning in his dark eyes. "What the hell does my car have to do with anything?"

Malcolm's rage built with every one of his former coworker's denials. "You used it to run Nicky over."

Omar's expression went from furious to incredulous. "Sweet Jesus," he breathed. "Is she okay?"

Malcolm sneered. "Don't worry. You won't be tried for murder. Probably just attempted murder."

Omar glared at him. "What the hell are you talking about? Are you accusing me of trying to kill Nicky?"

"Stop pretending," Malcolm shouted, the control on his temper slipping further.

"I'm not pretending," Omar shouted back. "I don't know what the hell you're talking about."

Malcolm studied his rival's angry expression and saw traces of confusion in his eyes. He didn't want to let go of his anger. Someone had tried to hurt Nicole, and someone was going to pay for that. But in fairness, it should be the right person.

Malcolm took a mental step back. He skewered Omar with a probing stare. "Where were you around noon yesterday?"

"I was here." The other man jabbed a finger toward the ground.

"Prove it."

Omar glared at him a moment longer, then returned to his desk to punch the intercom button. "Shelly." His tone was short and sharp.

"Yes, Mr. Carter?" the birdlike voice responded.

"Could you please bring in the receipts from yesterday's lunch with the accountants?"

"Right away, Mr. Carter."

"Thank you." Omar leaned back against the front of his desk, crossing his arms and his ankles. His Hugo Boss suit pants retained their crease. He fixed Malcolm with a baleful glare, which Malcolm returned. Neither broke eye contact when Shelly knocked on the door before entering.

Omar didn't move. "Give the receipts to Mr. Bryant, please."

Malcolm accepted the receipts, two papers stapled together. The charges were itemized and tallied on the receipts, which were dated, with the time stamped. Omar's signature appeared on the credit card slip. The date was Wednesday; the time was 12:23 P.M. Malcolm returned the slips to Shelly.

"Thank you, Shelly." Omar waited until the receptionist had left the room before continuing. "Even if I were inclined to run someone over—which I sure the hell am not—do you actually believe I would do it with my own damn car?" He returned to his desk and dropped into his chair. "I have personalized plates, for God's sake. How stupid do you think I am?"

Malcolm raised an eyebrow but refrained from commenting. He acknowledged that Omar had a point about the personalized plates. He hadn't thought of that earlier, probably because he'd been blinded by rage in search of an outlet. He rubbed the back of his neck.

"If it wasn't you, who was it?" he asked himself aloud.

Omar leaned his elbows on his desk. "I don't know. How's Nicky?"

Malcolm saw the concern in Omar's eyes, mixed with remnants of anger. "She has a concussion, but she'll be fine. She spent the night in the hospital so they could watch her." Malcolm glanced at his watch. He still had a couple of hours before he'd meet her at the hospital to take her home.

"So what happened? I take it you don't think it was an accident?" Omar shifted back in his chair. His temper seemed to be abating.

Malcolm envied the other man. His own anger still searched for a target. He looked Omar in the eye. "I'm sorry I accused you of trying to hurt Nicky. I thought . . . Well, I thought wrong. I apologize." He turned to leave.

"Mal."

Malcolm turned and watched Omar approach him.

"We were never friends," his competitor continued. "But we were colleagues. Tell me what happened. Maybe I can help."

Malcolm regarded him skeptically. "I thought you suspected me of being involved in Ty's murder."

Omar's gaze slid away. "I never believed that. I just said that to try to convince Nicky to buy back her movie rights." He looked back at Malcolm. "I didn't realize the two of you were married. You're a lucky man."

"We're not married." Malcolm's tone was flat.

Omar frowned. "I saw the article in the *Preview*. Are you telling me Nate was wrong?"

"Yes, your boy was wrong."

"Well, that's good news." Omar's grin faded in proportion to Malcolm's increasing frown. "Okay. Well. Come on. Tell me what happened yesterday with Nicky. Maybe I can help."

Malcolm mentally flinched from Omar's suggestion. The idea he couldn't protect his woman on his own hurt. The pain was almost as sharp today as it had been six years ago. But Nicole had told him she wasn't leaving, so he'd better find another way to protect her, even if it meant getting help.

Malcolm studied Omar. His rival had a lot of contacts in the city, he thought, looking around the office at the photos of Omar posing with political officials and corporate power figures. The other producer's connections, including his friendship with Nathan Rutherford, could prove useful in catching the stalker. Nathan had proven himself to be a very good investigator, Malcolm thought, remembering the reporter's recent foray into his personal life.

"Someone is trying to hurt Nicky," he began. His voice carried more reluctance than he'd intended.

"Sit down." Omar gestured to one of the teak wood visitor chairs. He rounded his desk to resume his seat.

Malcolm lowered himself into the chair and briefed Omar on the calls and letters Nicole had received, bringing him up-to-date with the break-in of her apartment, the mystery man on the running path, and yesterday's attempted hit-and-run.

Omar stared at him in amazement. "And you don't have any idea who's behind this?"

"I thought it was you."

"Well, you thought wrong." Omar's outrage returned.

"I know that now."

"So now we just have to figure out who it is."

"And why."

\* \* \*

Nicole pushed aside her hospital identification band to check her wristwatch again. She sighed and stretched her back. It wasn't even 10:00 A.M. She was dressed and ready to leave. There was nothing to do now but wait until Malcolm came for her this afternoon.

She looked at her watch again, this time studying the cracked face. *So close.* She remembered the headache that now was a mild throb. *So lucky.* She could have cracked more than her watch. She let her arm drop onto her lap as she half-sat, half-reclined on the hospital bed.

A knock on her room door diverted her attention. She looked up, but her visitor wasn't Malcolm coming to get her early.

"Frank." She was surprised to see the young man standing in the threshold. He regarded her with disconcerting intensity, or perhaps it was just that his sapphire sweater deepened his violet eyes.

"Hi, Nicole." Frank entered the room. "I heard about your accident. How are you?"

"I'm fine," she lied. "Thank you."

"I'm glad." He nodded toward the empty bed. "Did you have the room to yourself?"

"Yes." She cocked her head. "How did you hear about the accident?"

"Malcolm told my father." Frank tucked his fingertips into the front pockets of his straight-leg Gucci black jeans. "So, what happened? Do you mind my asking?"

"No, I don't mind." Nicole kept her voice light as she started her story. "I was leaving Joyce's house. Do you remember Joyce Allen?"

Frank nodded, rocking back on his heels. "Tyrone's fiancée."

"Yes. I was leaving her house, and as I started to cross the street, a car came out of nowhere. It would have hit me if Joyce hadn't screamed my name. But when I turned back to her, I lost my balance and fell onto the sidewalk. Hence the mild concussion that kept me here overnight." Nicole lifted her arms to encompass the hospital room.

"Wow." Frank shook his head in wonder. "You're so lucky Joyce was there." He folded his long frame into the chair next to her bed.

"Yes, I am." Nicole tried not to get tangled in images of what might have happened if Joyce hadn't been courteous enough to watch her walk to her car.

The comfortable squeak of nursing shoes advancing toward her room caught her attention. A willowy young nurse appeared in the doorway. She aimed a quick, appreciative look toward Frank before focusing on Nicole.

"Good morning, Ms. Collins." The nurse's husky voice sounded too full for her slight frame. "I'm Lucy Dunn. I see you're ready to leave us."

"Yes." Nicole watched the young woman smooth first her curly blond hair and then the slim skirt of her uniform. "But I appreciate your taking such good care of me while I was here, Nurse Dunn."

The nurse beamed at her. "Oh, it was our pleasure, Ms. Collins. You were an ideal patient." Her hazel eyes snuck another peek at Frank.

"Thank you." Nicole allowed some of her amusement to escape in the form of a smile.

Lucy slid repeated glances at Frank as she fussed around Nicole, checking her pupils and the bump on the side of her head. Her small hands were competent yet careful. Frank seemed unaware of the attractive nurse's preoccupation with him. Instead he chatted about possible plot twists of a science-fiction novel Nicole had recommended to him.

"I'm glad you're enjoying the story." Nicole extended her arm so Lucy could check her blood pressure.

"I can't put it down." Frank's smile made his model good looks even more appealing.

Lucy's glance lingered a bit longer on Frank this time

as she wrapped the blood-pressure cuff around Nicole's arm. Nicole wondered how Frank's mother would feel about young Lucy's interest with her son. The nurse seemed nice, but Ava probably would not be pleased. Nicole doubted the overprotective mother would approve of anyone. She seemed much too possessive of her baby boy. Poor Lucy. Poor Frank.

Lucy looked directly at Frank for the first time, seeming to gather her confidence. "Are you taking Ms. Collins home?"

"Well, we hadn't discussed it." Frank glanced at Lucy before turning back to Nicole. "But I can take you home, if you'd like."

Lucy smiled admiringly at Frank. "That's so kind of you."

"Not at all," the young man protested. His Superman-like lock of dark hair fell forward.

"I appreciate the offer, Frank. But Mal's meeting me," Nicole said, rolling down her sleeve once Lucy removed the blood-pressure cuff.

"Well, since I'm already here, we could call him and let him know I'm taking you home." Frank sat forward in his chair. "It would save him the trouble."

"He's already on his way."

"Then we should call him right away." Frank flipped open his cell phone. "Maybe he hasn't driven that far."

Nicole frowned at Frank's persistence. "No, really, Frank. I'd rather wait for Mal."

Frank held out his cell phone. "Are you sure?"

"I'm sure, but thank you for offering."

Lucy looked uncomfortable with the exchange. "It was a nice offer. I'm sorry. I hadn't realized you'd made other arrangements."

Nicole waved away the nurse's apology. "Don't worry about it."

Lucy smiled, her humor restored. "You're healing very well, Ms. Collins. But no more picking fights with the sidewalk."

With a smile, Lucy strode out of the room, casting a parting glance at Frank on her way.

"It was a good idea," Frank said after Lucy disappeared.

"Yes, but I would hate Mal to go out of his way to pick me up only to find I'd accepted a ride with someone else."

"I understand." Frank's tone conveyed his reluctance. "But it's not out of Malcolm's way to pick up his wife."

Nicole stared at Frank, wondering if her concussion had affected her hearing. "What did you say?"

"Hi, Nicky. Frank."

Malcolm appeared in the doorway. A wary expression sharpened his gaze. But Nicole wasn't as anxious to leave now. Nicole cut her gaze back to Frank.

"What makes you think Mal and I are married?"

Frank looked uncertain. He glanced between Nicole and Malcolm. "The article in *Silver Screen Preview* said you two were married."

Nicole's lips parted, and her eyes grew wide in surprise. She turned to Malcolm, unable to form the question.

"I was going to tell you, but then the accident . . . I forgot," he said, walking into the room.

"You two aren't married?" Frank asked, standing.

Nicole shook off her surprise. "No, we're not." *Not anymore.* She wondered how and why the trade magazine had found out about their former relationship.

Frank's brows gathered. "Then why did the *Preview* say you were?"

"I have no idea," Nicole prevaricated.

She looked at Malcolm, who quirked an eyebrow at her. She glared at him, certain he was to blame for this invasion of her privacy.

"That's weird." Frank shook his head, rocking back on his heels. His gaze swung between Malcolm and Nicole again. "Well, I'd better get out of your way so you can get home."

"Thank you for coming," Nicole said.

"Oh, sure. See you around." Frank's parting wave encompassed both of them.

* * *

He kept a white-knuckled grip on the steering wheel
and an eagle-eyed stare on the hospital entrance, not
wanting to miss Nicole and Malcolm's exit from the hospital. He ignored the sweat trickling down his back. The
car was hot and stuffy, although the day was cool and
windy. But he didn't roll down the windows. He didn't
want to do anything that would distract him.

He couldn't believe the answer to his problem had
been right in front of him the entire time. The solution
was so simple, so obvious. To protect his family, he would
have to assume the role of caregiver.

Nicole had betrayed his family, and if she didn't make
amends by calling off the movie project and buying back the
rights, he would be forced to separate her from his family.

He sat up straighter as he saw Malcolm assist Nicole
out of the hospital in a wheelchair. His gaze tracked
them as Malcolm helped her out of the chair and, with
the help of an aide, assisted her into his car. Malcolm's
manner was solicitous and gentle. Even from this distance, his affection for her was visible. Nicole was important to him. And, if he didn't miss his guess, Malcolm was
important to her. Maybe more important to her than his
family. He squeezed the steering wheel tighter.

In the past, he'd been reluctant to remove Nicole. In
her role, she was too important to his family's continu-
ance. He'd considered her irreplaceable. But now he realized Nicole could be replaced. If he was forced to get
rid of her, he would assume the responsibility of continuing his family. The balance of power had turned. He
was the one in control. He didn't need Nicole anymore.
And, if she didn't remember where her loyalties lay, his
family wouldn't need her, either.


Nicole went to the family room to wait for Malcolm.
He was in the kitchen loading the dishwasher and

cleaning up the remains of the wonderful dinner he'd prepared.

"Is there anything else I can get for you?" he asked, entering the room.

Nicole lowered herself onto the sofa. "No, thank you. I'm fine." Her lips curved teasingly. "Between the delicious lunch you prepared earlier and that fabulous dinner, we know my appetite wasn't affected. You're spoiling me."

"I want to spoil you." He took her hand as he sat beside her. "I almost lost the chance to do that. It's going to be a while before I'm able to stop hovering."

Nicole squeezed his hand before rising to wander the room.

"I know what you mean," she said over her shoulder. "It sounds trite, but being reminded of how fragile life is made me reconsider what I'm doing with mine."

She paused in front of the mantel, staring into the empty fireplace. "Don't get me wrong. Overall, I'm happy. The only regret I have is the unresolved issue between us."

"I regret that, too."

Nicole breathed in her courage before turning to face her ex-husband. He stood beside the sofa, studying her with a wary but steady gaze. "Mal, I need to know the truth, no matter how hard it may be to hear."

"What is it?"

She took a fortifying breath. "Do you blame me for our baby's death?"

She felt Malcolm's shock, and then his expression changed to irritation. His reaction reassured her better than any verbal denials ever could.

"I never blamed you. Never. I've told you that before."

"Then why did you file for the divorce?"

Malcolm gusted an impatient breath. He prowled the room, dragging one hand through his hair. Nicole felt his inner struggle.

"Because I blamed myself." His voice was low and hesitant.

Of all the things he could have said, that wasn't the response she had expected. "Why?"

Malcolm stilled and faced her. "I felt like a failure. I felt as though I couldn't take care of my family. I couldn't protect you."

"Why would you need to protect me?" Nicole strained to push her defenses down. Now wasn't a good time to be hypersensitive about what she considered to be Malcolm's old-fashioned view of the roles husbands and wives play in a marriage.

"You shouldn't have had to continue working during your pregnancy. And when you stopped talking to me, I thought you blamed me, too."

"Never," Nicole exclaimed. She rushed to him, putting a hand on his muscled forearm. "I never blamed you, Mal. I stopped confiding in you because . . . Well, Mal, talking to you was like talking to a wall. I'd share all my pain with you, and you never gave anything back. It was a lonely feeling."

He gave her an apologetic smile. "You told me that. And I'm sorry. I didn't realize that's how you felt."

Nicole stepped closer, sensing their body heat wrap around them. "Does your offer to start over still stand? Can we try to put the past behind us?"

A brilliant smile added a twinkle to his brown eyes and brightened his features. He pulled her into his arms and covered her mouth with his. She melted against him, his embrace making her warm and restless.

She skimmed the tip of her tongue against the roof of his mouth, groaning at the taste of him. The heat of him. He growled low in his throat, a hungry, hunting sound that stoked the furnace inside her. She swayed against him as his long, nimble fingers stole under her sweater and skimmed her waist. His arms curved around her, his fingertips playing the length of her spine. Nicole shivered, and he pulled her closer still.

He broke the kiss, and through heavy-lidded eyes, Nicole watched him feather his fingers over the healing scratches along the side of her face. He tenderly kissed the bruise above her right cheekbone. Pain darkened his eyes as he recaptured her gaze. "I could have lost you."

Nicole pulled his head down to her and sealed his lips with a kiss meant to take his pain away.

His lips left hers to sip along her jaw. Malcolm's tongue traced the shell of her ear, sending shivers to the very heart of her passion. Her body became weightless, supported only by her desire. Malcolm's mouth returned to hers, his tongue slipping past her lips to toy with hers. Stroking, sucking, pulling at the hunger within her. Her passions raced toward the begging point. She moved restlessly and felt the mattress beneath her.

Confused, Nicole opened her eyes. She looked around and realized that while she'd been dazed with passion, Malcolm had carried her to his bedroom. He smiled into her eyes. She returned the gesture and pulled him back into her arms.

Malcolm shivered as Nicole's hands slipped beneath his shirt. Her short, neat nails journeyed from his shoulder blades to the small of his back. Helplessly, he bowed into her. Nicole separated her legs beneath him, and he settled between them. She lifted her hips against him, undulating her need against his own. But he had more to share with her than his physical desire. He wanted to share his joy. Joy that she was safe and that they were back together.

Blood thrummed in his ears, but he cautioned himself to slow down. Their previous coming together had been fierce and hot. But this time he wanted to cherish her. This time was a renewal of their promise to each other. Malcolm wanted to show Nicole how much he appreciated her giving them a second chance. He wanted to prove himself worthy of her.

He gritted his teeth and, with an effort, rose to his knees on the mattress so he could undress her slowly, careful with her still-sore right arm. But Nicole wouldn't stay still. She sat up and pulled his shirt off him to suckle his nipples. Malcolm's legs began to quake.

"Not yet, Nicky," he whispered, pushing her away from him so he could take off her sweater, mindful of her bruises. He feathered a finger over the light scrapes on her rib cage. "I'm so sorry," he whispered.

Nicole cupped his cheek to lift his gaze to hers, then kissed him softly. When she pulled away, her ebony eyes were hot with desire. She leaned back from him and took off her bra with her left hand. Then she pulled him close to rub her naked torso against his. Malcolm moaned at the sensation, every pulse in his body racing.

He felt her hands at the waistband of his denims. He helped her slip his pants off; then he reached for her jeans. When they were both naked, she pushed him onto the mattress for a full-body caress. Her firm, silky body moved all over him, and her tongue found hot zones that pushed his body temperature toward combustion. He rolled over with her and pinned her to the bed.

She wrapped her legs around him, locked her ankles behind his hips, and rubbed herself against him. He felt her taut stomach muscles flex beneath him. The heat from her body battered against him like waves from the Pacific Ocean.

Malcolm covered her mouth with his own and stroked her tongue with his as he sank into her—long, slow, and deep. Every pore of his body wanted to be filled with her. Nicole arched into him, writhing under him. He moved within her, meeting her arches with counterthrusts. Malcolm gave her everything he had, then begged her to take more. She gave back tenfold.

Nicole stiffened beneath him. Her body pulsed around him. He stiffened above her, falling into her— and landing home.

Nicole wiggled farther under the covers, scooting back in search of Malcolm's warmth. She'd traveled almost

YOU BELONG TO ME

halfway across the mattress before realizing she was alone. Rolling over, she opened her eyes and scanned the empty room. Daunted but not down, she rose carefully from the bed. She hoped a hot shower would ease the residual stiffness from the accident. Memories of the previous evening brought a happy song to her lips. Laughter and love had lifted her mood and blocked out the violent events of the past month. Had it only been five weeks since Tyrone's death?

Nicole paused midlather. Yes, it had. She'd returned to Los Angeles the second week of March, and it was now mid-April. A lot had happened in that time, and there was a lot more to do. Nicole shrugged off the threatening dark cloud and turned off the water. She wanted to extend their romantic interlude a little longer. Later she would think about the murder investigation and the person who wanted to add her to the body count.

The knock at the door helped distract her. Malcolm's voice called through the barrier.

"Shake a leg, lazy bones. I'm about to put breakfast on the table." Amusement laced his words.

Nicole smiled in response. "Does that mean you're hungry?"

"I'm starving." He prolonged the two-syllable word for effect. "You wore me out last night."

Nicole chuckled. "I'm sorry, stud muffin. How inconsiderate of me."

His rumbling laughter, deep with wicked memories and full of satisfaction, carried through the door to her. "Very. If you hurry, maybe I'll let you make it up to me." His voice faded as he moved away from the door.

Malcolm's teasing fully restored Nicole's good mood. "Twenty minutes," she called, not certain he'd heard her promise.

She entered the kitchen precisely twenty minutes later. She hoped she didn't look like she'd just thrown herself together, although that's exactly what she'd done. Malcolm waved her to a chair so he could serve her. Steam rose from the plate of pancakes and turkey bacon. Her coffee and orange juice followed. She felt pampered and decadent as she waited for him to take his seat.

"I'd like to make a toast." He sat and lifted his juice glass. "To embracing the future."

Nicole lifted her glass. "To the future." She took a sip before placing her glass on the table. "What are your plans for today?"

Although she wanted to enjoy the glow of their reconciliation as long as possible, Nicole had to admit she was still shaken by Thursday's events. She looked forward to getting her courage back. In the meantime, she hoped Malcolm didn't have any plans that would take him away from the house for an extended period of time today. Even though it was Saturday, with his hectic schedule, he may have to go into the office.

Malcolm hesitated before answering. "I'm meeting with Omar to discuss a limited partnership for the *InterDimensions* project." He sipped his orange juice.

Surprised, Nicole stopped eating. "You don't think he's a suspect anymore?"

Malcolm set down his glass. "No." He told her about his meeting with Omar the day before. "I don't think Omar would commit any crimes while driving a car with personalized plates."

Nicole forked up her pancakes. "I wish you had told me yesterday about your meeting with him."

Malcolm's eyes narrowed. "We had other things to talk about yesterday, like the *Preview* article that claimed we were still married."

Nicole nodded. "Or perhaps this is another example of your not wanting to trouble the little woman with business matters." Her tone was deceptively mild.

Malcolm dropped his hands to his lap, a stony mask covering his face. "That's not what I said."

Nicole took a moment to readjust her attitude, hoping to salvage the situation. "Would you be able to meet with Omar here? I'd rather not be alone today."

"Of course. I'll ask him to come over." Malcolm finished his pancakes and sipped his coffee.

Nicole waited a beat. "Do you want me to join you since you'll be discussing the *InterDimensions* project?"

Malcolm shook his head, putting down his coffee cup. "We're going to be talking about forming a limited partnership to produce the *InterDimensions* movie."

Disappointment pinched her. She rose from her chair and placed her dishes in the dishwasher.

"Where are you going?"

Nicole shrugged. "To lie down."

He stood and stepped toward her, concern knitting his dark brows. "Are you in pain? Do you want some aspirin?"

Nicole raised a hand to stop him, anger making her movements jerky. "I'll be fine."

He came closer. "I'll help you upstairs."

Nicole allowed temper to snap in her eyes. "I'll manage just fine on my own. Enjoy your business meeting."

She took advantage of his surprise to whirl out of the room.

# CHAPTER SEVENTEEN

Nicole closed Malcolm's bedroom door with mature restraint, then marched to the bed and punched his pillow. Twice. After releasing some of her anger, she walked over to the windows. She looked at the tree and the bushes in Malcolm's front yard before switching her attention to the red tulips in the neighbor's garden across the street. Nicole turned her head left and right, straining to see as far down both blocks as possible. No silver BMWs in sight.

She turned away from the windows and strolled back across the room. Her bare feet sank into the thick, champagne carpet. Nicole stopped before the chest-of-drawers where Malcolm had a small CD player. From the tray, she selected a CD that suited her mood and pressed the PLAY button. Erykah Badu's voice offered sisterhood and sympathy. She lowered herself onto the edge of his bed and lay back on the king-sized mattress.

Why wouldn't Malcolm let her help him with the business side of the *InterDimensions* project? Was he still trying to take care of her, or did he think she had nothing to contribute?

Erykah Badu sang on. Her lyrics drew a picture of another woman who wondered about her role in her man's life. The doorbell rang, and Nicole frowned at the ceiling as she pictured Malcolm and Omar discussing their limited partnership. She swung one leg in time with the music.

Why didn't Malcolm tell her yesterday about his meeting with Omar? Was it really just an oversight, or was he deliberately trying to exclude her from his business dealings? If the answer was the latter, why didn't he want to share that part of his life with her? Tyrone had shared his business concerns with Joyce.

Restlessly, Nicole stood and wandered around the room again. She felt as though she'd lost control of her life. She couldn't convince Malcolm to see her as a partner in this business project. She couldn't find the person who had killed Tyrone and was threatening her and Malcolm.

She lay back down on Malcolm's side of the bed, his pillow cushioning her head. Fatigue crept over her, but she shook it off.

Nicole remembered how solicitous Malcolm had been when he'd brought her home yesterday. He'd been so afraid for her. He hadn't told her so, but he didn't have to. It had been on his face and in his actions.

Nicole's eyes grew heavy, but she struggled to stay awake. What did it matter whether Malcolm discussed his work with her? Why did she feel left out if he didn't ask for her help? She'd fallen in love with him as he was; why was she intent on changing him?

Despite the trauma of the past five weeks, the past four years had shown her she was happier with Malcolm than she'd been without him. Sleep pulled at her again, and this time she allowed it to carry her away.

"Nicky? Nicky?"

Malcolm's whisper roused Nicole from her nap. She found her ex-husband sitting on the corner of the bed. Her drowsy gaze saw the concern in his dark eyes, and noted his well-muscled arms braced on either side of her. "Umm. What time is it?"

He smiled faintly. "Just after eleven. Omar's here. Do you feel up to joining us?"

Nicole blinked, suddenly wide-awake. Her heart lifted

with the invitation. "But I thought the two of you were going to discuss your business partnership?"

"We already have." Malcolm stood up. "We're on to more important topics now, like catching a killer."

Nicole had proof that people in the film industry had lost their grip on reality. That proof was the two men sitting with her in Malcolm's great room.

Malcolm spoke with marked irritation. "Why does it have to be Rutherford?"

"Do you know a better media contact?" Omar's Southern California drawl flavored the question. "Nate has the pull at the *Preview* to make sure our announcement gets the right play."

Nicole shook her head in disbelief. They wanted to play up the announcement of their partnership to lure the murderous psycho fan to them.

"How do you know the killer reads the *Preview?*" Malcolm asked.

Omar's lazy chuckle danced around the room. "If it's not the *Preview,* which magazine is it? Admit it, the *Preview* is giving this project more play than anyone else. You're just upset because Nate made up that story about your marriage."

Nicole was still angry with the *Preview* reporter for his invasion of her privacy. Apparently, so was Malcolm. He rumbled an obscenity that made Omar chuckle again.

"Jackass or not, he has the pull we'll need for the coverage. We'll need the exposure to flush the killer out," Omar said.

"This plan isn't without risks," Malcolm cautioned. "Are you prepared for that?"

"I've never run from a fight." Omar sounded offended.

Nicole had stayed quiet long enough. It was past time to interject a voice of reason into the debate.

"Do you really think it's a good idea to do a full advertising campaign with TV, radio, newspapers, and magazines promoting the movie? This guy killed Ty just for buying the movie rights. A promotional campaign that expansive is like putting bull's-eyes on your chests."

Determination hardened Malcolm's gaze. "I'm not planting my hands under my ass while that nut job comes after you."

"Instead, he's going to come after you." Nicole didn't care whether fear shone in her eyes.

"That's a risk I'm willing to take," Malcolm murmured.

Nicole was astounded. "I'm not expecting you to hide in your room. I'm just asking you not to pin a target on your chest."

"Nicky," Omar interrupted. "It's not like that. It's a good plan. Mal and I will watch out for each other. And we're going to let the police in on it."

Nicole threw up her arms. "Great. They can complete the homicide report afterward."

"Maybe I'd better go." Omar stood. "Call me later, Mal. Bye, Nicky. It's good to see you're feeling better."

"Thank you." Nicole nodded, deciding not to mention the slight throbbing in her head. It probably had nothing to do with her concussion and everything to do with her fear for her pigheaded ex-husband.

Malcolm escorted Omar out while Nicole waited impatiently for his return.

She pounced as he reentered the great room. "This is too risky, Mal. Please don't do this."

"I'm not going to sit around doing nothing while some head case gets away with terrorizing you." He walked restlessly past Nicole and leaned against the fireplace mantel, arms folded across his chest. The sleeves of his dark blue jersey wrapped around his flexed biceps. His long, hard legs were covered in black Lee jeans. He looked big, tough, and dangerous. Invincible. But even Superman was vulnerable to kryptonite.

Nicole wanted to pull her hair out. Or perhaps pull out Malcolm's. "Why can't you wait for me to get that chat room membership list from Scott?"

Malcolm shook his head. "Analyzing the list would

take too long. Besides, we don't know whether he'll give us the list. Meanwhile, the killer knows who you are, what you look like, and where you live."

Nicole tried willing him to be reasonable. "You're being impetuous in a life-and-death situation."

Malcolm paced toward her, impervious to reason. "It's time to take control of the situation and turn the tables on him. I need to do this. For you. For myself."

Nicole could feel Malcolm's will and determination and knew he was set on his course. The fight was draining out of her. She gathered her forces to try one last plea.

She cupped his cheek. "I don't want anything to happen to you."

Malcolm held her gaze and placed his hand over hers. "I don't want anything *else* to happen to you."

Two days later, Nicole sat in Malcolm's great room updating her calendar with her agent on the other end of the phone line.

"Are you ready for the *A.M. L.A.* interview tomorrow?" Denise's voice sounded tinny on her speakerphone. The woman redefined multitasking.

"Not really. I don't feel mentally prepared."

"What's to mentally prepare for?" Denise shuffled papers. Nicole could hear her automatic stapler chomping on her desk. "They always ask you the same questions, anyway."

Amusement warmed Nicole's tone. "Thanks. I'll remember that as they're thinking up new and creative ways to torture me."

"What are you worried about? You always do great. The real dilemma is what to wear?" Her friend sighed dramatically.

"I thought I'd wear my cream suit."

"Well, that's a thought. Not necessarily a good one, but it's a thought."

Nicole quirked an eyebrow. "What's wrong with my cream suit?"

"Nothing—if you're going to tea," Denise elaborated. The crackling sounds told Nicole the other woman was stuffing envelopes. "That suit's not really helping your image. It makes you look more like a society matron than a sci-fi writer."

Nicole didn't know whether to be amused or offended. She chose amused. She'd had enough heavy emotions for a while. "All right. All right. What would you recommend I wear?"

"Girl, I can tell you what I'd recommend you *do.* Go shopping for something new."

Nicole didn't intend to run errands without her bodyguard, and she didn't think Malcolm had time for the trip tonight.

"Funny, Denise. I don't have time to go shopping. The interview's tomorrow. So, of the clothes I do have, what would you recommend?"

"Well, did you bring that red skirt suit?"

Nicole took the cordless phone upstairs to her closet. "No."

"Hmm." Denise picked up the receiver, disconnecting the speakerphone. "The sapphire blue suit won't do."

"Good, because I didn't bring that one, either." She rifled through her outfits. "What do you think of the emerald-green suit?"

Denise snorted. "I think you need to go shopping."

"I like that suit." Nicole pulled it out and held it against her. She imagined herself wearing it in front of millions of strangers. The image changed, and she saw Denise's point. She returned the suit to the closet and looked again.

"Did you bring the black pantsuit?"

"Yes." Nicole flipped through the hangers until she found the trim suit with the nipped-waist jacket.

"Good. Wear that. Put your hair up and wear dangling earrings. You did bring dangling earrings, didn't you?"

"Yes, I did. That will look great. I wish you were here. You have a way of steadying my nerves."

"You'll be great. Well, now that our business has been concluded, catch me up on the murder investigation."

Nicole filled Denise in on the accident and Malcolm's plan to use the media to draw out the murderer.

"You were in the hospital?" Denise screeched. "And you didn't call me?"

Nicole winced at Denise's volume. "I'm sorry, Denise. Everything happened so fast. Today is the first day I was able to call you."

"Humph. Well, how are you feeling?"

"Better, thanks. The headache is completely gone now."

"Good. And I like the sound of Mal laying a trap for that gutless stalker."

"I understand his wanting to take control away from the maniac and pull him out of the shadows. I could even buy into the plan—if I wasn't afraid he'd get hurt."

"Nicky, you're his ex-wife, not his mother. Learn the role."

"I know I'm not his mother. But I can still worry about him."

"Yeah, but within reason. He's a grown man." Denise's exasperation snapped in Nicole's ear. "Someone killed his best friend and is now trying to kill his ex-wife, a woman he obviously still loves. Instead of running for cover, your man is stepping out with this challenge. You wanted a man who would stick in a crisis. He's proving he can do that and more. Instead of holding him back, you should be cheering him on."

Nicole considered Denise's words. Had she held Malcolm back in their marriage? She knew she had a tendency to coddle the people she loved. Derrick had pointed out her habit in their relationship, and she had since backed off. Did she do the same thing to Malcolm?

"I am cheering him on."

"Humph. Well, cheer a little louder and smother a little less."

* * *

Malcolm shifted in his chair. He looked around the table in his company's conference room. He couldn't believe he was playing host to both Omar Carter and Nathan Rutherford. Tyrone must be spinning in his grave.

"I thought you two hated each other," Nathan asked with his usual lack of tact. "What makes you think you can work together?"

The question was directed toward Omar. Malcolm waited with interest to hear his temporary partner's response to this very revealing question.

Omar chuckled. "Who says I have to like the guy to work with him?"

Malcolm groaned inwardly. He started to step in when Omar continued. "I don't hate Mal. I've never hated him. I admire his work. He's very talented."

Malcolm was taken aback at Omar's sincere tone. "I have a lot of respect for Omar's abilities as well."

"I never said I respected you, partner. Let's not get carried away." Omar winked.

Malcolm smiled, getting used to Omar's sense of humor. Maybe this interview wouldn't be so bad.

Nathan turned to Malcolm. "Does that mean you're intending to replace Tyrone with Omar?"

Malcolm stiffened. He'd been too hasty in adjusting his opinion of the interview. He took a moment to temper his response. "No. I'm not looking for a replacement."

Omar jumped in. "No one could replace Ty. I wouldn't even try. He was a genius. But a project of this size requires two people to handle its production." His chuckle sounded a bit forced. "Steven Spielberg couldn't handle it on his own."

"Why would you sign up for this project, Omar?" The reporter changed gears. "Scandal and death are associated with this production. Suppliers are jumping ship. Why are you climbing on board?"

"I believe in this project." Omar spoke with firm

sincerity. "It's successful on paper. It'll be a success at the box office, too."

Malcolm decided on a more direct approach. "Someone doesn't want us to make this movie. For whatever reason."

Omar quirked a brow but didn't try to rein Malcolm in as he described the threats and attacks against Nicole.

Nathan wrote furiously. "That's where the real story is."

"If you want to put it that way." Malcolm's tone was dry.

Nathan continued scribbling even as he spoke. "You two are competitors who are now joining forces. Do you think these threats are coming from another competitor?"

"We don't know who's behind these threats," Omar said. "They're written as though a fan sent them."

"But whoever it is, we want them to know nothing is going to derail this project. We're moving forward."

Nathan looked up from his reporter's notebook. He gave Malcolm a challenging stare. "One person has already died. From what you've said, Nicole almost did. Aren't you afraid?"

"What I am is determined. I own the movie rights to this project, and Omar and I are going to produce it."

"No matter what happens?" Nathan pushed.

"Right," Malcolm confirmed.

"No matter what," Omar echoed, capturing Malcolm's gaze.


"I'm glad you both came." Nicole clasped Malcolm's hand and smiled at his partner.

Omar glanced dubiously around the walk-in-closet-sized guest dressing room in the *A.M. L.A.* studio. "I'm looking forward to watching the taping."

"That makes one of us," Nicole joked weakly.

Malcolm squeezed her hand. "You'll be great."

"Have you ever been interviewed on television before?" Omar asked, flipping through a magazine he'd found on a corner table.

"No," Nicole admitted.

"Well, don't worry about it. No one ever listens to those interviews, anyway. Especially not morning show interviews." Omar looked up from the glossy pages. "All they really care about is what you're wearing and how you look. And, honey, you look marvelous." He stretched out the last word in a poor Latin accent.

Nicole laughed. Glancing at Malcolm, she saw him smile as well. She was glad the two men were getting along.

A make-up artist/stylist had just left. The young man had tidied her hairstyle and applied the television make-up. The guest dressing room was so small that, while the stylist was fussing over Nicole, Omar and Malcolm had waited outside.

Now, the quarters were a bit cramped while the two men kept her company. Omar sat sideways on a cushioned bench so no one would trip over his long legs. Malcolm leaned against the vanity table while Nicole perched on a stool, her knees tucked between his thighs.

"Well, this is cozy." A strong female voice interrupted. Nicole turned to see Denise squeezing into the room behind her and settling into the last free space.

"Denise. I can't believe it," Nicole said, startled. She popped gingerly off the stool and squeezed her way over to the newcomer, wrapping her in a tight embrace. "I can't believe you came. Thank you."

"Girl, you should have known I wouldn't miss this. But I have to say, I thought it never rained in Southern California?" She swiped at droplets of water on her blazer. "It's pouring out there."

"We get the occasional weather patterns, just to keep us on our toes," Malcolm said.

Nicole shifted until she faced Malcolm and Omar.

"Omar Carter, I'd like you to meet Denise Maitland, my agent and best friend."

"You remember that, girl. Diamonds aren't a girl's best friend. Agents are," Denise joked before roaming her gaze over Omar from the tip of his Italian leather shoes to his Bill Blass suit to his salon-cut hair.

Omar stood and extended his hand. "It's a pleasure to meet you, Denise."

"The pleasure's all mine, cowboy," Denise purred as she caressed Omar's hand. The long, slow gaze she slid over his lanky frame made Nicole blush.

She interrupted her agent's optical foreplay. "Denise, I'm sure you remember Mal."

Her agent pulled her gaze from Omar. She leaned forward to take Malcolm's outstretched hand. "I'm very sorry about Ty. He was a class act."

Malcolm took her hand. "Thank you for the flowers you sent to his funeral service. They meant a lot to me and to Ty's family."

Denise nodded, then turned back to Nicole. "Why don't you sit back down, honey? That'll give us more room in here."

Nicole slid back onto the stool.

"That's better," Denise continued. "Now let me get a look at you. Turn into the light."

Denise moved so Nicole's face was in the light, and her back was to Omar. She bent over awkwardly to study Nicole's hair and make-up.

"You look great. Just a little too much forehead." Denise used her pink-tipped fingernails to adjust Nicole's hair. "Much better."

Denise stepped back, then came up short. She straightened and brushed a hand across her hips. Looking over her shoulder, she cocked an eyebrow at Omar. "Is that your knee, cowboy, or are you just happy to see me?" She stroked the tip of her tongue over her blush-tinted lips.

Omar's startled expression prompted a coughing fit from Malcolm. Nicole shook her head, used to Denise's ploys with attractive men. But she didn't feel a need to protect Omar. She was certain once he caught a bead on her, Omar would give back to Denise and more.

"When are you going back to New York?" Nicole asked her agent.

"My flight leaves at eleven tomorrow morning."

Malcolm conquered his coughing jag. "Where are you staying tonight?"

Denise moved aside so her back wasn't to Omar any longer. "I've booked a room in a nearby hotel."

"Why don't you stay with us?" Malcolm offered.

Denise smiled with surprised pleasure. "Thank you for the offer, but I don't want to impose."

"It's not an imposition," Malcolm insisted. "I have a spare room."

"Or you can stay with me," Omar suggested. "I have a spare pillow."

Nicole smiled. It seemed Omar had taken Denise's measure.

"Perhaps you should slow down, cowboy." Denise winked. "I may be too much woman for you."

Omar laughed. Denise's gaze lingered on him again before returning to Nicole and Malcolm.

"Excuse me." Malcolm struggled with another coughing fit. "I'm going to get more water." He grabbed the pitcher and slipped out of the room.

Nicole checked her purse under the vanity. "I forgot my cover flats in Malcolm's car. The host asked to use them as props." She spotted Malcolm's keys on the vanity. "I'll be right back."

"Oh, hold up, girlfriend." Denise moved to block her on the stool. "I'll get them. I don't want you going out into the rain before your interview and messing up your appearance."

Nicole hesitated. "Are you sure?"

Denise extended her hand for the car keys. "Of course. Where are you parked?"

Nicole told her where to find Malcolm's car in the parking lot. She also described his vehicle and where'd she'd placed the book cover flats. "Take my coat so you don't get too wet."

Denise shrugged into Nicole's brown trench coat. "I'll be right back."

"Thanks. I owe you," Nicole called as Denise left on her quest.

Malcolm headed back to the guest dressing room after an unsuccessful search for a water fountain. From the other end of the hall, he heard hysterical screaming. Clutching the empty pitcher like a weapon, he sprinted toward the sound and found a crowd gathering around a young woman.

"Our guest! Our guest!" the woman screamed. "Someone ran her over in the parking lot."

Shock quaked through him. The empty plastic pitcher dropped from his numb hand. In the split second before his body went into fight-or-flight-mode, a dozen thoughts flooded his mind, all centered on the woman he loved more than life. Nicole was in trouble. Nicole was hurt. Nicole was dying. His mind rebelled from that thought. Fury and rage denied its possibility.

Malcolm muscled through the crowd until he cleared a path to the entrance. His anxious gaze searched the parking lot as prayers tumbled over and across his mind. *Please, God, don't take her from me. Not now that she's with me again. Not ever. Please, God.* His heart stopped, and his prayers were silenced when he saw the heap of clothing sprawled across the asphalt like discarded rags. Damaged book cover flats were scattered around it.

Tears burned Malcolm's eyes. He forced himself to move forward, toward the brown trench coat he'd helped Nicole put on that morning. He dropped to his knees beside her and tenderly turned her limp body over. Confusion froze him as he gazed down at Denise's bloodied, battered face. Shaking off his surprise, he searched for a pulse in her neck, her throat, her shattered wrists. Nothing.

"Denise!" Nicole screamed behind him.

Malcolm rose and turned in one movement, his first thought to protect Nicole from the sight of her friend's lifeless body. He wanted now more than ever to keep her safe from everyone and everything. Even at the cost of his own life.

He stepped toward her. "No, baby, stay back."

Nicole didn't seem to hear him. She raced toward Denise. Malcolm moved to intercept her. He grabbed her hurtling body. Wrapping one arm around her waist, he buried her face in his chest. Nicole beat at his shoulders, crying hysterically.

"Where is she? Denise! Denise!" Her voice was wet with tears.

Malcolm held Nicole closer, his heart breaking for her. "Oh, baby. I'm sorry. I'm so sorry. She's gone."

"No!" Nicole screamed. She stopped struggling and gripped his shoulders as though to keep from falling off a cliff.

Nicole had no idea how long they'd stood outside, Malcolm holding her while she'd bawled. Omar had joined them. She hadn't wanted to believe Denise was dead, but Malcolm and Omar had verified her friend no longer had a pulse. Nicole had asked them to bring Denise's body into the building, but they had reminded her that moving the body would compromise the crime scene. She didn't want to do anything that would hamper the police's search for her friend's murderer.

Tears still streamed down her cheeks, but she had regained some of her composure as they returned to the television station. Her body trembled, but she wouldn't fall, not with Malcolm's arms to support her.

The trio stopped in front of a pale and shaking young woman, who someone had identified as the accident's lone witness. She sat holding a glass of water and wadded tissues. A curtain of straight, mouse-brown hair shielded her face. The talk-show host knelt before her, and an older gentleman stood nearby directing people in preparation for the police's arrival.

"Excuse us," Malcolm interrupted.

An eerie silence covered the crowd when they recognized Nicole.

"I thought you said she was dead," the host questioned. "What's going on?"

The young woman's thin face grew paler with shock. Her light gray eyes were dazed. "I saw you dragged under a car."

Nicole's stomach heaved at the description. She clamped a hand over her mouth.

Malcolm's muscled arm wrapped around her shoulders, bracing her. "Do you need to go to the bathroom?"

Nicole shook her head. She took a deep breath, willing the nausea to pass. "Why did you think it was me?"

"Your coat," the woman answered. "I recognized your chocolate coat. You were holding it above your head as you ran back across the parking lot."

Nicole swallowed the lump in her throat. Who had done this? Rage and grief frothed inside her. Malcolm's arm tightened around her as her body began to shake again.

"Could someone get us a chair, please?" he asked.

Someone positioned a chair behind Nicole. Malcolm pressed her onto the seat. She took a moment to form her next words.

"You saw my agent, Denise Maitland." Nicole felt it important these people know Denise's name. She didn't want her friend to be an unidentified body. "I loaned her my coat. She went to get my cover flats from the car." Nicole paused as her voice broke and guilt made an appearance.

"I'm so sorry." The woman's gray eyes looked stricken. "I saw her when she came in looking for you. I pointed out your dressing room. I'm Stacey, the production assistant."

Nicole recognized the regret in Stacey's eyes even as fresh tears pooled in her own. "Thank you." Nicole's voice was so thick with tears, she feared Stacey wouldn't understand her.

Stacey took the box of tissues from her lap and passed them to Nicole. She nodded at Nicole's thanks, then looked away. Long, slow breaths lifted and lowered her thin shoulders. "I've never seen anything like that."

Nicole needed to compose herself so she could find out who had struck down her friend. But the harder she tried to calm down, the harder the tears fell. Her chest heaved with rapid, shallow breaths. She felt Malcolm lay a supportive hand on her shoulder. Nicole wanted to tell him she would be all right. She needed to ask some questions, but she couldn't think. She couldn't clear her mind of the image of Denise being dragged through the parking lot.

She squeezed her eyes shut, and other images of Denise played behind her lids. Her first meeting with her agent. Denise's enthusiasm for the *InterDimensions* series. Denise encouraging her with her mystery series. Her friend bullying her into finding the self-confidence to promote her work through media interviews and book signings. Denise extending her hand for Malcolm's car keys and wrapping herself in Nicole's coat.

A lump blocked her throat, trying to cut off her air. Someone folded her hand around a glass of water. Through her tears, she saw Omar's face.

"Drink this," he urged.

Nicole gulped the water, unblocking her throat. But she still wasn't capable of forming the questions she needed to ask.

And then she heard Malcolm asking for her. "The car that struck Nicky's agent, what did it look like?"

Stacey shuddered. "I don't know a lot about cars, but I paid close attention to this one so I could give the information to the police."

"Whatever you can tell us would be appreciated," Malcolm assured the production assistant.

Stacey nodded. "It was a black four-door Lexus SUV."

An image of a black Lexus SUV with tinted windows parked across the street from her apartment flashed through Nicole's mind. Could that vehicle belong to the murderer? Could he have sat in his car watching her every morning as she ran? Her stomach muscles clenched in dread.

"Did you notice the license plate?" Malcolm's voice sounded strained.

"Yes," Stacey whispered. "I almost forgot. I made a point of looking for it so I could tell the cops. It's KZY-2525."

Malcolm's grip tightened on Nicole's shoulder. "Shit. It can't be."

# CHAPTER EIGHTEEN

*A.M. L.A.* aired a repeat of a previous episode—after filling in viewers on the events of the morning and Denise's murder. Even during a crisis, the producers considered their ratings.

The police had taken custody of Denise's body. They'd promised to expedite the examination so Nicole could make arrangements to return to New York with her agent's remains.

It had taken a surprising amount of effort on Malcolm's part to convince Nicole to let Joyce stay with her. She had been listless on their way back to Malcolm's house after the police interview. But when he'd suggested asking Joyce to stay with her, Nicole had insisted she wanted to be left alone so she could rest.

In the end, he'd waited until Nicole went to bed. Then he'd called Joyce and asked her to stay with Nicole in case she woke before he returned. Assured the other woman was on her way and would retrieve his spare house key from under the welcome mat, Malcolm and Omar had driven to Leo's home. He hoped they'd find Frank at the other man's house.

"I think we should have asked the police to come with us," Omar said.

He'd made the comment before. Malcolm explained

again why he disagreed. "Leo's a good friend. I don't want to show up at his house with the police and ask him to surrender his son."

Omar drummed his fingers on the passenger door handle. "This is going to be hard no matter how you do it."

"True." Malcolm slid into a parking space in front of Leo's house. "But bringing the police would feel like a bigger betrayal."

"True," Omar echoed, climbing out of Malcolm's car. "But we'd better be on our guard. It's not like we're accusing his boy of throwing a baseball through our window. Things could turn ugly."

The two men mounted the steps to Leo's house and knocked on the door. While they waited, Malcolm braced himself for this meeting with his mentor.

"Mal. Omar," Leo greeted them with pleasure and the customary twinkle in his blue eyes. "What a great surprise. Come in. Come in."

As they crossed Leo's threshold, Malcolm looked around for signs of Frank.

"So what brings you gentlemen here?" Leo closed the front door and moved closer to them.

"We need to talk with you, Leo," Malcolm began.

Leo studied their serious expressions. The twinkle in his eyes dimmed with concern. "Sure. Let's go into my office." He turned to lead the way down the hall to a room decorated in silver and black. Leo gestured to the deep-cushioned seats before his desk. "Can I get you a drink?"

When both men declined, Leo relaxed into the executive seat behind his desk. "You men look as though you're heading for the electric chair," he commented with a strained chuckle. "It can't be that bad. What can I do to help?"

Malcolm's discomfort increased with this display of his mentor's generosity. He hated carrying this message to someone who felt like family. "Leo, this is very difficult to say."

The older man looked from Malcolm to Omar. "What's wrong?"

Malcolm was grateful Omar was letting him set the tone. He took a deep breath in an attempt to ease his tension. It was a useless exercise.

"We believe Frank may have been involved in threats against Nicky and Ty." Malcolm briefly filled Leo in on the phone calls and letters he, Nicole, and Tyrone had received.

"My son, Frank?" Leo's eyebrows almost disappeared beneath the locks of hair falling over his forehead.

"Yes." It hurt Malcolm to watch his friend turn into an adversary.

Frost entered Leo's eyes. "What makes you think that?"

Omar stirred in his seat. "The letters were written by a fan. Frank is a big fan of Nicky's books."

"So are thousands of other people." Leo sat up, glaring at Malcolm. "And you said that you thought the threats came from a competitor."

Malcolm steeled himself to deliver the next blow. "A new development made us reconsider that theory."

"What development?" Their host leaned back in his chair, his beefy arms crossing his chest.

Malcolm dreaded the words he had to say. "There was another hit-and-run today."

"At the *A.M. L.A.* studio parking lot." Omar's voice picked up the story. Malcolm was grateful. "Nicky's agent was struck and killed by a driver who apparently mistook Denise for Nicky."

"Dear God. I'm so sorry." Leo paused to collect himself. "But what does that have to do with Frank?"

"The car was a black Lexus SUV," Omar said.

Leo leaned forward, anger snapping in his eyes. "Frank drives a silver BMW."

Omar and Malcolm exchanged looks, both remembering the silver BMW that had tried to run over Nicole.

"But Frank occasionally drives Ava's car, which is a black SUV," Malcolm pointed out.

"I don't know anything about my son driving his mother's car."

"I've seen him with her car," Malcolm said. "And her license plate number is KZY-2525."

Leo stilled. "That sounds right."

"And that car was used to kill Nicky's agent," Omar concluded.

"Yes." A new voice entered the conversation. "But Frank wasn't driving it."

Malcolm and Omar turned to see Ava DeCaprio framed in the doorway pointing a gun at them.


*Denise was being dragged under the SUV while Nicole watched helplessly. Her agent's body thumped across the asphalt parking lot, trailing blood, flesh, and pieces of clothing. Denise kept screaming, "This was supposed to be you." Over and over again the words slapped at her, leaving guilt and grief behind. Bells rang and Denise shrieked.* Nicole woke screaming.

She lay back, staring at the ceiling. She struggled to catch her breath and banish the nightmare from her mind. Then the thumping started again. Nicole shot up in bed, looking wildly around the room until she realized the thumping was someone pounding on the front door.

Nicole struggled out of bed, pulled on her robe, and padded downstairs. A peek out the side window revealed Frank standing alone on the porch. Nicole frowned. He was rocking on his heels and studying his watch. Something was wrong.

She pulled the door wide so he could enter. "What's wrong, Frank?"

The young man burst into the room. "You've got to come with me. It's the stalker. He has Malcolm."

Nicole's heart thumped once, then dropped. Her hand flew to her throat. "How do you know?"

Frank spun toward her, his movements jerky. "We don't have time. You've got to get dressed and come with me."

His urgency tried to pull her in, but Nicole had to stay calm. For Malcolm's sake. She backed up a step. "Go where with you?"

Frank stalked toward her. "To help Malcolm. The killer has him."

"How do you know?" Nicole watched him. Something was wrong. "How did you get involved?"

"I've always been involved."

She saw him raise his arm before everything went dark.


Leo stared in shock at his wife. "Ava, what's the meaning of this?"

"What's the meaning of this?" Ava repeated, seeming on the verge of hysteria. "You never could understand, could you? You don't have what it takes to be a good father. If you did, you'd understand what this means."

"Could you explain it to us?" Omar asked.

Malcolm glanced at Omar. He hoped Ava hadn't heard the irritation in the other man's voice. He didn't need someone pushing her over the edge while she held a gun on them.

"He's a horrible father," Ava said.

"That's not true." The words were out of Malcolm's mouth before he realized he was going to say them. But he knew Leo was a proud, affectionate parent.

"He was never around," Ava accused. "I raised Frank by myself. Like a single parent."

Leo stood behind his desk. "Ava, that may have been the case in the beginning, but things changed."

Ava tracked Leo's movements with her gun. "Are you calling me a liar?" Her tone was menacing.

"I don't think you're remembering the situation correctly." Leo seemed wary, but he wasn't backing down.

"Frank is my whole world. And I'm his whole world. He's my baby boy. I need to keep him safe."

"So do I." Leo braced his arms on top of his desk.

"No, you never did," Ava screeched, waving the gun wildly. "You wanted him to play sports. How would that have kept him safe?"

"But when he decided against joining a team, I didn't pressure him."

"I had to talk him out of it." Ava tapped her chest with the gun. "I told him he would get hurt. I told him he'd have just as much fun reading about adventures in the books I bought for him. But then he found those stupid *InterDimensions* books, and they took my place in his life. That bitch stole my son from me. All I ever heard was 'Nicole Collins' and '*InterDimensions*.' Those characters became his family."

"*InterDimensions* became his family?" Malcolm asked.

Ava switched her attention and the gun to him. "Yes. That's how he referred to them. I hated them. But I decided that if I couldn't stop him from reading those books, I would read them, too."

"Ava, did Frank tell you he was going to try to stop the movie project?" Leo reclaimed his wife's attention.

The gun swerved again as Ava turned to face her husband. "He told me he didn't want them to make the movie. I told him he should do whatever was necessary to protect his family."

Malcolm saw the blood drain from Leo's face. "You told him?" The words sounded choked. Leo's lips worked to form more words. "Did Frank kill Ty?"

Ava smiled. "No, of course not."

Leo hung his head between his shoulders and sighed heavily. "Thank God."

"I did," Ava continued. "And I killed Nicole's agent, too. But that was an accident. I meant to kill Nicole."

\* \* \*

Nicole came to slowly and found herself staring at huge, purple orchids. She blinked and realized she was lying on her side on a sofa. But this wasn't Malcolm's sofa. Confusion became fear with her memory's return. She spared a moment to control her anxiety. She needed to stay focused.

She rolled over, and the movement woke the pain in her jaw. Another memory came back, one of a fist flying toward her face. Anger surged, but she squelched that emotion as well. She needed to stay in control.

Nicole looked around. She froze when she saw Frank sitting on the opposite sofa studying her. A book sat on his lap; a gun lay on the table beside him. Frank's stillness disconcerted her. His expression gave nothing away.

"What are you thinking?" she asked.

A long pause preceded his answer. "I'm wondering what kind of person would betray her own family. A family she created."

Frank was her stalker? She'd befriended him and shared meals with him. And he had killed Tyrone and Denise. He'd completely fooled her.

"What family am I betraying? And how am I betraying them?" She needed to understand why he had killed her friends.

"Don't pretend to be stupid. I won't accept that from you." His words were all the more frightening for being delivered in a mild tone.

Nicole made herself match his composure. "I agree I'm not stupid. But that doesn't mean I know what you're talking about."

"The family," Frank repeated, as though willing her to understand. "The *InterDimensions* family."

Nicole's gaze dipped to the book on Frank's lap, recognizing the cover of her third *InterDimensions* novel. She met his stare. "And how am I betraying them?"

Frank looked down at the book and stroked its cover. Captain Mallory and Lieutenant Commander Albright joined various other characters in an action pose. "By making this movie. By letting outsiders control the family and their actions."

Nicole pushed herself into a sitting position, swinging her legs over the side of the sofa. She pulled her robe more tightly around her. "Is that why you killed Ty and Denise? To punish me for betraying the family?"

Frank still caressed the book. "It wasn't to punish you. It was to get you to realize your mistake and change your mind."

Nicole didn't think it would help her cause to tell him the *InterDimensions* characters weren't real. She looked around the room. It was decorated in muted tones with modern furniture and plush wall-to-wall carpeting. A glance over her shoulder showed French doors and the darkness beyond.

"Where are we?"

"My parents' Malibu beach house."

His measured tone and calm demeanor were misleading. Nicole reminded herself he was unstable. "Are you going to kill me?"

Frank lifted the gun from the small, cherrywood table. His familiarity with the weapon made her uncomfortable.

"Not exactly. It doesn't seem very heroic to shoot the creator of the *InterDimensions* family. I've decided to have you walk into the ocean instead. There's something much more honorable about the *InterDimensions* creator proving her loyalty to the family by taking her own life."

Nicole braced her hands on the sofa and cocked her head inquiringly. "You expect me to just walk into the ocean?"

Frank's violet eyes twinkled, reminding her of his father. "If you don't, then I'll have to shoot you."

"Why did you kill those people?" Leo came around his desk.

Malcolm tensed as he watched his mentor take slow, measured steps toward the gun.

Ava held the weapon steady on Leo's chest. "Because they were going to make that movie and Frank didn't want them to. They were upsetting my baby. But, of course, I don't expect you to understand. All you care about is yourself."

"Ava, what you did was wrong. Do you understand that?" Leo kept walking toward her, his arm outstretched. "Give me the gun."

"Don't come any closer, Leo. What I did, I did for my child. How could that be wrong?" she scoffed.

Leo stopped in front of her. Malcolm and Omar stayed perfectly still.

"Give me the gun, Ava," Leo said. "And tell me where Frank is."

"No. What are you going to do?"

"What I have to." Sadness weighed Leo's voice. He reached for the gun, but Ava stepped back jerkily.

"No. Stay back."

Leo followed her and reached again for the gun. And then it went off.


Frank stood and gestured with the weapon. "Get up."

Nicole battled a nearly overwhelming feeling of helplessness. Time was her strongest ally. She needed it to come up with a plan. Surely, sooner or later, someone would realize where she was and come rescue her.

"If you kill me, what will happen to the *InterDimensions* family?"

"I'll take care of them. You said yourself that you liked my *InterDimensions* story."

Nicole stared at him. *This young man has really lost his mind.* It was a terrifying realization.

"Come on. Get up," Frank repeated, waving the gun again.

Nicole rose slowly, adjusting her robe more tightly around her and knotting the belt. All she had underneath was a light T-shirt and underpants. She forced herself to keep her attention on Frank and not get distracted by the gun. The weapon was far too frightening. She kept her gaze on Frank's eyes, but they were almost as scary in their lack of emotion.

Nicole remembered the punch Frank had landed to her jaw. Thinking it might come in useful, she allowed herself to sway on her feet, pretending to steady herself on the arm of the sofa.

"What's wrong with you?"

"I felt a little dizzy for a moment." She made her voice breathless. She gave him an accusatory look. "You punched me, remember? And I'm still getting over that concussion from when you tried to run me over."

Frank's expression never changed. "Let's go." He waved the gun toward the French doors.

Nicole could see the night through the glass. This wasn't the way she had hoped to make her escape.

She led the way to the doors and waited for Frank to release the locks. He pulled one of the doors open and stood aside for her to precede him. They stepped onto a deck, its winding staircase leading to the beach. Crashing waves rolled in forty yards away. Nicole shivered. Her mind rebelled against taking one more step toward that watery end.

"Let's go." Frank stabbed her in the back with the gun's muzzle.

Time. She needed more time. She swayed again, putting her hand to her forehead.

Frank waited beside her. "What is it?"

"Just dizzy." Nicole took a hesitant step forward, grasping the banister as though afraid that, without its support, she would fall.

"We're almost there," he encouraged. "You're doing the right thing. You owe it to the family to sacrifice yourself for the shame you've brought upon them."

Nicole paused two steps down. "What do you mean?"

"Because of you, the family is now associated with Tyrone's and Denise's murders."

"I thought that was because of you." It was hard, but Nicole masked her anger over his accusation that she was responsible for her friends' deaths.

Frank prodded her again with the gun. "No. My mother killed them because of you. Because you were going to make the movie."

Nicole froze. "Ava killed them?"

"Yes." Frank paused on the step beside her. "Now, enough talking. We have to get going."

Nicole moved slowly, setting both feet on each stair before going on. Frank kept pace beside her. She stepped with care as part of her ploy, but also because she was dazed by Frank's latest revelation. He and his mother were involved in this campaign of terror. She wondered if his whole family was crazy.

Halfway down the staircase, she determined that if she was going to execute her plan, it was now or never. She pretended to stumble and crashed heavily into Frank, causing him to fall the rest of the way down the staircase. She ran down the steps after him, leaping over him as he settled in a heap at the bottom of the stairway. Gaining her feet, she ran hard through the sand in the direction of what she hoped was traffic noise. Her robe fluttered in the wind. Her bare feet sank into the sand.

Lights were scarce along the beach. Trash cans and beach markers appeared in her path without warning, hindering her pace. Her eyes had trouble adjusting to the dark because she had to run through the intermittent lights.

"Stop!" Frank yelled, foolishly to her mind since she had no intention of slowing, much less stopping.

Nicole heard his heavy breathing behind her. He seemed to be gaining ground. She strained to increase her speed but was hampered again by recycle bins growing in her path. As she dodged a barrel, Frank flung himself on her, and she fell face-first onto the sand. She ignored the ringing in her ears and fought to crawl from under him. He pulled her to him and flung her onto her back as though she were a rag doll.

Nicole gritted her teeth, refusing to be intimidated by Frank's wiry strength. Her arms worked furiously, struggling to evade capture as he fought to subdue her. The ringing in her ears grew louder. Bright lights flashed in her peripheral vision. She tossed and strained away from him, feeling her strength begin to ebb. Frank threw a leg over her in a misguided attempt to gain leverage by straddling her. Instead, he gave her the opening she needed. Without hesitation, she slammed her knee into his groin.

He screamed, slumping over to one side and writhing in agony. She rolled to her feet away from him. Headlights speeding down the beach momentarily blinded her, and she realized they were police cars. The flashing lights in her periphery and the ringing in her ears had been the police coming to her rescue with sirens wailing. She ran toward the lights, waving her arms and shouting.

"Nicky!"

*Malcolm.* She turned toward his welcome voice and threw herself into his outstretched arms. He caught her, and she let him hold her close. Hold her as though he'd never again let her go.


Nicole lay on the sofa cradled between Malcolm's thighs, her back against his chest. A blanket kept them warm, reinforced by the heat from the flames dancing in the fireplace. They'd given their statements to the police, who'd sent them home after arranging for them to return to the station in the morning for additional questioning. Nicole wasn't looking forward to the appointment, but at least Malcolm would be with her. She didn't want to go anywhere without him for quite some time.

Malcolm shifted behind her, and she retucked a corner of the blanket.

"Are you comfortable?" She hoped he was so she wouldn't have to move.

"Yes. Are you?"

"Yes." She sighed with contentment and closed her eyes.

"I almost lost you again tonight." His deep voice rumbled in the silent room.

She thought of Ava holding a gun on him, Omar, and Leo. "I almost lost you, too."

"We've had too many close calls."

She rubbed his thigh under the blanket. "It's over now, Mal. Thank God. I'm glad Leo's going to be okay."

Malcolm and Omar had told her about Leo struggling with Ava for the gun. The weapon had gone off, catching Leo in the shoulder. Luckily, the doctor had been able to extract the bullet. There wasn't any internal damage. All he'd needed were a few stitches and a sling.

"I was so afraid I wouldn't reach you in time. We sped all the way to Malibu after Ava told us what Frank had planned. I kept thinking I was going to run out of time. I was going to fail you. But you saved yourself, Nicky."

"I was so glad to see you." Nicole realized they both needed to talk. Their police statements weren't enough to put the night to rest. "I didn't know whether I would be able to get away from Frank. When I saw you, I knew I was safe."

Malcolm covered her hand as it rested on his thigh. "I realized tonight just how stupid I've been."

Nicole twisted around to look at him. "What are you talking about?"

"I let my insecurities come between us again." Malcolm pressed a finger against her lips to stop her interruption. "I wanted to keep you safe, so I left you behind when I went to talk to Leo. I didn't share with you my suspicions about Frank."

Nicole pulled his hand away from her mouth. "You had asked Joyce to stay with me. It's not as though you had intended to leave me alone. It was bad luck Frank got to the house first."

Malcolm kissed her. It was an awkward kiss because of their position, but it was still one of the most loving caresses she'd ever received.

"Every time I try to take care of you, something goes wrong," he whispered against her lips.

Nicole adjusted her position on the sofa so that she faced him. "We do a better job of taking care of each other."

Malcolm reached out to pull her down against his chest. He weaved his fingers through her hair to hold her against his heart. "You were right when you said we gave up on our marriage too soon. At the time, I thought two years was long enough for us to try to move on after we lost our baby. I was trying to shock us out of that frozen state we were in."

Nicole tipped her head back to look into his chocolate eyes. "If you'd wanted to know whether I thought we were through, you should have just asked me, Mal." Her lip quirked upward. "The divorce papers were a bit extreme."

Malcolm sighed. "Yeah. Well, words don't always come easily for me."

Nicole rubbed his thigh again. "That's something you're going to work on, right?"

"Right." Malcolm kissed her hair. "I'm really sorry, baby. Please forgive me."

Nicole propped her forearms on Malcolm's chest so she could gaze at him. "We both made mistakes. One of which was trying to change each other after we were married. You wanted a woman you could take care of. I wanted a man who would be my partner."

Malcolm cupped her shoulders. "I am that man now."

Nicole shifted upward to kiss him long and lingeringly. "I believe you. From now on, we'll lean on each other instead of trying to be strong on our own."

Malcolm stroked her hair. "It was a long time coming,

but you're right. We see each other more clearly now. What I see is our future together. And that's all that matters."

Malcolm claimed Nicole's lips to seal his promise with a kiss.

YOU BELONG TO ME

# EPILOGUE

Nicole stood in front of the hot, bright lights outside the movie theater. She watched the male news reporter smile into the camera, waiting for his cue to begin.

His smile widened when he got the signal.

"Ladies and gentlemen, joining us on the red carpet are the producers of *InterDimensions: The Movie*, Malcolm Bryant and Omar Carter. And the author of the *InterDimensions* books, Nicole Collins-Bryant." He turned to them. "Your movie premiere. How are you feeling?"

"Very excited," Malcolm said. "We have a really good turnout tonight."

"Yes, it's tremendous," Omar agreed.

Grinning, the reporter turned back to the camera. "The turnout's understandable, though. This project rose like a phoenix from the ashes. The movie actually was jeopardized, Nicole, when one of your fans threatened you and actually killed Malcolm's first partner, Tyrone Austin, and your agent, Denise Maitland."

A cloud settled over Nicole at the reminder of the deaths of her friends. "Yes, that's true. But we're grateful to the police for helping us find the people responsible and bringing them to justice."

The reporter continued. "A tragedy, to be sure. But it does have a happy ending. Not only has the movie been completed, but you and Malcolm were married last year. And it looks like you'll soon have an addition to your family," he said, referring to Nicole's obvious pregnancy.

"Yes. Our first child is due in eight weeks." She smiled up at her husband from the cradle of his arm. "Another reason to be grateful."

Malcolm shared a loving smile with her.

Reclaiming the spotlight, the reporter wished the trio a successful night and moved on to interview the movie's stars.

Two hours later, as the final credits began to roll, the audience erupted into applause, which dwindled to a respectful silence when the last frame appeared: "Dedicated in loving memory to Tyrone Austin and Denise Maitland."

## ABOUT THE AUTHOR

Patricia Sargeant dreamed of becoming a published author since childhood. She credits her family and Romance Writers of America® for helping her realize her dream.

Patricia and her husband live in Ohio. For more information about Patricia and her books, visit her Web site, www.patriciasargeant.com.

# Check Out These Other
# **Dafina Novels**

**Sister Got Game**
0-7582-0856-1

by Leslie Esdaile
**$6.99**US/**$9.99**CAN

**Say Yes**
0-7582-0853-7

by Donna Hill
**$6.99**US/**$9.99**CAN

**In My Dreams**
0-7582-0868-5

by Monica Jackson
**$6.99**US/**$9.99**CAN

**True Lies**
0-7582-0027-7

by Margaret Johnson-Hodge
**$6.99**US/**$9.99**CAN

**Testimony**
0-7582-0637-2

by Felicia Mason
**$6.99**US/**$9.99**CAN

**Emotions**
0-7582-0636-4

by Timmothy McCann
**$6.99**US/**$9.99**CAN

**The Upper Room**
0-7582-0889-8

by Mary Monroe
**$6.99**US/**$9.99**CAN

**Got A Man**
0-7582-0242-3

by Daaimah S. Poole
**$6.99**US/**$8.99**CAN

## *Available Wherever Books Are Sold!*

Check out our website at www.kensingtonbooks.com.

Look For These Other
# Dafina Novels

**If I Could**
0-7582-0131-1

by Donna Hill
$6.99US/$9.99CAN

**Thunderland**
0-7582-0247-4

by Brandon Massey
$6.99US/$9.99CAN

**June In Winter**
0-7582-0375-6

by Pat Phillips
$6.99US/$9.99CAN

**Yo Yo Love**
0-7582-0239-3

by Daaimah S. Poole
$6.99US/$9.99CAN

**When Twilight Comes**
0-7582-0033-1

by Gwynne Forster
$6.99US/$9.99CAN

**It's A Thin Line**
0-7582-0354-3

by Kimberla Lawson Roby
$6.99US/$9.99CAN

**Perfect Timing**
0-7582-0029-3

by Brenda Jackson
$6.99US/$9.99CAN

**Never Again Once More**
0-7582-0021-8

by Mary B. Morrison
$6.99US/$8.99CAN

### *Available Wherever Books Are Sold!*

Check out our website at www.kensingtonbooks.com.